DARK JUSTICE

ALSO BY J.L. HUGHES

R.A.Y. A Step Too Far

PRAISE FOR DARK JUSTICE

Think homicide detectives don't take their work home-think again. Unravelling this criminal entanglement will leave you breathless.

HEATHER GRAHAM, *NEW YORK TIMES* BEST SELLING THRILLER AUTHOR OF THE *KREW OF HUNTERS* SERIES

To paraphrase Brad Pitt's character in the hit movie *Seven*, Ladies and Gentleman we have a Serial Killer!

JON LAND, *NEW YORK TIMES* BEST SELLING THRILLER AUTHOR OF THE *CAITLIN STRONG* SERIES

In DARK JUSTICE, a prolific serial killer's methods echo the murder of homicide detective Jade Carmichael's mother, launching her into a relentless pursuit. This story will keep you on edge, up late, and haunt you long after the final dark twist.

D.P .LYLE, AWARD-WINNING AUTHOR OF THE *JAKE LONGLY* AND *CAIN/HARPER* THRILLER SERIES AND CO-CREATOR OF THE OUTLIERS WRITING UNIVERSITY

DARK JUSTICE

BROKEN JADE
BOOK 1

J.L. HUGHES

**ROUGH
EDGES
PRESS**

Dark Justice
Paperback Edition
Copyright © 2025 by J.L. Hughes

Rough Edges Press
An Imprint of Wolfpack Publishing
1707 E. Diana Street
Tampa, FL 33610

www.roughedgespress.com

Editing by My Brother's Editor

Paperback ISBN 978-1-68549-367-7
eBook ISBN 978-1-68549-432-2
LCCN 2025931559

DARK JUSTICE

PROLOGUE

I wonder if you knew me, would you save me or kill me? This is the answer I seek, one that keeps me breathing and propels me to survive long enough for you to know me. I believe you will take my life, even after I show you who I am, why I am. I believe this because I know myself.

And you…are a lot like me.

It wasn't late, maybe seven o'clock by now, but time had no meaning underground in the place he took me. The darkness of it created a perpetual midnight. The air is heavy with the scent of cement dust, bleach, and an unmistakable metallic undertone, the fragrance of fresh human blood.

My blood.

This is violence. I know violence. It's not as if I knew kindness, love, security, and then had it taken, the foundation of life ripped away to leave me falling into an endless sea of despair. I was always falling. I was born falling. My father made sure of that.

I lock my gaze onto my feet as his eager footsteps approach, my Doc Martens to be exact. I can't make eye contact with him. It would make the torture worse. The shoes offer no relief. They are scuffed on the bottom side of my right foot. Likely from him dragging me across the basement floor. Still, if he notices, I will be punished for that as well. My uniform must be perfect at all times, as his is. The world is not permitted to see a fracture or failure. That would put him at risk and alert them that things may not be as they seem.

Life from the outside appears upstanding, well-planned, the exception, an example of fortitude and accomplishment. He is very good at outside appearances.

One might say he is a master.

He is certainly mine. Why is he not yours?

No one crosses him. He is an authority. But today, like most days, I angered him. I've become capable of concealing compassion because his senses are so tuned to seek and destroy it, but he is still better than me. I will exceed him one day but not today.

The beautiful girl in the art room, she is why he is angry. I'm forcing her out of my head in case his gaze penetrates. He doesn't like pretty girls. She smiled too big, too bright, at me, and he saw it. No one is allowed to care. That is a risk. If they care, and I feel it, I may escape his control and never become the protégé he fought for so long to create.

He doesn't realize, and I will never admit, the time for me to escape his reign has long passed. I am him.

And the girl is already mine.

The familiar drain of strength and senses washes in as my blood washes down the tube and into the funnel. The room, already cold and dark, becomes frigid and black. With the last of my energy, I twist my right foot angling the scuff mark to be in contact with the concrete beneath. When I pass out it will remain hidden. I will have trouble walking when I am released, but I can shine the shoe after I recover.

I will recover. Without recovery, he could not torture me again. Where would he find gratification if not in re-administering pain? Two years until graduation, and he will unleash me on the world. I will survive long enough, endure so I can find you.

This is not the worst day. This pain is familiar, and living in it is how he molds me. I prefer to suffer it alone. Alone is better.

He drives me to crime scenes whenever the opportunity presents. This is to prove life is unfair, agonizing, heartless, and to become so is to swim comfortably in its ocean. When I was young, he left me behind the blacked-out windows of his truck, tape over my mouth so I could not scream. Close enough to feel the shock and devastation without anyone noticing my presence.

Weeks ago, he drove to a candy store, a playground of every

manner of defiling the human soul. Well stocked with pills, vials, and powder of every potent life-wrecker currently known, swallowed, injected, and snorted. The candy store owner owed him a favor, jacked up, and he expected to be paid up. My father didn't leave me in the truck this time. He said he wanted me to feel the energy of their lair firsthand. I walked in as he did, fearless, cold. They argued for a while, money and drugs changed hands, and then the man, if he could be so labeled, asked a question.

"And what do I get as collateral to make sure you don't give my location away?"

At first thought, an anticipated question. With a thousand ways my father could've responded. No option I contemplated came close.

"My son. He…is your collateral," he said, a grin escaping his lips. "Inflict damage to the merchandise that can be detected, and I'll ensure you suffer worse. Other than that, have fun until I return."

My scream could've shattered the carcinogen-smeared glass from its fractured, paint-chipped window frame, had I voiced it. I did not. Stealing myself for what came next. Five hours, thirteen minutes, and forty-three seconds. According to my Jaeger LeCoultre Reverso sports watch, that was the time he left me to be played with.

I don't like candy stores or their owners. If I can get rid of one or two along the way I promise, I will.

Perhaps you won't view my work as merciful. I will not inflict pain on the innocent, condemn those who have not first judged themselves, or allow them to survive in the shadow of violence as I am. I will do my best to ensure another of me is not created while I live. What will you do when you see all I have done?

Will you seek justice as I am? Redemption for all that has gone so ruthlessly wrong? I warn you it is a dark path.

In the end, which winding one of ours will be deemed most wicked? Both are certainly cursed. I hope you can remember I didn't ask for mine. It was given.

I feel my body go limp in a wave of submission, fully dependent on the shackles suspending it, the fetters digging into my wrists, bearing my weight as final insult before all light is consumed by the cloak of evil.

Tell me, will you choose to kill me?

ONE

Murder was the legacy her mother left her. She wished she could remember hearing her scream, but she never did. The visions of her mother's elegant feet dangling inches off the ground, the blood dripping then pooling below them was never accompanied by a scream. From the crack between the buffet doors, Jade Carmichael witnessed too much and not enough. Terror kept her still. She couldn't recall even breathing though she had. She heard him. The animalistic ravages as he brutalized everything beautiful. A scream would've been easier. This was the insight no other cop on the force had. She watched a killer, frenzied in the passion of torture and murder. Heard his joy as he plunged into a sacred heart and broke Jade's. For him, it was over too soon. For her, it never would be.

Those that knew Jade Carmichael said her upbringing, or lack thereof, gave her radar for violent criminals, an edge. She traded a natural family for one comprised of those in law enforcement. None would call her lucky. Nothing lucky about an eleven-year-old girl watching her mother succumb to a violent attack.

No one saw the world as she did. Thank God. Her brain never shut off. Hyper fantasia freeze-framed every violent excerpt from each crime scene into memory. Tetrachromacy painted her vivid nightmares with the breadth of Van Gogh, but seeing life for exactly what it was didn't paint a pretty picture. She envied others their muted, blurred, innocent perspective on days like today when hers couldn't be denied.

Jade wasn't one to overreact or lose her composure. She'd witnessed too much in her thirty-some years, in front of the knife, behind it, and under it. Bullets too. She faced pure evil and lived with its scars, scars so deep they separated her from the rest of humanity. Violence introduced itself early in her life. Some feared she knew it too well. Well enough to exact it with purpose to save a life, perhaps even to take one. Either way, she didn't apologize for what it made her. Its enemy.

Tonight, she ran as if an insurgence of mercenaries were primed to unleash a barrage of molten steel at her back. Her 1460 combat boots dug in, stayed solid, and came out of every crime scene weathered by death, their soles resembling hers, scarred in service. No one drove her but her ghosts. They were many.

The freshly painted back parking garage was desolate, too new to attract vagrants or to be entrusted with the luxury rides of its select tenants. Her boots slammed into untested pavement with reverberating blows announcing her pursuit for blocks. She didn't care. He knew she was coming. If he hadn't figured out she was the lead homicide detective after him by now, he would tonight.

When your mind houses wicked memories, your senses turn against you. A scent, sound, touch, taste, or glimpse can transform into a dangerous catalyst reviving trauma. The accelerated rhythm of her heartbeat reminded her how quickly her mother's had stopped. She watched the rise and fall slow and end, and no one came for her.

She flew to open the metal access door to the building and hit the staircase without breaking stride. Her partner's voice, spit from the cell phone pinned to her ear, broke the echo of her panting.

"You can't save the dead, and I don't want you joining 'em, Chancer." Detective Kane Kolton knew, partner or not, Jade would dismiss his counsel. "You're so damn—"

Welcome static interference robbed him punctuation.

"Broken?" Bursts of air exploded from her lungs between words. "Damaged?"

"Headstrong." Kane's voice deepened. "You're not thinking things through. What is it between you and this guy?"

"It's…something familiar," she said. Evil forced her to grow up, forged by it, it was…familiar. "What did I tell you when we started this thing?"

"The us thing? You said I'd get hurt. And what did I say would happen if you kept rollin' the dice?"

"I'd get dead." Years earlier a spiritual guru told Jade there were six doors of death offered before a soul exited life. She was counting down and hoping her suspect's target was too.

"She damn well better be alive." Her head throbbed as she rose through the floors. "Or I'll be pissed."

"This isn't a game, and it isn't about saving the next victim. It's about your mother."

"She's been gone twenty years, Kane. And I'm not exactly strolling down memory lane." Her words belittled the truth. Legacies existed to be fulfilled. Reformed by hers, she accepted her fate. He wouldn't until given no other choice.

"That doesn't stop you from seeing her face in every victim's." Kane's raw honesty wasn't particularly enduring, however accurate.

"You're offering advice to someone who has survived what, to you, is unimaginable, and you call it compassion." She was running out of breath and time. "It's about you not me, not what I need."

"What do you need? I want you alive at the end of this," he argued.

She paused, scanning the space. "I won't stay on the sidelines ever again. You want to support me? Stay out of my path. It's not one you're meant to walk."

"I know." His voice softened. "Jade, stop chasing ghosts."

"You don't get it." Her feet flew. "They're chasing me."

Jade dropped the call. He'd expect that. Before she dumped the phone, text bulleted across its screen. *Redemptor Fiduciarius Claves Regni Caelorum.* "The Redeemer holds in trust the keys to the Kingdom of Heaven."

Fuck it.

Traversing the cement lattice to the eleventh floor of the apartment building, she tossed the device back in her pocket. Her legs sprang up the stairs freshly fueled, each footfall in rhythm with the drumming in her chest. She left the cop she arrived with floors behind at the 'out of service' elevator and would've been happier if he wasn't there at all.

The killer's mastery of ancient languages was a tell not a talent. He could've said, "Another one bites the dust." Why he announced himself in Latin remained a mystery. What he did after did not. For Shadow Hook's police department, it marked the discovery of another victim. This twenty-first century demon hunted in daylight, preyed on the best of society, then vanished leaving a trail no more tangible than a wisp of smoke. For Jade, there was a draw to this criminal she couldn't explain. He'd crept under her skin and ignited a smoldering fire into a flash burn.

Papers in Upstate New York labeled him the Redeemer after a crime reporter leaked the word was left scrawled across a wall at the second crime scene. Their quaint community had been cast into a new darkness. Not the welcome shade of the lush forest draping the hill that protected their lakeside sanctuary and gave it its name, but a sinister gloom that weighed on its residents, casting doubt from neighbor to neighbor.

It wasn't the first homicide etched in memory. The last one left an open wound that still smarted twenty years later, but it'd been kept quiet, private. These new crimes reawakened bad memories, failure, and exposed their quiet town, soiling its reputation. Leaving Jade and Kane chasing a new toxin in a world choking on fumes. Fumes—lethal, resilient, and airborne.

The killer left no room for error. No trace evidence. No leads. No witnesses. Like her mother's murderer decades earlier, he killed with a mastery that, thus far, evaded punishment. She couldn't let that stand.

After seven months of living in his wake, Jade's solid composure showed cracks. Dark fractures.

"Wait for SWAT." Detective Damek Wenzel caught up to her. Hands pressed on knees, Wenzel spoke between heavy breaths squeezed from lungs worn by years of nicotine poisoning. His eyes surveyed apartment 1427's impenetrable door. "Let the city boys break it down."

Jade studied the deep cut wrinkles framing his arrogant confidence. He'd worked his way up from street cop to detective having never ventured into the nearby New York metropolis. She knew firsthand, he wouldn't have made the cut. Wenzel's scope of experience was, to say the least, limited. Much like his character.

He lifted his stocky frame upright and nodded in the direction of the solid mahogany door. "Or you could knock and ask politely, something you city girls don't do. Maybe he'll invite you in."

"Fuck you, Wenzel." She didn't hide her disdain, especially not when well deserved.

"There's something wrong with you," he barked.

"You're just figuring this out, Detective?"

Strange how her coarse demeanor shocked him. The fact she was younger, a well-seasoned homicide detective with a Black partner, and the lead in the case became corrosive, eating away the flimsy, pallid skin of Wenzel's ego. Perfect time to tear a hole in it.

"I guess there are a few doors you can't open." His panting lost rhythm, and his lips pulled tight into a smirk. A decorative marble ledge protruded out three inches on the wall behind him. For a second, the mental image of his face making contact distracted her. His out-of-shape, half-cocked approach could cost lives. Not today, not on her watch.

"I'm getting inside that fucking apartment." Scanning the hallway, her eyes landed on a large ventilation duct a few strides from the doorway. "Lock your hands." She motioned for Wenzel to help her reach its entrance near the roofline.

"There's no way in hell you'll fit, and even if you—"

"It's not a request. Either you offer, or I climb you like a ladder and not in the good way." Jade pushed down hard on his shoulder and kicked her size eight boot into his folded hands harder than necessary.

Muscling off the metal cover plate, she threw it to the floor not mindful of its trajectory. Wenzel ducked. His hands swayed, shifting her balance, then steadied.

Inspecting the sides of the shaft, Jade pushed on the metal casing testing for stability. The lower panel had little give. The sides popped out slightly with pressure. The roof, solid, metal over cement. Suffocating confinement.

"On three," she warned. "Remember this, while you call for SWAT, anything happens to me in there, and Kane and Jackson will come for you." She flashed him her pirate's half grin. "You'll wish you died with me. One, two, three."

Hoisting her frame through the opening, she disappeared into the air duct. Wenzel's protests trailed after her. She banked on the rest of him staying behind.

No modern-day heroes.

"Asshole." She swallowed hard. Kane was serving precious time on suspension instead of the case because of Wenzel's goading. She refused to fall into the same trap by getting physical, though she would've paid to land him on his ass.

If not for Wenzel's ineptitude, she wouldn't be crawling alone through dust in a two-foot square shaft. It wouldn't have gone down this way. Kane would've convinced this victim to stay out of the open. He was smooth, she was jagged.

Sara Keller, a doctor working in children's oncology, became the fourth of the Redeemer's known targets. Jade suspected there were more. The bastard had handed them to her, fearless in his anonymity. Dr. Keller fought their insistence on police protection—her patients all carried death sentences.

"If I'm not saving them, I might as well be dead," Dr. Keller declared. "This is what I live for." Jade related more than she admitted.

When the dust settled, Keller agreed to everything but altering her work schedule. Three days later she disappeared from the private hospital. Eighty hours of surveillance footage gave them nothing.

Dr. Keller's voice echoed in Jade's head. She edged her way deeper into the cold shaft. A dim light cast a glow across the metal ahead. She squinted, protecting her eyes from intrusion. No sound. Why couldn't she hear him? He had to be there. Facts and intuition pointed to this site.

Approaching the illuminated cross section, a faint resonance reverberated from the left tunnel. Scraping the back of her hand against a raised screw-head, she drew her weapon, bloodied. Without elbow room, she ran the risk of being stuck traversing the right angle.

Sara Keller. *This* was what Jade lived for.

Pushing her upper torso through, she wiggled amid dust and construction debris to inch her hips and legs in the same direction. Something scurried past her feet before they cleared the corner.

Rats.

The metal walls amplified her struggle. Echoes funneled past her.

Gun in hand, she cranked it back. Click. Click.

The bastard didn't deserve a warning, but if he were still there, he'd expect her either way.

Light grew brighter and shallow whispers, almost recognizable, arose from an interior hatch. The tunnel proceeded ahead several oppressive feet before coming to another 90-degree turn. Odds were, she had the right apartment. No guarantee.

A cover plate protected the hatch from inside the shaft. Jade switched her gun to her right hand, stretched her left arm free, and slipped the cover off.

Leaning her weight on her free arm, she hovered over the hole and peered through its screen at a sitting room. A fireplace crackled under a marble mantle.

Wrong apartment?

Jade shifted to assess options. Both directions made her throat tighten. Back through the rats to a triumphant egotistical bastard or forward into a dark abyss. Forward, always. A scraping sound drew her eyes down.

Entering the room with his back to her, the Redeemer dragged in what remained of Sara Keller.

Jade wanted to leap down on him, break his neck during her fall, and rattle off his rights while she loaded him with lead. Not exactly 'serve and protect' mentality. The airshaft held her captive.

His large frame obscured everything before him. Thick dark hair, broad shoulders.

Jade's position made it difficult to determine height. Tall, an arm's reach from the ceiling. If she fired, she ran the risk of hitting Sara, who may still be alive. If he were armed, he'd retaliate. A vision of cattle funneled toward a slaughterhouse brought the metal walls in closer.

His hands manipulated her like she was a rag doll, carving, slicing at will, but that wasn't this killer. That was the memory of her mother dying. This splice of vision awakened the old. She fought it back.

Her deep, controlled breathing depleted oxygen in the confined space. She pushed her face nearer the screen.

The killer stood directly below. Wasn't the first time she'd been on the fringe of evil. His hands donned a second skin, surgical gloves stretched to form a milky liquid sheath. He remained hunched, back to her. Jade couldn't ID him. He released Sara's upper torso. She thumped to the floor. Another woman discarded. Jade's breathing became level, drawing fuel for her rage as he walked out of view.

Sara was ashen and mercifully unconscious. Blonde waves framed her delicate face. Nothing like the crisp doctor Jade questioned at the hospital.

She wore a soft pink, sleeveless dress, its flowing edges crumpled. Jade hated crumpled silk. She trained her eyes on the woman's stomach. Slowing, shallow, shivers. It rose and fell, barely alive.

Where the hell was backup? Her claustrophobic trek had taken only a couple minutes. In her mind, an eternity. So close to ending a killer's reign. So close to saving a victim's life. So close to cheating death.

Too close.

Toxic spray exploded from below eating through the thin coating of Jade's eyes. She hadn't heard him approaching from the concealed side of the room. Blind, thunderous bursts rained in on her ricocheting tin and rubble. She registered three before panic stole her breath.

Her lungs fought for air against dizzying waves convulsing her stomach muscles. A scorching sensation burned up her left thigh. She was ripped from the shaft. Her right hand reached back, grappling at the vent opening finding no edge to cling to. The other held fast to her Glock. Lacking visual contact with her assailant, she couldn't fire.

She hit the floor with an unforgiving thud. Air burst from her lungs. Throwing off the impact, Jade stood firm, blinded by pepper spray and gulping for oxygen.

His hands were on her, but she wouldn't go down easy.

Life taught her to fight and fight hard. A deep breath, one strong kick, and she broke contact. Pain in her left leg ran interference through her thoughts.

His breath lingered close in the air, not foul, cleansed. He wore cologne, expensive, subtle, sickly seductive.

Swiveling in a semi-circle, she blinked rapid fire trying to reclaim her vision. A blur hovered before her, feet away, watching. Before she squeezed the trigger, it deked left, a snake slithering out of range. On the floor beside her lay Sara Keller. Jade dropped to her knees and reached for the woman. Pain erupted in her thigh. She leaned in listening for breath. No sound.

Her hands searched for a pulse. Faint. Sara wouldn't make it without medical.

An explosion rang out in the adjacent room, then another. Jade's reflexes had her gun arm extended over Sara's body, trained in the direction of the noise, before its echo stalled. No one. The hazy doorframe stood empty. An easy target, she gambled the coward fled, dismissed the chase, and fought for Sara's life.

Unable to determine trauma visually, the fingertips of her free hand traced Sara's ribs for fractures. None. She breathed life back into Sara's lungs.

Each compression, a tug of war with death. One she refused to lose.

Sara coughed, her arms flailing. Jade's damaged eyes captured the picture as if watching a static-filled, 70s television. Fragmented raspy tones fell from Sara's lips. No words formed.

The door to the apartment imploded.

Obscure forms with weapons drawn flooded the place, the voice behind the commands was familiar. Sara's tortured body became limp beneath Jade's hands. Two officers scooped Sara up, carrying her to help. Others searched outer rooms. She'd given Sara a chance. Slim at best, but a chance.

Jade rose, rubbing, despite training, her burning eyes, but couldn't maintain her balance. The adrenaline rushing through her veins was replaced by something leaden. Scorching pain reminded her of the loud bursts that preceded her fall from the shaft. Her world faded to black. Thick arms scooped her up from behind.

She recognized Detective Jackson Swan's voice. "Right here, kid. Look at me."

"Can't see, bastard sprayed me…I'm hit. Keller?"

"Stay with me." Jackson's voice morphed to a low drone. "Medic! Hustle, man."

———

In Jade's nightmare, Sara Keller wore a death mask. The angular features of her face sunken, stretched. Rigor had set in. Her lips were frozen in an emaciated scream. All but her eyes appeared less than human.

Those eyes.

They dug under Jade's skin sending tremors along the length of her spine. Staring into the lifeless pools that registered Sara's last emotions, Jade didn't read terror or fear. Instead, contempt.

Air trickled from a body not breathing. Then a voice, unnatural and inhuman, hissed behind Sara's still lips.

"You should've saved me, should've stopped him. You could've prevented my death. What about my patients? All those innocent children depending on me…you…you can't save anyone."

The coroner's men arrived. In crisp white jackets, they snatched Sara's stiff frame and threw it onto a gurney.

"No. Not yet. What's the matter with you?" Jade leaped to grab Sara away from them. "She spoke to me. She isn't dead. What the hell are you doing?"

"Cleaning up your mess—"

"Ms. Carmichael? It's okay, Ms. Carmichael. You're safe here." The night nurse coaxed Jade back to consciousness. "Do you know where you are?"

"In hell." Jade's voice rang back coarse and resigned.

"Hardly, though the nurses in the psych ward might agree. You were in rough shape when they brought you in. You should be happy to be here."

"Rough shape happened years ago. How long have I been out?" Her eyes burned.

"It's Thursday morning, three a.m."

"Sara? Sara Keller. What's her status?"

"She's alive." The nurse adjusted the IV and nodded to eye drops on the side table. "They said it'd be your first question."

"Thank Christ," Jade whispered, more to herself than the nurse while administering drops into both eyes with little relief.

"Don't thank Him yet. She flatlined twice. She's in a coma. Prognosis isn't good."

With a fresh cup of coffee in hand, Kane entered the room. "How's our patient?"

"Awake." On her way out, the nurse admired his form. "I'll leave you to talk."

"Thanks, Frankie," Kane said.

"Frankie? You're already on a first-name basis?" Jade admired the kindness he delivered with such ease. There were many days she couldn't deliver the same.

"Heck, yeah. Her sister attended the same school—"

"I don't want to know." Jade pulled herself upright in bed. "What are you doing here? If Grey finds out, your suspension will become permanent."

"No, it won't—"

"Gambler." Jade flipped the covers back to inspect her damaged thigh.

"Wanna bet? Passed him in the hall earlier, he wishes you well and wants to kick your ass almost as much as me. Oh, and said to remind you to buy silver. It's down."

"Is that all?"

Pulling a rolling chair near the bed, Kane's expression lost its humor. "I could've lost you. What the hell would I do then?"

"Go on." She answered too fast.

"I'm serious, damn it."

An unforgiving size thirteen cowboy boot kicked the door open and bounced it against the back wall with a resounding slam. "Hey, you're awake."

"Hi, Jackson. Guess I'll live to annoy another day. How did you convince the nurses to let you two cards in here after hours?"

"It's all the return business we've been giving them." Jackson flashed a Texas grin and handed one of the two cups of coffee he carried to Jade. "How ya feeling, kid?"

"Like I've been shot. Sara Keller?" She noticed her once new boots tossed in the corner, rain, dirt, dust, and pepper spray marred the leather.

Kane glanced at Jackson and back again before answering. "Doctors say her chance of regaining consciousness is minimal. Can't say if there's long-term damage."

"There is." Jade reclaimed her blankets and set the coffee on the side table. "I would know."

Jackson strode to the window, stared into the darkness, gulped down half the steaming brew then came to Jade's bedside. "She a strong woman, too, a survivor."

Jade's mind traveled the road they were all down, envisioning the tortured memories their survivor would carry if she regained consciousness. "It's not always a blessing, Tex, to survive."

Jackson and Kane exchanged an all-knowing glance. She read every regret in it, and they knew it, but no one spoke a word.

TWO

"You've done enough!" The words were spoken in an African dialect all too familiar to Lorenda Lainey. "End your interference, or I will."

The man with the mahogany skin had no cause to veil his threat. No one at the fundraiser but her understood his rant, and even if they did, his hostility was no secret. His private band of soldiers had fought her foundation's efforts in his country from its inception.

Security closed in on him before his grip on her arm inflicted significant pain.

"I'm fine." She pulled her arm free, stepped back, and made eye contact with the man she knew as Puma. "It's sad you can't recognize a helping hand when one is extended. You'd rather cut it off." These words she spoke only for his ears. Switching back to English, she continued. "Please escort my guest to a table at the front. I believe tonight's address could prove enlightening."

The heat of his disgust sent warm shivers down her back as she walked away. She was fairly certain he wouldn't stay for dinner.

African children, broken like china dolls, scattered into pieces across a barren burial ground. These haunting mental pictures fueled Lorenda's resolve as she crossed the stage to plead for future funding.

"I thank each and every one of you for making Home Land Africa a resounding success," Lorenda said from the podium.

He was wrong. She hadn't done nearly enough.

"As program coordinator, I couldn't be more grateful for the generosity of our sponsors." She scanned the crowd and made eye contact with a few particularly generous contributors. "Without you, the potential for healthy, self-sufficient communities in war-torn areas wouldn't exist. I raise my glass to you…and…to our Africa."

The clanking of wineglasses cued the orchestra as Lorenda left the stage. For those in attendance, the end of her toast marked the beginning of the celebration. Pristine waiters brought out gourmet meals while guests shifted their attention to each other.

"You did good, Ren." Harrison Wordsworth stood, backlit, only his outline visible. The man behind the scenes. He owned the foundation and commissioned Ren to manage it ten years earlier. They'd accomplished amazing things together. Along the way she learned its founder was far more comfortable in the driver's seat of a jeep racing across Africa's heartland than in a crowd of socialites. This, despite his fortune.

His was among Shadow Hook's aristocracy—families of past presidents, hidden global leaders, and quiet game changers. In Ren's opinion, the best of them.

"Will it ever be enough?" Ren joined him behind the curtain taking care not to stand too close. "Our newest site in Tanzania is in terrible shape, the worst of the bunch. How does one rebuild when the workers are children and amputees?"

"With help." Wordsworth smiled knowingly before his large frame drifted out a back door.

Nearing fifty, he harbored the charisma of a much younger man. A healthy man—everyone had secrets. His were well masked like the limp he'd merged into a swagger. Working hands-on with locals and volunteers to construct hospitals, homes, schools, and shelters had given him purpose and youth. His hair, wildly reminiscent of a surfer's, was bleached golden by African sunlight. His skin bore the chestnut glow of a summer construction worker. In her eyes, he remained unweathered.

Ren made her way through the crowd to the open bar.

After a series of handshakes and hugs, she found her director, Monda Munguzi, in the midst of thanking one of their most prominent sponsors. The man accepted Monda's gratitude graciously and kindly ignored the fact that she refused to surrender his hand.

"Hey, Ren. I was telling Mr. Isreal what a tremendous difference his contributions have made with the school site."

Ren exchanged a polite grin with the man she knew as Isaiah, stretching her hand out to give reason for Monda to relinquish his.

"I was hoping I'd run into you before I had to leave," Ren said. "Care to join me for a drink?"

Isaiah Isreal was, without question, the most exquisite creation in the room. In a banquet hall adorned by works of art, both living and inanimate, his presence dulled those around him. Humble, rich, philanthropic, and single. Everyone in the place vied for his attention. Angling to be seen with the devilishly handsome, obviously wealthy target.

It made having a quiet drink with him impossible.

"That is, if you don't mind escorting me to my office first." Ren slipped her hand into his folded arm.

"I'd be delighted. Escaping the vultures?" He flashed a grin.

Monda grimaced her disapproval, then ordered a martini. Ren couldn't hold back a modest chuckle. The lucky woman leaving with Isaiah was the only one with no romantic interest.

"Glamour becomes you." Isaiah's emerald eyes drifted over her French roll and down the open back of her gown before he led her across the room.

He cut a pathway through a horde of onlookers. Glancing back, he asked, "How was your last trip?"

"Difficult." Ren dodged the occasional jealous glare. "I wish we could've accomplished more. Had to return to replenish resources."

"Heard you were there over Christmas."

"Yeah. Celebrated with a few hundred of those I love."

He paused to wrap his arm around her waist then led her through a tangle of people in front of the executive elevator. She had to admit, it was nice, his doting fed the ego. Using her key card, she activated the lift. When it arrived, they stepped in alone.

Isaiah waited until the doors closed then asked, "Ren, how are you doing, really?"

"Fine. Busy. You know, a lot of pressure, but fine."

Isaiah's brow furrowed. "What about the threats?"

"I shouldn't have said anything." Ren slumped against the back wall. Her reflection deflated. "It's part of the job."

"We've been working together for two years. I trust you with my money. You can't trust me with this?" Isaiah moved closer, his reassuring smile infectious.

"Of course. I'm sorry. I don't want anything to ruin tonight."

The elevator stopped, and the doors opened. "Okay. If you ever want someone to confide in—"

"Thanks, Isaiah. Really. You're a good friend."

"Good friend? Humm?"

His lips formed a cagey grin as he scanned the empty hallway. They stepped out, and the doors to the elevator closed behind them, blocking out the light. Low overnight lanterns scattered down the expansive corridor cast them in silhouette. He moved into her personal space, pinning her softly between the wall and his body.

Harrison's face flashed before her. Every woman downstairs would gladly trade places.

"Yes. A very good friend."

Night pressed against the windowpane of Ren's office and transformed its clear glass into a black mirror surface. She'd read the prophet Nostradamus relied on such a device to stare into the future. After a long pause, she decided her gateway was flawed. Everything beyond it remained a blur. She set aside the two empty champagne glasses off her desk space.

Plans for her next site evaluation were finalized. Part of her wished she were headed back to Africa with Harrison and purpose. Every year, life here became more foreign. Home was a far-off land where tents and jeeps replaced skyscrapers and sports cars.

Ren stood with her back to her desk, its surface covered by photos that cataloged the realities of a violent world stripped of disclaimers. If anyone witnessed the stark evidence of the atrocities captured on film in Africa, they'd surely decide her love for the place twisted. She'd searched through the pictures after Isaiah left.

A picture of Harrison wounded in a February attack laid atop the pile of painful images. His injuries were far from fatal, but the memory haunted Ren.

Only Harrison's trusted driver knew the depth of their relationship or that she'd finally agreed to make it official in an African ceremony when they returned.

Oddly, the attack, the purity of the pain at the thought of losing him before she'd made the ultimate commitment, dissolved her long-standing resistance. Like Africa, Harrison became a fleeting but desired home.

Parched land held no secrets. Its history lay open and still set eyes ablaze with its beauty. If only the same could be said of her when utterly exposed. She too held scars.

Ren gathered the morbid photos into a file folder and locked them away in a drawer.

She hadn't confided in Harrison about the personal threats. The menacing messages she'd received. No surprise. Ren mastered the art of discretion. Their donor, Isaiah, knew. He'd been with her when the last one arrived.

They were appearing with increasing regularity. Annoyance had evolved into deep-seated fear. A fear she harbored alone.

Isaiah offered a shoulder, one she didn't accept. It was Harrison's heart she relied on. Life in the shadow of a clandestine relationship with a billionaire caused complications. She didn't intend on adding to them.

Longing to trade the foreboding quiet of the empty office for the chaotic comfort of the celebration, she shut down her computer, grabbed her purse, and headed for the door. Two steps away, her cell phone alerted her to an incoming text.

She debated, then pulled it from her bag. Harrison said he'd contact her to confirm their late-night plans. She refused to relinquish control of her life to a lunatic. A quick skim of the screen deflated her brazen confidence.

A warning floated in the black reflective surface.

You'll return to your beloved Africa in a box.

How was it this vile invader tapped into her thoughts at the most vulnerable times? Staring at the words, she stumbled backward away from the threshold. Clutching the edge of the desk for stability, she listened for signs of an intruder.

The building remained hollow.

Setting her handbag on the desktop, she rummaged through its contents in search of the detective's number. She'd written it on the back of a napkin at Isaiah's urging. He suggested she involve the authorities. Initially she'd been against the idea. Not anymore.

Turning her purse upside down, she littered the desk's surface with pens, a checkbook, Kleenex, hand cream, and lipstick. No napkin.

Scooping the scattered items over the edge, she dropped them back into the bag and rifled through her coat pockets.

A ding down the hall signaled the elevator's arrival. Jolting upright at the sound, she peered around the corner of her office. The corridor flooded with light when the doors opened.

No one exited.

Focused on the safety of the crowded lobby level, Ren collected her things haphazardly, dumped them back in her bag, and ran for the elevator. The doors were closing. Empty. She jumped in.

Her breathing calmed with the passing of each floor. When the doors opened again, the clanking of wineglasses and laughter swept over her. A stranger handed her a glass of champagne as she exited the elevator. Feeling foolish, she gulped down half the glass while he yelled, "Cheers to Africa," then disappeared.

Standing amid the drunken crowd, Ren scanned their faces. All reflected the moist afterglow of too much alcohol. None were threatening. These were her people. Damn thief, stealing her sense of security. And she'd let him, whoever *he* was.

Ren's guard lowered. Then a slap on the back spun her in a circle of terror. A young man danced across the vestibule singing an off-key rendition of "Africa" and out into the night. Time to follow.

Dodging partygoers, Ren made her way to a door leading to the rear parking garage. A passkey granted her entrance to a well-lit row of stalls. Her Audi waited alone under a streetlamp. She pushed the fob, and its lights flashed on while the car unlocked.

Her pumps clicked too loudly, announcing her presence with every step. Yet another reason to miss well-worn hiking boots. Halfway to the car she caught her train on her left heel throwing off her balance. After an awkward pirouette, she stamped her foot back on solid ground, free of the entangling material. She lifted the hem and twisted it in a full circle inspecting it for tears, then realized she was standing under the streetlight with her dress up around her hips in the middle of the lane.

Heavy shoes echoed behind her. She dropped her gown. Its material coiled around her legs. She dared not take a step. Then recognized the man's laughter, a friend.

"Hey, I thought you left a long time ago," she redirected, discounting her embarrassing performance.

"I waited to make sure you got home safe," he said. "You really are more comfortable in denim, aren't you?"

"Where's your car?" she asked.

"The limo picked me up from the airstrip with everyone else."

"Can I take you home?" Ren dangled her keys. "I could use the company."

"You've been busy with guests and contributors tonight. I thought you'd never ask." He escorted her to the passenger door. "Allow me. I'll drop you off and send the car back."

"Thanks. I'm a little shaky."

"My pleasure. Too much celebrating?"

"No. Long day." She carefully lifted her gown stepping in. "You can relate."

"I can." Returning to the driver's side, the man slipped behind the wheel adjusting the seat. The doors locked automatically when he put the car in gear. Ren stared through the glass sunroof into the night. Approaching storm clouds cast a dark veil over the stars making the sky appear painted black. She dropped her head back into the comfortable leather.

He pulled into the onrush of late-night traffic. "Are you certain everything's all right?"

"I'm fine. Really. Just can't wait to be home." Ren tucked a loose strand of blonde hair behind her ear. Her mind drifted down the list of preparations before she could shed this life for her homeland. She pulled a Kleenex from her bag. The detective's number fell out of its folds. She crumpled it back into her clutch.

The menacing text message tainted the world around her.

The car turned left, merging onto the Brooklyn Bridge. Since 911, Manhattan nights were much quieter than in previous years. Many had left. A strong police presence gave visitors a sense of security. For them, the tragic loss birthed a new kind of peace. Ren pondered this thought.

Moving from the Long Island Express Way to Grand Central Parkway, they passed the Calvary Cemetery. The moon reflected off its gravestones, the illumination speaking to her. She didn't like what it said.

"Why so deep in thought?" her friend asked. "You're pretty quiet over there."

Traffic thinned, and soon the rich foliage of forest trees lined the highway. She found this stretch of road heading toward lake country therapeutic. Few people knew she owned a place outside the city. Shadow Hook was her retreat, as it was for many others. The town, of now close to twenty thousand, had been a merger of two smaller towns, one on the upper sunlit side of the hills surrounding Shadow Lake and the older crest of homes clinging to its edge. Harrison's family owned one of the original colonial homes towering atop its prominent estate ridge. She occupied a nice lot on the far edge of the lake. Not necessarily a legacy lot, but a home she was immensely proud of. It needed work and balancing that, with travel, hadn't been easy of late.

"I'm sorry, did you say something?"

"I asked what you were thinking."

"Going down my 'to do' list," Ren said. "I've a lot to accomplish before returning to Africa and so little time."

He turned to meet her gaze. A menacing shroud flooded his eyes, as if the night had seeped through a crack in the window and coated his retinas with an evil film. When he spoke next, his voice deepened, and the contours of his face became sinister.

"So little time," he echoed.

No. He couldn't be. A wisp of hope circled Ren's confusion. Perhaps this man she had freely called friend scared her for the pleasure of a twisted joke. She read his eyes. She squirmed. They fed off her terror. No joke.

"I warned you."

"Warned me?" Thoughts collided. Ren searched the highway for life. Desolate.

"You would return in a box. I never kid about such things."

His words dropped like hand grenades between Ren's ears as the car veered onto a gravel road. She struggled to read the mile markers. Her vision blurred. Panicked, she reached for the door handle and tugged against it.

"Security locks," he said. "Standard in most vehicles. You don't want to jump, trust me. That wasn't any ordinary champagne you guzzled."

"I did." Ren fought to form her words, her body no longer following her cues. She didn't know if the door would open, and she'd die smashing to the ground or somewhere else. What did she know? Either way, it was over. "I...trusted...you."

"You're not the first," her captor whispered. "You won't be the last."

THREE

"What do you have to become to take a human life?" Dr. Abraham Maxwell asked.

Jade's attention averted to a lightning strike splitting the night, illuminating the distance beyond the window of his new office. Her eyes followed its trajectory down the hillside to the lake's edge before coming to rest on her reflection.

"Human," she replied, her tone deathly void. She waited a moment, allowing time for her answer to penetrate, then continued. "Merriam-Webster Dictionary's definition of inhuman is 'brutal, lacking acts of kindness.' I've seen brutality, trust me, it's human."

"To be human is to be brutal?" Dr. Maxwell settled into his over-sized armchair. Its new construction squeaked beneath his weight.

"No. Humanity doesn't equate to violence or cruelty. It's a choice. A choice made by a human mind disconnected from a truth most of us share."

Moving closer to the office window and the darkness beyond it, Jade placed her left hand on the cool pane. On the other side, rainwater trickled past her fingers echoing a chill down her spine.

"What truth?"

"A respect for life. The knowledge that it's sacred in any form…it's the inner dread that surges when the lights dim during an execution."

"Inhuman?"

"Yes. To be inhuman, inhumane. And the Redeemer…he's all human. He's gone so far down the rabbit hole he found the door to hell."

"Has he taken you with him?" Maxwell asked.

Jade stared into the night not answering. She hated storms. How they drew her. Storms meant trouble. Not the inconvenient trouble of slick roads and soggy clothes, but as a precursor to death.

Transfixed by the shimmering rain against the blackness beyond the window, her mind jumped tracks, derailing.

"Jade…where are you?"

"Can't you tell, Doc? I'm at the door."

Maxwell's office reminded Jade of an antique library. Its warm colors and stern interior encouraged hushed tones and inner contemplation. No question, the man deserved the many plaques adorning the walnut bookcase behind him. A shame his qualifications proved lacking to her cause.

"Which door?" Maxwell's patience had no end while Jade's had no leash.

"Pardon?" Jade scanned his diploma from Johns Hopkins directly overhead noting the year he graduated with honors before making her way to his couch.

"Stay with me. Which door?"

"The last one. Sara Keller's." There was a haunting within her voice. She recognized when it surfaced and wondered if he did too. Stretching across the distressed leather, she turned away from him. "She lived in an executive concrete apartment. You ever been in one of those?"

"Yes." His tone revealed a mild annoyance.

"Should've known. Of course, you have…you can hear a pin drop when that door shuts behind you." She drifted back to the scene of the crime.

"The door to the apartment or the door to hell?"

Cagey.

"They're the same thing, Doc. That's my point. They are *exactly* the same thing. Not all mahogany doors guarantee entrance for the damned. This one did."

"It's not the only door to Hell, though, is it?"

"It's a brick wall, Doc…that back alley you're heading down is closed off by a brick wall. Brick walls don't move."

"Then we'll dismantle it, take the bricks down one by one. Clear a path."

"I'm no mason, and neither are you. You know better. And I doubt you know your way around a sledgehammer."

"Let's discuss your department's concerns."

Smooth how he navigated pain and made inroads to her psyche. He had practice in both.

"I wondered when you would broach that." Jade reached for the water glass on the table across from the sofa. "Tell me, if you saw someone dying in front of you and a killer escaping at the same time, how would you prioritize?"

"I'd do what you did. I'd save the girl. But I'm not the lead detective tracking a serial killer. You are."

"I couldn't see. I couldn't have stopped him." A defensive edge caged her voice.

"Are you certain of that, or are you being dismissive?"

"After seventeen years of living and breathing these assholes, I think I can safely say it is my educated opinion!"

"I believe you…I'm not convinced you believe yourself."

"I have my reasons." Setting her water glass down without drinking, she glanced at the clock on the mantel. Seven minutes left.

"Then, the official report shall read that, having assessed the immediate situation, and considering your physical condition and the previous patterns of your suspect, you determined the primary course of action was to remain with the victim, administer CPR, and save her life."

He rattled it off like a grocery list. Jade's stomach turned.

"Yes. And if she ever recovers, she may hold the key to the bastard's undoing."

"How is she?" Max's voice softened.

"No change. Doctors don't know how long her brain was deprived of oxygen or the extent of the damage. Now, we wait. Wait for her to wake up, for a break in the case, for the next victim. You can bet your ass he won't be waiting. He's out there. Right now. Planning his next move. Hiding behind another door."

Again, the storm lured Jade's focus. It reminded her. Damn weather.

"And you blame yourself for that?" Max pulled her back.

"I was in the room with him, Max." She shifted in her seat. The leather muttered beneath her. "I stood inches away, and all I fucking learned was he uses mouthwash and expensive cologne."

"You came close. He hasn't taken a new victim since your encounter, has he?"

"Not that we know of."

"In the past he announced this to you directly?"

"Or Kane. Last time he tipped off Wenzel." This fact didn't make sense to her and her tone revealed it.

"Not one of your favorites."

"You know it."

"How do you feel about him changing guard, contacting someone else?"

"What do you mean, how do I feel? I don't give a damn who he contacts. I want to catch the bastard, not become pen pals."

"Fine. Why do you think he changed tactics?"

"He's playing with us, evading. That's what he does. He lives and breathes the game. He won't stop. And he doesn't make mistakes."

"He did. You ended up in the room with him."

"I ended up shot, out cold on the floor, not him." Jade's relaxed composure disintegrated. Her back stiffened, a cobra preparing to strike. "This animal survives to kill. His purpose on earth is to inflict human suffering, and he is a master. He knows our procedures, forensics, and evidence collection. He's left us nothing at the scene, and he's a hell of a shot."

"You respect him, his intelligence?" He wasn't condescending, merely confirming facts.

And they were correct. "He's way ahead of us."

"How so? You came to his door and saved Sara's life."

"That proves nothing."

Max's expression, usually bland, blossomed with disbelief.

"I gained breadcrumbs. He gained dangerous insights."

"Why?"

"He knows how far I'm willing to go." Jade's response flew from her lips before she could tame it.

"You think this is personal?" Max was leaning in.

"Of course it's fuckin' personal. People are dying on my watch. He puts them under a microscope and examines them like specimen. He knows their routines better than they do. By the time we're involved, he's so far ahead he's laughing. I can practically hear him. To stop him you throw him behind bars and weld the door shut. We're not even close. He could walk into this room and stand beside me, and I wouldn't know it.

"Hell, you wouldn't know it."

Her last words hung in the air. Max stared at his desk for a moment. At times like this, Jade knew she contributed to the thick wave of silver hair that sat above his ears. He shifted back into his chair then launched another inquest.

"If this man is willing to risk everything to carry out these murderous impulses and possesses the intelligence you ascribe, it stands to reason he'd be a formidable opponent. What I want to know is why you carry responsibility for his actions. You really need to talk about the first door, Jade."

Max was bent on resurrecting a past long dead and buried.

"You need to discuss the first murder you witnessed." His forehead crinkled with fatherly concern. "You're still reliving it, aren't you?"

He tried and failed. Dear Max, brilliant, devoted, and persistent as hell. Jade trusted him completely. He knew pain like she did. That didn't mean she'd willingly unleash inner demons in his presence.

"I need to go." She slid off the sofa, snatching her leather coat. "I'll see you again."

"You will." Selecting a card from his day planner, Max stopped her at the doorway. "I know you're uncomfortable involving outsiders. An old acquaintance of mine is in town. Her name is Rachel Leigh. She's a PhD who specializes in the study of serial killers and is a leading forensic psychiatrist. She's attending a conference in New York, staying at her family estate in lake country. She may offer worthwhile insight."

Jade slid an arm into her jacket, stared past him, focusing on her dark reflection in the storm-ridden window, then accepted the card.

"Better zip up." He helped her with the twisted arm of her coat. "The weather's wicked."

"It's not the only thing, Max. Take care."

"Call me if you have any—"

"I will."

Jade disappeared down the dimly lit hallway through the waiting room doors, sensing his eyes on her back. She never turned to meet them. He'd been her therapist for years. He cared and not about the money the department paid him to keep her head screwed on right. Their sessions offered a place to safely unload her burdens.

Not all of them. The darkest ones stayed, like the killer she hunted, hidden in shadows and silence, ever threatening.

Thunder clapped a daunting applause when Jade exited the brick building. She pulled her collar up tighter to her neck cutting the icy wind. Her body flinched and tensed, compensating for the raw pain in her injured thigh muscle. The rain gathered construction dust in the area turning it to paste, infusing the air with a dank must.

Sharing the parking lot with only two others, her Mustang sat illuminated by a streetlight. In a few short weeks the parking structure would fill with expensive toys owned by high priced saviors and slayers —shrinks and lawyers, local and from neighboring towns. She reached for her door, heavy drops bouncing off the windshield.

She hated storms. Hated the cold they awakened within. A reminder of home.

Wiping the rain from her brow, she surveyed the area. Stone and mortar walls enclosed the parking lot save for one open side to the street. Scattered boulevard trees drooped, made sullen by Mother Nature's poor mood. A stretch of paved sidewalk paralleled the building street-side and ran across the parking lot, disappearing beyond the blur of the evening downpour.

Empty.

Sliding behind the wheel, she closed her door. The radio blasted an old Stones tune with a turn of the key. The lyrics repeated, "shattered...I'm in tatters." She let it play.

Light refracted from the rearview mirror as she backed out. Her field of view shrank behind narrow slits. With her foot on the brake, she turned to inspect the bright source. Couldn't locate it. Her phone rang, the first three bars of "Paradise Circus," she answered, pulling onto the main road. The forensic report on Sara Keller was in.

"Don't tell me. Let me guess. We have nothing."

She blended into the mild flow of traffic, then swung left, cutting off a merging car and headed for the lab.

"Semen? You're sure? That's a first. Don't bother. I'm on my way."

FOUR

Streams of distortion transformed Kane Kolton's cabin's windowpanes into carnival glass. The world beyond bent and melted. Perfect. Kane's mood personified the dismal weather. In boxers and an open bathrobe, he stood watching a wasted day pour down the drain.

He'd built the lake cabin with his father and grandfather a decade and a half ago. The last project they shared. His grandfather still spent time there. His father, the South African surgeon, passed three years earlier from a brain aneurysm.

From his first day on the force, his father lectured him. Forever fretting about how Kane's life could be snuffed out in the line of duty. He was a "Black man in a White man's world." He was wrong. When he looked in the mirror, Kane saw the tone of his skin. He also saw the soft green shade of his eyes inherited from his platinum-blonde Irish mother. He was a man in a man's world. He meant to drive that point home to his father. Before he could, he died performing a life-saving surgery on an eleven-year-old boy with a similar heritage. The boy lived. When the child's parents sought out Kane to express their gratitude at the funeral, he saw grateful people, not the color of their skin.

The memory made him hate Wenzel all the more. The thick bastard was the reason he had time to contemplate. He put him here instead of by his partner's side.

The gray cabin on the shoreline gained character with age. Offers for purchase came every spring. Isolated in a cove, it was prime lake-front. Kane would never sell. Too bad he had no children or wife to share it with. The only constant in his life was his partner, and she was driving him insane.

He listened for Jade's voice to break over the police band radio—a sorry substitute for working side by side on the trail of a killer. After months of tolerating Wenzel's bullshit, he'd reached his limit. Wenzel landed on his ass, Kane here, under what he referred to as house arrest.

Airwaves crackled, and Kane recognized Detective Jackson Swan's voice.

"Jade, did forensics catch up with you? We've finally got good news," he said. "I called your cell. Your phone's not on."

"Battery died again. Cordless charger isn't working. I'm five minutes out. Want to meet me there?"

"You bet, kid."

Kane smiled. Jackson had been doing double time to make up for his absence. He owed him.

"I'm two blocks out," Jackson said. The airwaves filled with the dialogue of other officers.

Kane couldn't stand to hear the case move forward without him. He couldn't shut it out either. Wringing his hands, he paced across the bank of windows that framed his living room.

He'd been warned. If he showed his face anywhere near the office or engaged in police work of any kind, his short suspension would become permanent. Worse, he promised Jade he'd stay put so they'd be back on the case together by month's end.

He exhaled. "Two weeks."

The annoying ticking of the antique wall clock was drowned by an echoing succession of rings from the house phone.

"Kane here." He held the receiver to his ear.

"Did you hear that?" Jackson asked.

"Yep."

"Too good to be true?" Jackson, a Texas Ranger's son, wasn't a big believer in easy breaks.

"What's your theory? I know you have one."

"This guy has given us nothing *then* decides to leave DNA? No way. It has to be from a legitimate donor."

"You're thinking boyfriend?" Kane ruffled his mass of blond hair.

"Yeah."

"Could be…"

"What?"

Grabbing a clean coffee cup out of the cupboard, Kane paused then said, "What if he didn't have time to clean her up? He was interrupted."

"Was he?"

Kane poured dark roast into his cup. The aroma filled the kitchen. "I've been meaning to ask you, how in God's name did he escape the building? I thought you had the location surrounded."

"We did." Jackson's words flowed out in a rush. "We aimed for ground level. No one pegged the guy for a gopher."

"Underground?"

"You bet." Jackson's voice trailed. "I'm outside the forensics building. Want me to hand the phone over? Jade's is dead."

Muffled fragments of Jackson mumbling out his car window cluttered the line.

"Tell her to call me later or text. She's afraid to talk with her fingers."

"I will, buddy. Stay sane."

Jackson's car door slamming shut echoed down the line. Kane hung up.

Turning his back to the rain, his eyes searched a nearby bookshelf coming to rest on the spine of a text titled *The Human Predator*. This was what his partners faced alone.

Kane's frustration swirled down his throat with the dark roast, smooth and bitter. His resentment wasn't for Grey Grant. In Kane's opinion, Grey was one hell of a police chief and a terrific leader. Everyone on the force knew the life Grey gave up to be in service to the town. A successful commodities trader, he was forever dropping hints of when to invest down their hallways. His land holdings were impressive. Not everyone had been to his estate. His team had. His summer cookouts were events not to miss. The cottage Kane was standing in was his because of a tip from Grey. Jade's place too. There was no question he was on their side. Circumstances forced him into a decision he openly admitted was detrimental to his team.

No. Grey's actions were rational, understandable, if undesirable.

Damek Wenzel, a forty-something racist dosser, deserved no such reprieve.

In bare feet, Kane sauntered to an old drafting table that housed case histories instead of blueprints. He set down his coffee and loomed above the wreckage.

There'd been three murders in Shadow Hook attributed to the Redeemer before Sara Keller was kidnapped. The first one had the markings of an isolated incident.

A woman in her early twenties found dead at an empty construction site with ritualistic writing around her. At first glance, a willing participant in a sacrificial killing. No signs of a struggle. No bruises or broken bones. After delving deep into the woman's past, Kane and Jade unearthed a history of drug abuse and dependencies. The company she kept had been, at best, questionable. She'd moved to Shadow Hook only a few years earlier and, as neighbors told it, "never left the city behind."

Close up, the crime scene photos read like an addict's worst nightmare. A needle protruding from an open vein, the user unconscious while her lifeblood drained out.

It might have been ruled accidental if three quarts of her blood hadn't been missing from the scene. Far more than her heart could've pumped out unassisted and, to date, unaccounted for.

Kane shuffled through his notes, translations of messages left behind and copies of emails sent by the Redeemer. The answers were there. Cryptic, encoded, indiscernible, but there.

When the second body was discovered, it became the link in a terrifying chain of events that threatened the integrity of Shadow Hook's police department. Tensions were at an all-time high after larger newspapers caught the story.

Kane stared at photos of the first victim, Eva Summers, ignoring the arm with the needle in it. Her left hand, clutched in a fist, had been pried open to reveal a clasp from a chain. A solitary triangular piece with three attachment rings designed to connect to other sections of a rather unique necklace. Heart-shaped, the 18-karat white-gold fragment formed an intricate lace pattern. Officers canvassed every local jeweler and searched online, failing to match it.

Kane memorized its structure, delicate, fragile in appearance, but able to withstand whatever force ripped the missing segments from her grasp.

Why had she held onto it so desperately while she died? Was it a family heirloom? Who walked away with the rest of it? And could it provide the link to her killer?

These were a few of the questions on the long list plaguing Kane.

The phone rang repeatedly before he hit the speaker button.

"Kane." He stared at the case file spread across the draft table.

"It's Grey. Hope you haven't made plans to try the lake."

Kane's eyes searched the photo of the first emaciated corpse left by the Redeemer.

"We have another message." Grey's low voice echoed. "It came through a couple minutes ago on your email."

"I'm listening." Kane waited for the worst. Of late, emails didn't herald good news.

"Time to come back." A long pause of silence passed between them, carrying all the things they didn't need to say.

Kane's finger traced the body in the photo, down to the area where the needle violated her arm. "I'll be there in an hour."

He hung up. Leaving the open file, he headed for the shower, anxious to know victim number five's story and how long they had before she joined the series of grizzly photos scattered across his drafting table.

FIVE

"Are you working the case or apartment hunting?" Jade bypassed Detective Wenzel heading for the living room of the high-end apartment where Sara Keller almost died.

"Smooth killing surface. What is it?" Wenzel wiped his hand across the slate-gray zinc surface.

"Who cares?" Jade focused on the tile floor beneath her boots.

"Pricey. It could be a great operating surface, is all." Wenzel called after her. "Easy to wipe down, sterilize."

"This isn't where he did his handy work. Forensics found nothing." Jade kneeled, her hand drifting over the high-pile carpet where the Redeemer left Keller's body.

"If the crime scene investigators came up empty, what exactly are you hoping to find?" Wenzel stopped swooning over the décor and came in behind her. He waited on the threshold, leaning around the corner belly first.

"Why would a killer with this MO bring a victim to a place with white carpet?" Jade wasn't seeking an answer.

"Maybe he—"

"He's throwing it in our faces." Jade's focus shifted to the ventilation shaft overhead. Memories flashed. She dismissed them. "How concentrated was the sedative in the victim's blood?"

"They couldn't give us anything definitive. Why?"

"You notice anything?" Standing, she moved in a semi-circle scanning the room. It smelled new.

"No signs of a struggle."

"When you add that to the information the building inspector gave us…"

Wenzel joined her directly beneath the open airshaft, then said, "Only three of the apartments are serviced by a shaft this size."

"He orchestrated the whole thing." Jade shifted weight off her injured leg.

Noticing her discomfort, Wenzel asked, "Still smarts?"

Jade refused to brood over battle scars with him. "What did the guy say the width is on that shaft?"

"Twenty-six inches, wasn't it?"

"Yes." Her eyes locked onto the location of the three shots fired. Three reverberating blasts rang out in her mind. She closed her eyes, using the vivid memory to guide her. Methodically, she inspected the roof damage, then, "Son-of-a-bitch…he wasn't aiming to hit me. He fired at the sides. I shifted into his path."

The bullets were patterned at the outer edges of the vent, two on the left, one on the right. Precisely placed.

"There's no way. He shot you at close range."

"He wanted me alive." Jade headed for the door.

"Are you saying he knew you'd crawl in? He planned the whole thing?"

"You can bet your ass, he knew. He counted on it."

"Well, that's a bitch." Wenzel stopped at the kitchen counter. He leaned on the zinc, making no effort to follow her into the hall.

"And why is that?" Jade waited in the outer corridor.

He smirked. "He knows you too well already."

Striding stiffly to the staircase, Jade could hear Wenzel chuckle behind her. Asshole. Unfortunately, the asshole had a point.

Jade equated hospitals with sickness, disinfectant, and fear of things to come. Fear set them apart from crime scenes. At a crime scene, fear transformed from a necessary survival mechanism to a useless, limiting emotion. Evil had already come and gone. Both places shared the stench of human failure that Jade detested, one more cleansed than the other, but ever present below the surface.

Inside County General's doors, her breathing fell short and shallow. Drawing deep breaths became undesirable when disease and death tainted the air.

Hospitals were a vital stop on the path to recovery. Not a place you wanted to visit or stay in for any length of time. Necessary. Dismal.

A few strides down the hall an old man had removed his prosthetic leg, and leaning his weight on the handrail of an open staircase, dragged his body up step by step. He wavered precariously between the sixth and seventh riser leading to a physiotherapy unit.

Determination. She exchanged a smile, walking past, never removing her sunglasses.

"Good morning," the veteran said.

"Morning." She hadn't found anything good in it. She was glad he had.

Sara Keller remained under guard in the intensive care unit on the third floor. Jade stepped into the elevator. The doctor assigned to Sara's case had called to say that an additional blood transfusion proved vital to her overall condition. Her recent tox screen came back clean. Despite this good news, he couldn't say when, or if, she'd wake up.

Exiting the elevator, Jade flashed her badge at the nurses' station en route to Sara's room. The heavy echo of her boots on the white tile floor belied her size. Today she wore Moncler Vivianes, subtle in buffed leather, strong and warm.

She hadn't laid eyes on Sara since administering CPR, even then she hadn't seen her clearly. The image that waited beyond the door wasn't what she expected.

Not depleted or pale, sunken or gray, Keller glowed. Her skin was neither white nor tan. A soft golden hue. Her blue eyes were closed. Jade remembered their coastline shade from the first time they met at the hospital. To see her here, if not for the obviousness of her surroundings, no one would guess she'd danced with death.

Jade found herself staring.

"Do you have any new leads on the maniac who did this?" The question came from a voice behind her, its resentment crisp.

Breaking from her trance, Jade turned to face a man sitting pensively against the back wall watching Sara. "I can't discuss an open investigation. I'm sorry. You are?"

The man wore tattered designer jeans and a rowing team T-shirt sporting a faded sculling logo, hardly the attire of a medical staff member.

"Dr. Johnathan Franks." He offered his hand.

"Off the clock?" Jade made mental notes on every detail from his athletic build to his tanned skin, brand of running shoes, and solid grip.

"Yes. Well, no—"

"Which is it, doctor?"

"I'm not one of Sara's doctors…I'm a staff member, cardiology. Her heart is doing fine."

"Why are you here?"

"Sara's my girlfriend." He rose, bypassing Jade to check the chart attached to the end of Sara's bed.

"I didn't know."

"You wouldn't." Franks diligently absorbed the information. "Most of the doctors in this place didn't either. We hadn't made it public. Sara wanted to avoid town gossip."

He paused for a moment, adjusted an IV drip, and brushed a hair from Sara's forehead. "Everyone knows now."

"I'm sorry." When his eyes met hers, pain had laid a recognizable film over their surface, a cloudy substance curdling with anguish.

"Find him." He pulled his chair closer to Sara's still form and said nothing more. His body language screamed "get out and do your damn job."

Jade angled to reach for the door handle and paused. "Were you supposed to meet…the night this happened?"

"What?" Franks swiveled.

"Did you have a date Wednesday night when she disappeared?"

"No. She was researching an alternative treatment for one of her patients…said she'd be working late. I told the other detective. Why?"

"Every detail helps." A distorted image of Sara's limp body in a pretty pink dress flashed through Jade's mind.

"If there's nothing more…" Franks turned his back to her. How this happened to Sara meant nothing to him. Neither did why it happened. It had, that's what mattered. This, Jade understood all too well.

"I will…" Jade's eyes stayed on Sara. "…find him."

Slipping out of the room, she veered left, taking the back staircase. These people were coworkers and friends of Sara Keller's. If the

Redeemer had been caught sooner, they'd be joking in the hallways, not fighting to save her life. Their judgment, real or imagined, caused a greater internal pain than the burning sensation Jade's wounded leg inflicted with each step to ground level.

She didn't tell Johnathan Franks Sara's rape kit came back positive for semen. This card she selected to hold close to the chest. Its value yet to be determined.

Although Jade had her fill of doctors in the last few days, there was one more on her list. Rachel Leigh had written countless books devoted to the study of serial killers. Three of those were recommended reading at the FBI academy. If Max endorsed her, she couldn't be all bad.

———————

"Detective Carmichael, Dr. Leigh. Thank you for seeing us on such short notice. Sorry to disturb you here at home." Jade extended her hand to an elegant woman with cropped black hair. "This is Detective Jackson Swan."

"Pleasure to meet you both." Leigh ushered them into her adjacent library closing the door behind them. "Max is a dear friend. We go way back. He said you'd be dropping by."

"Have you been following the Redeemer case in the papers?" Jackson asked.

"Of course, Detective. It's what I do. Every year we spawn a new mutation in violent human behavior. I wouldn't offer much in the way of insight if I didn't make it my business to stay current. Have you narrowed in on a suspect?"

"I know him inside out," Jade said. "Not the name, the criminal."

"In that case, have a seat. Let's see if I can help you identify him. Would either of you like coffee or a glass of water?"

Never one for hesitation, Jackson said, "I could spit dust. Coffee would be great."

Jade grabbed the chair with the best view opposite the bank of windows behind Rachel Leigh's desk.

The room smelled of aged books and almond vanilla. Odd pairing, but it worked. The library sat at the front of the estate home, left of the foyer. Everything was bright and relatively open, not well suited for disturbing conversation.

Leigh spoke into an intercom connected to her assistant's quarters. "Iris? Could you bring in fresh coffee and three cups, please?"

Jackson scanned the matching antique chairs but remained standing. "Hell of a view you have here." He stared out the window to the garden. "Does this property border the Churchill lands?"

"You've done your homework. The grounds were designed in the fifties. A more elegant time." The woman's confidence and pride were not openly displayed. Subtle. Deeper. The signature of hard-earned achievement. She wore a chic Hugo Boss suit in a cream weave with black patent heels and a matching belt that accentuated her tiny waist. Sophisticated, not pretentious.

"What can you tell me about the Redeemer that the papers haven't said?" she asked.

"He texted messages to us before each of the murders. Latin." Jade shifted in her seat, unable to find comfort. "The first few times his messages were cryptic, but they've become blatant."

"Interesting. Does he give specifics?"

"Yes, on the victims. He profiles them in fragments narrowing in on his target, leading us to identify them. Then, when he's at the kill site, he sends a final warning."

"Does the information give you a chance to find these women or the illusion of a chance?" Leigh leaned across her desk in Jade's direction.

"The illusion of a chance?" Jackson settled his large frame into the delicate chair next to Jade's. "What'r you fishin' at?"

Jade smiled at Jackson's discomfort. His cowboy boots clashed against the Persian rug. He followed her stare to his feet, then turned his attention back on the doctor.

"Is he allowing you an opportunity to stop him, or is he taunting you?" Leigh clarified.

"Good question," Jade said. "There's a window, a small one—"

"Who has received the messages?"

Leaning forward far enough to fall out, Jackson inched to the edge of his chair. "Jade, for the most part…and her partner, Kane. With the last victim, he sent it directly to Detective Wenzel."

"Is this person working the case with you?"

"Not by any choice of ours," Jade said. "Tensions between Wenzel and my partner run high. They erupted recently, resulting in Kane's suspension. I blame Wenzel for the whole mess."

"Is this public knowledge…the tension between you?"

"No. I wouldn't say that."

"I might." Jackson dodged Jade's glare.

"Do you think it's a coincidence the Redeemer chose to involve someone you're at odds with?"

"Actually, I think when it comes to this guy, nothing's a coincidence." Unable to remain seated for a moment longer, Jade contemplated how Leigh would read her pacing the room. Opting to appear useful, she opened the door for Iris and the coffee tray.

"Have you brought a copy of the case file?" Leigh asked.

"Right here, Doc." Jackson slid the thick file across her desk while Iris poured him a cup of coffee. "Interesting late-night reading."

"I can imagine." Leigh rested her folded hands over the closed package.

"Something else, that's not in there." Jade motioned for Jackson to forget the coffee and follow her to the door. "We found semen on the last victim. I spoke to her boyfriend earlier…they weren't together that night. In fact, it sounded like she blew him off with an excuse about working late."

"All right." Leigh waited for the connection.

"Sara wasn't dressed for work." Jade caught an inquiring gaze from Jackson, who was smarting from gulping back scalding hot brew. "Not even close."

Leigh jotted a few words down on a piece of paper and rose from her desk to walk them out, her expression armor masking a web of thought.

"Don't stand up," Jade said. "Call me when you have something."

"I will." Settling back at her desk, Leigh had the file open before they passed the doorjamb. "You'll hear from me soon."

Jade's gait faltered. Time in the uncomfortable chair had stiffened her bad leg.

"Are you injured?" Leigh asked.

"He shot her," Jackson offered. "Hit her in the leg when she rescued Sara Keller. It's in the file."

There were times when Jackson's forthright personality wasn't so charming. "I'm fine," Jade said. "He didn't mean to hit me."

Leigh furrowed her brow. "You're certain of this?"

"If he wanted me in a pine box, I'd be there."

Leigh stood, set the file down, and walked to Jade's side close enough to peer through the tinted lens of her glasses. "Don't ever believe your part in the game will keep you safe from his rage." The seriousness of her warning added tension to the angles of her face. "In truth, it makes you more vulnerable. He has a point to make and is not above using you to make it."

Jade didn't speak. It was what she'd suspected for some time. The killer's siren song was personal. Jackson thanked Leigh and led the way out.

The fresh air beyond the brass doors came as a relief. Walking across the paved drive to the car, Jackson asked, "You think Sara knew him?"

"I think Sara did more than know him."

"Who else have you told?"

Jade leaned over the car's roof. "No one, and it stays that way. This could be it, Tex, the lead we've waited for to turn the tide on this bastard."

Clearing the front of the car in a few lengthy gaits, Jackson came to the driver's side ushering her to move.

"I'll drive," he said. "You think."

SIX

A true servant of God always keeps his promises. A savior is waiting to be redeemed. Kane read the Redeemer's message.

Then read it again.

"Bodies are littering my lawn." Captain Grey Grant slammed his open hand beside the case information spread on the wall of Shadow Hook's police department's investigation room. "This is the latest translated text, sent to your email. He's calling you back into the game."

"Your lawn, but I'm back to bagging them."

Grey turned from the bulletin board and faced Kane, his pale-blue eyes worn by years of consistent worry. "Which makes me question how he discovered you were suspended."

"Wouldn't be hard." Kane ran his hand through his blond waves. "He placed a few calls. This guy's no idiot."

"Still, have Neco run down any incomings. We need everything we can find."

Kane nodded. "We've narrowed the possible targets to five."

"We've made contact with three. Two are still MIA." Grey handed over the file.

"Not good." Kane flipped through the information. Faces of women, photos taken by loved ones unaware that a sick twist of fate would land them here, in a homicide case evidence file. Kane's wristwatch gained a few octaves, ticking with punctuation in his ears.

The Redeemer wouldn't wait for them, especially after being interrupted with his last victim. Sara Keller survived. He had to know it. Chances were that knowledge would only serve to inspire vengeance in a beast swimming in it.

He closed the file.

Propped on the corner of a desk, Kane settled in. His eyes drifted over the catalog of death and evasion. He walked to the bulletin board and removed a blueprint of the building they found the Keller woman in.

"Jackson said he escaped underground?" Kane stared at the complex layout.

"Through some kind of geothermal shaft," Grey said. "He'll fill you in. Should be here soon."

Kane drifted from one end of the board to the other, tapping each of the initial photos taken at all four crime scenes. "Remote locations. All abandoned or unoccupied."

"Uninterrupted time with the victims," Grey reasoned.

"I don't know, Cap. Evidence doesn't suggest any of his handy work being done at the discovery sites. Too clean." Kane turned his attention to Grey. "You taking heat yet?"

"We were given more funding than any other county because of my connections, and we're coming up empty while bodies mount. What do you think?" Grey rubbed the creases above his brow. "I'll shield us for as long as I can, but the clock is ticking."

"Yeah."

Damek Wenzel strolled into the room, inflated like a peacock. "And to what do we owe this pleasure?" He headed Kane's direction.

"My office, Wenzel." Grey squashed what was sure to be another of Wenzel's ineffective tirades. The captain made for the set of double doors. Wenzel's reluctant exit from the room wasn't tolerated for long. "You got something else to do?"

"I was—" Wenzel protested.

"Want to keep your job?" The expression Grey wore zapped all notions of comedic intention from his question.

Wenzel's scowl failed to intimidate as he scurried in step with Grey.

From behind, they made the perfect odd couple. One tailored, strong, with harnessed wisdom, the other sloppy, weak, and dripping of arrogance—an armed menace. The doors, sporting "Detectives Only" in large black lettering across fogged glass, closed behind them. Kane turned his attention back to the evidence.

Backing up, he put space between himself and the wall, offering a clear view of the entire case. A chair sat a couple feet to his right. Instead, he dragged the desk he leaned on earlier over, placing it in the dead center of the board. Crime scene photos hung in a row at eye level. He removed a toothpick from his back pocket, unwrapped it, and placed it in his mouth.

The key to catching their killer lay buried in existing information. His mind would unearth it, piece-by-piece, fragment-by-fragment, body-by-body. The FBI wouldn't let it sit in his hands without results for long. He loosened his watchband and rubbed the pinch-marked flesh of his wrist.

The evidence exposed a graveyard game of hide and seek.

Grizzly images transformed into calculated outcomes in a pattern of equations, his job resided in recognizing the x-factor. The killer's methodology spoke a secret language. The trick was not to lose its truth in translation.

The Redeemer's victims were successful, accomplished women in their late twenties to early thirties, attractive, unique contributors to society. The head of a renowned wildlife preserve fund, a Black professor, an Asian athlete, and most recently, a White surgeon. A span of ethnicity, all prominent citizens, not easily preyed upon outcasts.

The murders were neither obvious in their violence, nor blatantly sexual. No violation after death, no signs of a struggle prior to. In the subtlety of the acts, the killer revealed a disturbing control more lethal than if he shredded his victims' alive.

No fear of discovery. No fear at all. Restraint. Rage. Killer combo.

Kane left his perch to inspect an enlargement of the first known victim's wrists. The coroner suggested she'd been bound with cotton padding to protect her flesh. A few stray fibers remained behind. No other victim shared this fate.

The Unsub had taken good care of the women prior to killing them. None showed signs of starvation, exposure, or dehydration. Not so much as a scratch on them. From this, Kane narrowed the field of possible assault locations. They weren't being hiked through the bush to a remote hunter's cabin. It had to be somewhere he could drive in and unload his unconscious catch without being detected.

Wherever these women met their fate, they weren't there long. The time between disappearances, text message warnings, and discoveries had decreased with each victim. The killer was excelling at his craft or bored. Neither bode well for the next woman on his sacrificial death list or for law enforcement.

Kidnappings had increased in regularity, from months apart to within days. The schedule was becoming taxing. Every day soiled with the threat of attack.

Toxicology revealed all four women had been sedated. This accounted for the lack of a struggle but brought up other questions. The Redeemer drugged his captives. How was the sedative administered? And what was the duration of its effects?

Their ability to analyze these facts was compromised by the blood-letting.

And what the hell was he doing with their blood?

Visions of vampire horror warped Kane's perspective.

The FBI profile they requested after the third kill made no bones about the pleasure this twisted creature found in human suffering. A docile participant couldn't feed his hunger. To exert his power and take theirs, he'd keep them mercilessly conscious until death. And, in the end, it always came back to sex. His sadistic torment was intimate.

Kane turned his attention on the body dump locations.

Time of death guaranteed three of the four victims were alive when they were abandoned at the sites. Though, nothing short of an act of God could've saved them.

None of the sites had anything in common. Owned by different companies, they ranged from abandoned warehouses scheduled for destruction, to a corporate head office closed for renovations, and a semi-vacant luxury apartment.

Kane's tongue tossed the toothpick over in his mouth as his mind memorized the settings, repeating them with each flip. Why these? If he was hunting for a deserted site, why not others? Still, it wasn't right. Their guy was too precise to be random.

He'd done his research to ensure his castoffs remained undisturbed long enough to expire. Easy to do in a growing county with a surplus of empty or abandoned sites popping up all over, spread across hundreds of acres and town centers.

Kane's revulsion filled the empty office. The Redeemer was taking up too much space, bleeding into Kane's psyche.

The unit's double doors imploded, and Kane bit down stabbing the toothpick into the roof of his mouth, filling it with the taste of blood.

"Kolton, the head coordinator for Home Land Africa is missing." Grey stopped the left door from closing with his size thirteen shoe. "No one has seen her since their fundraiser three nights ago."

"Three nights?" Kane spit the bloody toothpick into the trash and flipped through the target file locating Lainey's dossier. He placed it on top. "Why so long?"

"Apparently, she kept in touch via email. It threw off suspicion for a couple days. Her fiancé showed up at her house to find it empty. He's downstairs. I'm having him transferred into an interview room."

"Which one?" Kane grabbed his leather jacket off the chair. "Which one?" He wasn't letting Wenzel clamp his greasy hands on a possible lead and have it slip away.

"Three." Grey's square features solidified to stone. "We're walking into a hurricane. Tread lightly."

"Why?" Kane's hand clutched the door. The taste of blood lingered in his mouth. "Who's her fiancé?"

"Harrison Wordsworth."

The name stopped him at the threshold. "The billionaire?"

"None other."

"Oh, this ought to be fun."

Grey's expression hardened. "His father was on my polo team, and our benefactor for the department's computer upgrade works with him."

"Don't look so grim. She's alive. For now." Kane didn't give a damn about net worth.

"Watch it. We have no clue where. Optimism aside, we both know the score…we're losing four to none."

Kane's lengthy gait had him halfway down the hall before Grey finished. Approaching interview room three, he passed a fellow detective, Amy Logan, and gave her a grin.

"Hey, Sugar Kane, glad to see you struttin' the dark halls again. You prying secrets out of the money man?"

Everybody knew Harrison Wordsworth and what he stood for. "Gonna try. You see him?"

"They brought him up five minutes ago. He smelled so damn good almost made me want to switch gears."

Kane laughed and rounded the corner. The light outside room

three indicated an interview in session. He swallowed hard against images of Wenzel tripping over his tongue. A repulsive aftertaste. He burst through the door.

"Mr. Wordsworth, I'm the lead detective on this case, Kane Kolton and…" The words left his lips before he made eye contact.

"I thought she was." Wordsworth pointed to Jade.

"Hi, partner."

Her smile brimmed with relief. After years together, they hardly required verbal communication. They read each other with a glance.

"Have a seat. May I call you Harrison?" Kane offered an uncomfortable plastic chair. "Glass of water or coffee before we begin?"

"Water." He lowered into a seat begrudgingly. "I want you both to know money is no object. I want Ren…Lorenda found."

"So do we," Jade said. "When did you realize she was missing?"

Kane left the room, fetched a clean glass from their break room, filled it with filtered water, and returned. He placed it in front of Wordsworth and sat down. Then he and Jade questioned the man relentlessly.

They didn't badger him without cause. The missing person's report covered most of their questions. They asked to gauge his responses, dry out his mouth, increase his body temperature with their pressure, and force him to leave DNA and a nice solid set of fingerprints on the water glass.

Wordsworth hadn't noticed all other visitors to the station were supplied with paper cups. If he had, Kane suspected the billionaire would reduce it to preferential treatment and nothing more.

"You said you'd made plans to meet after the fundraiser." Kane sat back in a chair opposite the moneyman. "Is it typical for her to cancel plans?"

"No. Never." Wordsworth's posture stiffened.

"You weren't alarmed when she didn't show?" Jade asked.

"I told you, she sent a text. It'd been a long day."

After forty minutes of repetitive conversation, they had what they needed, a set of prints, DNA, and leads.

Wordsworth confirmed that Lorenda Lainey's car left the fundraiser and hadn't been seen since. Like her, it never made it home.

Aside from a search for the vehicle, they didn't have much. Several people saw Ms. Lainey leave the building alone. None of the witnesses were credible, all under the influence. There was no camera operating in the parking area. No CTV footage for miles.

"Could Lorenda have been seeing someone?" Jade asked.

"For what?" Wordsworth's body language stiffened defensively.

"Were there other men in her life?" Jade persisted. Kane didn't interfere but managed to throw her a visual caution flag behind Wordsworth's back. "Anyone moving in on her?"

"Men vie for Ren's attention all the time. She's a remarkable woman. They don't stand a chance with her, and she makes sure they know it."

"It's not my intention to offend you—"

"Too late." Wordsworth stood his full height towering over Jade despite her three-inch heeled boots. A tremor unsteadied his hands, and he shoved them in his pockets.

"Listen, Harrison." Kane stepped between them. "Someone has taken your fiancée. We need to find him to find her. Think of anyone who might have shown a special interest in Lorenda."

Wordsworth backed up, shifted his weight, and stared at his feet for a moment. "Wait. There was a young guy at the office who joined the African away team. I know he pressured Ren to come on board. Something about him…"

"Do you know his name?" Kane said.

"I don't remember. I know who would."

"Who?" Jade said.

"Isaiah Isreal."

"And who's he?" Kane escorted Wordsworth to the door and away from his water glass.

"One of our long-term sponsors. He made a point of knowing those involved."

"Why?" Jade asked.

"They're spending his money." Wordsworth jotted a number on a business card and left it on the edge of the table. He turned back around before clearing the threshold. "Ceremony or not, she's my wife. I want her back. She is not replaceable."

The bereft billionaire exited the hallway at the other end. In blue jeans and a rugby shirt, he didn't appear made of money. Unsteady. Broken. Despite his bank account balance, Kane found himself feeling sorry for the man. Jade did too. He read it in her eyes when she joined him at the doorway.

"This is what killers do—turn everyone, even billionaires, into beggars," she said.

"The text came in over an hour ago," Kane said. "We don't have much time."

Jade pushed by him. "The texting. He checked all his messages since?"

Before Jade ran after him, Wordsworth rounded the corner headed back in their direction.

"I thought you might need this." He handed over his BlackBerry. "Only use this one for family."

"We appreciate that. Thank you," Kane reached for the device. "When did you receive the last message from Lorenda?"

"Right before I drove to her lake country house. It's all in my statement."

"And since?" Jade asked.

"It's empty. The password is Vegter, African for warrior. Ren's idea." Wordsworth turned to leave. "I'll expect a call when you have a lead."

"Of course." Jade grabbed Kane's arm, forcing him behind the interview room door and out of the billionaire's earshot. "You know what I'm thinking?"

"The Redeemer sent all the messages."

"Yes. And he quit sending them after Wordsworth showed up at the house. The guy was there. Watching the property."

"Page Jackson. Have him come in from the opposite direction and meet us there."

"There'll be no more messages from Lorenda," Jade said. "Wordsworth's a widower."

"Tell Tex to come in quiet."

SEVEN

Ren clenched her eyelids tight, the lone shelter that remained. The pictures the killer had strewn at her feet were unbearable to witness. Indefensible slaughter reduced to black and white.

Without uttering a sound, she prayed. Prayed for forgiveness. Prayed for salvation. Prayed for rescue, expected deliverance. The Redeemer drove her to a remote location in the country. No one to hear her screams. She didn't waste strength on futile cries for help.

"Is it painful?" She stared, fully exposed.

He came close. A slither of purity lit his eyes.

"That is always the first question…I have no interest in causing you physical pain. Only in redeeming you."

Liar. She'd known men like this. Heartless.

"How is it your mission to cast judgment on me or any other?" She knew the question could infuriate her captor. After forty-eight hours in his possession, she'd passed the point of giving a damn.

"I'm not judging you."

"The hell you aren't."

"I'm redeeming you. You don't understand. Sacrifice is the window to enlightenment."

The needle didn't pinch going in. Smooth. He'd done this before—many times before.

"How many others?" She wasn't sure what made her ask, morbid curiosity or confirmation of her worst fears.

"I've lost count."

Ren exhaled. Hope slithered away on a wave of breath.

"Remain still. There'll be no pain." He left her tied down on the crude slate floor with the capped needle sticking out of her arm. A cold confidence marked his gait crossing the room for supplies.

Keen killer.

In hours, by his hand, her life would end. He'd end it devoid of the slightest sympathy.

The story stole headlines. She couldn't help wondering if the women before her experienced the same silent terror. No way to bargain with a thief who wanted nothing from you but your life. The papers said county police linked four deaths to this man. They were wrong. His sober manner announced a much higher body count.

"Why this way?" Ren said.

"The method is sacred." He returned with clear plastic tubing. She amused him.

Clamping tubing on the capped needle inserted in her arm, he released the flow of blood by flipping a small lever. He inspected his work and retreated into shadow.

Wind howled beyond the walls. She couldn't see windows. She heard them clatter in darkness, afraid for her. They knew what was coming. They'd seen it before.

She quivered on a slab centered in the room. Custom made for the purpose of death, it sat inches above the main floor. Its edges were elevated a grade higher than its center, to hold the spill of blood. The space they occupied was garage-like, but ostentatious. Everything had a pristine shine. The floor carried not a speck of dust. From her vantage point, she could see across its surface, a high-gloss shimmer.

Traces of glue tainted the air. Far from the pure scents of Africa.

Don't think of Africa, Harrison, or the wedding she'd never have. She'd see them again, but not in this world.

"I had a life!" The strength of her outburst surprised her as much as him. He closed the gap between them in a single stride. "You son-of-a-bitch. I have people who love me, depend on me. I contribute to the world in ways you can't imagine!"

She expected to be broadsided by a blow to the temple or subjected to a vicious rebuttal. Fury filled her chest, the fight in her returned. If she could rattle him, maybe he'd slip up.

Dead eyes. No emotion.

In a steady voice, absent of mercy, he said, "They had lives." He pushed the scattered photos closer to her. "You'll never know what their contributions to this world could've been. They had people who loved them, depended on them. All their lives are in ruins. Parents. Siblings. Friends. The list is endless."

Her lungs deflated in a gush. The impenetrable force that steeled her resolve tore without warning. This was it, the beginning of the end.

"Did you know one of them?" The question had hovered behind her lips since she woke to find herself surrounded by the images of dead children two days earlier.

The Redeemer hooked the open line of the tubing into a blood bag and returned to answer her question. He leaned in, face to face, holding her eyes in a hypnotic stare.

Flipping the lever, causing a rush of Ren's blood to snake down the clear tubing, he said, "I am them."

EIGHT

The body was posed.

Unlike the others, drawn and wilted in a display of death and despair, where life and hope were abandoned, its position was orchestrated.

Jade recognized the outstretched lines, the cruel subtleties of each angle. The form stalled her breath and left her in cold silence. She'd seen it before.

Kane entered the room behind her, his line of sight not quite as raw. Still, he halted a stride beyond the doorway.

"Stay back, boys." He threw an arm out, blocking the tactical team's entry forcing them around the long way. "Can't afford scene contamination, not on this one."

Jade's gun arm remained stiff in front of her. Despite the "all clear," she couldn't retract it. Her body refused to holster her weapon.

The victim lay on her side in white linen, arms extended one atop the other pointing to the feet, hands touching in prayer, legs straight out, pressed together. Her head unnaturally twisted into the floor. The face wrapped in a linen cloth—a portrait of shame.

A portrait, all too familiar, burned into Jade's soul.

Her trigger finger vibrated. Rage surged inside her chest, laboring her breathing and erupting behind her emerald eyes.

It flowed off her in waves.

Kane came up from behind, slid his hand down her arm, removing the Glock from her grasp.

"Hey, partner," he whispered. "Breathe."

His calm, alluring tone belied the fear glittering in his eyes.

"Call the ME." Jade spoke loud enough for the boys in blue beyond the threshold to hear and peek their heads around the corner. With her back blocking their view, she reclaimed her weapon and holstered it. "We need TOD."

Kane's perplexed expression faded before their backup noticed.

"Caught me off guard." She patted his broad back. "I'm good."

Stepping cautiously around the left side of the body, she bent forward and slipped on gloves. "We need to know what our window was, if he gave us one at all."

"She's fresh." Kneeling, Kane placed his hand on the victim's back. "Almost warm."

Examining for signs of rigor, Jade agreed. "Dr. Leigh said the chance to save them might be an illusion. She's right."

"Maybe we should pay the good doctor another visit."

"Better call Grey. He deserves a heads-up on the shit storm Wordsworth will rain down on the department when he hears his future wife is dead."

"Damn." Kane pulled out his phone.

Jade waved hers at him.

"No. Let me do the honors. God knows I'm already blacklisted. No sense in you joining me." Kane drifted into an empty outer room and embarked on a dissertation of facts, excuses, and mumbled regrets.

Jade leaned over Lorenda Lainey's body, circling what remained with eagle eyes, scouring the area for evidence. A hair, a fiber, a drop of blood, God, she demanded, give me something.

With her flashlight she traced the outline of the body. She paused, illuminating the swathed face. With her phone, she photographed every angle. Then she lifted the cloth. Studying the expression, she tipped her head closer. "You fought him, didn't you? Good for you." A stray hair hung over the victim's left eye. Jade slid it aside then stood to retrace the body. A fragment glistened back at her, partially exposed beneath the right hand.

"Thatta girl."

She removed an evidence bag from her pocket and kneeled down, cautious of her boot placement. On closer inspection, the scrap appeared to be a black piece of plastic.

Everything mattered.

With the edge of her collection bag, she slid the piece out, tipped it inside, and raised it to eye level.

Kane trudged back into the room. "Tell me you have something."

"Torn piece of plastic. How bad—"

"You don't want to know." Kane started off left, away from the body, then paused and came right. "Wordsworth is on his way to the station. Someone in the department is supplying him inside information. I'm sure he's paying for it."

"This is one bit of news with too high a price...even for him." Jade's flashlight illuminated the horror.

"Their wedding day is less than two weeks away." Kane joined her beside the corpse. "She waited too long."

Their eyes met. Neither spoke. The volume of their silence weighed heavy in the air.

"Sorry...I didn't mean to interrupt," said an officer. "Jackson called up from the gate. We have reporters incoming."

"I'll handle it." Kane rushed to the door. Jade expected him to glance back, say something. He did neither.

Standing at full height, she surveyed her surroundings for the Redeemer's message. He always left one. At the first murder scene it couldn't be missed, scrawled across the wall in blood—not the victim's and, to date, untraceable. Since then, they were less obvious, in inconspicuous locations written in dust or smeared through steam on a mirror.

How many unsolved cases were the work of their boy? How many times had he left messages? And, how often had they been missed? She'd modify her search for back cases with similar MO dreading the results.

The house, like half the town, was cast in shadow. Leaving the lights off, Jade circled the room, cataloging the placement of everything from furniture to crumpled papers.

The murder hadn't taken place here, apparent from the phone that sat unused inches away from their victim's final resting place. If an ounce of life remained in her, she would've sought help.

A lone wineglass sat on top of a hand-carved cabinet. Jade was eyeing it when footsteps echoed behind her. An officer entered the room on his cell phone. A small table sat adjacent to the threshold. On it, a large white pad, a handsome black fountain pen, and an old-fashioned telephone. The officer, with his own Bic Roller in hand, leaned over the pad to jot down his caller's information.

"What? Give me that again slowly," the officer said.

"Freeze!" Jade traversed the distance between them and had her hand between his pen and the paper before he could retreat. His pen punctured the flesh on the back of her hand.

"Hold on," the officer said into the phone, muting it by pressing it into his chest. "What's the—"

"Crime scene, jackass," Jade scolded.

"There's nothing on the pad," he defended.

"How would you know? This guy doesn't put up billboards or leave crumbs for amateurs."

"It's Grey on the phone. He has a message for you and an address."

"Then pass me the phone. And kindly remove your damn pen."

Not realizing his writing tool remained embedded in her flesh, the officer jolted his hand away and relinquished his phone. Jade smiled. "Thanks?"

"Tommy Lennix."

"Thanks, Tommy." He'd endured the lashing with restraint. Good kid. "Can you find Detective Swan for me?"

"Sure thing. The guys found a boot print outside. They taped it off. Twelve or better."

"Thirteen? Every guy I know wears size thirteen," Jade whispered. "He wouldn't be that stupid."

She glanced at her newly acquired laceration, then at the pad of paper. Holding it at an angle with her flashlight beam centered on its surface, she scanned it for indentations. Something had definitely been written on the preceding torn off page. The remaining impression wasn't legible. The lab techs would have to work their magic.

Sounds of discontent resonated from the cell phone. "—bad connection. Jade? Jade, can you hear me? Damn cell phones." Captain Grey wasn't a man of patience.

As she raised the phone to her ear, headlights from an approaching vehicle cut through the victim's living room curtains illuminating two wicker boxes sitting opposite the cabinet with the wineglass on top.

"I hear you. Hold on a second." Jade skirted the dresser, standing a couple feet from the boxes, and absorbed the images before her.

The entrance of sloppy footsteps cast a shroud of annoyance that made her neck tense.

"You searching for African antiques?"

Jade wondered how Detective Wenzel made it past Kane and into the house without injury. She applauded Kane's restraint while questioning her own.

Holding a hand up in a gesture to silence him, she gave Grey the go-ahead.

"Yeah. I figured as much," she said into the phone. "Yep. Give me it…that's close."

Grey advised her Amy Logan had finished the search for potential sites and came up with an empty lake house under construction within Shadow Hook's newest district. He then hung up. She continued speaking into dead air.

"Okay. He just walked in. You want him to check it out?" She let seconds drift as Wenzel waited anxiously. "I'll give him the address."

Wenzel moved in, expecting her to hand over the phone. When he closed the gap, she hung up.

"A tip on an empty property near the riding stables. Grey wants you to check it out."

The tip was real, however negligible. The rest, a lie.

"What's the address?" Wenzel made for the door. Jade gave him the details and breathed a sigh of relief when his car pulled out.

Desperation to impress made for a willing gander.

Lainey's body was dumped in her own house between the time Harrison Wordsworth visited the place searching for her and when they arrived to investigate. The Redeemer wanted them there. He'd lured them into the area.

History guaranteed their discovery meant he was long gone.

The arrangement of the victim mimicked the position Jade's mother had been found in when she was murdered over two decades earlier. Max said she imagined every victim wore her mother's dying face. Today, it was easy to believe.

The killer knew her most intimate nightmare, replicating it with precision. The display reflected an ancient Roman death scene of one of the most celebrated virgins and martyrs—Caecilia, a virgin believed to be guarded by an angel.

Vicious reminder.

One she needed no translation for.

Decades passed, and the rage remained raw. She wanted to rip open her chest and let it bleed. As if somehow, that would release the darkness trapped there. Nothing helped. Nothing ever would unless maybe...more than wanting, she needed this killer in custody. Stopped.

Jade's head dropped. The wicker boxes were at her feet. Her gaze drifted over their surface, making note of the outer measurements. Shifting to the cabinet, her mind placed the boxes neatly inside, most certainly their prior storage space. The wineglass stood at eye level. Her flashlight cast a gleam over its surface. No prints, lip marks, or dust.

Jade studied art history in college and recognized period pieces of furniture. The cabinet's worth would be wasted on others, though it certainly exuded obvious quality. No owner with an appreciation for antiques would dare risk its finish to a drop of stray wine. The goblet's placement, like the body's, was deliberate.

Jade reached for the cabinet's lower doors and flung them open stopping short of impacting the decorative front panels. Inside, in glow-in-the-dark chalk, the Redeemer left his mark. She typed the words into her phone and waited for the translation.

It read, "Home Sweet Home."

"Find anything enlightening?" Jackson's voice bellowed in the dark room. Startled, Jade slammed the cabinet doors shut and spun on her heavy heels.

"Jesus, Jackson. You'll give me a coronary."

"Sorry. What did you find?"

"His message. You'll love this. Home Sweet Home."

"Son-of-a-bitch. My sister has that in her kitchen."

"Everyone does."

Kane entered the room at the tail end of their conversation. "Everyone does what?"

"The message, Home Sweet Home," Jackson said.

"Nice." Kane walked further in to inspect the cabinets.

"How did Wenzel end up here?" Jade asked.

"Came in the back when I was dealing with reporters," Kane said. "No worries. Grey's looking for a reason to transfer his ass to Siberia. It won't take long for the weasel to slip up."

"That's what worries me." Jade gave Jackson a nod. He walked to the light switch and flipped it on. Harsh illumination. The body lay directly below the brightest overhead. It glowed gory in its scarcity. A tribute to the knowledge all humans were comprised mainly of fluid. Its skeletal structure and the ashen skin were a drawn mockery of the once vibrant woman in the award photos adorning the walls. The Redeemer had sucked all the lifeblood from her.

Gallons.

An unlikely vampire, his thirst would never be quenched.

"No blood, no lividity." Jade pulled a black tape measure off her belt and threw it to Jackson. "Distance from the body to the furniture."

Jackson caught the tool, gave a nod, and got to work.

Jade passed Kane, heading for the door.

"I want to know what the hell he's doing with their blood," Kane said.

"Swimmin' in it." The words fell from Jackson's lips without volition as he stared at the body in horror. "Firewood before the deep freeze. He's stocking up."

"Jackson," Jade redirected his attention. "The distances, can you make sure—"

"I got it, kid."

"And seal the scene until I come back. Intact."

"Heading for the lab?" Kane asked.

"I want a report on this fragment. Time's not on our side."

"I'll go with you—"

"No. You're needed here. Wenzel will be back. Text me."

"You never answer your texts."

She turned once, the dead woman calling to her, the image burned over her childhood nightmare. Perfect match. Any moment Kane and Jackson would read it in her eyes. She couldn't allow that, wouldn't allow that. She needed air. The all-too-familiar smell of human stench was rising again.

"End of April," she whispered the words, then louder, "What's the date?"

"It's the seventeenth," Jackson said, his expression questioning.

Kane's head dropped, but he said nothing.

Jade walked out into a slew of field boys, calling back to them, "Process the scene. I'll call you later."

Their voices trailed after her.

"Let her go," Jackson said.

"I can't."

"The date?" he asked.

"Yeah. It's the same day she lost her mother."

Outside, her Mustang was boxed in by a patrol car. She found its owner and lambasted him. The guy laughed then realized she was serious, hopped in his front seat, and pulled out of her way. His fender barely cleared her bumper. She never let up on the gas, narrowly missing Wenzel returning to the scene along the cramped drive. She read his pissed off expression through the windshield.

At the entrance, she threw the car hard left. The field of lights danced in her rearview. There was someone she needed to see.

Alone.

NINE

Mother nature, choked unconscious by a triumphant evil, fell silent. No sunshine. No rain. No wind. The world forfeited a day. Dread hung in its place. It rattled down the length of Jade's spine, resting uncomfortably in her lower back.

Aged oaks gathered their tips in a protective arch over Max's street. Nice neighborhood, typically the sunny side of town. Cast in shadow by the dreary weather, its manicured landscapes and well-seasoned estate homes held the promise of the hard-fought American dream. Its residents hid behind decorative doors, worlds away from a dark reality Jade couldn't escape.

Her Mustang splashed to the curb, its unmistakable throaty engine's growl echoing in the otherwise silent night. Dim lights glowed in Max's library—cocktail hour. He'd have heard her pull up and be at the door. This wasn't her first visit. It wouldn't be her last. Banking on that certainty was a gamble in her line of work, one that paid off so far.

Her keys slipped from her hand and under the car as she exited the vehicle. The absence of sunlight made it impossible to see beyond the car's underpanel. She searched the damp pavement, finding only gravel and muddy debris. Catching something sharp on the tip of her finger, her arm jerked back. She lost balance and regained it, thanks to the wide soles of her MIA Maeva's, narrowly avoiding full contact with the soiled ground. She inspected her wound. A bead of blood formed above a deep pinprick.

"Great." Rising, she scanned the pavement in both directions. "Not exactly a junkie's hangout."

A reflection caught her eye. Car keys. She retrieved them, hit the automatic lock on the fob, and headed up Max's walkway.

Her mind cataloged a hundred possible approaches to the same delicate subject matter. Max would make it difficult. He'd exploit every avenue to force her to reveal more than she wanted. Expecting nothing less, she came armed.

Never disarm, even when you lay down your weapon.

She needed a closer inspection of her mother's case file. She'd recompiled it over the last twenty years—everything except the crime scene photos. The department, Captain Grey, Max, and her father all agreed it was in her best interest to avoid revisiting the murder in such graphic detail, like it wasn't forever etched in her mind. She hadn't spoken to her father in years and wasn't about to. That left Grey and Max.

Max was the most likely to fold. His sensitive patient records were stored at the house during office renovations, and he mentioned they'd continue crowding the place until his new assistant started. His insatiable desire for an inroad into Jade's steel-trap psyche gave her the ultimate bargaining chip.

"Evening, Ms. Carmichael." Max opened the door long before she reached it. "I had a feeling I'd be seeing you. I'm glad you called. This case is stirring up old demons."

"You have no idea." Jade passed under his arm and into the main foyer. The house was warm and inviting despite its formal nature.

"You're bleeding." Reaching to take her coat, Max noted a trail of blood down her finger.

"It's nothing." She kicked off her wet vintage militaries in her usual haphazard fashion. "Dropped my car keys, caught on something."

"I'll fetch a bandage."

She stopped him from walking by. "It's time." Her words were smooth and soft.

"Time for what?" Max's expression obscured a nervous curiosity.

"Time to talk about the first door."

"You're sure you're ready?"

"It's vital to the success of this case. Avoiding it will only cost lives —possibly my own."

His features solidified into an unresponsive doctor's mask. The spark behind his eyes gave him away. It always did. She'd learned to read his irises. They laid bare a varied depth of interest depending on the burn, a quick flash, a silken gaze, or the unmistakable deep flame of intrigue flickering today.

"The study." He strutted ahead, swiveling back to ensure she followed.

The library off his study sat in relative shadow. A fact Jade appreciated. A lone reading light illuminated the area encircling Max's favorite chair. Jade sunk into the billowy sofa across the footrest from it, comforted by the dark void. He accommodated her eyes' inability to adjust timely to changes in light by leaving them dimmed. Aware of this defect, he'd never disclosed it to the department. Jade was aware of his defects too.

They shared appreciation for each other and secrets.

Max disappeared in the distance, then resurfaced in the glow from the bar light nearby. He handed her a bandage coated in antiseptic ointment.

"What are you thirsty for? I assume you're on the clock."

"Always. Ginger ale, if you have it."

"Of course. Shame though. I acquired a Queen Elizabeth cognac, very rare."

Jade absorbed her surroundings while Max poured.

"We should have our sessions here," she grabbed her glass. "Your new office is great, don't get me wrong. It's a bit—"

"Too cerebral. Aloof even." Max settled into his chair, set his cognac on the side table, and leaned in. "Why do you feel confronting the past will aid in breaking this case?"

"The killer knows about Nina's murder." She eased into the dark waters of the past knowing he'd follow. "The last body dump was a recreation."

"You're certain? No possibility of coincidence?"

"Unless my memory's failing."

"Have you mentioned this to—"

"No." Jade sat upright, shifting to the edge of her seat catching a sliver of light over her face. "I'd need to inspect the crime scene photos to be sure. I can't risk Grey doubting my stability. Kane suspects. Won't take him long."

She opened the proverbial doorway and waited for him to inch through.

"What if this *is* directly linked to your past? What if *you* are the central key to the suspect's plan? You need—"

"I need to see the photos, Max. It's the only way." She revealed her intention, leaving no time for contemplation. "I know I couldn't have saved her. I was an eleven-year-old child. I've seen criminals of that caliber in action. I wouldn't have survived to stop a single one of them if I hadn't stayed hidden. All the logic in the world doesn't stop me from kicking the shit out of myself over it. She was my mother, my everything."

Throughout her dissertation, Jade avoided eye contact. She focused on the golden liquid swirling between ice cubes in her glass. When she turned to face Max, his expression brimmed with awe. No typical shrouded emotion. He was beaming with pride. Whether he attributed this breakthrough to his own work as her doctor or was simply relieved to see progress, she wasn't sure. It didn't matter. The moment rendered him speechless. Jade smiled sorrowfully and swallowed back her ginger ale.

"Where do we go from here?" she said.

"I can't allow you to see those photos." Max inhaled, preparing to say more, so she closed the gap.

"Then I can't allow you to continue treating me."

It hit the mark. He reared in defense. "Jade, it's in your best interest—"

"I can't trust you if I don't respect you. I can't respect deliberate interference with this investigation. I told you my life is at risk."

"If it sets you back, especially in light of the case—"

"If I need you, I'll call. You have to trust me."

"You're demanding I toss out the code of ethics?"

Max was on his feet. She stood inches away and several below. "I'm demanding you help your patient save the lives of countless women including her own."

"I really hope you know what you're doing. This is the first time I've seriously questioned your judgment." He rubbed his forehead, a nervous tick.

"There's nothing wrong with my judgment or my sanity. I'm doing what I'm paid to do. Use every means possible to catch a killer. I need your help."

She reached out and pulled his hands away from his face, allowing him the rare opportunity of physical interaction and direct eye contact. Reserved for Kane alone, and he knew it. "I need your help, Max. People are dying."

"Don't make me regret this." He left the room. She hoped to retrieve the file. Her eyes flowed over his chair to the table where his expensive cognac had disappeared from the tumbler, tonight he'd need a second. His footsteps fell heavily overhead, his private office. The empty chalice sat on top of a brochure. He closed a filing cabinet. Its airtight seal echoed above. Stretching to a vantage point, she slid the paper at an angle and read the print.

"Africa: The Withering Womb of the World"

Max's footsteps reached the bottom of the staircase. She shifted the paper back. He rounded the corner, the folder filled with photos of her mother's defiled body in his hands. Begrudgingly, he handed it over.

"Anyone else have access to this? Other than trusted staff?"

"Not even them." Max paused. "Movers, maybe for a very short time. If someone was determined—"

Jade stuffed the file under her arm ready to leave. "Someone is."

Jade's house smelled of aged books. Strewn on every surface, dim lights illuminating intellectual texts. Their titles, graphic and callously prepared to send shivers down the spine, were left exposed in inappropriate places.

Jade ate with them, slept with them, even bathed with them. A treasure trove of avenues into brutality, written by brilliant minds dedicated to undermining the most devious among us.

Her collectibles.

Floors of reclaimed hardwood, walls of exposed stone, and a multitude of shelves framed her criminal archives. A den fit for a life engulfed in darkness but held in the hope of light. Her acceptance of life, good and bad, softened her outer edges summoning solace. High ceilings and open skylights fittingly bathed her home in natural light.

In the wide hallway leading to the open living space, an inset glass case held her awards and photos of those she loved—all of them on the force or in aid to law enforcement.

Her family.

In the center of the two-story great room, Jade sat on the plank floor with her back against a crooked leather couch. The furniture was awkwardly placed, shoved around the room on demand to suit her mood or knocked about on account of it.

Steam rose from black coffee in the mug beside her. She breathed in its aroma. It wasn't intended to keep her awake. A rare individual who developed an adverse reaction to dark roast, black tar soothed her like chamomile tea.

She slid the leather ottoman forward and slightly to the left with her feet. Far enough to cut the answering machine from her line of sight. She found its flashing indicator light annoying. Not all the calls, just the one she knew was waiting. It was fine to pretend she didn't exist, to send her to military school when she was too young and broken to go, but on the anniversary of her mother's murder, her father was compelled to check on her. She didn't answer the phone today.

A visual catalog of her mother's death lay inside the file folder on the floor in front of her. She'd organized the Lainey crime scene photos to her left. Lifting her coffee cup, she swallowed the burning liquid, grimacing as it hit her throat, she opened the file.

The pictures were black and white. Her eyes registered the bloody mess all the same.

Unlike the Redeemer, Nina Carmichael's killer spilled her blood with impunity. It seeped into the carpet, spreading its way to the buffet. From behind cabinet doors, through a crack between the seal, she witnessed a life taken, a most sacred life.

Her mother's last act was to hide her suffering behind closed eyes. Flashes of them glossy with regret burst into Jade's memory. She'd mouthed the words, "I love you always," when he tied her feet. Then, there was nothing more to say. She turned away so Jade couldn't see the pain. And she never made a sound.

Neither did Jade, for almost two years.

By the time she reclaimed her voice, there was no one left to speak to. Her father tried family therapy. When that failed, he sent Jade alone. After three specialists and a battery of psychoanalysis, he gave up. The more she grew into the mirror image of her mother, the more her presence tortured him. Before she turned fifteen, he broke, sent her away, and moved on with a new life. She'd forever be a morbid reminder he couldn't face.

He wasn't alone building walls. Jade couldn't forgive him either. He failed to protect her mother and, by default, her. Her distance made him pay but never enough.

She traced her mother's outline in the photo before her. Beautiful. Filled with dreams. And dead.

Lying in the exact position of the Redeemer's latest victim.

Jade searched the photo for specific details, couldn't focus past the date stamp. Then, there it was, the torturous pain that consumed without warning. Her hands shook. She had to know if he'd taken the pose from intimate knowledge or if he'd had police access. She turned the photo upside down, swiveling her mother's face away from her. It didn't help. The file slipped out from behind the photo, spilling its contents across the floor between her legs. Grabbing for them, she knocked over her coffee. The dark liquid raced toward the merciless images of her dead mother. She glanced around. No towel, napkin, or blanket to be had. She ripped off her white T-shirt and slammed it to the floor between the photos and the spill. Her face was so devoid. Like Jade's life forever after.

Dark liquid soaked into the white cotton until nothing pristine remained.

Jade thrust the photos in a heap back into the file with her stomach heaving. Then crumpled in a ball in blue jeans and a bra, she melted into the floor and sobbed. Alone.

Eleven-year-old daughter of deceased found on site, unresponsive.

Kane couldn't imagine a much colder description. As he read between the dark lines of Jade's past, a cold breeze drifted through the station, across the room, and over his desk. It made impact somewhere between the nape of his neck and his lower back, triggering an unsettling wave through his veins.

Searching details, he read on.

Jade had been trapped behind the buffet doors, a place her mother shoved her before her assailant entered the room. Forced to witness an unspeakable evil at such an impressionable age, it amazed him she'd survived. She stayed silent and endured. That hadn't changed.

She didn't come through it unscathed. Her scars toughened her milky skin, drove a raspy edge to her smooth voice, and carved her emerald eyes to refract every direct stare.

Jade, jaded. He loved every part.

And he couldn't save her from the past. Hell, he couldn't protect her now. As he absorbed the mirror image of her mother's murder in their last crime scene photos, that fact glared back unforgiving and unmistakable.

She hadn't answered his calls since she'd left the scene. Reluctantly, he'd contacted Max. The doctor's involvement with his partner rubbed him the wrong way. Max held secrets. Secrets that empowered him. Maybe, on a deeper level, it was jealousy. Jade pried confessions out of hardened criminals, but Kane had never heard her make one.

She kept her nightmare close and everyone else at a distance, even when he lay next to her. She hadn't shut him out completely, she could've. Her father was proof of that.

Kane knew what time she'd left Max but nothing of what transpired. As usual, the guy claimed doctor-patient confidentiality leaving Kane drifting in the wind. "Damn doctor." Jade had an allegiance to Max, he knew things she wouldn't share.

He rubbed the back of his neck, twisting out the knots formed from pouring over evidence. In twenty-four hours, he'd gone from desperately wanting back on the Redeemer case to wishing it'd never landed on his desk.

Jackson's place was ten minutes west of Jade's. He called her landline and her cell. When she didn't pick up, he decided to swing by. The case had taken on a new intensity. One aimed in Jade's direction. It made him itchy.

Her car wasn't in the driveway. He stepped out of his truck and strolled over to the garage window, his cowboy boots casting spray across the sodden pavement. Cupping his hands to block out the streetlight's glare, he peered in. The Mustang reflected back, still damp from its trek over wet roads. He walked back across the drive.

Standing at the bottom of the stairs leading to the house, he turned on a flashlight and glanced up.

A dim glow lit the transom window above the front door though no welcoming lights were on outside or directly inside the foyer. If Jade was home, she'd left a light on somewhere deeper inside the house.

The steps passed behind the umbrella of a handsome weeping willow that smothered out the streetlight and left the impression of a towering mushroom. Jackson tipped the flashlight to ground level as he passed beneath. The step's shallow depth barely accommodated the length of his boots.

Pounding his heavy hand against the wooden door garnered no reaction and forced him to use the iron knocker. He hated that thing. Why she wouldn't install a doorbell like the rest of the world he'd never understand. Jade had a reason. Jade always had a reason.

No answer.

Not content to give up, he made his way through low bushes and across the yard to the back of the house. The slope of the land gave way to an elevated back deck. Jade insisted on privacy, and the height it afforded added seclusion. Light from her great room illuminated the space. With no other options, he grabbed a corner post and swung up one leg at a time. Throwing his large frame over the railing he landed hard enough to wake the neighbors a half-acre away. He expected Jade to burst through the doors cursing at him. No movement. His heartbeat echoed in his ears.

At the window, he scanned the room for signs of life. After a brief moment, he spotted her gun and badge on the table closest to the fire-place. A lamp sent a glittering light over the metal. An array of combat boots littered the room. No fire roared.

She was home. She had to be.

He rapped his fist against the glass calling her name.

"Hey, kid, open the door, would ya? Jade, where are you at?"

Nothing. A dog protested in the distance.

Shifting positions to another window he searched more carefully. The jumbled furniture was clear of bodies, the rug in front of the fire-place empty, no one approaching from the hall. Then, a small portion of her foot protruded from behind an ottoman in the center of the room.

The night fell cold against his skin.

"Jade!"

He searched the windows for an opening, knowing with her security locks, the doors wouldn't be easily forced. The long vertical window at the far end opened. Locked. He pulled out his weapon and smashed it hard against the glass. The outer pane shattered, while the inner one remained intact. His eyes searched beyond it. Jade's foot hadn't moved. Again, the butt end of his gun impacted the glass where the security latch connected inside. It broke enough to cut his hand reaching in to disengage the lock. He forced the window open and squeezed his large frame inside.

"Jackson? What the hell are you doing?" Jade spoke detangling her headphones.

"I thought...why the hell are you wearing noise-canceling head-phones? We've been calling you for an hour." With excessive force, he slapped broken glass off his jeans.

"Jesus, you're bleeding." She grabbed and inspected the wound. "Edgy cowboy."

"Jade!"

"The neighbors bought a puppy. I couldn't concentrate."

"You couldn't concentrate?" He shook his head at the destruction he'd left behind.

"Thought you were as smooth as molasses in the Texas sun." She laughed her way to the kitchen. "Edgy."

She didn't notice or care she was shirtless.

"Edgy? While you're in there, put on some clothes. Headphones?" He collapsed into the sofa waiting for a bandage and her to quit laugh-ing. Then his boots grazed the scattered photos at his feet.

No pretty pictures. No reason for laughter only deep-seated dread.

Jade returned, shirt and first aid kit in hand. She set the shirt aside, retrieved the bandage, and proceeded to wrap his injured hand. By the third loop, she paused to answer his stare.

"You're worried." Her smile added wattage to the dull glow in the room.

"Real worried, kid." Her emerald eyes were impossible to read. He tried. She retreated, her attention on the white gauze. Her touch was kind and open, a contradiction to the gateway to her thoughts.

"Time to swap out the windows for something sturdier."

"Then how will I break in when you're ignoring us?" He inspected her work and grinned approval.

"Military school," she said. There were so many reasons for her to be hard. Her touch was soft. Her heart was too, he thought, but only to a point.

She smiled, rose, and threw the shirt over her head leaving it crooked. He stayed seated. "You think you're a lone wolf. We're all behind you, you know. You're just out in front of the pack." A moment passed. "I'm worried about the path you're choosing."

"The path's set, Tex." She stood and headed back to the kitchen with a handful of supplies. "I've been alone too long to believe it's not. I didn't choose it, just walking."

"Running more like. Watch your step," He stood, scooping broken glass into a pile with the edge of his cowboy boot. "The ground's a minefield."

TEN

Gravel dust swept up by turning winds snaked across the rooftop as architect Venice Beil and her construction manager exited the elevator. They weren't alone. The graceful element of Venice's walk, despite the hardhat and steel-toed boots, made her appear adrift. His stare followed the debris encircling her, twisting up her lithe body, making landfall in her steel-blue eyes.

She couldn't have seen him even if she hadn't been blinded by filth. He, the one they'd labeled the Redeemer, remained a darkness noticed too late.

The annoyance at Venice's side slid closer than necessary during his dissertation on the progress of the building.

They all did that, hounds begging for attention. Sexy lured so easily it created pathetic, wanton drones from potentially decent individuals.

The manager uttered a statement meant to amuse her. Venice smiled politely then shifted the conversation back to business—ever the eager architect. He couldn't hear much more, out of range. The dissatisfaction of her response registered on the man's face. Their visitor wore out his welcome. Grinning, the Redeemer checked the watch beneath his tightly stretched glove. Time was on his side.

An updraft breached the edge of the rooftop, hitting the man with a force that sent him quaking. It caught Venice as she stepped back from the lip, almost sending her to the gravel. The construction manager lunged at the opportunity to put his paws on her, seizing her shoulders, jerking her to him.

Visions of the manager screaming to his death down fourteen floors comforted him. A shame it wouldn't come to pass. This work called for a live patsy.

Incensed by the rejection, the manager made his exit and headed back alone. He didn't know that with each footfall he closed the distance between himself and an invisible enemy deciding his fate. His ignorance was laughable, but the moment called for silence.

The Redeemer blended into darkness. A craft he'd honed by years of it bleeding into him.

They'd become one.

He sent chills softly whispering, sensed but never seen.

Brushing dangerously close, the manager appeared as predicted, stocky, weathered, and aged by nicotine with repulsive, meaty hands. He stepped onto the elevator pawing at some imagined tendril tickling the nape of his neck and was whisked away from certain death oblivious to the frailty of his existence. If not complicated by the fact he'd be the last person to see Venice alive. Identified on surveillance cameras entering the building with her and again leaving alone—difficult to explain for such a meager mind. His fingerprints might even be traceable on the shoulders of her jacket.

Convenient.

Detective Carmichael wouldn't buy it, certainly not after the interview stage. Her adversary was too cunning to announce guilt in obvious ways. Jade knew him better than that. And he knew her.

Every lead had to be followed regardless of validity. This new morsel he'd hand her deserved, at minimum, an uncomfortable grilling.

Venice surveyed the area, scribbling notes on her organizer while walking the perimeter. The building wasn't an architectural masterpiece. However, with his help, it'd stand as a monument of stone long after she crumbled to ruin.

Through beams, he watched the elevator disappear, carrying a scapegoat to ground level and beyond the point of registering screams. Though there wouldn't be time for any. His eyes followed it down until a scraping sound diverted his attention.

She'd made her rounds to come full circle on the rooftop standing at the gates of judgment. So close he could reach out and touch her.

How could she be numb to his presence? She faced the opposite direction, her back to him. Her copper hair, wind whipped into a fiery mane, drew the light as if starved for wattage. He reached out to touch it. Fingertips grazed over warm strands. She froze where she stood.

Not so numb after all.

Kane rubbed his eyes then squinted as the afterburn set in. Instead of relief, the effect was sandpaper on tissue already red and raw. He'd poured over Sara Keller's hospital videotapes all night, not willing to accept the results from the lab techs. No slight against their abilities. Their eyes were not his, and that was reason enough.

He narrowed the footage to fifteen minutes. Spliced periods where nondescript individuals exited the building—two through the front, five out the rear employee doors.

Four men on the footage were eliminated. He searched for the Keller woman. The techs expected her to be carried out, forced against her will by her kidnapper, or ushered out unconscious on a gurney or in a wheelchair.

Kane's tired eyes darted across the screen, looking for the alternative.

Sara Keller left willingly or…worse.

He froze the image, zoomed in, and enhanced its clarity. Then glanced at the empty bottle of aspirin on his desk. Sara Keller, in disguise, walked out the back door unaccompanied straight into the arms of a killer. He replayed the footage twice before leaving to rummage through Jade and Jackson's desks for painkillers. He was in for one hell of a headache.

This changed everything. Each fragment of evidence painted a clearer picture of the Redeemer, his motivations, his targets. It awakened the prospect that he'd known the victims—Sara for certain—before they were chosen. He may even have held long-term relationships with them all. They'd cross-referenced known acquaintances and come up empty. The guy would likely use different names, and an array of disguises.

As Kane tossed Jade's second desk drawer, the stream of possibilities rushed forth carried by the throbbing pain in his head.

"I'm not stashing booze or money in there. What's the attraction?" Jade entered the room to find him buried in the contents of her desk.

"No. I…" He flipped the cap off an Advil Migraine bottle and dry-swallowed two before glancing up.

"Have you been home? And what are you…Jesus." Jade skirted his desk and came face to face with Sara Keller's incognito image. "She met this bastard willingly?"

"Appears so." He treaded wearily to the water cooler. "You know what this means?"

"We're worse off than we thought. We can't protect his targets if they're protecting him. She walked right into his hands."

"Who did?" Jackson came in on the tail of Jade's discovery. "Man, you look like horseshit." He sauntered by Kane catching a glimpse of the image Jade was transfixed by. "Damn it to hell."

"It's more personal than we thought." Kane stared at the case board, gulping water down in an effort to dislodge the pills stuck halfway down his throat. "Where's the connection? I could see the killer targeting the Keller woman. Maybe she failed to save someone he cared about?"

"Revenge?" Jackson said. "If that's the case, how could one event tie a doctor, an African aid worker, and these other women together? Not likely."

"Doesn't matter," Kane focused on the victim's faces. "If he knew them, he's hidden in the history, buried somewhere behind every one of them."

"Did we hear back from the lab on the plastic from our last scene?" Jade moved away from Kane's desk to allow Jackson a closer inspection of the footage.

"Common plastic. They couldn't identify specific the origin," Kane said. "It's a fragment of a larger piece—"

"Like everything else we…" Jade's voice dropped off.

Kane turned to face his colleagues. "They *did* find traces of a substance left behind."

Jackson abandoned the frozen image of Sara Keller's worst mistake. "What substance?"

"Drywall dust."

"He's using empty buildings." Jackson sunk into his oversized chair then rolled it closer to the board.

"They'll probably link it to the apartment where I fell in on him." Jade converged with them in front of the row of victims, pausing before the photo of Lorenda Lainey. Disappearing in its details, she spoke without volition. "Your death didn't need to happen, nothing but a fuckin' waste. It served no one, not even you." She rejoined the living, asking, "How did this lunatic dupe such a smart woman?"

"She was distracted." Kane stepped back to lean on the edge of his desk. "Never saw it coming."

"Well, that makes half the damn population sittin' ducks," Jackson said.

Kane glanced at Jade then back to the victims. "Some more than others."

"Is that a warning, Detective?" Jade's voice held its defiant undertone.

"Someone who's still limping from his last attack shouldn't need reminding."

"So my vision was clouded by something other than mace?" Jade distributed her weight equally on both legs, tempting her injury.

"This guy has dug under all our skins," Kane said. "But his fascination is with headstrong women." Jade's eyes darted to the folder he held. Although hidden by other papers, a section of her mother's crime scene photo was exposed.

"He knows them." Jade strode by the line-up of photos. "Studied them."

"Knows how to manipulate them." Kane slid the folder behind him on the desk.

"Unless…" Jackson walked over to the African aid worker's picture and pulled it off the wall. "She didn't want to be saved."

"What are you suggesting?" Kane shook his head. "You think the victims cooperated…with their deaths?"

"I've heard crazier theories." He placed the photo back on the board. "It explains the doctor's willing exit from the hospital and the absence of a physical struggle."

"So would drugs," Kane said, weighing options.

"Seriously," Jade grabbed the picture of Lainey's gaunt corpse. "No one chooses to go out this way!" She slapped it down in front of them, incensed. "I ought to know."

Kane studied the photo, not that he needed to. The image was forever cemented in his psyche.

Jade stood before him, inches from his body. "Her priorities might be backward. Doesn't make her a masochist."

Kane glanced at the photo one last time, then locked eyes with her. "They don't suffer the aftermath. Their loved ones do. *Didn't* make her a masochist," he corrected.

"What?" Jade asked with her head turned, analyzing the board.

"She's dead," he said. "Past tense. She isn't anything anymore."

Jackson reached in and removed the morbid image, inserting it back in the empty hole on the board. "I'm going down the hall to make a fresh pot of tar. I'll be back in ten. Play nice." He made eye contact before leaving. "We need combined brain power for this one. Circle the wagons. There's a link somewhere."

When the door shut behind Jackson, Jade spoke first.

"What the fuck was that? Blaming the victim won't work here or with me. Ask Beau."

"I'm not your father—"

"Good to remember."

"You're taking unnecessary risks. I know why. Solve it from the outside, don't get sucked into the heart of it."

Jade headed for the door. "I don't work like that and guess what?" She pointed at the Redeemer's wreckage. "Neither does he."

"You're leaving?"

She never acknowledged him. Kane stared back at the dead women's faces listening to Jade's combat boots fade. He wanted to grab her, shake sense into her, and break down her walls. He'd tried for five years. He was as far inside as anyone had ever been. There was a line he couldn't cross. A minefield capable of blowing everything he'd built with her up to this point to smithereens. He couldn't risk it. They'd come too far. The recognition of her brilliance on the job lent some comfort. Still, he couldn't help seeing Jade's shadow placed over top of the faces before him.

He barely heard her come back in, and with her four-inch crap kickers on, that was saying something.

"I think we're safer in here." Jackson finished his conversation with Jade as the doors shut behind him. "Bookin' nightmare out there."

"Don't be so sure," Jade teased, smiling on approach. Her rage back in hiding.

"It's in their background," Kane said as the pair returned to the board. Jade moved well inside his personal space, claiming him as only she could. He stepped around her. "We know their careers. None of them are married. No kids."

"Ambitious women, haven't had time?" Jackson offered.

"Haven't made time. Two of them were on the path to marriage… two that we're aware of."

"He's killing them off before they commit?" Jackson questioned.

"Before they have a chance to give life." Kane's words were idealistic. Gut instinct said they had merit.

"Marriage completes you? You—"

Kane didn't let Jackson make it personal. "Commitment poses a threat to our guy."

"It poses a threat to a lot of us." Jade's tone, lighthearted, annoyed.

"Some view it as the ultimate opportunity." He cut back.

"You think this guy dated them?" Jackson asked. "Always a bridesmaid?"

"Yes, and maybe not so far back."

"The dress." Jade flipped through a file, pulled out part of a report, and read it aloud. "…wearing a pink cocktail dress."

"What?" She'd lost Jackson.

Jade continued, "Keller. She blew off her fiancé, but her outfit said date night. Casanova?"

Kane stared at the victims' faces. "These women were hiding the same secret."

"Cheating is a filthy business with dire results," Jackson said.

"Such insight." Kane teased.

"You're not speaking from experience, are you?" Jade asked.

"I'm an upstanding gentleman," Jackson said.

"While you're up standing, you want to fetch breakfast? I'm starved," Kane said.

"You laugh, Kane." Jackson headed for the door. "Hurry up. I'll swallow your sarcasm, but I'm not doing takeout."

Kane hesitated for a moment, glancing back at the beseeching faces, then followed behind Jade and Jackson.

"Swan and Paddle, Paddle side?" Jackson asked on the way out.

Jade reached over and rubbed the two-day growth on Kane's chin. "No one else will let him in." One touch from her laid claim on him and those eyes. She searched his for the, "yeah we're okay," until he gave it.

"Lucky for you, I have family connections in this town." Jackson laughed.

They weaved through people crowding the station to the front of the building. A gang bust consumed the place with wall-to-wall chaos.

"You two only wish you had as solid a work ethic," Kane yelled, shoving the door open.

"This from a guy who just came off suspension," Jackson said, escaping the building.

"Listen—"

"Hey, Sugar Kane." Amy Logan burst out the front door down the steps after them. "You have another one. Your phone must be off."

Pulling the cell phone from his pocket, the icon flashed repeatedly that he'd missed an incoming text. The phone was on, fully charged, with volume up, and useless beneath the noisy reception area. He opened the message while the others encircled him. They read the expression on his face before he uttered a sound.

"No grub then," Jackson said.

"Nope." Kane tilted the screen to his partners. "His prose decimates the appetite."

ELEVEN

Human hands are the cruelest weapons. The Redeemer studied the lines and contours of his before sliding them into a new set of gloves, revisiting their darkest acts.

Knives cut indiscriminately through many things given an accurate degree of pressure. Guns fired bullets that tore from a distance. And poison, poison wreaked havoc beneath the surface, lethal and unknown.

No. He brushed a finger down the length of Venice's throat. Human hands put these cold weapons to shame by the duality that set them apart.

They caressed before they killed.

A strong pulse brought the still flesh over his victim's jugular to life. It rose and fell in a relentless erotic rhythm. With her head swiveled sideways, the vein was pronounced. He studied its tempo for sixty seconds, calculating the speed of exsanguination based on her resting heart rate.

Adrenaline would soon disrupt this perfect cadence, replacing it with erratic rhythm. There were drugs for that. He knew and possessed them all.

Her head fit comfortably in his hand. Peaceful. Unaware.

He dropped it to the bed.

He rose, making his way to a nearby drafting table.

"The lines are clean and true, I'll give you that." He inspected the architectural renderings of her building. "There's symmetry, but no passion."

As if dismissing him, she moaned then fell silent.

"I expected more. You possess passion. At times, it rules your life. One could even say it set the foundation for the fragile lattice of self-destruction that was your youth. Complex beauty—no backbone."

Her moan intensified, offset by the icy tone filtering into his voice. She'd always struggled with his censure. She had good reason.

The bland blueprints failed to bolster more than a moment's interest, lacking the captivating essence of their creator. He studied her, arms and legs chained wide open. Flashes of her rejecting the construction manager's less than subtle advances danced in his memory, she never rejected him. She wasn't stupid. Sophisticated. Refined. And leery—fire on ice.

He returned, sitting near her chest. "Apologies, darling." He removed the gag from her mouth.

"It's fine." She licked moisture back across her lips. "It's just…we agreed not to discuss business when I'm tied up."

"Baby, I wasn't discussing business. I was discussing passion."

"It made you mad, Jimmy hitting on me." She adjusted in bed.

"It made you hot that I was watching."

"Yes. The question is, what are you going to do about it?" Her eyes begged.

"Kill him."

"Would you?" She waited, never one to rush. "Kill for me?"

"Yes."

"You wouldn't." The doubt in her expression said she didn't know him at all.

"I would." His voice echoed back too solid.

She pulled her head off the pillow, bit his chin, and seized his mouth as he bent to release her bite. Her passion was endless, nasty, deep, and unbridled. She came up for air, gained enough to whisper. "Prove it."

"You think you can handle me," he whispered back. "You can't, kinda wish you could."

"Try me." He straddled her, hovering over her midriff. She fought to touch him, affect him. She'd never get the chance.

He leaned down. She rose up. "I have," he said. "Too many times."

She opened her mouth to speak. He silenced her with the rag. He unlocked the chains from the hooks one at a time. Her eyes stayed on him. Curious. No panic. He seized her right wrist in the solid grasp of his left hand and dragged her body outside across the gravel surface of the roof. She came to life a little more with each step. By the time he tossed her head and shoulders over the roof's edge she was decidedly protesting. Suspended by a cinch of chain at her waist, her face twisted around the curses muffled by cloth.

"Quite a view, isn't it?"

Her arms flailed, her legs fought to retreat, dust kicked up in plumes by her efforts floated past. She'd lost all composure and clearly wasn't enjoying this downward perspective of the building.

With a sharp jerk, he pulled her back to level ground.

"You let fear overrule the opportunity for insight."

She couldn't breathe. He removed the rag. Coughing out a cloud of filth, in a disheveled pile at his feet, her true nature emerged. "What the hell is the matter with you? I could've fallen!"

"You didn't."

"What's happening here? We didn't agree on today." She scrambled to regain composure. Searching the background for her clothes. She noticed the scrapes on her ankles and legs. "What the hell? What's going on? Why are you here?"

He waited. She stopped scanning their surroundings. Her eyes drifted to his hands. He'd never worn gloves before. She liked his hands, but not today.

When dread brought her eyes to his, he seized the moment. "To even the score." He struck and landed a single blow to the head in the precise location of the injury she sustained two days prior. She hit the ground like a bag of hammers.

He couldn't put full force behind the strike. Her death would not be so simple.

Still, the action permitted a modicum of satisfaction. As did the knowledge that there'd be more where that came from.

Venice Beil wasn't where she was supposed to be. Kane and Jade found her apartment empty, her office too. Kane was routed directly to an answering service when he called her number. And, when he reached them, none of her clients or colleagues had seen her since early morning. The metal industrial clock in her warehouse loft tracked time in silent motion. Kane stood beneath it listening to its imaginary gears grind down hope of finding more than a corpse.

"I hate this." In the hour they'd been there, Jade's search had escalated from riffling through papers to pitching draft tubes. "This woman has seven active sites and consults on a dozen others spread across three counties. God only knows where he cornered her."

"It doesn't matter." Kane walked to the doorway. "She's dead."

"We don't know that." She stopped riffling through papers.

"The hell we don't. We interfered. You got too close. He's using her to teach us a lesson. You read the text. He didn't write in obscurities. This is payback."

"Where are you going?" She stepped out of the mess she'd amassed to follow him to the doorway.

"The station. Any link we're going to find will be there."

Jade grabbed his arm before he turned the handle. "So will a heap of trouble and a swarm of camera crews."

He couldn't think past the case.

"Harrison Wordsworth," Jade reminded.

"Terrific."

"Grey called me on the way over to give us a heads up. He's gonna take serious heat on this one."

"Might as well use it to our advantage."

"How do you intend to do that?" Jade dusted off her jeans.

"Don't know. We have eleven blocks to figure it out."

On the way to the station, the lab called. They'd identified the plastic fragment from Lainey's crime scene as remnants of an older model Mustang, early nineties, part of the headlight apparatus.

Jade relayed the news as Kane drove.

"She drove an Audi, this year's model. Nothing else registered in her name." Jade worked on the onboard computer digging into vehicle registry documents.

"Should I be checking your headlights?" Kane flashed a grin.

"Funny."

"Start with Lainey. Can't rule out a previous victim or the next one on his list. Go all the way back. When was she licensed?" he asked.

The odds of a killer keeping a car part from twenty years earlier were slim. Their suspect was too clever to leave evidence behind without reason. The part was planted. Its connection gnawed at Kane.

"Strange. There's nothing here before her twenty-eighth year. Long time to wait to assert your independence," Jade said. "Doesn't add up."

"She didn't strike me as the hitchhiking type. What about a learner's permit?"

Jade was working on the computer when he turned into the station parking lot. Creases cut into her forehead when it brought up Lainey's first DMV photo. She swiveled the screen his direction. "She was a kid. Why wait thirteen years in between?"

"Good question, and I know who we should ask. Follow the cameras."

Harrison Wordsworth had transformed from the moneyman behind the scenes to a frontman for vigilante justice. When he came to the station claiming his fiancée was missing, he'd slipped in concealed in casual clothes. He left in a well-used Jeep. Today he wore the marks of power and distinction, stepping out of a Rolls-Royce limousine, surrounded by bodyguards dressed in Armani suits.

"Shit. Let me out." Jade abandoned her search as the media circus came into view. "I'll push him inside before he destroys us."

Kane slammed his foot on the brakes. She sprang from her seat, injured leg and all.

"Mr. Wordsworth. Thank you for coming," she said before the door slammed shut.

He slid the car into an open space reserved for Captain Grey and rushed to provide a block between their visitor and trailing journalists.

"Detective, Detective, are you any closer to catching this madman? What assurances can you offer the community?"

"I'm glad you asked," Kane said. His acknowledgment stopped the reporters cold. They hadn't expected a welcomed response. "Thanks to the help of Mr. Wordsworth and other witnesses, we are narrowing in on our suspect. We know he's choosing specific targets, individuals he has had personal involvement with—"

"Have you identified the killer?" another asked.

"As I said, we're narrowing in."

He hated reporters. Grey was probably on the other side of the station doors holding a silver platter and a machete for his head when he walked through. They had to be told something. It might as well annoy the hell out of the Redeemer. Kane prayed his animosity for the bloodsucking son-of-a-bitch crawled through the camera lens, reaching beyond a transfixed audience to land like a bad rash.

"Has the FBI been called in on the case? It certainly appears warranted."

Kane's grasp on his car keys tightened to an uncomfortable clench. "No one knows our community better than Shadow Hook's detectives assigned to this case, and *no one* has a more personal interest in seeing justice carried out. What assurances do I have? I'll tell you this, we'll bring him in, and he'll pay for his crimes if it's the last thing I do."

He'd hoped to play it cool. He failed.

He meant what he said. His delivery of those words cast the mob into silence. As he escaped behind the station doors, he wondered how he'd live up to them. He wasn't the only one.

"What the hell was that?" Grey said. His scowl and ushering of Kane down the hall meant he was pissed without the luxury of time to dwell on it. As they walked, the tension between them narrowed the corridor until Kane was certain their feet would entangle fighting for space.

"Harrison is threatening to place a bounty for blood on this guy."

"Bad analogy." Kane focused straight ahead during Grey's reaming.

"You made an impossible pledge on national TV, and your partner managed to offend him in under five minutes. Do I need to waste time telling you what's at stake?"

"No, sir. I'll make him listen. I'll handle it."

The stress cracks never left Grey's face. He marched on, leaving Kane to enter the conference room where Wordsworth waited alone.

"Don't get up," Kane said, entering the room. Wordsworth sat in a wingback chair transported from Grey's office. No more uncomfortable plastic. "Before you say your piece, hear me out."

Wordsworth fumed. Beneath the searing surface, his loss burned him to the very core. Rage made him frail. A statue of ash.

"Nothing you say will—"

"This isn't about you or your feelings. It's about your fiancée and her right to justice. I put my head on a chopping block on national television to prompt this bastard out of hiding. He doesn't need another target, so you won't be giving him one! He knows the women he kills. You need to focus on everyone who had contact with Lorenda—"

"You're not suggesting—"

"Infidelity is the least of your problems. I don't think, the department doesn't think, she was having an affair. Considering the lack of evidence, that'd be a blessing. Who did she trust?"

Kane studied Wordsworth's body language, the head in the hands, the shuffling of his feet, the uncomfortable shifting in his chair. His eyes issued a transparent window to a broken soul. He wasn't their guy. Of that, Kane was certain.

"Think." Kane came around the table and pulled a chair close. "Who?"

"She argued with an African—"

"We know. It's not him. We know she left the building alone. Who would she trust to get her home?"

"My driver, but he was with me."

"Who else?"

"The event planner, a woman, a couple team members. Your men have probably checked them out."

"Write down their names and contact information." Kane handed him a pad and pen.

"And maybe a couple key contributors."

Kane tapped the pad with a finger. "Them too."

"It's useless. She's known them for years. They never showed any signs—"

"They never do."

Something hit home. Wordsworth's hands clamped onto the chair as if it were the only life preserver in an endless sea. He waited a moment to compose himself before he spoke again.

"You're right. They never do. I won't be without Lorenda for long. I probably won't ever see you apprehend this garbage—"

"We'll catch him. Don't give up on us. We haven't—"

"You don't understand, Detective. I won't live long enough. I'm dying. Maybe tomorrow, maybe a month from now. With Ren gone, I don't care either way. She knew. No one else."

Kane expected the conversation would elicit no new leads. He started it to redirect the grieving man's attention off lawsuits and onto their team. Instead, it opened his eyes to a Greek tragedy.

"There's a gap, well over a decade, between her learner's permit and her driver's license. Tell me why."

Wordsworth paused, switching gears. "She was in a bad accident, kids died."

"I have to ask, was it her fault? I'm sorry."

"For what, Detective? Indelicate questions? The kids? Her murder? Or me dying?"

On his way out of the building, circling wolves cornered the moneyman. He said nothing in response as guards ushered him into the waiting Rolls.

Kane briefed Grey as soon as he was gone.

"Damn lucky." Grey caught the highlights on the flatscreen in his office with the door shut.

Kane stood stoic beside him. "Not so lucky."

Grey lost interest in the screen and slid back behind his desk. "His compliance won't do a thing to save Ms. Beil."

"No." Kane ran a weary hand across his forehead, smoothing out embedded tension.

"Find something that will."

"Yes, sir."

"And get that piece of crap out of my parking space."

"It's gone." Kane headed to the door with keys in hand and had almost made it when Jade poked her head into the hallway and waved him back inside.

"Can it wait? Grey's having my car towed."

"Nope. Max is here. Dr. Leigh is with him. You need to hear what she came up with."

Kane tossed his keys back into his pocket and followed Jade into a meeting room. Max and Dr. Leigh waited inside. Leigh stood to introduce herself. Max needed no introduction and never moved from his seat, his eyes locked on Leigh's case file.

"Pleasure to meet you." Kane extended his hand to Leigh.

"I hope you feel the same after this meeting," she said.

"Your opinion of this degenerate can't be any worse than mine."

"Might surprise you." Max shifted his attention off the case file.

"Max." Kane crossed the room and loomed over Max's shoulder. "What's up, Doc?"

Jade rolled her eyes at Kane's intentionally demeaning humor then said, "Leigh thinks we've missed a crucial aspect in the killer's profile."

"What aspect?" Kane directed his attention to Leigh.

"He is after one of you." Leigh waited, letting the gravity of her words fill the room.

"How? Why?"

"You said you suspect he knew the victims before he attacked them...knew them intimately. What makes you think the same logic doesn't apply to you?"

"He's the hunter, they're the prey, we're the forest rangers," Kane said. "It's not the same."

"Not in your eyes, perhaps. Everything I've read suggests this predator has specific targets and a particular agenda fueling these acts. He's advancing to a final resolution. His timeline is narrowing approaching his ultimate goal—"

"What goal? Proving what?" Kane demanded.

"I don't know." Leigh's composure held like her certainty.

"How does that help us?" Kane paced the room. Standing in one place became intolerable. "Profiles are intended to direct the focus of investigations this isn't—"

"Wait a minute," Max chimed in. "Rachael spent years learning what makes these predators tick and—"

"We both appreciate your help, Dr. Leigh," Jade said. "I'm sure you understand our mounting frustration."

Kane ignored the apologies. "Tell me something I can nail him with. What made him is meaningless if it can't help us stop him."

"No link has been established between any of the victims thus far, correct?" Leigh asked.

"That's right," Jade said. "Nothing obvious. We're searching their backgrounds for commonalities, so far..." Jade's lips pressed tight in contemplation.

"Keep trying. It's there. Have you tested their blood?" Leigh asked.

"Of course. All positive for sedatives," Jade said. "I'm sure you read that."

"No." Leigh spread the victims' photos across the table in front of them. "I mean for genetic links to each other."

"Brutal." Kane studied their faces for shared features. "The blood. He's made a point out of taking their blood. You're telling me we've been chasing this lunatic for months misinterpreting the blood's relevance?"

"It wouldn't be the first thought." Leigh set her file down. "It's symbolic in its genetic link, I believe."

"I'm sorry." Kane put his hands flat on the table and stared at the photos beneath him. "We've searched. There's nothing we've unearthed that even hints at that."

"That's the other piece of the puzzle."

Kane shook his head in disbelief. "Brilliant."

"Quit being hard on yourself, Detective. He hasn't made it easy for you."

"Women are dying, ma'am."

"He wants you to feel exactly as you do—responsible. That's the reason for the clues exposing the victim's identity before he kills."

Kane stood at full height again. "We don't figure out the clues in time, and they die."

"Yes. And the blood…is on your hands."

———

Venice was first aware of the pain at her left temple. The sharp ache and consistent throbbing were familiar. She experienced the same days earlier after slipping on grease and cold cocking her head against the car door. The doctor said she'd come as close to a serious concussion as she'd ever want to. The pain intensified. It sent piercing reverberations down her neck and into her limbs. She fought to open her eyes. Seeing only black when her lids complied.

"It's a blindfold. Don't bother straining to see. It's better you don't."

Terror replaced the pain. She remembered the moment before she lost consciousness. The gloves. The "payback" he rained down on her. What was worse, he wasn't finished, and she hadn't a clue why he started. He'd never been violent before.

"Why?" Her voice sounded thin and foreign. If he'd gone to the trouble of tying her up and blindfolding her, why hadn't he gagged her? That fact was anything but reassuring. Talking him out of whatever he'd planned seemed the only option. "You know me. We've always had a good relationship."

"You see what you want to see."

His voice had developed an eerie undertone. Not the man she knew. Darker.

"If I offended you in some way—" she tried.

"Offended me?"

His laughter was cynical, colorless, and inhuman.

"Why am I being punished?" She forced every shred of strength into her voice. It rang back as weak.

"*That* is the crime."

His footsteps gained volume as he approached. She steeled her body against another lancing blow and couldn't loosen her muscles when it didn't land. His breath drifted over the portion of her face that remained exposed. Horror mixed with confusion, for he still smelled the same. Smooth. Sophisticated. The man she'd known. The one she trusted. The one who didn't exist. A bitter churning levitated from her stomach into her mouth. She swallowed hard against it.

Think.

Her mind spun reels of every conversation she'd had with him, this psycho, in the other life before he transformed. Playing with bedroom matches had always been a gamble, but this? As she launched her apology, he cut her off mid-sentence.

"This isn't about me, you stupid woman. It has nothing to do with me."

"If it's not personal, then why—"

"You really don't have the slightest clue, do you? As I said, *that* is the crime."

He remained close. Her memory struggled to grasp something, anything that might lead her to a revelation that could stop this insanity. Desperation prevented her from registering the pain immediately.

He was doing something to her. Pressure on her upper arms, a twinge by her left wrist then the right. Sweet Mother of God. He'd said it was better if she didn't see. His voice remained cool and confident. Whatever he was doing, it was on the ugly back of what he'd already done while she was unconscious.

She needed to see. Didn't want to see. Needed to.

"Do you want a hint?"

His question threw her. She'd succumbed to a mentally paralyzing dread. Hint?

"Are you still in there?"

No. God no. I'm not here.

"This could be fun."

Sick bastard.

Stay focused.

She tried again. "We're all entrapped by our sins. Some of us handle these offenses internally, not in an obvious manner—"

"That's for damn sure."

"Whatever it is I've done, I've carried the guilt unbeknownst to the rest of the world."

"Not good enough." He twisted something rubbery. It snapped. She jerked away from the noise. Pain scorched through her from too many places to count.

"What have you done to me?" Behind the blindfold, tears rolled, tears no one would see. She prayed they would stain the cloth masking her vision, declaring her life mattered to her.

"The burden is on you. I am here to redeem you, nothing more."

"Here to redeem me? You think I...redeem? Mother of God. You? You're him? You're—"

"Wonders will never cease."

They had a relationship. She assumed something made him snap. The truth raped her of hope. He wasn't her monster. He was *the* monster, the one stealing the headlines.

She didn't want to recall the articles she'd read, the gruesome details. The words flashed in psychedelic waves across the backdrop of her blindfold. Horrific premonitions of what awaited her.

"I don't need to be redeemed." Any approach was better than accepting this fate. "The hell you don't."

Wrong thing to say? Was there a right thing?

"I meant, I've prayed every day for forgiveness."

He didn't respond immediately. The seconds that passed devoid of voice carried empty fear. She forced herself not to speak, not to cry, not to breathe above a sigh. It hurt. Everything hurt.

"Forgiveness for what?"

She had no answer. And the price of silence would surely cost her life.

"For the actions I won't speak of."

He fell quiet once more, and she fought to suppress the voice of fear that built from a whisper to a scream. His feet shuffled around her, a predator circling wounded prey deciding where next to strike.

It was better, he said, if she didn't see.

He bled his victims dry.

This was the atrocity he committed while she laid vulnerable and unconscious. Vile preparation. Not to steal a life, to steal it slowly. She'd have full awareness of it seeping from her hands to his with no means to stop it.

Jesus.

This was how she would die.

He sensed her epiphany. She'd been quiet for too long.

"You're guessing. Heartless bitch!"

He was laughing.

His laughter hurt.

Then, the sound of a lever clamping into a new position, a draining one.

Kane unclipped his weapon and smacked it down on the bathroom sink's edge. The sound caught Max off guard. He spun in a wet pirouette, hands soapy.

"Where are you running off to in such a hurry?" Kane blocked the exit. He leaned over and locked the door from the inside.

"I told you, I have somewhere to be." Max's expression wasn't one of fear.

"You're going to be late." Kane loomed two steps closer.

"We have a real problem, you and I." Max eyed the paper towel dispenser but didn't move.

"You think? Where do you get off heaping the responsibility for this case on my partner's shoulders? You, of all people, know what she's dealing with."

"I didn't do that. I'm trying to help."

"You're failing miserably—"

"I don't think—"

"No, you don't think. Jade is rushing headlong into the heart of this case. Half her fellow officers think she has a death wish, and you're supporting her reckless behavior!"

"I am not, I understand her more than—"

"Shut up, Doc. I'll make this clear. If anything happens to her, I'll be coming for you with a fury few would survive."

"Kane—" An unrecognizable fire lit behind Max's eyes. His calm was unnerving.

"Don't interpret. There's nothing to read between the lines here. Suggesting responsibility?"

"In her mind, the blood was on her hands long before I got involved."

Kane cranked the dead bolt open, picked up his gun, and held it loosely aimed in Max's direction. "Don't forget to dry, your hands are dripping."

Leaving the room, Kane crashed into an outbound Texas bull. Jackson steadied him, spinning him to face the building's main entrance.

"You've got to quit staring at your feet. It's dangerous."

"Only when you're around, mate. What's up?"

"Site three. It's a bad one." Jackson's wide Texas grin was replaced by a sorrowful grimace.

"As opposed to the others?"

Before the station doors closed behind him, Kane glanced back to see Max enter the hallway, devoid of his prior haste. Jade was in the parking lot getting in her car, and for the time being, he stood between the two. Where he always was, the buffer of protection, the vest blocking the obvious shots. It was the stray bullets that worried him.

The one he couldn't see coming.

TWELVE

Jade offered the rookie his dignity, drifting by undaunted as he bent over and heaved into an empty evidence bag.

First timer hit hard by the transformation from human being to desecrated flesh. The kid was smart enough not to contaminate the site. She'd interview him after she dealt with the corpse turning him greenish gray.

She walked the grid to the body absorbing data marked by the CS team along the way. Scuff in the floor dust. Papers strewn. Broken pen. Rubber tubing. Endless lengths of rubber tubing that snaked away from a single source. She had to stop, nowhere to place her flap-down Troopas.

The tube ends were open. Tainted by bloody residue from the drainage that occurred hours earlier. The metallic scent lingered near the victim. It grew stronger when Jade crouched for closer inspection. She slipped a glove on her right hand.

No wonder the kid threw up.

"Nothing here that won't repulse," Jade whispered. "He was mad at this one."

The attending ME nodded agreement. The body was battered.

Jade waited until he wrapped up, and she was alone before removing the victim's blindfold.

"I'm taking this off now. Open your eyes where you are. I'll take care of things down here. And don't look back." Anger rose, and she swallowed hard.

A plain black bandanna collected in a stream of evidence that led to nowhere. Crusty, hardened like paper mâché. Jade stared at it. Stained by makeup. Stained by tears.

Bastard.

Bag sealed and properly stowed, she turned her attention back to Venice Beil's body—a house for the brutal memory of another woman taken by violence. A hundred and ten pounds left. No more. Driftwood.

Jade's focus shifted from the torso to the sunken face.

The victim's eyes were closed. She lingered on this detail. Venice was blindfolded. There'd be no reason to close her eyes. The circumstances of her death railed against her shutting them voluntarily like Jade's mother had.

"Theo, we need to dust the eyes for prints." The medical examiner, a veteran, shot her a glance beckoning clarity. "Not the lids, the eyeballs. I think he messed with them."

Jade sprang to her feet, leaving the body and ignoring the entanglement of tubing. She swept by other officers, including Wenzel. Near the door, she slid a hand over the shoulder of the kid with his head between his knees. She fought the urge to join him.

There was no time for weakness. If her instincts were right, she'd found a conduit to the killer. If they were wrong, she'd validate the rumors of self-destruction. To catch him, she needed live bait, and she wouldn't risk any life outside her own.

In the police break room, Jade couldn't bring herself to lay the crime scene photo of her mother next to the Redeemer's victims. She knew the puzzle wouldn't make sense without it. If the possibilities eating at her were correct, Nina Carmichael's death represented a key component.

She couldn't lay it down.

The picture remained tucked inside the file folder, stashed beside her right hip, pushed deep into the cushions of her chair.

The other women were completely exposed in their most horrific form.

Headshots above, bodies below. Happy snapshots of them alive placed in such close proximity to the gore book photos of their deaths enhanced the cruelty of the act. Jade slid the table aside, laid all the photos on the floor in a circle around her, and ran her hand through them until they were in complete disarray. The cut-up, montage technique worked for David Bowie. She loved Bowie, UK artists in general. Heritage.

Perhaps this was what Jade needed, the trigger to release the hidden elements of the killer who eluded her.

There existed a commonality in the faces she fought to absorb. She selected the headshot of Lorenda Lainey. This image spoke the loudest. Jade struggled to silence everything but.

The dead woman's once vivid eyes revealed a yearning. Jade rose to her feet with the photo still in hand and paced the break room, circling the area she'd strewn with the misery of unfinished lives.

The stench of stale coffee churned up with each lap. That and the saccharine scent of day-old donuts left open on the counter. The aroma paled in comparison to the metallic odor of blood encircling the body at the last crime scene. It clung to the sensitive fibers in Jade's nostrils, potent, refusing to fade.

She scrutinized her surroundings. Designed to mimic the comfortable family rooms sitting empty in the homes of the detectives, the space captured the melancholy, nothing welcoming. An oval mirror hung above a sideboard table, though no one entering wanted or needed a visual reminder of their defeat and exhaustion.

Jade caught her reflection. It stopped her.

It was there. The same yearning evident in Lainey's eyes. Not just a yearning, one masking a black hole of emotional trauma. And guilt.

She spun on her heels beside the table. Dropping to the floor, she grabbed at the faces, pulling them into a pile in front of her, leaving a mass of dead bodies at its center. "Jesus." Amy's shock registered in her arrested body language.

"Sorry, Amy. Didn't hear you come in." Jade absorbed the room anew.

"This is what he does?" Amy didn't appear capable of shifting her focus off the macabre pictures, drawn by the evil responsible for them.

Jade stood, blocking Amy's sightline. "What's up?"

"Hum? Oh, Dr. Leigh's here. Should I walk her back?" Amy leaned past Jade, captivated by the faces amassed under the table's edge. "Good women, eh? They had it together."

"Looks can be deceiving." Jade stared at the picture of Lainey.

"Don't have to tell me. You should try dating them. Half the women I go out with are hiding some dark personality trait. By the time you figure it out, you wish you hadn't shown them where you live."

"Send her back."

"What?"

"Leigh."

"Oh, yeah. It's a shame. They're 'take home to meet mom' girls. There aren't enough of them."

The door closed behind Amy, and Jade sat back on the floor. She turned the photos to face her. Amy was right. They were the kind of women you were proud of. So why hadn't any of their relationships made headlines until they were dead?

"I brought coffee. Black, right?" In blue jeans and a polo shirt, cup in both hands, Leigh exuded a casual, crisp appeal only those raised in wealth pulled off. "I assumed you were onto something, or you wouldn't have called me in. I brought fresh. Figured we'd be here for a while."

Leigh never reacted, even after she'd had time to soak up the graphic images.

"You do want the coffee?" she asked. "Haven't known a cop to pass up fresh brewed before."

"Thanks," Jade accepted the cup. "I think I've stumbled across a link..."

Jade rearranged the photos with her back to Dr. Leigh. First discovered to most recent, heads above, bodies below.

"Missing one. Is this your mother's file?" Leigh had the folder in hand and open before Jade could stop her.

"I don't—"

"I respect how difficult this must be. Hiding from it won't make it any easier and—"

"And?" Jade stood eye to eye. Leigh wore delicate high heels. Jade wanted, if only briefly, to throw her off of them.

"And he might be banking on you doing that. I know about the date match."

Jade slipped the photo out of the folder and set it on the table in front of them. Leigh had a point. "I think his hatred has something to do with his mother."

"He wouldn't be the first. Why?"

"Look at their faces," Jade said. "What do you see?"

"Alive or dead? Are we reading expressions?"

"Alive." Jade's eyes searched Leigh's. Her blunt response was unexpected. Perhaps too many years analyzing multiple murderers, making them her life's work, numbed her. She was single, childless, too. It was almost comforting.

"Aside from the obvious, they all managed to avoid certain key stages of life." Leigh stared directly at Jade. "Marriage, motherhood."

"Exactly. Why did you? I have an excuse. Cop's life."

"I have my reasons."

"Reasons you don't want to discuss with me."

"I—"

"I don't want to know yours. I do think we'd better start searching for theirs."

"Background dossiers?"

"In the pile to your left."

Leigh reached for the stack of files glancing briefly at a second, larger heap on the right side of the table. "And that?"

"Possibles."

Leigh's expression begged for clarification.

"Related cases in nearby towns we might have missed."

"There has to be twenty or more," Leigh said.

"More. Some date back eleven years. Long shots, but they all involve bloodletting with comparable victim profiles."

Leigh set down the background dossiers and picked up a handful. "May I?"

"I called you."

Jade examined the faces of the dead women, all deserving of a justice they'd never receive. Kane's words repeated in her head, "She isn't anything anymore." What justice mattered when you were dead? The question irritated her. Jade's very existence hinged on granting such a justice, and in the end, these women didn't give a damn. The futility of it gnawed at her until Leigh interrupted her self-loathing.

Leigh had been leafing through the pile until a file stopped her. "I remember this case, a particularly brutal execution by the killer. I thought it'd been closed."

She handed over the file. Jade set it in front of her and opened it.

"I remember it because the man I was dating at the time thought we could've been sisters," Leigh continued.

Jade turned to the victim's headshot. Both had straight black hair. The victim's hair was longer. There were similarities in their features. The woman wasn't a dead ringer for Leigh by any stretch. She glanced back at Leigh.

"I know. I didn't see it either. I think he was making a play for moving in."

Jade perused the details of the case. There was an eyewitness report. It didn't read as remarkably credible, but they had to start somewhere. She flipped the file closed and headed for the door.

"Find something?"

"Probably not. Only one way to be sure."

"I'll be here when you get back." Leigh offered to safeguard the paperwork.

"I booked the room," Jade said. "No one will disturb you. If you need anything, ask Amy Logan up front."

"Take care. The closer you get to him, the closer he is to you. You may be drawn to him because of your past, but he isn't your mother's killer."

"I know," Jade said. "He's a far more organized killer."

"Good luck, or should I say happy hunting?"

"Both."

Jade left the pristine doctor in a room full of depravity never fearing the gruesome images had potency enough to soil her. Like Jade, her armor was noticeably impervious. How it became so was not.

"I appreciate you stopping in, Isaiah. I know your time's limited." Grey sat in the wingback by his office window and offered the adjacent chair to the department's benefactor. "Haven't seen a case this bad in…well, ever."

"No one has time for anything these days, Grey." Isaiah accepted the chair, but perched on its edge rather than settling in. "Priorities."

Isaiah Isreal had given generously to many organizations in recent years, not the least of which was nearest to Captain Grey's heart. His single contribution provided funds necessary to significantly update Shadow Hook's major crime division's computer system, landing it leagues above surrounding towns. Grey welcomed the donation, but it'd stirred pressure from those not so fortunate to share Grey esteemed connections. Now, it left Shadow Hook looking overqualified and underperforming. Hauling Isreal in for questioning was not how Grey envisioned thanking him. Attempting control over the delicate situation, he did it anyway.

"The Lainey woman's death is weighing heavy on us—"

"Her connections?" Isreal inhaled deeply the fresh brewed coffee aroma.

Grey motioned to a coffee machine on a shelf left of his desk. "Can I get you—"

"Never touch the stuff." His face belied his pledge.

"Smart man." Grey poured one cup from the carafe and swiveled back around to face Isaiah. "Kolton and Carmichael are narrowing in, but not fast enough and—"

"Say no more. What can I do?" Isreal's instant support was a relief.

"Do you remember anything about that night, the last time you saw her?"

"I do." His manicured hands rested comfortably on his lap. "I remember how anxious she was to get back on the plane."

"Did she say why?"

"I think being here made her nervous because of the threats. I mentioned it to your detectives."

"Do you recall anything specific?" Grey prayed for a tendril of possibility.

"About the messages? I saw one, some time ago. Weeks even. I'm sure you have the date in her records. He criticized her charitable efforts, but I couldn't recite it word for word." He rubbed the back of his neck, searching memories.

"Anyone suspicious?" Grey knew where he was headed and hoped Isreal followed.

"You know my involvement. I'm called in during financial discussions but prefer to keep a low profile."

"How close were the two of you?"

"And there it is." Isaiah tapped his fingertips together mulling things over in the private confines of his mind. "The uncomfortable question you knew you had to ask."

"There it is," Grey repeated.

"This is where it gets complicated."

Grey offered nothing and gave nothing away. You couldn't with men of Isaiah's intellectual caliber.

"If I divulge the existence of an affair, I'll be subjected to intense scrutiny and not just from the department. I could jeopardize a reputation I've safeguarded and fostered since adulthood."

"It's possible." Grey leaned out of his chair closing the distance. "On the other hand, if it's discovered that you've concealed the nature of your relationship—"

"I'm screwed either way." He stretched his neck left and right weighing options.

"Yes. You are."

"I slept with her once. Well, one weekend, one unbelievable weekend two years ago. Never since."

"Whose idea?" Grey fired questions maintaining momentum.

"To end it or start it?"

"Both."

"It was mutual. I knew if we were working on the same project, it'd interfere. She agreed. The weekend was enough."

"Okay."

"Can you keep it out of the papers?" Isreal's expression challenged Grey's ability.

"Do my damnedest. It'd only hurt the investigation." Grey stood. "Thanks for coming down. If anything comes to mind…"

Isaiah rose from his chair, pausing at the threshold on his way out. "I'll be in touch." He filled the doorway or maybe that was how Grey saw him.

"You said they were narrowing in," he added. "Is that the truth or the party line? It'd be nice to think my donations account for something."

"They're getting close. Carmichael believes we missed prior cases. Her search unearthed a couple significant new leads. She's fleshing them out."

"Good to hear. The wolves are circling. You wouldn't have called me if they weren't. Like they say, the path to hell is paved with good intention."

Isaiah vanished behind the doorjamb. Grey couldn't help wondering if the department would ever see another cent from him. Philanthropists didn't generally appreciate having near strangers delve into their romantic entanglements. A phone call from him, and they'd all be out of a job.

He sympathized on a personal level. He wouldn't be okay with someone poking around in his past. Everyone had secrets, some more threatening than others.

Grey leaned into the hallway. Isaiah and Jade were blocking the view twenty feet away. Isaiah stepped close to Jade making room for other detectives to pass. He wore a cagey grin. If he was making a play for her, he was on the wrong field, yet there existed a symmetry between them. Both unique, powerful, and isolated in their own right. Grey nodded at Isaiah and called out to Jade, "You on your way?" He hoped to break up their conversation before Jade said something off-key. There were land mines everywhere.

"Yep. Just leaving," Jade confirmed, pulling away from Isreal.

"She's at Burlington?"

"Yep."

"Dark as hell out there after sundown. Take a flashlight to the interview, or you won't find your car. Parking's a block away."

"I'll call in when I'm through."

"Can't wait." He directed his attention back to Isaiah. "Thanks again."

"My pleasure." Isaiah smiled at Jade, whispered something that made her laugh, and left.

Grey vacated the hall for the refuge behind his closed office door. He'd done what he could to avoid disaster. Handled questioning all the power players with kid gloves. The news bites were escalating with the pressure. They'd be burning allies soon enough.

His pocket watch confirmed he was officially off the clock. Collapsing in his swivel chair, he pulled open a hidden drawer in the built-in shelving unit behind him, slid his Beretta aside, and reached for the small bottle of double-barreled.

His eyes searched the walls, coming to rest on the leather footstool blocking a corner adjacent to his desk. The occasional detective sat on it when other options weren't available, but no one ever asked why it was there when he never used it. Not as a footstool anyway. When he was working cases, he learned hiding in plain sight was the most effective method of concealment. He used what he'd learned. So far it worked.

He rubbed at the tension across his forehead, swallowed back a single shot, replaced the lid, returned the bottle, and embraced the burn.

He'd also learned secrets didn't stay hidden forever, and his own were creeping to the surface.

THIRTEEN

The sanitarium wore its lavish price tag with class. Its occupants' families paid dearly to keep their broken dolls housed safely from the world, from themselves, and from bad memories.

And Jade was there to awaken one.

"Miss Simms is on the grounds attending art class. I'll take you back."

Ushering Jade from the visitor's door, the woman introduced herself as Nurse Jewel. Her hair said early fifties. Her energy shaved off years. In moments, she'd delivered the history of the colonial building, their motto, and how its operation set industry standards. She was proud, and by initial impressions, with good reason.

Nurse Jewel escorted Jade down a lengthy hallway where cathedral ceilings and architectural grandeur opened to the grounds behind the main building. Through three sets of double doors, a landscaped paradise explained why art classes would be held outside despite the luxurious amenities available within.

Down a bank of wide stone stairs, across a marble sitting area, over snaking pathways to courts of interest, and onto its perfectly manicured lawn, Jade absorbed the lush environment and its community members.

Caregivers, as Jewel referred to them, wore matching uniforms, crisp white with gold accents. And the same mask, a combination of pride, purpose, and pleasantry.

The art class perched on the crest of a sloping hill claiming the best view of the gardens. Seven residents sat in front of large unfinished canvases creating masterpieces out of their misery. This place was a quiet, but respected, financial contributor to Shadow Hook's high society.

Jade scanned their faces as she approached, wondering which witnessed the horror that lay locked away and unsolved for the last two decades.

One woman with flaming red hair wore the scars of a more personal assault down the left side of her face. A cruel tapestry of flesh carved by an unholy artist.

Not Miss Simms. Her scars slashed deep, ugly grooves in the confines of her psyche. They couldn't be seen and, according to Jewel, hadn't been healed.

A dark-skinned woman caught Jade's attention. She wielded her brush with the grace of a ballet dancer. The performance made admirable by the grip of the hand on her only existing arm.

Jade broke away from Nurse Jewel heading into the class space. The nurse caught up and stopped her abruptly before walking within earshot.

"Miss Simms isn't up there." The nurse directed Jade to a bench nearby.

"You said art class." Jade closed the distance to the bench but didn't sit.

"Yes, but not painting. Miss Simms can't see."

Jade stared at the nurse for a moment. "Her file never said anything about her being blind."

"Well, it wouldn't." The nurse's tone revealed annoyance.

"You just said—"

"I know what I said, Detective. There are a few minutes left of the class. You'd better sit down."

Irritated, Jade claimed a seat.

"Miss Simms suffers from Convergence Disorder."

"That was in the file." Jade gave her the opening to explain.

"It manifests differently in every person. Medically there was nothing wrong with her eyes, but after witnessing the events that brought her to us, her mind severed the connection that allowed her sight, a protective reaction to extreme trauma. The murder served as a trigger to an off switch. And that is what you are here to discuss.

"Isn't it?"

The woman's eyes were a muted gray-green, but Jade felt their force. Not knowing how to respond, she said nothing.

"It has taken us twenty years to coax this broken woman to a place of peace. We don't want those efforts undermined." Sincerity underlay her words.

"It's not my intention—"

"You'll pardon my frankness, Detective, it never is." Nurse Jewel stood and directed Jade to a circle of artists sitting before stone tables, sculpting on a lower bank to the left of the bench. "She's the one with the long black hair."

Jade didn't stand, unexpectedly aware of the damage left by the gunshot wound to her thigh compromising motor function at a whim.

"She wanted to meet with you," the nurse prompted. "She thinks she's ready. You'll excuse me. Twenty years of shattered souls has made me protective."

"Injustice has that effect." Jade spoke without volition, understanding why the nurse left, unwilling to be party to what came next.

Jade stood as the class disbanded, some walking away of their own free will, others with assistance. They didn't appear unhappy. Miss Simms remained seated, saying goodbye to her classmates as if studying at Berkley. Smiles and aspirations.

The interview would be harder than anticipated. Jade made her way over.

"Elizabeth Simms, I'm Detective Carmichael. You can call me Jade."

"Call me Beth. I know who you are. Have a seat." She offered Jade a place at her left. Jade sat, meeting her at eye level. A distant drift said nothing was being captured behind the stunning blue outer rings.

"I'm sorry—"

"Don't start that way, Detective. If you do, we'll never get through this. How about I tell you what I experienced, what I remember? You can ask questions along the way."

The woman's candid approach threw Jade off guard and made her grateful she couldn't see her reaction, though she probably sensed it.

"Okay," Jade said. "You first."

"You don't wake up one morning thinking you'll die or that someone's waiting to kill you. Watching that reality play out for someone else is no less devastating. It wasn't for me. I was a kid. This will have cobwebs on it."

"One unearthed detail can spin a lead." Jade retrieved a pen and pad from her bag.

"For the sake of the future victims, I hope so." Simms brushed her long locks aside, giving Jade a close profile. She was striking, stunning at worst, and completely unaware of it. "If he has aged since then, and the Redeemer and the man I remember are one and the same—"

"If he's aged?" Jade never missed spoken details, perhaps because she'd been unable to give them for so long following her mother's murder.

"Time has no better grip on a man like him than you do, Detective."

Jade sat back on the stone seat getting a wider perspective of her witness.

"If it's him, you'll never see him coming." Simms certainly wouldn't. Jade contemplated her risk factor. Had her silence protected her like Simms's blindness?

"And why is that?" Jade stared into Simms's sightless eyes.

"To be in the presence of a beast as hideous as him blinded me for life."

"Nurse Jewel explained there was nothing medically wrong with your eyes."

"There wasn't when I lost my sight. Vision is like anything—you don't use it, you lose it. My eyes have been useless for so long the muscles were degraded beyond repair years ago."

"I'm sorry, I didn't—" Jade couldn't help her compassion for this woman.

"There you go again."

"You said he was hideous?" Jade listened intently, then harder, to every shred of emotion.

"He is."

"That'd explain his rage against beautiful women, but it's seldom that simple."

"It isn't," Simms agreed. "What stole my vision was the fact that I couldn't trust it. What I saw was the most handsome creation I'd ever laid eyes on turn into the vilest creature that walked the planet. The man you're looking for could tempt you into anything, even giving your own life."

Jade studied Simms's face. Its lack of crow's feet, worry lines, and time-etched creases. Unhampered by age spots, sun damage, or the layering of makeup. Even up close, it was beautiful, and she'd never see it. What she had seen was the face of the Redeemer. Of this, Jade was certain.

"Do you remember details?"

"Of his appearance? Nothing that would help you now. He had dirty-blond hair, perfect skin, a masculine jawline, and alluring hands, the kind you wanted all over you."

There was nothing obscure about the passion underlying her description or the intensity that time held no claim on.

"I can't remember his eye color. I've tried. I can't remember it at all, like that detail was erased." Simm's eyelids fluttered as if fighting to clear film from the memory.

"Did you know anything about his background?" Sensing heightened emotion, Jade shifted tactics.

"Lies. His lies."

"You spoke to him. Could you identify the sound of his voice? I know it's been decades, and you've fought to forget—"

"Yes."

"Yes?"

"I remember his voice. I could identify it, but that won't help you."

"Of course it will."

"To identify it, you first require a sample," Simms said.

"Yes."

"To get a sample, you'd have to get close to him."

"And?"

"If you get that close, he'll kill you." Simms reached out, placing her hands on Jade's face, reading it in the most intimate and uncomfortable way. "You're young, balanced features, beautiful, a strong jaw, like his. He'll kill you if you get any closer. He's already planning it. And it will be brutal."

Her confidence unnerved. It spoke volumes. This woman wasn't an unsuspecting witness to the Redeemer's first attack. She'd been a willing candidate who'd been denied.

"Why do you think he let you live?" Miss Simms had waited twenty years to answer. "Beth, why?"

Her head bowed into her hands, and the eyes that granted no vision spilled a surplus of silent tears. They couldn't blur, but Jade bet they burned.

"I loved him. He knew it, so he killed her instead. She was my sister, and she died because I loved a monster."

The peace Nurse Jewel claimed required years to cultivate had never existed in this woman. Stillness. Acceptance. Denial.

No peace.

"It should've been me."

"Don't." Jade pulled the woman's hands from her face. "There is no way off that road. Don't go down it."

"By sparing my life, he made me die a thousand deaths, and he knows it. He never stopped. I suspect there are many more cases unattributed to him that should be. He is brilliant. He'll have amassed considerable wealth. You should expect he has every advantage over you. You can't win, Detective. You'll be lucky to survive. Or not."

"I need an insight into him, and you're it. What did he love? What did he do?"

"He loved the way I made him feel. He did…everything I can't erase."

"You know what I'm asking you." Jade sprung from her chair finding the air close to this woman heavy and claustrophobic. "I need details. Where did he meet you to have sex?"

Simms turned, following Jade's movements with eyes that held memories and denied reality. "We met in a building that was under construction. He knew the owner had a key. Give me your pen and pad. I'll write it down for you."

Jade hadn't said anything about the pen or pad, and she'd barely used them. She handed them to Simms, who perfectly scribed an address Jade was familiar with.

"It wasn't sex."

Retrieving the items, staring at the penmanship, Jade asked, "How would you describe it?"

"I said I loved him. He loved me too."

Jade hovered over Simms, speechless. Angry and with no target to vent at.

"Yes, Detective. He is capable of love…and the worst possible hatred."

Simms stood, then disappeared down a path leading back into a residential building. She reemerged in the distance, met by Nurse Jewel who had been waiting to put her back together again. Jade didn't rush to follow. She knew if she fell on bent knees, there was no way she'd be granted access to Simms again.

The information she'd provided was personal, tragic, and terrifying if only because the knot forming in Jade's chest told her Simms was right.

Worse still, Simms's courage to come clean about her past made Jade's failure to do so a blatant reality. Answers were waiting for her. Answers that could save lives, and she'd ignored them for the sake of pride.

Simms turned as if glancing back at Jade, her sightless eyes condemning and challenging her to confront everything she'd turned a blind eye to.

Was this where neglectful parents went after abandoning their children in ruin? Pristine suburbia. Jade studied the stately forest-green house with the linen trim, inviting with its manicured lawn and waterfall feature, wondering how the hell Beau Carmichael ended up here, living the dream after leaving her in a nightmare. Anyone else would see it as inviting. She saw it for what it was. A dangerous, well-orchestrated lie.

She sat out front long enough for her sweaty palms to leave residue on the steering wheel. The car was cold. She was enflamed.

This was the home of her father, but never her home. The soft grass had been played on by his children, but not by her. The picnic table out back had weathered many family feasts. It heard the laughter and relived shared stories. She was in none of them. A dreaded secret he never spoke of.

She hated this man. Vowed to never speak to him again, and now she was walking to his door, breaking her own rules.

With every step her stomach twisted in refusal as if fighting to turn her back around from the inside.

His Jaguar, the lone car in the drive, said he was home.

There was no prepared speech. No wise words arming her. Determination. Women were dying. He didn't care. How could he? He hadn't done anything to protect her mother or her, so why should he care about mere strangers?

Jade's hands shook. She wrung them out like wet towels, then rang the bell and waited.

I hate you! That was what she wanted to say when he opened the door. Hate you for letting my mother die, for discarding me after I lost so much, for being a useless idiot.

When the door opened, the words didn't come. He was older than she remembered, older than she'd made him in her mind. And he'd never been useless or an idiot.

"Jade?" His expression contorted with confusion. "Umm. Come in."

She said nothing. Glancing back at the cool grass sloping to her waiting means of escape, she stepped across the threshold, keys in hand.

"Are we alone?" She scanned the area.

"Yes." He stepped back. "Grace took the kids to their grandma's for the week. Do you want to sit down? Has something happened?"

"No." Jade absorbed the endearing pictures set in frames on the sideboard, the smell of fresh cut flowers from the nearby vase, and all the comforts of home she'd been robbed of. "Why?"

"I haven't heard from you in years, and you're here, so I assumed—"

"Not that. Why did you leave her that week? What were you fighting about? Why did you give up on me?" Her stare locked him in place, leaving no wiggle room. "Why was it so easy for you?"

"That was so long ago, and it wasn't easy."

"The hell it wasn't! I can't imagine abandoning my child in the black hole you left me in. How could anyone do that to their own flesh and blood after—"

"I didn't. You'll never understand." His voice held defiance out of place. "I knew there was no saving you. No force on earth could've parted her from you. There was no saving her either. I gave eleven years—" His hands clenched air like a safety rope.

"And then you gave up! For this?" Jade spun around, waving at all the sentimentality. "To build a pretty lie. This façade of a perfect life!"

"This isn't a façade. This is the real thing! Not perfect, but real. That's what you'll never understand. That life before, that was the fantasy. The dream that turned into a nightmare again and again!"

He was angrier than she remembered, or maybe his anger never registered in her young, damaged brain.

"I didn't come here to listen to you whimper about how rough things were for you. My mother died at the hands of a monster, and I'm the one carrying that visual to my grave!" She wasn't about to give him a second of sympathy.

"You have no idea what you're saying." He retreated into the kitchen, the fire in his voice overtaken by a smoldering defeat.

"Then you explain to me. What am I missing?" Jade left her Giuseppe Zanottis on, stomping in behind him. "All I know for sure is that you left, and you kept leaving."

"I tried—"

"You should've tried harder!" She paced in a circle ending at the same impasse.

"There's always more you're holding back not saying. What haven't you said?"

"You're here because of the victims in the papers, aren't you?" He held a spot against the counter by the coffee maker. The view to a garden primed for a magazine cover behind him.

All she could see were dead women's faces overlaying it all. "Yes. Them too."

"I thought—"

"Don't say you were thinking of me, save it." Jade backed up closer to the hall.

"I thought they might be enough to make you come. I knew nothing else would." His left hand gripped the soapstone counter's edge.

Jade rocked her left foot front to back on the thick leather sole of her boot. "Look, I stayed away. I gave you your freedom from me, the memories, from all of it. You owe me."

"And you think that will save them? You think it'll save you?" He paced the kitchen, avoiding eye contact.

"What have you kept from me? How much?" She wondered before, watching him now, she knew. "I heard you fighting the night you left. What was it over? You know I blamed myself?" Rage rose from those smooth soles all the way up, gaining strength every inch. "I was eleven! I thought it was over me."

He quit pacing to stand inches from her. "It was." His expression held no malice.

"My fault?" She cursed the quiver in her voice.

"No. That's not even logical. It was over you, not because of you."

He sighed, deflating before her eyes. "That's the unbearable part of all this. You didn't ask for any of this. Did nothing wrong. You didn't ask to be born into this mess. Your mother wanted you so much. She bonded with you the second she knew you existed. There was no talking her out of it—"

"Out of what? Out of having me? You didn't want me even then?" Something deep inside broke. She read it in his eyes. He didn't need to speak.

"It was never about me or what I wanted, but now, since you've made it, I'll tell you." He was pacing, lawyer-like. "I wanted your mother. I wanted her safe. I was young and afraid to be a father—"

"Damn good reason for that," she admonished.

He shook his head. "I wanted you! God help me, I did. I wanted you safe, but she refused to move. Refused to leave this place that brought her so much pain, so it followed her, caught up to her, and killed her."

Jade couldn't find words, too intrigued to argue back. He came close, searched her expression, then stepped back and shook his head. The quiver moved from her voice into her core, shaking its way out.

"You know I passed the bar first time in the top three percent? You won't hear my advice any more than she did."

"What advice?"

He looked her dead center in the eyes. "If you don't drop this, walk away right now, run, you'll end up just like her."

She read it in his body language, the inflection in his voice, the resin filling his eyes—he was afraid for her, terrified. And then she felt it, sympathy. He had tried to protect his wife and failed. That weight had never lifted. The realization threw her train of thought off course. Why had she come? What was she doing bringing all this pain back up and crushing him with it in the kitchen of his happy home?

"Jade?" He glimpsed realization in her eyes, and in his, a light appeared, a burst of hope buried in a lifetime of regret.

"I have to go." She turned to leave. He stopped her.

"You need to choose your future over the past. I want that for you. I always did."

"Why didn't you want her to have me? You weren't ready to be a father? Was that it?" She was hurting, and it showed.

"It wasn't about me being your father." He stepped out of her path. "I was honored to be your father. I still am."

"Then, why?" Pain exploded beneath her chest. She could feel the reopening of old wounds physically tear. It made her gasp for breath.

"There's so much a parent does to protect their child, so many things we pay for that can't be understood or appreciated by the young. My first loyalty was to your mother." His stare drifted to a place back in time. Where? What was he seeing that she couldn't? "I'd suffer anything for her, and I did, but I don't know what the right thing is now that she's gone."

For all his stature, his wisdom and accomplishments, he appeared lost, broken, a whole lot like her. She never saw it before, the regret. It shrouded him too.

"What do you mean? What right thing?"

"I mean, how can there even be a right thing in the midst of murder?"

"Her murder or the women today?" she asked, her feet planted inches from his. For the first time since before her mother died, she didn't want to back away.

"It doesn't matter, does it?" He reached for her face. To his surprise, she didn't pull away. His eyes lit, the way her mother's had whenever she did anything sweet or funny as a child. "You're so precious."

"Dad, tell me." Slow tears pooled.

He watched. "I promised her many things." He kissed Jade's forehead, lingering there, pouring years of missed tenderness onto her.

She couldn't move. This was what she'd waited for but couldn't receive. He did love her, always had. She'd come armed with a lifetime of questions. Questions fueled by unquenched passion. Questions she couldn't grasp. They'd slipped too far away. Instead, she stayed protected in his embrace, gazing through the haze of the liquid shedding her eyes.

"Do you know who killed her?" She heard the words as if it hadn't been her who formed them.

His wedding band became too tight. He twisted it loose staring down at it, maybe seeing the one that occupied his finger first. "I'm not breaking any more promises. Run, Jade, while you can. Please do for me what she wouldn't. I'm not the bad man, but he's coming...he's coming for you."

She never spoke. Feeling tears burning her cheeks she refused to argue. Instead, her heart clung to his warning. Her dedication to justice, that fire burning red hot for vengeance, wouldn't let her stop. She understood, whatever he withheld, he'd done it at her mother's request. It was the only thing he had left to give her. Jade would never ask him again to betray her trust, even for the truth. She'd unearth it on her own.

Defenses down, she hugged him. His embrace was strong, honest, and hard to break free of. He couldn't shelter her from her fate. No one could, and she wouldn't allow them. No matter the volume of his love, it paled against the strength of her will.

She was the image of her mother.

He confessed, "I always loved you. You will always be my daughter. Come home when you've caught him." And she was gone, across the rich lawn, inside the car, blinded by pain, fortified by love, back into a war he believed she was guaranteed to lose with one lingering question. He'd said pain caught up to her mother and killed her. He wanted her to move away. Did that mean he knew a monster in Shadow Hook was after her?

FOURTEEN

Jackson lived in Upstate New York, but Texas lived in him. No surprise his property transported visitors to his home state, from its iron gates and riding arena to the long barn and ranch-style home with thick timber accents. Jackson was built with good stock and old money. His grandfather made a fortune breeding racehorses, though he refused to ever "plant his carcass on an equestrian saddle." Jackson rode western too but wasn't quite as opposed to the more sophisticated riding approach. After all, his mother had been an accomplished jumper before she fell for his dad and the ranch she lived and died on.

Perhaps it was why he guarded her cherished horse with such fervor. The dapple-gray had an unpronounceable Arabian name so he nicknamed him Thrash, for the mess he made with his hay. He'd trailered him in from south Texas to live out his years pampered under Jackson's watchful eye in Shadow Hook. Though Saratoga was a short trip down the highway, he'd vowed never to sell him. He'd been with Jackson for years and was past his prime, but perfect for teaching locals to ride. Checking him over while giving him a brush down, Jackson took pride in the force to be reckoned with.

"Stop slamming those hooves. There's not a ton of room in this stall. I swear you're still itching to race, aren't ya?" The horse blasted air out his nose and over Jackson's arm. "Are you kiddin' me? Full of attitude just like her."

Finishing with Thrash's mane, Jackson stood back to appreciate the animal. "You still got it buddy." He patted the horse's neck with a firm hand before gathering his grooming gear. His back was turned when Thrash reared and smacked Jackson into the stall wall.

"Jesus, Mary, and Joseph! What in Sam hell has you so riled up?" Jackson shoved Thrash back to his side of the stall. The horse refused to settle. Hooves dancing, head jerking up, Jackson scanned the ground for mice. "I'll be damned if I'm gonna sift through your mess of hay again for rodents. It's late buddy, and I'm logging long hours. Calm it down a notch."

The horse eased up, twisted his neck from side to side as if stretching out the stress that plagued him, and dipped his face into the water trough. Jackson tossed his remaining tools into a bucket and headed for the gate. "Man, you're edgy."

Jackson locked the gate, walked a few yards down the center of the barn to a storage closet and placed the equipment inside. He had crossed halfway to the far end closest the house when Thrash protested an indignant neigh. "Oh, keep it down. The mice are trying to sleep."

A night like any other, chores filled the gap that could've been regret for what was missing in Jackson's life. All those things he veered away from until they quit coming. He wouldn't dwell on them and did a fair job at avoidance.

Maybe that was why the bullet came as such a shock.

Slamming to the ground, clutching his right side, Jackson mopped the floor with his body scrambling for cover behind a load of new stall doors. His horses screamed and reared at the opposite end of the barn. Thrash was warning him. Thick-headed, he didn't listen. Still, they protested.

He prayed his assailant didn't silence them.

A bullet's force on contact pales in the wake of its afterburn, and as sure as the blast's echo reverberating off the barn walls, Jackson knew the fire would follow.

Most people wait for the pain as shock sets in, reeling in the proverbial "why me." Not homicide detectives on the heels of a serial killer with a thirst for blood. When the bullet tore through somewhere mid-abdomen, Jackson thought only of the gunman and how to avoid another round.

A second report splintered the top edge of the pile over Jackson's head. He flattened his frame against the floor. Glancing down waist level, he was relieved to see red blood not black. He tore his See Camp from his right boot, the 14-ounce gun was easier to dislodge than the one beneath his wound.

And there it was, the burn.

Combating the searing pain, he listened for movement between him and the stalls, gun in one hand, bloody mess in the other. A soft scraping sound filtered across the far left side of the tackle room. He rose off the floor, crouched low, then swiveled around the back left of the unsalvageable doors. On the toes of his boots, he rotated sound-lessly to a space between an outer wall, the pile, and the place he'd been shot.

Searching shadows against the adjacent wall, he noticed nothing out of place. His familiarity with the building afforded an advantage.

The horses fell silent. Only two of his six were in the barn. Undergoing extensive remodeling, Jackson didn't want the younger animals spooked by construction. The two remaining horses he refused to board out. An impressive buckskin named Leather that he'd owned since its birth. And Thrash. He'd vowed to provide him a life of luxury until he dropped dead. Preferably not from a gunshot wound.

Scanning right, Jackson studied the length of hall flanked by five sets of stalls. The horses occupied the furthest two. He was about to shift his attention elsewhere when a dark mass emerged from the far end.

It paused, turned toward the dapple-gray's stall, and fired.

The gun's flare illuminated the man's profile for a fraction of a second. Jackson was too distant and too angry to make out any details. Before the shooter rotated around and put a bead on Leather, Jackson exploded into the hall.

He sent the first shot low, aimed for the intruder's legs. His injury and the See Camp's loss of accuracy after twenty feet cost him his usual precision. The bullet slammed into the back wall sending splin-ters behind the shadowy mass.

Leather reared and smashed into his stall door anxious to trample their enemy.

Jackson's second shot followed a ghost into the night beyond a swinging exit gate. The gate crashed closed. Leather snapped the bolt closure off the door and broke free of his stall. Jackson crumpled to the ground, the room closing in on him.

The last image he registered was that of a friend standing guard above him.

"He shot my mother's horse! Murdered Thrash! The son-of-a—"

"Jackson? Where are you calling from?" Kane left the shop the same time as Jackson, both desperate for sleep. It hadn't been an hour, and Kane's phone was filled with the gruff voice of a severely pissed off Texan and wailing background noise. "Are those sirens?"

"The ambulance. Shot me too, but Thrash! For the love of Christ, what does this asshole have against horses!"

An EMT confiscated Jackson's phone. Kane listened to them being yelled at then one got on the line. "We're bringing him to County," an annoyed voice said. Jackson was protesting. Kane heard him yell he'd be fine, "just grazed," and the line went dead.

It was a toss-up what would infuriate Jackson more, an attack on home turf, being shot, or the death of his mother's favorite horse.

Kane guessed the horse.

The hospital confirmed Tex's wound wasn't critical. Jackson went into surgery, and Kane spent two hours at the ranch inspecting the crime scene. Jade met him there after her witness interview. She sent him back to the hospital with a message for Jackson and stayed behind saying she'd catch up with them back at the station.

They all harbored an aversion to buildings with red crosses on them. Kane arrived as Jackson was being prepped for release, which he'd demanded. Kane walked the hall to Jackson's curtained cubical staring at the clean shirt he brought and the floor tiles.

"Heard you were causing trouble. Time to bust you outta here." Kane's comment was met by an icy glare from the nurse administering to Jackson's bandages.

"Stay still, sir. Shouldn't be going anywhere. Infection in this type of wound can have dire consequences," she said.

"Then you better strap it on tight. I don't want it coming apart on me."

"I assume if you'd seen him, you would've mentioned it when you called from the ambulance." Kane shifted around the nurse to stand in the far back corner of the curtained-off trauma room. Jackson leaned on his left side while the nurse finished work on his right. He'd been xrayed, stitched up, and injected. The wound tore through skin and muscle tissue but managed to miss vital organs. The nurse changed the initial dressing, apparently with some resistance.

"By the time I had a clear view, I couldn't see straight." Jackson was inspecting the nurse's handy work. "That ought to hold up."

"For what? You're not seriously leaving," she said. "You're in no condition—"

"You don't want me hanging around causing a ruckus. I'd only get more ornery."

Kane chuckled, welcoming another cold shower from the nurse. "Did he jump you?"

Jackson glanced up. "He was waiting. Knew where to hide and when to pounce."

The nurse halted her final touches. "There's no way the doctor will release you."

Jackson yanked a crumpled paper out from under his leg. "Already has, darling. Knows I'd cause too much grief." He glanced back at Kane. "Fox in a henhouse."

"He's been watching the place," Kane said, more to himself than Jackson.

"He could've been a better shot." Jackson shifted to an upright position.

"If he was, you'd be dead," the nurse said. She left with a glare that held all the warmth of a freezer.

"That's my point." Jackson waited for her footsteps to recede. "He aimed to miss."

"You think he wasn't aiming to take you out?" Kane asked.

"Down not out."

"Why?" Kane tossed Jackson the clean shirt he'd been carting around. "Why now?"

Jackson stretched on the new shirt like it was lined with glass shards. "The immediate threat isn't the why, it's the how. He is watching all of us."

A shiver ran down Kane's spine, and it wasn't aftershocks from the departed nurse. He wasn't worried about an ambush at the cabin. Jade's headstrong determination made her reckless and irresponsible with her own safety. An easier target than she'd admit. And those targeted for death were women. Tex was living proof.

Jackson slid off the bed leaving the pressed shirt hanging out over his bloodied jeans. "He marked Jade and me. My fear is you're next. He gambled the farm on being a hell of a shot. If our luck runs out, his first mistake will have one of us in a pine box."

"The bullet is from a Beretta nine-millimeter," Kane said. "Interesting weapon."

"Cop's gun." Jackson collected his things off the bedside table into a hospital bag and threw the curtain back. "Let's go. I hate this place."

They passed the nurses' station, and Jackson's attending glanced up from her paperwork to flash them an admonishing scowl.

"Feeling's mutual." Kane laughed out loud when they hit the elevators.

"Are you kidding? She loves me."

"Speaking of, Jade asked me to tell you to quit competing with her. Said her wound was more serious. Yours is uglier."

"That's not fair. She hasn't even seen it."

"I have." He grinned. "That's not all. She said it doesn't matter what you do, she'll always be the first one to take a bullet from this guy."

"Man."

"I know. Harsh." They shared a smile then Kane paused before they exited the elevator. "Seriously, you scared the crap out of her... and me."

"I know. I'll tell her it's payback for the headphones."

"She's going to make you pay for that window."

"Small price. I saw her half-naked. Well worth it."

Kane smiled slyly before they crossed the sidewalk to the parking lot. "Only half?"

"Quit worrying, Romeo. I know my place. You do realize the dangerous game you're in, don't you?"

"This guy's a real monster."

"Not what I meant. You've all your eggs in one basket, and it's sitting in the middle of a firing range. If anything ever happened to—"

"Nope. Don't go there. I can't." Kane dug for his keys avoiding eye contact.

"Sometimes these things aren't our choice. I love her too. Too much at stake." Jackson stopped blocking Kane's pathway.

This time Kane locked eyes. "I can't quit her, Tex. And I can't make her quit. It's always after the next case." Kane walked on a few steps nearer the vehicle and hit the fob.

"It isn't in her to quit. That's the problem. Neither one of you know when to. Stubborn like mules." Jackson eased into the passenger seat and closed the door.

"You're one to talk." Kane lingered, drinking in the night air before ducking in. "You owe her big time," he bellowed.

"For what?" Jackson asked from inside the car.

"Vet bills. She saved Thrash. Vet showed up as fast as us. Said he was grazed. It's like he knew to play dead. But I'm pretty sure he's as pissed about it as you are."

Kane heard Jackson laugh, yelp in pain, then chuckle again.

He wasn't laughing. Jackson was right. He had two unsolvable situations, both with the potential to kill him. Jade wasn't a woman you came back from. Self-sacrificing like no other but shattered beyond mending, and he'd fallen for every broken piece.

FIFTEEN

The Redeemer knew better than most, beauty was had by monsters. He scrutinized photos of those he'd disposed of until nausea seized him. Reflected light cast from the spotlight illuminating their faces sent shards back at him outlining his shadow. The shadow and he were one and the same. He turned his back on the images to stop from retching.

He couldn't face them again. He needed a moment to compose himself. The potency of their lies swelled like cotton in his throat leaving him gagging.

Coiffed hair, clear complexions, bright eyes, and none of it revealing a shred of truth behind the masks. He knew. His vision penetrated the illusion. And they'd all paid for their sins. Not enough. Not nearly enough.

He pushed the photos he'd taken of their final moments over his surveillance shots. Grotesque finality brought a righteous comfort, relieving his stomach.

Analyzing next steps, he reviewed the fifteen victims on the drafting table. Success demanded decisive planning. He needed coffee, black and strong. He abandoned the drafting table, gliding out of the room soundless as a specter.

Martial arts training as a kid taught him to move catlike. When he broadened from a gangly one hundred twenty pounds to a hulking man double the weight, no one expected he'd sustain his silent nature. They were wrong, again.

A barista machine sat in the corner of a café bar in the vestibule outside his office. Industrial-sized and imported from France, it could handle the workload of the busiest Starbucks. Yet, cappuccino or latte, its talents were a singular treasure. He reveled in its robust aroma and admired the precision of its delivery. Placing a rust-colored cup in the holder, he programmed in a double and left to adjust a nearby thermostat.

The furnace kicked on with a soft hum seconds before being drowned out by the machine producing the finest espresso in the city.

Carrying the piping-hot brew to the drafting table, he settled back into his chair, stole a tentative satisfying sip, and pulled out the dossiers on his adversaries.

They'd be thanking him not chasing if they understood his mission. Unfortunately, archaic laws of justice afforded no honorable results.

He stared at the photos of Detectives Kane, Jackson, and Jade. They were quite the pack, and they were closing in. Howling near his den. Time to throw them a bone of misdirection. The arcane clues he'd fed them conquered and divided. He drew unique satisfaction watching them scramble to salvage a lead out of scraps.

Their will was admirable. He'd become close to each. He knew their motivations—Kane to prove his dead father wrong, Jackson to live up to his, and Jade, well she was unique. She lived under a self-imposed death sentence, regretting survival.

He knew another with the same affliction. Institutionalized. How interesting their meeting would be. He wished he could've been the fly on the wall. No. Flies were ugly, dirty, and all-around disgusting. Dragonfly. Better. Cleansing the garden of bloodsucking mosquitoes and other pests. Yes. He wished to be a dragonfly perched on a petal.

Jade's isolation, her moralistically infused philosophies, and fierce resolve made her a kindred spirit. Exceptional gifts came with price tags. Hers were costly.

Kane would anticipate him coming. Jade and Jackson had both been marked. All their lives exposed. Nothing sacred. He'd memorized their routines, homes, family and friends in painstaking detail. No escape. A realization sure to resonate with those he allowed to live.

He'd chosen the fortunate two with great care and contemplation.

Though he questioned if jealousy played a role. Contemplation was not only the path to enlightenment, it paved the way to attainment for those with intelligence, discipline, and will.

Character traits he possessed in spades. And patience. Tremendous patience.

All countered by the team who sought to apprehend and destroy him. Their persistence was relentless, their determination fueled by every death.

And there'd be more before it was over.

More persistence. More determination. More death.

Despite their best efforts, they failed to identify him. He walked among them, noticed but never seen. They'd opened their door to a wolf. Granting him insider access to their every move. One worried him. Trouble from the beginning.

Patience.

The temperature of the room dipped. He studied his surroundings. New woodwork scented the air. Moonlight cut through a crack in the heavy drapes illuminating the walnut shelving and rolling ladders, a thirteen-foot fireplace adorned by family crest and swords, plaques of achievement, and well-appointed artwork. A soft shaft of light embraced "The Madonna," a painting acquired on a trip to Italy three years previous.

The corpses drew his attention downward.

Each pawn a worthy sacrifice. None as meaningful as the first on the journey of redemption. She rivaled the idealistic subject of the Italian painting aglow above him—the antonym of everything motherly, pure, and nurturing, and yet a heartless whore.

The drafting table had been Venice's. Made of fair quality and craftsmanship, it joined his collection for sentimental reasons. Gratification came from having such memorabilia in plain sight. He ran a hand down the length of it. Smooth reminder. Killers far less worthy coveted silly keepsakes, trinkets of jewelry and locks of hair. He furnished his home with grand acquisitions.

He raised the espresso to his lips and indulged. Perfect. Hot without the burn. A rich dark brown with golden hue. Bold. Sensual. Full-bodied flavor. He set the cup down and reviewed his work. He didn't need to. The planning was in his head, a map drawn over decades. The visual was merely for pleasure.

But the pleasure was thinning as his files thickened.

Ignoring his usual kit, he extracted a Beretta from a drawer hidden in the shelving unit and headed for the door.

Selecting a Ralph Lauren coat from his wardrobe, he tucked the weapon in at the small of his back beneath the heavy wool.

Twilight called forth deeds that daylight wouldn't dare witness, and this one required a service revolver.

SIXTEEN

Max's phone rang unanswered. Jade called all three lines to no avail. She needed to speak with him, needed someone sound to run her theory by.

Max was more than the department's shrink. A staggering success rate unearthing skeletons, a personal fascination, resulting in vast knowledge of infamous killers, reinforced his reputation as the go-to guy on countless cases.

He kept what she coined 'monster memorabilia' in his home office. Books owned and autographed by Ted Bundy, childhood artwork drafted by John Wayne Gayce, and a knife collection once the property of the suspected Monster of Florence.

Strangers either feared him or questioned his motives. Not Jade. She'd known him since childhood and witnessed the scope of his compassion and dedication to victims, the force, justice, and her own sanity.

He wasn't a threat. He was an enigma. And he'd suffered in ways only she knew.

She drove to his house.

Jackson and Kane were waiting at the station, thankfully both in one piece. Conjecture wouldn't fly with them. Clarification was convincing. She needed to be, hands down, fucking convincing.

Arching branches heavy laden with thick foliage blocked out any trace of moonlight down Max's block. Streetlights more than compensated for nature's curfew. The one nearest his place was burned out.

A dark void. Their town had lots of those, just not near him.

She'd wait. He had to come home sometime.

Checking her appearance in two-inch sectors in the rearview mirror offered a fractured composure. Futile and the only option. Max didn't have mirrors on the main floor of his home. The décor and atmosphere made it a natural thing until you entered the guest washroom. A serene Monet stole the place of a common mirror, and though it transported the admirer to tranquility, it didn't help you check for lettuce between your teeth. Jade understood the lack of mirrors, privy to a history he didn't share with most.

Certainly mirrors existed on the upper floor. Jade never had reason to venture into that private domain. Max had never given her one.

She accepted her disheveled state and flipped the visor up.

Outside the window, the night was still. A funeral pall blanketed the area surrounding Max's house. It lay in utter darkness, but for Jade it signified a beacon of hope.

She'd gained an inroad to the Redeemer's psyche through information garnered from her blind informant. What remained was how the new pieces fit into the larger puzzle. Simms confirmed that the Redeemer's motivations started young.

What triggered them?

She had ideas. She needed Max.

Simms knew nothing of the killer's family, only that he came from wealth and had the brains to amass more. This gave him means.

Some event left the Redeemer mentally scarred and twisted by a compulsion to exact revenge. The motive.

The killings fed his inner hunger. Increasing cruelty and shorter rest period between victims revealed a diminishing satisfaction from the act. The addiction.

The death drug was waning.

And he possessed a magnetism that lured prey to him and drew from them an acceptance of their fate. Opportunity.

Alas, the makings of a serial killer.

Jade refocused her vision from the memory of Venice Beil's defiled body to the street and found herself staring at the broad outline of a man approaching from the far side.

He didn't see her inside the darkened vehicle. She made no move for the door. Instead, her eyes followed the man's path seeking its destination. He crossed between two cars at an angle that placed him at the foot of the stairs leading to Max's door.

Wearing the hood of a poncho-styled raincoat, his identity remained concealed. It wasn't raining.

The man moved in sync with the quiet night.

She reached but stopped herself short of opening the door when he ascended the stairs. The way he drifted up them said he'd done it a thousand times.

In seconds, Max vanished inside, and the lights came on.

Her enigma had become more mysterious.

Jade slipped out of the car and was halfway up the walk before realizing her hand was resting atop her weapon. For an instant she forgot her place. Hunting when out of the woods was akin to fighting outside the battlefield. She had no set terrain, nothing off limits, armed by instinct.

She dropped her hand to her side, shot up the last few steps, and knocked on the door. A few heavy, advancing footsteps and it opened.

"Sorry to intrude so late." She stood outside.

"We're both night owls, no trouble." He opened the door wide allowing her access. "Please, come in."

The raincoat was hanging on the first hook in a row of options. She glanced at it then back to Max.

"Your neighbors will start talking," she joked.

He smiled, retreating to allow her room to remove her heeled Allsaints Caceys.

"I have a confession to make." She stood inches away. "I watched you come in."

"You did?" Surprised but not alarmed.

"Didn't take you for a night walker. It's not exactly prime conditions for a stroll."

"Please, join me in the study." He ushered her by him and followed behind. "Am I detecting your investigative curiosity?"

She plunked down in her favorite seat and smiled up at him.

"The weather's dreary," he said. "An improvement over the suffocating depression I listen to some days. Helps dispel the cobwebs. You relax, I'll get us coffee, and we'll talk."

She scanned the room. Everything surrounding Max attested to his intelligence, here and at the office.

He returned with two cups, handed her one, and sat in a large armchair.

"I think I'm getting into this one's head," she began.

"You've been working it around the clock." Max shifted for comfort more than usual, the mental burdens of patients weighing on him.

"The pieces are there. It's placing them." Jade admired him. Like her he never said no to his calling or shrank from its toll. And there was one.

"Okay."

"His motive derives from a childhood issue, as does most. I'm guessing mother."

"Typical."

"Accurate." She settled in her seat and sipped the hot liquid. It warmed going down. "He started killing over two decades ago and close to home."

"Someone he knew? The intimate nature of the killings points to that possibility."

"His addiction is a fierce habit. He can't quit."

"Also typical." Max swallowed back a sip and held his cup, twisting it in his hands.

"The ritual is payment." She leaned in closing the gap between them as if the conversation called for discretion though no one existed to overhear.

Max tilted his head inquisitively.

"I think we've been focusing on the wrong evidence," she continued.

"How so? Sounds like you've surmised a workable profile."

"The bloodletting."

"It's his method and a ritualistic one with religious connotations—"

"It has nothing to do with religion, Max. Frankly, I'm surprised you didn't identify this earlier."

"I've disappointed you."

"No, no. I didn't say that." Jade clasped her hands together and searched the dark oak plank boards. "I don't know if I'm right. Truthfully…I don't know much. I'm not sleeping."

"Do you need something for that? I can prescribe a mild sedative that'll turn your mind off long enough to—"

Jade glanced up. "Thanks, no. I need to stay on this one."

Max pushed the prescription pad he'd eagerly written on away. He always had one handy. A partial word, beginning with the letters ZO, wasted the page.

"What's the theory?" Max flipped his Mont Blanc pen over with a dexterity that said he'd mastered sleight of hand.

"I think it's about draining the life out." Jade rubbed her eyes. Friction deepened the burn left over from her encounter with the mace.

"Literally." Max shifted into a thinker's pose.

"No. Figuratively." Jade stiffened. "Someone sucked the life out of him. This is payback."

Max weighed her summation before responding. "Your perspective collaborates Dr. Leigh's. The common thread between victims is his undoing."

Jade's eyes were blurring in tandem with the clarity of her thoughts. Blues music filtering in from Max's kitchen was beginning to lull her. She smoothed hands over her brow, then swallowed down more coffee. She let the cup dangle, holding it from the top rim. "Why these women?"

"And who in the department?" Max asked.

"What?"

"Don't forget what Leigh warned. According to her, one of you is a high risk."

Jade shrugged. "We're cops, Max. We're all at risk, all the time. We know that. Jackson and I particularly."

"If she's right about this—"

"I'm starting with Elizabeth Simms."

Max lost interest in his pen, dropping it to the side table with a thud that said it'd slipped. "Who?"

"Beth Simms. Her sister was the Redeemer's first victim. I'm sure of it. Same MO, same ritualistic righteousness, and she was a close kill. The way Simms described her sister's death, it had to be him."

"Have you shared this with Kane or Grey?"

Jade set her cup aside. "Not yet. I needed to talk it through."

"What about Leigh?"

"Don't know. She's familiar with the Simms case. She thought it'd been solved. The murder happened in her neighborhood."

"Interesting." Max tapped his fingers together.

"Damn. I hate that word." Jade stood, walking the room. "Talk to me."

Max stood with her. "We've come full circle. Sound theory. Focus

your efforts on that first unsolved. He's a scholar. Check college gradu-
ating class lists for honor students, scholarship recipients, even valedic-
torians. I'd say his first kill was close in age, within a year or two. And
put Simms under a microscope. Affiliations, clubs, hangouts, they
should be in the original case file. If she was there, there's a chance he
was. He wouldn't have been as careful back then. Someone knows him.
He was the kind that stood out."

"Simms said he was exceptionally attractive," Jade offered. "Not
that I put much stock in the twenty-year-old memory of an infatuated
blind woman."

"It explains the allure," he said over his shoulder, turning his back
to her.

"So does chloroform."

Max laughed, walked to the table and collected her empty cup.
"Second cup?"

"Your coffee's the best." She hesitated. "No thanks."

Max approached. He towered over her. She was reminded of his
substantial size, a formidable protector.

"The boys might have come close on the Simms case. Revisit their
suspect and witness list. I'll bet he's in there." He eyed her injured leg
and the dark circles forming under her sleep deprived eyes. "I'll be
right back."

He gestured to the kitchen and disappeared while she headed in the
opposite direction for the front door. She laced and belted her shiny
boots. He returned with a baggy containing tiny white pills.

"Here. When you can, get some rest. They take half an hour to
kick in, and it'll taste like you were eating metal the next morning, but
you'll sleep."

"What is it?" Jade shoved the bag in her jeans pocket.

"Zopiclone. Can't hurt you. You hate medication. It's candy to
some. Don't think I hand it out regularly."

"Thought never crossed my mind. Thanks." She opened the door,
masked by the shadow of the threshold. Night air crept by her. "I got to
go. Jackson and Kane are waiting."

Max leaned against the doorjamb. "How is he?"

"Jackson? Tough Texan. He's pissed about his mother's horse."

Max laughed, then stared past her.

"What? You have that look."

"Didn't take this one for an animal killer." He put his hand on her shoulder then withdrew inside. "Take care of yourself. You headed to the station?"

"Have a stop to make. Simms gave me an address." Jade started down the steps. "Building's still standing. Thought I'd check it out."

"Your partner's worried about you. Don't keep him waiting too long."

Jade stopped at the midpoint landing. "Above and beyond, Max."

"It's the job."

SEVENTEEN

Detective Wenzel sunk low in his car cursing under his breath while he waited to end Kane's career. The exasperated air rose in hot plumes fogging his view to the station's back exit. Sadly, it lacked its regular dose of nicotine and so did he.

His discomfort was worth the chance to follow Kane home for irrefutable proof of transgressions sure to ruin him.

Jade wouldn't have been promoted if she had a set of balls. Jackson was as dense as he was thick. And Kane? Kane had been out of the way until Grey called him back. The evidence was in front of Grey, and he refused to see it.

That was about to change.

Jade and Kane were having an affair, throwing protocol to the wind, and screwing more than each other over. He didn't suspect. He knew. Confirmed at a company party, in a public washroom no less.

A crack in the bathroom door gave window to the main event, from beginning to sloppy end. He'd followed them then too, to no avail. He needed something Grey couldn't dismiss.

This would be different.

He was prepared. Could've used a sweater vest under his coat. The chill was worth the photos he'd capture with his new zoom lens. He'd send them in anonymously and damning. Unbecoming conduct for certain.

Jade wasn't at the station. He'd waited past dinner, and she hadn't showed. Outside the night lay still. A few late travelers broke the monotony. Otherwise, the street appeared abandoned.

The Texan's large silhouette hovered near the exit. He came out, descended the stairs, and disappeared to the left. An engine started. Wenzel waited for fumes to mark its location. Jackson's truck exited the lot and headed south in the direction of their regular steak house. Kane would follow soon.

Sitting in the cold while they dined on bone-in didn't sound appealing. He'd come too far to quit.

He endured plummeting temperatures inside his Volvo as the engine sat cold. A drift of exhaust was enough to tip off a detective to a tail. He wasn't about to give Kane any warning.

Staring out the window wasn't satisfying, but cigarette smoke trails risked exposure. He chewed nicotine-infused gum instead. A warped mixture of peppermint and chemical crap that left a disgusting taste in his mouth like his tongue had been used to hotwire a junker. It scented the air with a sickeningly sweet minty undertone. The scenery was as uninspiring as the gum.

Parked at a forty-five-degree angle to the exit, he had a clear line of sight to departing cars. Kane's Land Rover was two rows in, just out of view.

His original strategy was to shadow Jade. He'd unearthed enough dirt to strike a nerve that sent Kane into a rage at the most inopportune time. The last wild goose chase Jade sent him on made it evident it was time to switch tactics.

He wondered about the other man though.

The big guy he'd seen tracking Jade two nights back. They would've run straight into each other if a strange twist of fate hadn't delayed him a few seconds. He'd stopped for smokes.

What was his name?

He'd seen him before when he'd followed Jade to the doctor's estate.

Was she having another affair? Women like Jade were complicated. He cared less how many idiots she had lined up at the end of her bed, as long as her conquests stayed out of his career path.

The obstacle outside his window was enough. He'd never seen Kane bring value to the department and couldn't understand why Grey would choose a man of his racial background over one of his own.

Kane descended the stairs and crossed beneath the lamplight. It cast a halo around his hair and leather jacket. He didn't get the appeal. Why Jade would be interested in a blond Black man. The women at the station lingered over him surely because he was strange, but not regal like the other man. The two were nothing alike. A sophisticated businessman versus Kane. She had to be using Kane, a stepping stone on the corporate ladder. The other guy had to know. He'd followed her for a reason. Maybe if he shared information the guy would rid him of Kane.

What was his name?

Kane's Rover pulled out, turning left, passing him without a glance. Couldn't have seen in, fogged windows saw to that. Wenzel waited a few seconds, started the engine, and followed.

"Time to settle the score." An exhale of artificial mint.

"Funny, exactly what I was thinking." The man rose like steam, silently, from the back seat, a Beretta pointed at Wenzel's temple.

The Volvo veered out of its lane and was dangerously close to losing its side mirror to oncoming traffic when Wenzel regained control.

"We need to talk," the man said. "I know the perfect place. Head out of town."

"You don't need a gun pointed at me. I'm happy to tell you what I know."

Wenzel detoured for lake country. The man guided his maneuvers with a nudge of his weapon, two lefts, a right, and eventually devoid of streetlights. If he'd thought the night was quiet before, it was deathly silent now. Soon the hum of empty roads beneath his tires served as confirmation his was the only car for miles, and the guy behind him didn't have to be a marksman to get the job done.

Not good.

Brazen, snatching a cop outside their building. Maybe his new fare was a cop? Made sense. They dated in the same circles. No time to meet civilians.

His throat tightened. He feared gagging on the nicotine-tainted juice flooding his mouth. He swallowed hard. The gum descended, catching at every possible site like a wad of caulking. He turned to see the man's face outside the rearview mirror. "I think we both want the same thing," he said.

The man searched highway markers giving Wenzel a peek at his profile. "I doubt that. If we did, I dare say that'd pose a problem."

He studied his assailant. His fear, for the moment, lay buried beneath vengeance. He'd make Kane pay for this hassle and countless others he'd caused. This *was* Kane's fault. He'd pissed the guy with the gun off by messing with Jade and drove him to kidnapping. His own resentment burned deep, and he wasn't sleeping with Jade, though it appeared he was the only one who wasn't.

"Kane's no match for you. Jade would be crazy to keep it going."

The man in the back laughed.

"I'm glad you find this funny." Wenzel stayed calm, working the guy's ego.

"You have no idea."

"What do you want from me? You want to know where they go? Where he hangs out? That sort of thing?"

"Nope."

"What then? You looking for a cop for hire?"

"You offering?" The man was smooth, calm to a fault.

"He's out of a job soon. Leave it to me. It's the least I can do." His brow beaded with sweat despite the cold car.

"You should be concerned with your own future."

And he was. Kane needed to go, and he needed out of this car.

"Point is...he won't be working with Jade much longer, so you won't need to follow her anymore."

"Follow her? Hmm. Is that how you saw me? Following her? You think I need your help?" The man glared. The reflection diluted the potency of his stare, but not enough.

"If you didn't, you wouldn't be here."

"That's your first mistake." Waves of anger coming from the back said Wenzel missed something in the exchange. Easily done with the muzzle of a Beretta at your temple.

"Once his career is over, he'll be no use to her. Problem solved."

"Not even remotely," the man said, shifting positions out of the rearview.

Time for the direct approach. "You want him dead? Is that it?"

Laughter filled the back again. Something within it made Wenzel wish he were driving a company cruiser with bulletproof glass and mesh wire between them.

The man motioned to an upcoming exit. "I get the distinct impression you don't approve of Detective Kolter."

"Kane's an ass. You ever spent time with him?" Ask questions. Keep him talking. Wenzel knew conversation saved lives. What he didn't know was why his was in danger to begin with.

"Can't say I've had the pleasure."

"Everyone treats him like he's a genius. I, for one, have no idea why."

"Because he's a genius. Graduated with a list of honors and has an IQ of 141."

"You admire him?" The man had done his homework.

"I do." The gun muzzle waved him to veer right.

"How can you respect him when you know he's sleeping with Jade?" Wenzel scanned the terrain. They were off the beaten path and not a country house in sight.

"He's not a threat to me." The laugh returned, too confident.

"Then what do you need from me?"

"Silence." The man slid into clear view, staring through the front windshield. A stream of moonlight cut across his face.

"Now I remember!" To recall under duress was so impressive, he jumped in his seat.

"Remember what?" the man asked, his voice not sharing in Wenzel's excitement. "You can pull into that turnout."

Wenzel slowed the car, steering onto the shoulder by a grouping of mailboxes for farm sites on the outskirts of Shadow Hook. Discreetly, he'd open the line to dispatch but hadn't hit the button yet. This was a decent, intellectual. He'd listen to reason. They'd come to an arrangement.

Wenzel peered over his shoulder. "Your name. I remember it."

"And that," the man leaned close enough to whisper. "...is your last mistake."

Wenzel pushed open the receiver. Heard the click of the trigger, the impact slam his head into the window, vengeance no longer his. Eleven seconds. That was how long he had to think of all the things he should've done with his life and to know his mother had been right. He wasn't detective material, she'd said. Too easily distracted.

EIGHTEEN

Jade never feared the dark. Darkness saved her life once. Now, the sensitivity of her eyes welcomed it. She keyed in the door code and entered the old textile mill prepared to feel her way through the labyrinth that lay beyond.

In the turmoil of refurbishment to accommodate a larger online business component, light was the first to be sacrificed. Switching outdated electrical wiring for the latest reliable cable, the seven-thousand-square-foot building was sentenced to intermittent blackouts.

Shame its timing corresponded with her investigation of the premises. She could've scheduled to come afterward, when renovations were complete, but she'd miss seeing it in its original state. Time was not on their side.

She'd contacted the owner from the parking lot of the sanitarium earlier for permission to access the site.

"It's a vicious obstacle course after sundown," he said. "Last guy who went in without a flashlight suffered a nasty leg wound after tangling with a cutting table."

Comforting.

She never entered anywhere without her Tac flashlight but now wished she'd brought something industrial. Hers offered fractional lighting. Its narrow beam caught an ominous array of metal monsters glistening back with claws and teeth that screamed stay out. The cotton and linen aroma lingering in the air drew her in its irony. That and an unquenchable thirst for insight.

The scent permeated the walls and lay heavy on everything between. Jade hadn't stumbled upon rolls of refined fabrics, but the fragrance assured they existed.

Scanning the corridor before her, she gained an appreciation for the obstacle course reference the owner made. Aside from rows of industrial sewing machines, presses, and threatening cutting tables, spools of wire, ladders, and tools littered the maze where once a clear aisle had surely existed.

Banking the flashlight right, she was startled by a hanging metallic silk fabric that transformed her reflection into a disturbing distortion. Her hand sought the refuge of her gun holster, rested there, then lifted, latch closure intact.

She negotiated waves of draped material, past linens, bamboo, and Egyptian cotton never knowing what she hoped to find—an inside track to the Redeemer, an intimacy to ensnare him.

She lingered in the stillness listening to a faint, distant, slithering sound. Images of spools of silk coming to life, snake-like, sliding across the floor came to mind. Validating her belief that sleep deprivation was a short track to insanity.

A machine of unknown origin came to life somewhere deep in the building sending reverberations down the walls. The fabric closest to her quivered in the flashlight beam, it was scared. She was not.

Advancing toward the sound, clarity said air conditioner. The night was muggy and brisk. Inside the temperature plummeted. She wore a short-sleeved sweater and jeans. The skin on her arm bristled with the draft of air filtering in from overhead vents.

If this was where the Redeemer brought his lover, his hide-a-way existed somewhere other than the vast open warehouse floor. No place sufficient for quenching sexual appetites in this front half of the building. Offices occupied the back. Allowing for window views of wooded grounds behind. Without doubt, one of those was where the killer and the sister of his first victim consummated their relationship.

The memory of Lorenda Lainey's posed corpse sent a gust of death into Jade's nostrils churning her stomach and flooding her mouth with saliva. Her flashlight beam slid over a table pausing at a box of Tic Tacs. She grabbed it, popped the lid, tapped out two, and tossed them in her mouth. Thinking they may come in handy, she threw the mints in her pocket and kept moving.

Bolts of fabric, packaged for shipment, lined the floor. Ahead of them, sample swatches overflowed on tables.

Finally, behind an artistic display of colored thread, sat the bank of offices. The current company had altered much, but she was assured no walls were constructed or removed and the original layout remained intact. Heading east to west, Jade threw light on each.

The first, the obvious home to an anal accountant, possessed neither the space nor atmosphere for ravenous copulation—she suspected the Redeemer knew no other kind. Other workspaces were cramped by furniture or exposed by shared windows. Nearing the far west, offices increased in size and views transformed ambiance from tedious to tranquil.

A bland but efficient eating area was expansive enough to play in. Jade dismissed the static domain. Not his style.

The buyer's office housed a luxurious sofa and an equally spectac-ular forest backdrop. Flanking suites shared similar benefits. A hallway between led to a staff washroom and a back exit. She peered out the outer door's narrow window. No seats for cigarette breaks. Nothing, save dense forest.

No. Not here.

Her gut instinct was a barometer for the trail of evil. It hadn't failed her.

Inside the largest office a narrow door existed left of the desk. It creaked opened to a stairwell. Jade ascended. The walls tightened with each step. Darkness folded in on itself. Misjudging distance, she banged the flashlight against the wall. It flickered, extinguished, and came back to life.

"Not now."

Pinning her arms to her sides, she sought the upper landing. Outside the stairwell, dim moonlight, blocked by heavy foliage, left the room awash in shadowy depths.

To her left, her flashlight found aged photos mounted on the wall, founding family members and supporting designers. Captions listed names and contributions. Jade removed the picture with the largest numbers, shone her beam on it, and snapped a photo with her phone.

A daybed stole center stage in the loft. Adorned in the most well-appointed bedding, it was encased on three sides by pillows and scenery. Inviting for brainstorming session or murkier strategies. Tucked into a nook, it hovered amid a canopy of trees. And, since all other windows occupied ground level, it offered complete privacy.

She ran her free hand across the coverings.

Sifted flour, softer than silk.

Setting the picture down, she turned her attention to a narrow door at the loft's far end. It opened to a modest but luxurious bathroom, complete with closet occupied by a suit, two shirts, and a selection of ties.

This was an owner's home away from home, a hard worker's retreat, and the first lair of a killer. The suit would've hung loose on Kane. No tag. Custom.

A bar area furnished with a small fridge and a bank of cupboards was located to the right of the bed. Magazines and business-related books lined a shelf directly across. A flatscreen and security monitor sat above. From here one could see everyone on the floor and approaching from outside.

Settling in the center of the bed, she glanced around, sweeping the flashlight in a semi-circle. "You saw them coming." She peered out the left window into the menacing shadow of the trees. "A high-hide for a low-life."

The silence broke under the inappropriately light ring tone of her cell phone.

The shop.

"Yep." Her curt response softened at the sound of Kane's voice.

"Where are you?" he asked.

"Checking out a lead. Leaving soon."

"What lead? Why didn't you call? I'll come meet you."

"Not necessary."

"Didn't pan out?"

"No, interesting, but I'm done. It's an old textile mill off Burbank Road."

"This is no time to be redecorating." He laughed.

"No kidding? I think he started here."

She scanned the room with her flashlight. A low creak funneled up the stairs then the air shut off. "I'll explain when I get there."

"If you don't make it back by midnight, I'm coming for you."

"Come away." She checked her watch. Time to leave. "See ya soon."

She placed the phone back in its holster and shut off the flashlight. Even with filtered moonlight cutting through the trees, any escape presented serious obstacles unless you'd studied this place in the light of day.

The Redeemer knew the layout.

Jade flicked the light back on. It shuttered then came to life. She grabbed the photo off the bed beside her. Difficult to discern faces. The picture was taken from a distance and time had muddied details. She reread the caption. All names were not listed, companies and significant individual contributors. They'd have to do a search to unearth the company's owners.

Like everything against them, this too would take time.

Time they didn't have enough of.

Someone knew him. She needed a name.

She'd take the photo, make a copy at the office, and drop the original off in the morning.

Moonlight hit metal and sent a shard of condensed light that made her squint. From the bed, the bar fridge was within reaching distance as was its lock—its reflective chrome finish, the blinding source.

All cops understood the necessity of suspicion, but the fridge didn't have capacity for a frat party of alcohol.

The lock seemed redundant.

Closer inspection piqued further interest. Jade recognized the make, virtually unbreachable and known to come with one master key that forced a tricky and expensive intervention if lost.

It begged the question, what was inside?

Chances were, it wasn't cold draft.

She fumbled with the lock, flipping it from side to side, and making a clatter of noise each time. She typed the model number and name into her phone, snapped a photo, dropped the lock back in place, and dialed the mill's owner.

He answered on the third ring with a dreary voice that said she'd woke him.

"Mr. Angelozzi, it's Detective Carmichael, I need to know what's in the bar fridge."

"Who? Oh, Detective. In the what?"

"The bar fridge upstairs has a lock on it, and I need—"

"Upstairs? It's the owner's. I'd suspect something expensive."

"I'm serious about this—"

"I gathered that by the late hour. I'm answering you." His tone sharpened with annoyance. "I don't know what's in it. I'm wondering how you got up there?"

"I walked." It was late. He wasn't the only one annoyed.

"The door should've been locked." He sounded confused.

"Well, it wasn't. I'm here. And I'd appreciate knowing what's inside the fridge of your private office."

"It's not my fridge," he said, calming. "I own the company, not the building. The owner of the building keeps that area off-limits. I've never been up there. If I'd known it had a bar…that stipulation was insisted upon on the long-term lease."

An unnerving clarity transformed the room around her. It wasn't the killer's first lair, it was his current lair, and she was alone, in the dark, inside it.

"I'll need all the information you have on this owner." Her words rushed out in the surge of adrenaline. "Did you meet him? Can you describe him? What's his name?"

"Only saw him once from a distance…years ago. I don't think I was ever told his name." Angelozzi sounded unnerved, reacting to the urgency of her tone.

"Can I leave through the back door?" Jade leveled her breathing by force.

"We never use it after business hours. I guess."

"I need you to view a photo line-up. I'll call you tomorrow." Jade hung up, trading the phone for the picture frame she focused the flashlight beam on the ground leading the way out.

The light caught something large and black at the threshold to the stairs, the toes of a set of boots much larger than her own and dangerously occupied.

Sweet Jesus. He'd left the door unlocked for her. An ambush. He'd followed her, come through the back, and set the trap before she made it across the cutting floor.

And she knew what he did to women. This time the dark was her enemy's friend.

"I'm young in that photo. Almost unrecognizable," the owner whispered. "Almost."

Jade traced up the feet, legs, and torso to the eyes of a killer until her light was extinguished.

NINETEEN

"He watches, malevolent, from the murky fringe of society and orchestrates murder in finite detail." Dr. Leigh's long black pencil skirt, matching patent stiletto heels, and white turtleneck projected onto the theater screen, exuding a stature more in line with her intellect than her five-foot-three frame. She wasn't sure how attending students, FBI, and police perceived her, and she didn't care.

"How he'll drug you. The blade he'll use to cut you. The gauge of rope he'll bind you with, and in what position, is decided long before you're taken. And that too will come without warning."

Faculty members fearful of society's filth contested her direct approach, suggesting she "tame it." She responded by spending the last two hours underscoring the raw truth.

The students needed to be scared. If they were pursuing a line of work that put them up against monsters, they had to know they were real.

"Tell me something," she asked the crowd. "How do you react to physical threat? Call it out."

The audience hummed under its breath then a few brave souls gave it momentum.

"Run," a jock in the third row boasted.

"Scream," a girl hidden somewhere mid-crowd said.

"I saw a guy clear a guard rail like a track star to avoid being crushed by a car once," a man on the left offered.

A police recruit stuck up her arm, waited for acknowledgment, then said, "Negotiate a way out."

Leigh smiled. "There it is, scream, jump, run, negotiate. All typical reactions, and all useless against a serial killer. You might try them *if* you're not paralyzed by shock.

"How about sex?" Leigh's redirect stirred hecklers, as she hoped. "What's your fantasy? Anyone willing to share?"

She scanned the crowd through harsh stage lights and caught a heated glare from a female in the fraud division sitting front row, a critic with no interest in the subject matter attending to fuel brewing complaints. A homicide detective beside her rolled his eyes then smiled at Leigh.

She grinned back and continued. "Come on, don't be shy."

No takers. Audience participation was crucial.

"Would all the gentlemen between the ages of twenty-five to forty-five stand up? If you're African American, Asian or Hispanic take your seat. Cameraman, would you pan this handsome crowd of future officers and give me some close-up full-body shots?"

Man after man, scrutinized by the lens, projected onto the screen. Leigh began highlighting qualities evident on the specimens overhead. "Ladies, gentleman, anything of interest—"

"A hard body," a flirtatious blonde called out.

"Great hands," a girlfriend said as her partner hit the screen.

"Big feet," a guy in front admitted.

"You can't see his feet," Leigh joked. The audience laughed, Leigh with them.

"What turns on a serial killer is the pain, suffering, and death of his victims." She paused for effect and walked the edge of the stage. "The more you run, the more you flinch, scream, or negotiate, the more you beg, plead, and cry, the better the high."

The men in the crowd were no longer comfortable standing.

"At any given time, there are as many serial killers at work in the United States as there are men left standing in this room. Better sit down, guys. They appear as harmless as any of you. They can come from any walk of life. They can, and have been, police officers, doctors, clergy, teachers, nurses, lawyers—"

"I believe that," an audience member blurted out.

The crowd erupted into laughter releasing a stream of nervous energy.

"The truth? There is no living creature on earth to compare to the lethal nature of a human predator. And if you're planning on catching one, you have to study every possible mutation to see him…or *her* coming. Don't make the mistake of thinking this an easy task. Many have tried and failed to recognize these masked monsters. If you don't believe me, ask Judith Ridgeway how she slept beside the Green River killer for decades, oblivious to his crimes and mounting body count."

Leigh returned the microphone to the podium.

"Thank you. You've been a great audience. Good hunting."

The mediator applauded as she left the stage. The audience rose from their seats and joined him—some more enthusiastically than others. Leigh returned to a reserved seat in the center of the front row as faces of serial killers flashed onto the screen in succession from long dead to the most recent breed.

A well-known FBI profiler was introduced and soon the show became far more graphic as a catalog of evidence photos and video footage confiscated from the lairs of captured killers told of their brutality in a way words never could.

Ushers soundlessly lined the exit rows with garbage cans on either side. Intended for vomit not trash, for those with weak stomachs and slow feet. Within minutes, exit doors streamed intermittent light down the rows as attendees left seeking refuge from a harsh reality, and time to contemplate a new career path.

Leigh sympathized.

She noticed a young reporter at the end of her row, sitting mercilessly with the clearest view of the gore book photos. Despite the horror, she transcribed with fervor in her notepad. Glancing away only to notice a garbage can being placed to her right.

A colleague snuck into the empty seat at Leigh's left and leaned over.

"You did great. Offended every desperate ego in the room and excited all the promising candidates," he whispered.

"Hope so." She spoke over her shoulder. "I hate to walk out on his speech, riveting as always. It's so late getting back."

"It's running over. He'll understand. I'll pass on your compliments."

"Thanks. And thanks for having me." She picked up her bag and inched off the chair to a crouch below head level then scurried down the aisle. As she passed the journalist at the end she said, "You've got a promising career, kid." She handed her a card. "Call me after graduation. The door is open, and the work is off the charts."

The young woman stared at the card, smiled, nodded, and went back to work.

She reminded her of someone else at that age. Maybe she'd avoid the mistakes Leigh made, the kind that threatened to derail your life path, maybe not.

One in particular haunted Leigh with such crushing guilt, she'd almost succumbed to it. Her wrists, though diminished to innocent creases by time, wore evidence of her early exit strategy. She awoke from that youthful nightmare with a tenacity that built her legacy.

The journalist's intensity reeked of the same high-octane fuel.

Outside, she wondered what drove the reporter as she approached her limousine. The driver, as always, arrived early and waited. She appreciated his punctuality, hating to be left standing alone in a dark parking lot. She hurried to the passenger side.

She preferred opening her own doors, and the driver knew it. After a year of her insistence, he'd quit getting out unless she had bags. In a singular motion, she ducked below the roof, slid into the back, closed the door, and reached for the seat belt. It clicked into place. She glanced up to see a man sitting across from her in the incandescent interior light. The hatred in his eyes said her survival tips just lost credibility.

He was holding the case file on the Redeemer. She'd left it in the car intending to utilize the long ride home for further analysis.

"You don't know me," he said. "I find that mildly amusing and somewhat ironic. You're fairly efficient. I'll give you that. In so far as the larger picture, you're as blind as a bat."

He'd reached across, seized her wrist, and twisted it over, inspecting the linear scar down its center. Then, he laughed, extracted a syringe, and shot her up with a vile of a milky white substance.

Her vision clouded as a metallic taste flooded her mouth. The muffled voices of students overflowing into the parking lot filtered in. She wanted to scream for help. Her vocal cords wouldn't respond, and even if they did, as she'd preached, there'd be no escape—it'd only serve to elevate his high.

He patted her limp hand, pulled her slouching frame into him, and whispered, "Have a nice nap. We'll talk in the morning. I have a busy night planned."

She wished those plans didn't include her. Wished she hadn't worn a tight skirt. And wished to God Detective Carmichael and her partner ended their suspect's reign before he ended hers.

TWENTY

Kane's dashboard clock read ten after midnight, Jade hadn't showed or called, and the damn Rover GPS system kept sending him to an address in California.

"Piece of…"

He swung his truck onto the roadside, pulled out his phone, and keyed in the textile mill off Burbank Road. It brought up a tracking map showing it off the main highway heading from Shadow Hook to New York. He locked in the most direct route and flew down the road with his lights whipping the night in strobe incandescence. No sirens.

When he traded pavement for gravel, he sent spray pockmarking route signs. The panic deep in his gut rising, his foot grew heavier on the accelerator. The one good thing about traversing backcountry roads at this time of night was their general abandonment.

General, not complete. He rounded a corner with too wide a berth and nearly caught the bumper of an oncoming SUV. That was the only label he could give it. It might have been black. Everything appeared black at night. He was fairly certain the driver was cursing him.

He had to slow down. Couldn't.

The case stole center stage in his mind, the knowledge he'd amassed wasn't enough. The major player was hidden somewhere behind the curtain. Kane was blind to the final act.

He threw on his high beams as a cautionary measure and sped up.

When the mill was within a few miles, he unsnapped his holster. Adrenaline in no short supply.

If Jade was getting in her car when he pulled up, he was libel to shoot her in the foot to prevent her from wandering off again without him. He hoped it'd be that simple.

Life seldom was.

He slid into the parking lot. Anxiety cratered into fear. Best-case scenario there'd be no sleep tonight, worse he'd be burying the only true partner he'd ever had.

The front windshield of Jade's car was smashed, the tires slashed, and the headlights beaten sightless. No Jade.

Kane flew from his vehicle, unholstered his Colt, and slid into a jimmied front door. He hit the light switch to no avail then followed his weapon with a flashlight searching the floor for some sign of her.

He sensed he was alone but couldn't risk calling her name.

A rustling noise further back became his target. Hunching low, bouncing from cover to cover, he made his way to the sound.

"Kane? Is that you?" Jade's voice started his heart back into rhythm.

"What happened?" He rushed to her, kneeling beside where she lay with a nasty gash on her forehead, on alert.

"I met our friend tonight." Jade reached for her wound, and her hand came back bloody.

"Can you stand?" Kane slid a supportive arm behind her back and lifted her.

"He didn't kill me."

"Any chance he's still here?"

She stood scanning the mill. "If I'd seen his face? I should've had him. He vanished."

"This is the most asinine thing you've done to date." Kane stared her up and down.

"I know he's connected to this place. We'll get a name." Jade leaned in, weak and disoriented.

"And you slam his victims for walking into his trap." He couldn't see any other injuries.

"He can't stay hidden forever." Jade stared into the darkness.

"He trashed your car, smashed out the lights." Kane ushered her to the door.

"He had every opportunity—"

"It's a miracle you're still breathing."

"He wants me in the game or—"

"One more slip and—"

"I'd be—"

"You'll be—"

"Dead." They spoke her fate in unison. Even in the dark of the abandoned warehouse Jade's green eyes shone with the restrained film of terror, anger, and defeat.

She faced him. "Why didn't he kill me? He hit me with something. I remember fading out. He whispered something."

Kane called the incident in, eyes trained on her. "What?" He held his phone to his chest.

"You don't die until I decide. He said it before I passed out."

Kane shrugged out of his jacket, wrapped it around her shoulders, and ushered her outside. "You're staying with me. It's not his decision to make. Narcissistic prick."

"Did you say something about my car?"

"Don't look." They exited the building. "I'll have the boys comb it. Leaving you alive pissed him off. He beat the shit out of your car. We're going home."

"I can't sleep." She slid into the passenger side of his truck holding a cloth to her head. She held his gaze. "He'll kill again and soon. I made him mad. Violated his domain." He closed the door for her and skirted the front of the vehicle to the driver's side. He couldn't help but compare the Mustang's beaten steel to flesh.

He leaned in. "Be glad it isn't you." He slipped behind the wheel and slammed his door, his rage inching near the surface. He knew the blame belonged to the man who'd disappeared back into the depths and left Jade bleeding on a cold cement floor. "What the hell were you thinking, coming here alone?"

He never glanced her direction. His grip on the steering wheel left heat marks. Seconds passed. She sat in silence while he regained his composure and remained so for the duration of the trip. They hardly spoke at the hospital. The doctor confirmed a mild concussion and bandaged her up. It wasn't until he turned the cabin's dead bolt locking them inside that his emotions erupted, unleashing months of frustration.

"A killer granted you life tonight." Kane glared at her. "You should be dead."

Her smack landed full force across his left cheek. She raised her hand with a follow-up. He arrested it midflight. His face stinging, he met her glare.

"What was that for? Speaking the truth, being hard on you, or picking you up off the floor?"

"For acting like I aimed to end up in a body bag. I'm working the case." She tore her hand from his grasp, kicked free of her partially laced boots, and stormed away.

"What case is that?" he called after her. "The Redeemer's or your mother's?"

"Not that again!"

He followed her into the family room. Rain slithered down the windows, silver snakes in the moonlight. "You're running around oblivious to protocol like a damn rookie!"

"Don't preach protocol to me, you son-of-a-bitch!" She stomped past him and threw his coat on the corner chair. "You just came off suspension."

"I was defending you—" He dared to block her exit.

"I didn't ask you to." She skirted his leg, coming in close then paused.

"You don't have to ask. I found you out cold on a cement floor with a gash across your head. You were unconscious with a demon hovering over you in a dark, secluded location. You do understand that!"

"I get it! There was no way to anticipate he'd still be using the place, or he had any connection, let alone that he owned it."

"There's not much we *can* anticipate. So why put yourself at risk? You ever stop to think of the consequences?"

"That's the whole reason I was there. I want him to face them."

"Well, you'll never see that day if you—"

Inches from each other, their eyes brimmed with uncorked passion. Kane's eyes drifted to the injury, now partially hidden by fresh bandages.

Jade shifted, concealing it from his examination. "You would've done the same—"

"I wouldn't, and you damn well know it. *I* think actions through. It's not just about you anymore." Kane spun her back to face him. "And he isn't coming for me!"

"You're so sure? We don't know who he's coming for! When. Where. We've got nothin' and—"

"That's the point! I went to that place expecting to find you dead. Do you know how that feels? Waiting to discover your worst nightmare? You make me live that every damn day. If I hadn't called you and asked where you were, he could've come back to finish what he started. I can't handle—"

She leaned in and kissed him hard on the mouth. He scooped her off the floor, carrying her to their bed. Her lips hungered with an acceptance her words would never admit. She'd been scared. He erased the fear. Love was an empowering antidote.

He bestowed it with passion enough to drown her doubt over and over.

He set her down at the foot of the bed. She tugged her shirt over her head grazing fresh bandages. He ripped his off while she stood unbuttoning his jeans. A size too large for her waist, her trousers dropped over her hips to the floor. He fought the snug hold of his Harley Davidson boots, molded by years of wear. His heel slipped free of the right, but the left wouldn't come loose. In an effort to twist out, he lost balance, caught the footboard mid-fall, and tumbled them both onto the bed.

"When they say 'fall in love,' they don't mean it literally." She crawled backward to the center of the bed.

He inched up, jeans at his hips, one boot still on. "It's a complicated descent." He whispered. "You ready for it?" Closing the distance, he hovered over her. "Let's make it interesting."

"Is that why you keep rescuing me? I intrigue you."

Her emerald eyes sparkled. He was drowning in them and couldn't catch his breath.

"Like no other ever will."

TWENTY-ONE

"A stockbroker discovered Wenzel's body on the way to work." Captain Grey listened as the first responder at the scene brought him up to speed on the latest in his department's list of failures. Each one, a nail in his coffin. Several he'd slammed firmly in place himself. Couldn't think about that now. "Blood splatter on the windshield. Says he didn't touch anything."

"I want him interviewed at the shop." Plumes of gravel dust followed Grey as he closed the distance to the ruins of one of his officers. Not his favorite. Not one he drank with or easily tolerated, but one of his.

The other officer on the scene wandered back to his vehicle leaving Grey and the ME alone.

"First impressions, Theo." Grey leaned into the open passenger side.

"Single shot to the right temple, weapon on the seat in proximity. Appears to be suicide." Theo glanced up from where he was leaning over the point of impact to Wenzel's skull.

"Appears?" Grey focused on Theo and not the brain matter spray. There was no escaping the smell.

Theo glanced up, remaining quiet.

"You smell that?" Grey asked.

"Cap?" Theo's expression said he'd made serious efforts to disregard this one sense.

"It isn't right, is it?" Grey asked.

Theo stopped, froze in place, and inhaled a long breath through his nostrils. His brows tightened to an inquisitive disbelief.

"Dust," Grey said. "Death diluted like the door was left open."

Theo examined the dash. "Air conditioning wasn't on. Mitch checked his calls. He'd pulled up your direct. Must've had something to say. Never dialed."

"Whatever he had to tell me, he can't say now."

Theo inspected the damage to Wenzel's jaw and mouth region. "Nope."

"I need TOD."

Theo pulled a long silver thermometer from Wenzel's abdomen. "Six to ten hours."

Grey walked back to his car and leaned across the roof in the direction of the adjacent cruiser. "Mitch, take a fine tooth to the back seat."

"You think he had company?" The officer hung back, waiting for Theo to finish up.

"It's possible. I'm not telling his family a thing until we're certain. Were the doors closed or open when he was found?"

Mitch nodded in the direction of the motorist in custody. "Said he 'thinks' they were closed. I'm inclined to doubt that."

"Where's the weapon?"

Mitch leaned into his car and pulled out an evidence bag. "Beretta. You know the model. It's a pretty old piece."

"Pass it over. I'll take it."

"Cap?" Mitch handed the weapon over the roof reluctantly.

"I'm heading there." Grey clutched the evidence bag in his gloved hand. He ducked, slipped behind the wheel of his Lincoln, shut his door, and started the engine. His hands were visibly shaking. He set the bagged weapon on the seat and gripped the wheel.

"Kolton." He instructed his hands-free as he pulled away.

"Dialing Detective Kolton." The automated voice responded.

Service worked so why hadn't Wenzel completed his call? Second thoughts or silenced?

As the ring tone ricocheted through the interior, Grey contemplated the answer. He worried about the words unspoken. He could hear those nails in his coffin rattling. His title acquired all the responsibility and provisional authority. He was fighting bad memories and wondering why he'd strived for such a position when Kane answered.

"You at the station?"

"I am," Kane said. "We have a lead. We're running background on the textile mill. I think we have a hit on the parent company. And I'm pretty sure I passed him on the way in. I'm analyzing camera footage at access roads, gas stations—"

"Were you with Jade last night?"

"I was. What's up?"

"I'll be there in twenty. Don't leave."

"Wasn't planning on it." Kane's confusion registered in his voice.

"Wenzel was hit last night. He's dead."

A pause hung heavy in the air. "Jesus."

"I'll bring you up to speed when I get in."

"Chief?"

"Yeah."

"I'm sorry."

"Me too."

"His wife?"

"We have to delay that." The road out was empty. Perfect isolation for a killer.

"Do you want one of us...Jackson at the scene?"

"Mitch is handling it. You passed the Redeemer last night?"

"Good chance."

"Stay on it. We need to know when. Timeline will be crucial. Where's Jade?"

"With Max. She has a minor concussion. Doc is sitting her out for a couple days."

"I want to see what you have. If he's responsible, last night was outside his standard MO."

"Not sure he has one, boss. You're sure it was him?"

"I'm sure." Grey lived way past denying his instincts.

"We're getting in his way." Kane read all the markers Grey did. One of the many reasons he promoted him to detective despite the racial blowback within the department.

"And we're paying for it in blood." A message alerting Grey to a secondary call flashed across the car's monitor. He knew the number. "I'll see you at the shop." He hit the button to take the new call back to his cell. He picked up, pressing the phone to his ear.

"You've got one hell of a mess on your hands," the man on the other end said.

"I'm well aware." Grey almost missed his turn. The car lurched through the correction.

"I'd say you're missing key pieces."

Grey pulled over and slammed the vehicle into park on an abandoned outer city street. "You plan on filling those in for me?"

"I could. Have you showed your detectives the earlier case?"

"No. I can't do that yet, and you know why. You have as much at stake as I do, Max." Grey threw off his gloves. His hands sticky with sweat.

"You have more. Meet me tonight at the club. Perhaps I can help us both out."

Grey hung up and swung back onto the highway cursing the start to a long, dangerous day.

TWENTY-TWO

Jade's cranium bowed, suspended by a metal vise tightened to the point of fracture, immobile, and awaiting repeated blows from the blunt end of an axe. Or that was how she envisioned the source of her pain. The headache that began when the Redeemer bashed her over the head erupted into the worst migraine of her life.

Kane drove her to the doctor in early morning, apologizing for every bump. Surviving on T3's, she waited for Max in his office. Cursing under her breath, the sniveling delinquent patient wasting his time.

In an odd way, she found the searing pain cleansing. Her thoughts were on nothing else. Even her beloved Gianvito Rossis were hitting the ground too hard, echoing up her spine, and reverberating across her swollen brain.

She fumbled with her prescription bottle in an effort to make out dosage limits. Instructions blurred. Squinting did nothing to clarify. She dropped the bottle, retrieved it off the floor groaning with the agony of elevating her head too fast.

She fought with the cap, smacked out another pill, and swallowed it down with the water Max's assistant had provided. Rolling off his lounger, she fumbled to the window and dropped the drapes.

Blanketing the room in darkness comforted her eyes but did nothing for her psyche.

She staggered back, stretched out on the lounger, and surveyed Max's space. She'd have no need to come here after today.

Her quitting the force would come as a shock. Somewhere between accepting that the blame for her mother's murder wasn't hers, watching a stream of women die before ever finding peace in their lives, and spending the night in Kane's bed, the decision was made.

Or was fear her motivation, the instigator behind her hands shaking and nightmares escalating into night terrors? Was she lying to herself?

No turning back. The drive that saw her through training and tightened her grip on the slippery ladder to detective was waning. Replaced by a compulsion to fill the void left by the family life she'd been denied. Kane saw her, even when she preferred he didn't. He knew all of her and kept coming. There'd be no one else that daring, that brave.

The clock was ticking on this one chance. Had the Redeemer's victims heard it too?

He stood in the way of her hanging up her badge. They'd catch him. As a team Jackson, Kane and she were formidable. They were too close to fail. She prayed more lives wouldn't be lost before they unearthed the malicious seed.

There were odd distractions, Wenzel's death for one.

Kane gave her the news. She'd called Grey. His death plagued her. The guy was tarnish on the badge no doubt, but shot point blank? His murder appeared cold and distant on the surface. It screamed of intimacy on deeper levels.

Max's shuffling withdrew her from the debate.

"Didn't mean to wake you." He paused closing the door behind him.

She slid upright. "You didn't."

"How's the head?"

"Throbbing like I've been hit by a tire iron."

Max smiled, threw a thick file on his desk, and collapsed on the sofa across from her. He sighed then said, "We have a lot to talk about."

"I don't think you're up for it. Rough case?" she asked.

"Daunting." He wiped his eyes. "Depression. A surefire avenue to prescription bliss during the downward spiral to a hellish torment that ends in a hedonistic massacre we'll all pay for with the lives of our most innocent. And my professional hands are tied."

She sat in silence giving him a moment to breathe. She could only imagine the litany of crap he'd endured.

"Sorry." He lifted his head, and their eyes met. "I know you understand that more than most. Helpless case. Though, I shouldn't admit it."

"Promise I won't tell. So you're human." This was the realism that bonded them.

His eyes brightened a little. "I know what your definition of human is, Jade. I don't think that's a compliment."

"Definitions can change." She rubbed her throbbing temples.

"Oh? Is that what you were thinking about when I came in?"

"No. Wenzel." The massage wasn't helping.

"The one who you blame Kane's suspension on?"

"Not anymore." She folded her hands.

"You don't blame him?"

"No point blaming a dead man."

"He's—"

"Gunshot wound to the temple. Brain splatter across his front seat on an abandoned road to nowhere." She questioned her raw delivery of the truth but couldn't recall a time when she'd mastered sugarcoating it.

"Are you investigating—"

"No. I'm done."

"I read the doctor's recommendation. You're sidelined for the—"

"No, Max. I'm done. Bringing the Redeemer to justice is my final act. I'm quitting the force."

Max's exhausted composure transformed. Stiffened by this astonishing revelation.

"Quitting? Just like that?"

"Hardly. It's been what? Twenty-five years of self-destruction, seven of mental anguish, and…oh, eight months of death wishes."

Max swiveled, taking in the storm outside the pane, then stood to meet it. "I knew you were leaving soon. One way or another. I knew it."

"I wish you'd told me. I could've hurried things along a little and found a renter for my place."

"You're moving?" When he faced her, his eyes were red and worn.

"Not far. Kane has a cabin on the lake—"

"You're renting the house from Kane?"

"Something like that." Jade rubbed the back of her neck. "It's the timing that bothers me."

"I agree. I don't think you're ready to be uprooting yourself so soon after—"

"No, Max. The timing of Wenzel's so-called suicide." She folded her hands between her knees. His prying days were over. "The guy was an asshole, but he loved himself more than any cop I know."

Max strolled back to his chair and assumed the familiar stiff, authoritative position. "You're not buying suicide?"

"No one is. We can't officially say otherwise but. Why kill him? He was too dense to be a real threat."

"Maybe not. Maybe he got in the way."

"This guy wouldn't risk killing a cop, inciting riot from the force for an obstacle."

"What then?" Max's blunt response divulged irritation.

"Shouldn't you be telling me? Are you okay?"

He leaned back, shifted his chair at an angle, and selected a thick reference book from the bottom row behind his desk. In hand, he opened it to reveal a deep hole cut within its center and a bottle of twenty-five-year-old MacCallans.

"Rough week."

"I hear that," she said, desperate for the T3s to take effect.

He offered her a swig, then withdrew his hand. "Can't be mixing this with meds."

"I've got a driver on call."

"Won't improve the headache."

"Can't make it worse." She waved the bottle back over.

He handed Jade the flask. She gulped down the aged scotch and returned it. "Smoother than the meds and probably more effective."

Max smiled, reclaimed his libation, and drank. "He would if Wenzel had damaging insight."

"Something we don't?" Her forehead crinkled in disbelief, even this caused pain.

"Even idiots get lucky."

"I wouldn't call him that." Jade chuckled, then winced.

"An idiot or lucky?"

"Lucky."

Max opened his mouth, but never gave voice to his thoughts. His assistant interrupted their conversation with news that Detective Kane had a car waiting for Jade, and his last patient's mother was in crisis on line three.

"Thanks, Max, for everything." Jade rose slowly from her seat, one hand on her head. "I wanted to say goodbye in person. Don't get up. I know the way."

Max stared strangely at her, then picked up the phone. "Hello...I need you to remain calm, Mrs. White. Is your son with you?"

Jade shuffled to the door, afraid the impact of a footfall would amplify the searing throbbing between her temples. Before she crossed the threshold, Max covered the receiver. "We still need to talk. It's a dangerous...the link between the Redeemer and the man from your past."

Jade nodded and then disappeared around the corner followed by Maggie.

"Should we schedule your next appointment, Ms. Carmichael?"

"That won't be necessary, Maggie. Take care of him."

Jade hobbled to the front of the building. At its entrance, she paused to assess the new digs. Forged to appear regal, they failed, and it didn't matter. She had no intention of coming back to see Max, at least not here. And soon, not as anything but a friend.

The motion of the car lulled Jade with an ease that surpassed any prescription. Buildings drifted by blending into a fresco of grays, blues, and greens.

"Chilled water?" the driver offered.

"Sure." Luckily, he was long armed so shifting positions wasn't required to reach the cold bottle.

Heated leather seats warmed her back as the cool water quenched the dryness of her throat. For the first time since the warehouse, the throbbing in her head subsided. She held that position of comfort, fearing the slightest movement would reignite the pain.

Max's voice played over in her mind. He was right. The link between her mother's killer and the Redeemer was dangerous. A truth she knew and feared uttering. As if vocalizing the words served to empower dark forces.

The killer in her past had gone unpunished, never captured. His ultimate act of cruelty, housing the memories of his brutality in her psyche. Worse still was the realization he and the Redeemer suffered a shared psychosis.

The killer she hunted and the one haunting her were not one and the same. Her mother's murderer would be too old to fit the profile. Besides the combined logic arguing against them being the same man, Jade knew they weren't. The way cops do. Her gut knew both. Linked yes, the evidence supported that, but fundamentally opposed.

The Redeemer possessed a deep-seated purpose, a refined violence.

She'd seen the other at work. Ragged viciousness. Not contained. Lacking principle. Her mother was a brilliant woman. The world didn't know it, not the way they could distinguish the Redeemer's victims. The victim profiles didn't match, highly visual accomplishment and success versus anonymous housewife.

Details of the cases overlapped, transparent blueprints in her mind, and when her eyelids became too heavy to hold open, the gory images became the things of bad dreams. Deciphering clues in her subconscious was nothing new. Her thoughts were never clear of demons, but there, in the back seat of the town car, the distance widened, her perspective elevated, and a calm swept in.

The Redeemer was hers to stop, and she would stop him. Shadow Hook took on a new darkness the day her mother died at the hands of a killer. A shadow that was meant to pass, not hover forever. She needed to step back into the light. They all did.

She wasn't expected back at the office for three days, doctor's orders. Kane insisted she stay at the cabin while recuperating. She could work from there unimpeded. He wouldn't be there much given the state of things, but said it gave him peace of mind knowing she'd be waiting. He had certainly done enough of that for her. So much so it'd be difficult for him to trust her decision until he witnessed it first-hand. She'd use the time to research avenues to stay in service in law enforcement without holding a frontline. She thought of Dr. Leigh. Holding a minor in psychology gave her options she hadn't entertained until now.

A safe distance from crazy where she'd meet it within the confines of a file, just like Rachel Leigh.

TWENTY-THREE

Know Thy Enemy. These words adorned a plaque above Leigh's desk and served as a daily reminder. Her current state of captivity made it blatantly clear she'd failed to heed the warning.

Fear ravaged her during the night. Buried beneath the shroud of a drug-induced haze, she woke determined to apply her IQ to save her life. Think past the terror; find her captor's weaknesses.

After twelve hours of isolation, focused on nothing else, she suspected she'd identified a few.

She'd awakened on a cold stone slab. No restrains. No gag. No killer looming over her with a torture trove. A pillow and blanket sat neatly folded beside her. They emitted the scent of lilac fabric softener.

She wrapped the blanket around her back and tested her legs. He'd injected her with a quick acting sedative. A lone needle mark scarred her left arm. She didn't speculate about what he'd done after she passed out.

Her clothes were intact. She wished she'd worn pants.

Lap after lap, prospects for escape diminished. Unless she became an Olympic gymnast. The only opening was a skylight twenty feet above. No ladder, stackable items, or irregularities to grip for scaling the smooth slate walls. The door, impenetrable metal, was sealed shut with a thick rubber overlay. No crack of light. No chance of freedom, even for her screams.

A corkboard displayed his work beneath the glow of low overhead lamps. She examined every picture. Some she'd seen before. Either he'd photographed the victims shortly before their bodies were discovered or he'd accessed police evidence. His case collection trumped theirs in volume and attention to detail.

The frames held distressing specifics zoomed into sharp relief. A clenched fist, a sorrow-stained face, blood, dried and crusted, on porcelain skin. The dead armed her with information only they could give. There was a photo of a man shot, labeled, Detective Wenzel at the bottom. She studied the handwriting not the wound.

The case file she'd possessed when abducted was left on a stone table below his visual catalog of killings. The order was disturbed. The contents were intact. He'd been through them but hadn't removed a single sheet.

One thing was certain. He knew what she thought of him.

Ice drizzled down the length of her spine. She pulled the blanket tighter around her shoulders.

Think. Amass clues.

What was here? What could save her life? No other could be trusted to rescue her in the past, some things didn't change.

The room held no cupboards or shelving. No medical supplies. No rubber tubing. His kill kit was missing. He'd bring it with him, but why? It could've easily been locked away in a…

She hunted for hidden compartments, safes, or floor vaults. Nothing.

He didn't use exsanguination on Wenzel, but he was a man in the way, not a female fitting the profile. Not the typical victim. Either was she, so why?

A crack where the floor met the wall caught her attention. Inspected and dismissed, she stood and returned to the corkboard to continue studying the victims. Twenty years their senior, she was old enough to be their mother. No mother deserved to see her child end this way.

A flush of tears blurred her vision. She blinked them away.

She thumbed through the case file. They'd compiled a fair amount on the Redeemer and were closing in. Perhaps he needed her to bleed out information, not blood. She selected a single paper. On it, the timeline of the murders was recorded beside the victims' faces. Inching closer to the board, she reached an arm up and smoothed her hand across the pictures, comparing them against the record. They weren't in chronological order in his display.

Telling.

A review of dossiers on each allowed her to compare birthdates. They spanned a decade. They hadn't gone to school together. The link wasn't there.

She reviewed their family backgrounds. None of the women were married. They'd realized that early in the profiling. None had ever been. No children either. New perspective brought new light to her original analysis.

God how she wished she were at the station brainstorming with Jade and not here.

One victim had a criminal record. She riffled through the case file searching for the information. The first known victim, Eva Summers, was arrested on a drug-related charge eleven months prior to her murder. This held no intrigue.

What drew Leigh to her file was what was missing. Leigh had done a follow-up call and reached Summers' arresting officer. He'd said he'd let Eva off easy and wished he hadn't because jail time could've saved her life. Leigh asked him why. He explained that she'd had a rough time coping with a vehicular tragedy when she was nineteen. He was a second responder at that accident. Five lives were lost.

When Leigh pressed him about who died he'd said, "Children. She lost control of her vehicle and killed four kids including the one she was carrying. She was seven months pregnant."

A dull ache shot through Leigh's heels sending shivers up the back of her calves. Her feet were numb. The slate floor wasn't heated or well insulated. She marched over to the pillow, snatched it off the raised dish where she'd slept, marched back, plopped it down in front of the row of pictures, and stood on top.

They were all killed before they could reproduce.

Everyone assumed he bled them dry driven by an obsession with their blood. The truth contradicted that theory. He discarded their life force. Eradicating it from the world. It was as if—

She hadn't heard a car approach, a lock disengage, or footsteps advancing. Breath by her ear and the reminiscent scent of expensive musk was an insufficient warning.

She spun on her pillow to face him, coming up staring into his chest. Without the advantage of her heels, which he'd removed, she was a full foot shorter.

"What crime did they commit that made them unworthy of motherhood?" If intellect was her only defense, she'd argue academics until time or her life ran out.

He stepped back. "Sin." He stared at her as if examining her for the first time. "Crime doesn't interest me."

Eyes of ice staring back, she understood, failing intervention, she wouldn't survive. Jade and Kane had to find her. He'd never let her go.

With his identity revealed, capture became inevitable.

"I see you made good use of the pillow and blanket I left you." His words and tone belied the depth of rage in his eyes.

"How could you possibly qualify as a proper judge of—"

"Of who'd be a good mother or not? Let's assume I know the type and the cost."

"These women were remarkable." Against physical dread, she turned her back to him, focusing her attention on their faces and not his. "Pillars of the community."

"It'd seem." He strutted over to a high wall panel, placed his left palm on it, and waited for the adjacent one to open. A three-foot wide by six-foot high section slid away revealing the entrance to an additional room.

"My office," he explained. "Do come in."

Reluctantly, Leigh followed and was shocked to discover a well-appointed space with an array of expensive women's clothes hanging neatly on a rolling rack at the back.

"Size two. They're for you, Dolce & Gabbana and Ralph Lauren. You can change in the dressing room." He pushed a button under his desk and another wall panel opened up. "Something warm." The shadow of a smirk stained his face. "It's cold here."

She swept through the items, yanked black pants and a turtleneck sweater off the hooks, and disappeared behind the wall. As expected, the shower, toilet, and sink were bare of anything useful with all the trappings of a bomb shelter. The expansive dressing mirror unnerved her. She didn't need visual confirmation of the panic and vulnerability spreading from her core and did her best to mask it.

His ability to predict and disable his opponents alarmed her. His air of calm unsettled. His charisma terrified, evil veiled beneath the aura of a charming gentleman. And there was something else, something underlying it all, more disturbing, that she couldn't find words for.

The clothes fit as if tailor made. He'd been expecting her.

Leigh couldn't help wondering if this was the routine the other women he'd taken endured before their deaths. Was she on the first step of the ladder into Hell? There were signs that his treatment of her veered from the norm.

Her mind swept back to the corkboard. The victims were found in the clothes they had worn when abducted. It didn't mean they hadn't been outfitted by him and stripped of their new threads before he killed them.

"Penny for your thoughts," he said.

"Is this typical?" She stepped out of the bathroom, reclothed, standing before his desk. Truth. He could read a lie, making deception inherently dangerous.

He sat behind the desk flipping a shiny coin between his fingers.

"Only for successful professionals with adequate financial security." He smiled with an ease that said they'd been old friends. "Kidding. You're asking me if you're special?"

The smile vanished. He continued flipping the coin, averting his stare into an invisible window in time.

"Not special, different," she clarified, deliberate with the ease of conversation.

He tossed the coin into the air, locked eyes with her, and caught it between two fingers with a scary accuracy. "Special. Yes. I didn't go shopping for the others."

"Are you going to kill me?" She held his gaze.

"I knew you were direct. Impressive." He rose from the chair towering over her even from a distance. "I hadn't planned on it." He searched her eyes as if anticipating a fluctuation in her resolve. "Yet."

"So you need me?" She knew every word uttered was a gamble. He'd thrown her into a high-stakes game of survival.

"Needed." He spoke that one word softly then shifted his weight from left to right and back again. "Perhaps I thought I'd enjoy your company." His voice regained its bravado.

She nodded no. "This isn't that simple."

He moved around the desk. She stepped back, nearing the exit.

"There is no escape without me. You will not die today by my hand." His brow furrowed while he studied her face. "I have no intention of raping you. Relax."

She forced herself not to blink or flinch. "Why rape?"

He broke his icy gaze. His eyes drifted over the lines of the roof, tracing the skylight, then fell down the slate walls to search the floor dust. "Pardon?"

"I understand why you'd rule out escape and death," she said. "I've read the files."

"Yes. We should discuss the flaws of your misguided assessment." She held his attention again.

"There were no indications of rape on your victims." A fact she regretted revealing.

"My victims? You act as if you're justified, or worse, accurate in labeling them without the benefit of their whole story. I don't like the sound of that." He motioned to exit back into the larger room.

"Why?" She walked to the threshold. He stuck his arm out blocking her. She froze. He pointed to the corner of the room. "Shoes," he said.

With no more interest than if they'd been in her own closet for years, she chose a pair, slipped them on, and left the room.

"They're not mine, possessions to be owned, nor are they victims." He sauntered out after her, placed his palm on the outer wall sealing the office. He moved close enough for his cologne to waft over her. "Do I seem the type who must force sex on women? Or require their fear and submission for my empowerment?"

"No." She faced him again. "You don't appear a monster, but you are one."

She stood at the center of the corkboard. Ran her hand over the images of the dead. "They didn't know to fear you. In the wild, predators reveal themselves."

He laid his hands on her shoulders and spun her away from the board. "Even lions hide in the grass. I gave them a choice."

"No one would choose this."

"You're wrong. When you decide on an action, you welcome its consequences. Ignoring them doesn't alter the course."

"That makes you brave, oblivious, or insane."

His lack of retaliation divulged more than anticipated.

She pressed on. "Why you?"

He stared past her at the board then walked to the opposite side of the room. "I quit asking."

Compassion rose inside her. Irrational. It had no rightful place in the wake of the wreckage of so many beautiful lives. "Why don't you stop?"

"I plan to…when it's finished. Not sure what'll be left of me by then." Regret softened his tone.

This wasn't madness. Not a random serial killing of women conforming to his victim profile. Rationale existed. A connection. She had to find it, unlock the nightmare that possessed him, and do it surreptitiously. If he became aware of how close she was to cracking his case, he'd kill her where she stood. Of that, she was certain.

"They knew you." She crossed the room to where he was and confronted him. "I mean, they thought they knew you."

"Yes." He pushed a panel. It opened to reveal a counter space complete with a sophisticated espresso machine, bar fridge, and all the conveniences of home. He read the shock on her face. "Searched the whole time I was gone and missed it? Gadgets. Wealth affords certain privileges and perilous extravagance."

She shook her head of cobwebs. She'd made direct accusations. Still, he appeared indifferent. Perhaps even slightly intrigued.

"Coffee?" he asked, while preparing water and cleaning the steamer.

"This is a pleasant fiction, kinder than reality. I know you…what you are, but…do I know you?"

His hand jerked, making contact with the steam rod. It burned instantly. He put his wrist under cold water and angled to see her. "You should."

Something in those two words made her stomach flip. Whatever vendetta he harbored, she'd made the hit list.

An operatic fragment ringing alerted her to the comparative silence in the room. He extracted a cellular from his jacket pocket and skimmed the screen. What he read there distracted him. He eyed the counter as if taking stock. "Have to leave you again. Eat. It's not poisoned. Not my style." His grin didn't comfort.

He sauntered to the door with a strong, confident gait, pausing at the threshold. "Don't waste time searching for weapons. Unless you're deadly with a plastic spoon there's nothing useful here."

"I don't want to kill you," she said. He faded out into the real world. She meant it. He glanced back. The feeling wasn't mutual.

TWENTY-FOUR

You can't save them. I stopped trying. So should you.

Kane stared at his phone in disbelief. Words, translated from the Redeemer's warped Latin filter, bled across the screen. Kane recalled every time he'd said similar words, speculating how horrible that was. The realization made his intestinal tract twist and tighten into a knot.

The Redeemer didn't have him hooked up to a bloodletting device. His commitment to a greater good traded for a leaden sadness, failure in the pit of his stomach, and useless rage.

"What is it?" Jackson, head and shoulders in case evidence, glanced up. He read Kane's expression and assumed the worst. "We have another crime scene?"

"He's won." Kane flipped his phone over giving Jackson a clear view. "He knows it. He's getting cocky."

"He isn't done." Jackson issued his Texas glare. "Either are we, pal. I'm willing to gamble that it's him who won't be saved."

"We've lost one officer, suffered three direct hits, our leads are an endless trail of dead ends, the body count is mounting, Grey's neck's getting scorched from high command breathing down it, pushing to hand it off to the Feds, and I'm thinking it's not such a bad idea. Nothing's on our side."

Adding insult, Kane bumped organized papers piled a foot high on the corner of his desk toppling them over the edge. They sprayed across the floor.

"See what I'm saying." Kane stared at the mess. "We could use a break."

Jackson snatched the papers left on the desk in an effort to stop the avalanche. A page caught his attention. He spun it around. "Jesus."

"Praying?" Kane scooped up the papers, examining the page Jackson held, an advertisement of sorts for a church choir. He stared at the words not grasping Jackson's revelation. The Texan shifted the sheet pointing to the bottom corner. A link to purchase rosaries featured an expensive version in pale pink. Jackson's finger was on the center of the piece.

Kane stared in awe. "Eva Summers."

"Not a necklace," Jackson said. "Important enough for her to cling to."

Kane dropped the mess back to the floor and marched to the evidence board. "Important enough for him to rip all but one piece from her hand. He wasn't taking her jewelry. He was denying her absolution!"

"Logan!" Jackson's voice echoed. Amy rounded the corner precariously balancing three coffees. "Your sole purpose from this point forward." He slapped the paper down in front of her. "Pull Eva Summers' history—"

"The first known victim?" she asked.

"There was a jewelry fragment concealed in her hand. A rosary. Find everything there is to know about it. We need this." He paused for effect. "And high tail it."

"I'm on it. I'll miss a terrific concert with a new date who doesn't forgive easily." She smiled.

"Have her call me," Kane said. "I'll make you her hero."

Amy relieved her hands of two coffees and strolled to her desk leaving Kane and Jackson alone in the mess of papers.

Jackson flashed a broad grin. "Ask and you shall receive."

Kane stood in front of the photo of the Summers woman. "Our blood letter's about to experience a whole different kind of depletion. I wish I'd gone to church."

Kane swiped his phone from where he'd dropped it on the desk. His thumbs worked the keypad.

"You calling Jade? She could use good news."

"Texting. Promised I wouldn't wake her."

"Tell her, there are penalties for people caught sleeping on the job, for me."

Kane glanced up, grinned, and finished letting her know about the new lead. He didn't wait for a response.

"Interview Summers' therapist again?" Jackson suggested.

Kane grimaced, scooped his jacket off the back of his chair, and headed for the door. New insights were priceless, didn't mean fleshing them out was always fun.

Kane entered Dr. Farnsworth's office with careful footing. The old guy was cantankerous on any given day. Kane learned the hard way during Eva Summers' investigation that he harbored a particular aversion to cops—especially those demanding he relinquish client histories.

"I have nothing to add to the extensive statement you acquired four months ago and a full day of patients waiting."

Kane hovered inside the threshold, the furthest point from the desk. "We understand—"

"I doubt that very much. Why are you here?" The old man closed the three open files he'd been perusing.

Knowing better than to burn a bridge he needed to cross, Kane said, "We've come across new evidence in Miss Summers' case. Thought you'd want to be notified given your involvement. If you're too busy—"

"Come in, close the door behind you. What have you discovered?" Farnsworth clamped his hand together over the closed files, his face brimming with entitlement.

Kane caught a glimpse of Jackson's condescending grin and wanted to slap him. They needed the information anyway they could get it. If that meant eating crow, so be it. Didn't mean Tex should enjoy watching it so much.

Farnsworth didn't offer them seats. If he had, they would've refused. Having height on the man seemed wise.

"She was the Redeemer's first victim. We've reason to believe her murder holds the key to stopping him." Kane expected Jackson to jump in. He played mute.

"I suspected as much." The man leaned back in his chair with an arrogance that made Kane wish it'd flipped him ass over teakettle.

"You were correct. We reviewed her history with you in—"

"She ever bring a pale pink rosary with her to sessions?" Jackson found his baritone Texan voice.

"Well…yes. I recall her rolling the beads during difficult discussions. They helped her relax, focus her thoughts."

Jackson's direct question disarmed the doc.

"You always notice your client's jewelry?" The question quantified the doctor's contempt.

Farnsworth's face contorted into an expression of renewed disdain. "What?"

Jackson stepped forward and loomed over the man. "Did she own more than one?"

"I don't know. She was attached to the pink one." The doctor regarded Kane with censure, unfolding his hands to order items on the desktop.

"She told you that?" Jackson's voice dug deeper than normal, reverberating off the woodwork. "Just spat that out like trail dust?"

"Well, no. No. She forgot it on the table once. She'd been particularly upset that session. Set it down to use the Kleenex. Left crying. I suspected she was using again. She returned in a state of panic. Rambling about how it was the symbol of her forgiveness."

"Where did she get it?" Kane asked.

"How should I know?" The doctor glanced up at the large clock above them. It was ten til the hour. "I have to prepare for my next patient."

"You remember anyone from her past who would've given her the rosary?" Jackson stepped back from the desk and sauntered around the room inspecting the doctor's possessions. "Anyone you know, not worth their stock?"

"She was an addict." Farnsworth's head swiveled in tandem with Jackson's milling. "Everyone was a risk. I'd check with the church in her area. Her license was revoked. If she was attending church, she was doing it on foot."

"Did you have any indication that there was someone new in her life?" Kane leaned on the desk opposite the doctor, blocking his view of Jackson and messing with his neatly displayed trinkets. "Any revelations?"

"I told you last time, I was on the cusp of a breakthrough before she died."

"And you didn't attribute that to the introduction of a new man?" Kane pushed.

"No. She trusted me. Confided in me, if—"

"You and you alone?" The doctor, patient, confidentiality crap had Kane's back up.

"Well—"

Jackson circled back to the desk, and the two cornered the doctor. "Women are having the lifeblood sucked out of them like a dead cow in a fly swarm."

The doctor eyed both men, stared down at his own hands, then back up. "She'd showed vague signs of renewed hope early the month before her death."

"And you didn't think that was relevant?" Kane pounced.

"It's in my notes. If you read them, you'd already know this." He pulled a notebook out from beneath Jackson's large mitt.

"You attributed it all to therapy?"

"I assumed—"

"Thank you, Doctor." Kane drifted out the door in need of fresh oxygen. Jackson followed, leaving the doctor's disdain behind.

"I'll reread the narcissist's footnotes tonight. See if we can pinpoint when she met the Redeemer." Kane said a few strides down the hallway.

"That piece of work could have—"

"No point, Tex. It's done."

A wisp of a woman in her twenties rounded the corner, Farnsworth's next patient no doubt. Jackson drew her eyes off the ground with a broad smile. "You don't need him, honey. He's a damn fool. You may have sauntered down the wrong path. Pick higher ground. Something better is waiting." The smile she returned said she believed him. Kane seconded Jackson's opinion with a nod and watched her disappear.

"Cross reference all the victims' distance to Catholic and Anglican churches from her area," Jackson said.

"They weren't all Catholic or even religious." Kane exited the building.

"Everyone needs absolution sooner or later." Jackson let the heavy door slam shut with punctuation. "Maybe these women bore their human stains earlier than most. If they did there'd be no record, it'd be juvenile. Wiped clean when they entered adulthood, nothing we could've traced when we searched their past. No way to link 'em."

Kane focused on the break in the clouds then on Jackson. "No mercy."

"So, we unearth it for them. Don't know about you, but I'm from Texas, pal. I was born to dig. This is just a different version of Black Gold."

TWENTY-FIVE

Wind whipped willow trees into emerald waves beyond the cabin's deck with a force that called for cashmere, so Jade stole Kane's favorite sweater from a hook on the way out. She leaned against the wet rail in yoga pants and a T-shirt using the extra-large garment as a wrap, lulled by the rhythm of the breeze.

Kane and Jackson were busy pursuing a new lead. She locked in on the Simms woman and the Redeemer's secret past.

Motive.

Max said when digging into the psyche, revelations are unearthed by focusing on the unseen. Recent events gave that theory merit.

She abandoned the weather and settled inside. She'd rearranged the case evidence into a random pile on the floor and placed a swivel stool in the center. Her David Bowie oblique strategies move.

Kane preferred a drafting table, Jackson the wall of his barn—before their Unsub's bullets splintered it, and maybe more after.

She claimed her place center of the ruins, pulled up one leg, and spun with the other. Faces of death blurred around her. In her mind's eye the victims were crisp and clear, as were their missed lives. She drew up her other leg and closed her eyes until the spinning stopped, oddly at the place it had begun.

They opened on the Redeemer's first love—the blind lover long before her years in the plush sanitarium. Sexy and seventeen in the graduation photo and oblivious to the part she'd play in the creation of a killer.

The picture reflected exactly how she'd appeared when he'd chosen her as a mate. What did he see? She needed his eyes now.

Chastity. Purity. Innocence. Unspoiled by choice. Beneath the obvious allure, these qualities stirred a fierce compulsion. The root of his revulsion. Jade targeted his mother as the origin of his rage. What happened when he was seventeen? Jade remembered that age and the difference between the girls who gave it away for the slightest attention and those who were selective, like her. From the outside, Elizabeth Simms appeared selective, but Jade knew better than most the outside didn't necessarily reflect the truth of the inside. Either way, no bastard had the right to judge, violate, or discard their lives.

She pivoted. Images, vast in number. Faces of women, all reminiscent of the most influential woman in her life, the mother stolen from her. She'd been everything a mother should be, loving, protective, kind, funny, playful, stern, and real. She gave her life without hesitation for a chance to save her child. She never cried out.

What had his done to him when *she* was seventeen?

Jade leaped from the chair, clearing the scattered pictures and landing with room to spare. She snatched her cell phone from the drafting table. The answer was there, so simple it'd been missed. His mother did the only thing a mother that age could've done. She gave him up.

Her thumbs flew without pause for several seconds.

> Kane, we need to search adoption records.
> We're looking for a seventeen-year-old mother
> going back thirty years. She abandoned him at
> birth or close to. That's the crime he believes
> destroyed his life. I'm sure of it. Not certain how
> the victims play into it, but we need to uncover
> pregnancies, abortions, or any child-related
> offenses in their past. Call me if you find
> anything. LUM

She hit send and repeated the process three more times sending similar notes to Jackson, Leigh, and Max, absent the "love you most" tag.

Reality said it'd be an uphill trek. Adoption records were often closed, and no one welcomed opening old wounds, particularly those involving family issues. She'd use every avenue at her disposal.

> Jackson and I are fleshing out church leads.
> We'll push in that direction. Good work for
> someone who's sleeping! Tex says you're
> forgiven, for now:) LUM

A smile lit Jade's face with a depth reserved for family, she set her phone aside and returned to her pile. She traded the stool for a pillow and began examining the evidence from a more intimate perspective. What sins did these women share? Were they the same? She could ask them if they weren't dead.

She flipped through the dossiers of possible remaining targets compiled against known factors, selected one and opened her computer. They'd searched backgrounds of each. She dialed back twenty years and dug in again, this time with a fresh agenda.

The pictures on the floor called out to her. Distractingly haunting. Flashes of her mother dying in front of her fractured her concentration.

"Jade?" As faint as the whispers of the willows, her mother's voice beckoned her.

She shook free of the memories. Her eyes fixated on a photo of the Summers woman. Jade recalled her long history of drug abuse. They'd been given a treasure trove of information from her guardians. Jade set the target's file aside, located Summers' and cleared a space in front of her.

Eva Summers was placed in a home for wayward teens in high school. Four months before graduation. Why go to the trouble of placing her when she'd be old enough to move out that summer?

Included in the information was a newspaper clipping from the previous February. Her sister and a friend died when their car slid off the road and wrapped around a tree. Jade's eyes scanned the text, then froze two paragraphs down. Eva had been driving, illegally and intoxicated.

She'd killed her sister, and her parents couldn't stand to have her in their home. There was her sin. And Jade was betting the Redeemer knew long before he killed her.

She read on, retrieved the other victim's name, and searched her computer. A follow-up article covered the funerals. A second girl in the car was older than Eva and also pregnant. Her family buried her and their unborn grandson. Four died in total.

The pieces were falling into place. All the answers awakened more questions. Did the Redeemer know the Summers woman back then? Was he the father of the unborn child she killed? How did this relate to his other victims? All of them couldn't be responsible for crimes against him. Or could they? Jade found the parents' last known address.

Time to shake the skeletons.

Jade questioned human resiliency as her cab approached the Summers' family home. She had counted on it for her own survival and for those stained by the dark. The Summers had too—they were still together, but they'd abandoned their child in her darkest hour. Too familiar. Sunlight broke free from scattered clouds and penetrated Mrs. Summers' garden as if God reserved today for her alone. Jade found her kneeling on a flowered pad beside a cluster of tulip bulbs.

"They'll be beautiful in a month or two." She spoke without raising her eyes from her task.

"They will. What colors?" Jade appealed to her heart gently. She'd lived through the loss of her baby girl in the car crash, then her other daughter's murder. Much of what she had been surely died with them. To Jade's trained eyes she was broken and fragile. Frail pieces.

"I love yellow, but it symbolizes jealousy. I suppose that's appropriate. Can't plant orange…or red. White's okay. White and blue, if they had blue."

"I've come to you because of Eva's death. More women will die if I don't stop him, and I need your memories."

The old women tended to each bulb with gentle care, brushing loose dirt free, preparing the perfect spot for them. Then she did something unexpected, placing a blonde curl of hair in each hole below the bulb.

"The iron feeds the flowers. They would've liked that."

"I'm sorry to unearth the painful past. There are other daughters at risk."

With weathered hands, misshaped by arthritis, she placed two bulbs in a single hole. She padded dirt around them. "Pink," she said. "Only two. My flowers shouldn't have died."

Jade leaned down and cupped water from the jug beside the woman. She sprinkled a little over the bulbs. "They'll grow strong in a new place," she said. The woman turned her head up and stared into Jade's eyes until the sun forced her to turn away.

Jade scanned the yard. Beautifully manicured and empty of what mattered most, a family to enjoy it. "Was Eva seeing someone? Did she have a boyfriend before the accident? Did the other girl who died? The pregnant girl, Marci?"

The old woman's words caught in her throat. "Oh, I miss them. I want to leave too. Be where they are. I wouldn't have sent her away. Her father. He didn't handle it well. God, forgive us. She was a good girl. They both were. Even Marci's family and fiancé forgave her. Why couldn't Earl?"

Earl was Eva's father. Jade's heart broke. She knew too well the pain of banishment. "You knew them? Marci's family, fiancé?"

A car rolled up to the side of the property.

"He's married, has three girls of his own, Marci's fiancé. Brings them by on Sundays." A smile transformed the old lady's face.

Clearly the Redeemer hadn't been the father of the unborn child. Dead end.

"She never had a boyfriend before the accident. I wish she had. All the men afterward, they hurt her. None as much as Earl. Oh, God forgive us."

"I'm sorry." Jade kneeled beside the women. "He knew the women before he killed them. I need to know how."

Mrs. Summers turned and faced Jade, her eyes staring through her to the mounds of dirt where the bulbs were buried. "The church. It's the only comfort. Sunday service."

Jade stood and shifted into the shadow. The old woman's pain consumed her world.

"You should go. Earl will be home soon. He gets mad when I speak to you."

Jade followed the cobblestone path to the archway exiting the garden, catlike. She was impressed her new combats didn't make a sound. The gate closed behind her. She turned to see a man in his sixties entering from the house porch. She disappeared behind the tall hedges that lined the corner property as the Summers' neighbors made their way to their car. Their conversation drifted.

"Beth said she was in the yard talking to God again," one said.

"Better Him then the alternative," replied the other.

Jade understood grief. She had to. She'd lived in its shadow most of her life. For her, it was the beast that fueled her to stop another family from suffering the same. For others, it destroyed indiscriminately from the inside out. And if you hadn't lived it, no matter the intention, you could never see how it turned all the colors in life black. It was the worst offense with no hope of justice, no hope at all, only darkness.

TWENTY-SIX

"I've considered every plausible outcome. They all end badly. You're in serious trouble, Grey." Max sat in the chair behind his desk refusing to sit directly across from the visiting police chief. He favored a safe barrier. He wasn't afraid of Grey, far from it. He avoided close proximity as if the toxic past clinging to Grey threatened to seep by osmosis into his flesh and poison him.

"That's brilliant. And to think, I questioned Kane's disdain for you. I didn't make chief by misinterpreting the obvious. The goal is to manage the fallout constructively. Who else knows?" Grey's nerves never showed in his face, but his clenched fists said panic was rising dangerously close to the surface.

Max wondered what was contained in the file Grey's hands crushed. The one he wasn't willing to hand over. Aged and deteriorated worse than Jade's mother's.

"You know as well as I." Max averted his eyes from the kept document, deciding it best to placate Grey. "Everyone who was around when he died has either transferred and is long gone or retired and no longer cares. Outside of that, you and I. No one knew what really happened. The case was sealed. When your chief died, the media didn't have the thirst for its pound of flesh. It does now."

"You're positive the signatures match?" Grey's stare allowed no wiggle room.

Max reviewed the decades-old case file before him. "There's a definite link. When were you planning on introducing this to them?"

"I wasn't. I've spent the better part of my career burying it. Hell, until a couple days ago I'd convinced myself I was wrong and—"

"You weren't. He killed Jade's mother. So now what?" Max had double-checked that his phone was locked in privacy mode twice before the conversation started. He rose to test the security of the door.

"I can't smear his name out there—"

"Smear his name? The man was a psychotic killer." Max toured his office.

"And a police chief who I shot and killed." Grey twisted in his seat following Max's movements. "Sit down!"

Startled, Max sunk into the sofa reserved for his patients, and instantly wished he hadn't. "If you wait any longer—"

"I know how bad it looks. He's long dead. I wasn't sure. There was no way to link him to this killer until Wenzel." Grey ran his hands through his hair and squinted, blocking out the sunbeams stretching through the window. Not hard to see the man was conflicted.

"His gun?" Max asked. "You're certain?"

"Ballistics confirmed. Not that I could ever forget. I've been searching for that weapon for the last twenty years."

"Tell her." Max stood again, this time seeking refuge and stature behind his desk. "Jade needs to know. If you withhold this, the blood is on your hands."

Grey rubbed his eyes. "It always was." The strain couldn't be blamed on the bright day. "You think she'll handle a blow of this caliber and still solve this case?" His blue eyes faded with defeat. "When did we become the bad guys?"

"I don't know that we did," Max lied. The cards he kept close didn't make him a good guy.

"You can't call us heroes."

"She's tough. This could provide the closure she's needed. She's always admired you. You did catch her mother's killer. Now, she'll know it."

Grey stood, made his way to the threshold, pausing to unlock the door with his back to the room. "Did I?"

"I'm pretty sure," Max said.

"Then his copycat is doing a real bang-up job."

Max's silence said enough. If the truth came out, it'd help solve the case. Grey would be hailed a hero, or it would destroy him. He'd do his best to manage the fallout, but Max knew defending against the unexpected wasn't easy.

In two strides, Grey disappeared from view, the door closed automatically, and Max inhaled a cleansing breath.

"Maggie," he spoke into the intercom. "I could use a double espresso. You cleared my schedule for the rest of the day?"

"Yes," she said.

"Good. I have an out call that can't wait. I'll be leaving soon."

Grey leaned against the cold brick wall outside his car. He'd chucked his phone inside with the file and slammed the door so he couldn't see either. An icy fire raged before his eyes. It crackled and hissed threatening his career and all it had meant. Far more was at stake. The lives of those he led and those he loved.

Silence protected the integrity of the cases the deranged police chief worked two decades prior. It did nothing to salvage those since.

Max was worried for him. It had showed on his face. No wonder he always lost on poker night.

Never gamble against criminals or cops—both are skilled at concealing their tells. Their lives depend on deception. Grey was well acquainted with the murky line between the two. He couldn't remember when he'd crossed it. He knew it wasn't intentional.

Kane was his best avenue. He wouldn't appreciate how he'd handled things but would relate to the circumstances. His love for Jade outside the office complicated his position too. Grey could use it to his advantage if necessary, but he preferred not to be reduced to threatening his best men.

The past had taken hold. Salvaging his career and credibility depended on reining it in. More importantly, so did the integrity of every case he'd been associated with. The thought of criminals using his skeleton as a get-out-of-jail-free card was sickening.

"Shit."

His phone's intrusive buzzing escaped the ventilation system. He retrieved his cell phone and was scanning messages when Kane pulled up.

"Thanks for meeting me."

"No problem, boss. You wanna tell me why we're outside Max's office and not at our own?" Kane stared at the building with disdain then joined Grey, leaning on the wall beside him, two sentinels on guard.

"What I have to say can't be overheard. Max knows. Only because he had previous knowledge of the case." Grey silenced his phone and dropped it into his pocket.

"Knowledge of what case?"

"You know about the chief of police's death back when I worked the division?"

"I heard. Accidental shooting. They used it to warn us when we were coming up."

"No accident." Grey left the wall, walked to his car, and leaned on the roof.

"Fine. How do you——"

"I shot him."

Kane straightened up and joined him at the car. "You...shot the police chief? Francis Carroll? Brutal. What the hell went down?"

After so many years, Grey expected it'd be easier to talk about. It wasn't.

Kane leaned in. "Why are you telling me? Why now?"

"He killed Jade's mother." There. He'd done it. The truth was out. Oddly, the air in Grey's lungs weighed heavier.

"What?" Kane struggled physically with the news, backing away.

"There were others before her. She was the last." Grey stepped back, allowing Kane space to process. "We thought Shadow Hook was safe again."

"How? How long have you known?" Kane paced to the erratic rhythm of betrayal. "This *is* about Jade! And you're divulging this now?"

"Not necessarily. It's not the same killer. Can't be. I killed him two decades ago."

"You're thinking copycat? Why the silence? Why did you wait so long to——"

"I didn't know. I suspected Francis was responsible for Jade's mother's death. We had nothing solid linking him then. The crime scene was clean. Jade became mute. I caught him attacking another woman two months later. The MO didn't match. We didn't have the resources or advances in DNA."

"Stop! How the hell can you claim to connect any of this without—"

"Ballistics. The weapon Francis Carroll used to attack his last victim went missing from evidence. We were moving into the new station. They blamed it...three years after Jade's mother's murder she was on record describing the same weapon, a Beretta with a symbol on the grip."

"What symbol?" Kane stopped a foot from Grey.

"A black dolphin. The same one used to execute Wenzel and left, deliberately, at the scene."

Kane's fight for comprehension showed on his face. He pounded his fist along the cement wall, patrolling the length of the vehicle like a caged lion. Grey sympathized. He'd suffered the same perplexity since he found Wenzel in a pool of his own brain matter.

"Who else knows? Did you miss a second killer?" Kane accused.

"Evidence said he was alone. The killings ending after his death." Grey opened the car, picked a thick file off the passenger seat, and handed it to Kane. "This is everything I have. Won't find anything through regular channels, and you can't try. If word got out about the chief, every animal he put away will walk, and our town may never recover."

Kane stared into the file on the roof of the car. Grey slapped it shut. "Jade may not process this well. I've protected her from the day she became his victim. I'd rather she didn't relive this."

"This is why you set her up with Max." Kane nodded at the building. "You suspected this would come out?"

"I didn't know anything for sure. Wish I could've ended it back then." Grey fought the coarse rasp creeping into his voice. "She's more than a partner to you. She's more than a damn good detective to me. My gut said I was right then, and what it's saying now won't make this easy. Use your head, everything that got you here, and watch your back. Have Jackson work it with you."

"It's good Jade's out for a couple days. I need answers." Kane bent his head, his back against the car, his hands stretched across his thighs, a racer's pose, afflicted with a nauseating bout of dizziness. "This, it'll kill her."

"It could." Grey walked around to the driver's door and opened it. "That's what I'm afraid of. This bastard has done enough. I won't have him destroy us all."

"What are you going to do?"

"See what else I can find out, unearth the monster and bury him in evidence…and pray." Grey sank into the car and closed the door. Kane scooped the file off its roof and backed away. When Grey pulled out, Kane stood solid, a twenty-year-old nightmare awakened and dangling from his grip.

TWENTY-SEVEN

Rachel Leigh stood center of the Redeemer's lair searching for a path to survival in the doomed eyes of the dead. Their disfigured, emaciated corpses said what she already knew.

He'd be back to finish what he started.

She'd reread the case file three times. Analyzed her conversation with him in fine detail. Studied every aspect of the information he'd left for her. The gnawing question was why she'd been allowed the opportunity.

He wanted her to complete the puzzle. She'd been cast as an integral part in his quest. The hell was in identifying her role.

Tears not shed burned behind her eyes. Rage, restrained, crushed her lungs. She couldn't breathe.

She ran at the photo board, smashing her hands into pictures. No one to vent to except his casualties, and what did they care? She collapsed to the ground in tears for seconds before the consequence of her outburst shocked her back into form.

He couldn't find her in this condition.

She sprang up, wiped her face with tissues left out by the coffee maker. She'd downed the coffee, two black, one latte. She poured what remained over the makeup stains and tossed them in the trash.

She checked the board. Luckily her slamming hadn't creased any corners. She straightened the few crooked frames and slid the pillow back in front.

After smoothing her hair and clothes, she inhaled and exhaled three cleansing breaths. Regained control.

"I'm made from strong stock. I will not fall apart or be broken by the evils of this world."

She'd recited the mantra before, a lifetime ago, during a situation that trumped her present unfortunate circumstances, at least, thus far. She wondered what triggered her to revisit a time she'd all but erased.

The prestige of her family demanded strength and success. Her father's expectations for his only child afforded her no room for failure even when life had other plans. Ugly plans. This framework drove her to great heights and paved the way to the comfortable existence she enjoyed. It also helped her forget.

Until today.

"Always a survivor, never a victim." She surveyed her environment. "Okay. What am I missing?"

An extra hot espresso.

The Redeemer snuck in silently the last time. She hadn't known where to focus her attention then. She did now. If the coffee burned, it could blind him long enough for her to escape the building. With no idea of her location, she'd be at a disadvantage, and outside would pose new risks. She didn't care. When staying guaranteed certain death, leaving by any means became an attractive option. Night had to be setting in. No clocks to check. Even if there were, she couldn't trust them. She needed to see the moon.

The machine used pods—no pot to smash over his head. When he returned, she'd be armed with paper cups and scalding liquid.

Glancing over her shoulder at the door, she brewed an Italian dark roast and prayed for the element of surprise.

Roses, peony bubble bath, moonlight, beeswax candles, a full goblet of Italy's finest, tranquil sounds, and a razor blade, therein lay the allure of Nikki Taylor's Saturday nights.

The perfect escape, plus or minus the razor blade.

Nikki put business to bed hours earlier. A rule she adhered to during her weekends at home. She gutted the stone estate after inheriting it from her grandfather, preserving its character while dispelling cobwebs.

A leader in pharmaceutical advances, she was a medical research genius who lived at the lab. Despite a six-figure income that afforded her a life at the Ritz, she spent most nights crashing on a warped futon three feet away from an array of drugs she created to save lives from any manner of affliction.

Transfixed by the gleam slithering down the edge of the straight razor, she wondered how many she'd save before the torment ceased.

No one who worked alongside her in the battle to discover the next cure questioned her solitary existence. Who in their right mind could tackle the demands of her life or intellect? She drove her team with a passion that broke some, inspired others. It came, as most do, from a dark place fiercely guarded.

She'd sought help, forgiveness from God and those she'd wronged. It hadn't helped.

The sharp metal called to her—an end to the self-loathing and guilt.

She joined a support group, under an alias and far from all who knew her. The confirmation of so many other sinners only deepened her depression. She quit the group after two months claiming she moved, placating them with a sizable donation. Another in the long list of futile amends.

She swallowed down the wine, placed the glass on the ledge beside the candles, glanced again at the razor, and sunk beneath the water.

The moon centered in the skylight above swayed in soft waves of distortion through the water. It glittered in hues of milky sapphire, incandescent and ghostly, haunting a starless night. The silence was peaceful, the memories, tormenting. She'd chosen week after week, year after year to endure them. That was her sentence. No easy way out.

She lifted her head above the waterline, alone in her thoughts and the sprawling estate. No time to dedicate to an animal. She'd tried fish, managed to kill them off in three months. For ambiance, she left tranquil sounds playing on the system in the den on the main floor, and the bathroom door slightly ajar. She dunked, silencing ocean waves. She hadn't found a way to silence her thoughts. When she broke the water's surface again, the disc downstairs skipped as if... bumped.

The razor was in her hand. Didn't take much these days to put it there.

The machine corrected, and the music resumed. Nikki strained listening for sounds out of place. Nothing unusual. She scanned the room for her phone and located it three steps away on the chair where she'd thrown her robe.

The warm water soothed. Getting out seemed paranoid and pointless. The disc was well played. She set the razor down at the far end, out of reach, and leaned into the bubbles. Someday she'd discover a cure to heal the masses with enough significance to curb temptation. She was close to one for ALS, a motor neuron disease. Soon. Not yet.

She caught her reflection in the dark window. Messy wet waves toppled on her head, smooth, pale skin, having had no time for the beach, and dark circles under her eyes. Her eyes revealed the scars of her obsession, signs of a haunted woman.

She dropped her head back into the tub pillow and stared at the moon, clearer now, obscured by soiled glass.

Music downstairs shifted to a medley of sea birds. Her favorite. She slid the candle closer to the wall to avoid knocking it with her wineglass. Its light licked the silver and gray tiles en route to the roofline exposing the source of the smear on the skylight glass.

She eyed it from one angle then tilted the opposite direction searching for clarity. The intermittent light made it difficult to read. Running lines with a symmetry that ruled out random weather marks. She twisted her head in an uncomfortable position. Her hair clip let go, sending her long locks over her eyes. She tossed them out of the way.

Breath shuttered out when her eyes gained a clear line of sight. Two large handprints glowed sinister.

Someone watched from above while she bathed.

She sprang from the water smashing her wineglass to the floor. Her feet absorbed stabbing crystal shards lunging for her robe. She'd left the razor out of reach.

He gave her no time to retrieve it.

"Hello, Nikki." He filled the doorframe.

She backed nearer to the tub. His eyes were ablaze. She recognized the fire, adrenaline resin. "Who are you? What do you want?"

"Your savior. I want redemption. Don't you?" He pounced.

No room to retreat. She fell into the side of the tub. He pulled her back up, his hands on her. He never saw the blade she wielded until it'd sliced deep into his forearm.

She broke free, slippery and fluid beneath his grasp, and darted for the exit. Slamming the door behind her, she added seconds on her lead. She slid down the banister, a childhood game her grandfather allowed was a game no more. At the base of the stairs, she smashed her palm into the alarm pad and sent sirens wailing. He hit the landing when her hand seized the handle of the front door. She flung it open, skirted around it, and ran full out for the neighboring property, a bloody trail of footprints behind her.

She prayed the sound of his heavy boots slamming into the ground wouldn't be the last thing she heard. She'd wounded him. He hadn't expected that. If her life was to be taken on a lonely Saturday night, it wouldn't be at his hands. That thought numbed her pain and drove her across the neighbor's lawn and crashing through the glass French doors of their parlor.

The Redeemer disappeared behind the tinted glass of the Town car, donned the hat and glasses waiting on the passenger seat, and crawled down the alley with the lights off. Five blocks away, he turned onto a high traffic street, hitting the low beams after he reached highway speed.

His left arm throbbed, wrapped in a towel stolen from Nikki's bathroom. He couldn't be certain he hadn't left DNA behind. If he did, his timetable would take a serious hit. He feared tonight's failure signaled the beginning of the end.

Inevitable as it was, it would finish on his terms not theirs.

He knew how the cops worked. It'd take time to access traffic cameras and narrow the field of potential vehicles. He'd ensured they'd never identify him through the windshield—its glass was specialized to distort images inside. A sharp turn into an underground parking lot, and the vehicle disappeared among the fifty or so others.

He chose a suitable spot midway through the maze of similar and identical makes and models, slammed the car into park, and popped the glove box. Inside, he removed a medical kit. Within its modified supplies, spools of sterilized wrap, antiseptic, and medical grade disinfectant. He shrugged out of his damaged leather jacket, mindful of the slash on the left sleeve. Closer inspection of the wound confirmed what he'd suspected. It required stitches and would leave a telltale scar.

A scar cops could trace.

He bit down on the leather jacket and poured antiseptic over the gash. The pain would get worse before he was done.

After bandaging his arm, he wiped the vehicle's surfaces down, then moved outside and swapped license plates. He changed clothes, packed everything in a duffel bag from the trunk, and walked back above ground. At the security booth, he entered a code, opened the door, and engaged the camera systems he'd disabled earlier.

A block away, he hopped into his Hummer and drove away. Fifteen minutes later he swiped a stolen security card through a door lock and disappeared into a warehouse basement. He walked over to an incineration tank and tossed the duffel bag inside. He waited, watching it burn for a few seconds to ensure its complete destruction. Then he pulled away.

Angry.

TWENTY-EIGHT

"Don't give me doctor-patient confidentiality crap. I carry a loaded weapon." Kane cornered Max on his way out of his cushy new building. His insider knowledge of Jade's demons always unnerved Kane, but Max's familiarity with Grey's skeletons set off alarm bells between Kane's ears and left him craving ibuprofen. The doc had become dangerously suspect. "Shall I remind you the damage your secrecy has caused or broadcast it on the eleven o'clock news?"

"Maybe we should discuss this in my office?" Max eyed the building's foyer uneasily.

Kane laughed. "Suggesting I get on your docket? After all the shit you've been sweeping under the rug and your history of failures?"

"I haven't failed Jade." Surprisingly, Max appeared truly incensed.

"Says who? You? Don't flatter yourself. Think I'll solicit a second opinion, Doc. She'd be far safer at a distance. You knew about the chief, and you said nothing!"

A group of executives passed by, glanced at the pair, sensed the discord, disbanded, and drifted through, a school of fish avoiding barracudas. Kane's coat was clutched in his hand, his weapon left fully exposed. The most curious eyed it, then him, and picked up their pace for the exit.

He didn't blame the guy. It wasn't the first or last time the tough Black man was eyed warily when it was the sophisticated White man who should be feared. Or did he have it right? At the moment, hard to say.

Kane didn't have height on Max, but a glimpse at his reflection confirmed the hard lines of a man capable of taking a life, someone menacing who, bets were, already had. Uncomfortable in his skin, Kane shifted his stance and rolled his shoulders. He couldn't help wondering who'd poured acid over his iron resolve. It had eroded. Months, even weeks, earlier he was a defender of life, all life, good, bad, or indifferent. Now?

Not so much.

And the more Max stonewalled, the more he valued the use of deadly force.

Max waited until the outer door closed, and they were alone again in the lobby. "Jade's reckless pursuit has much more to do with you than me. She's quitting the force because of her love for you and her longing to build a family she believes will replace the one she lost. I'm not her keeper. I can't convince her to tread lightly here! This killer's throwing her mother's murder in her face and...are you listening?"

Max's voice lost its ability to penetrate abruptly after he mentioned her quitting. It drifted back and gained volume. He realized Max was losing his composure.

"Stop yelling. When did she tell you?" Kane's shoulders released.

"Tell me what? About the copycat body staging?" Max asked.

"No. When were you told she was quitting?" Kane smoothed his voice into interrogation mode.

"The session after her doctor's appointment." Max studied him for reaction. "Did you not know?"

"Of course I knew! What else did she say?"

"I can't discuss anymore. I've said too much already. The point is this case has gone deeper than under her skin. It penetrated her core. No one could persuade her to back down now. She believes solving it will put closure on her mother's death. And, in light of the connections to Grey, her logic is solid. I can't keep her safe. At least I'm aware of my limitations. And I can't break confidentiality! Even if it's killing me."

"What the hell is that supposed to mean?" His shoulders solidified into iron again.

"You can't protect her. You're too involved to accept it, and until you do, you're endangering her further. You're as much a loose cannon verbally as she is in action."

Kane rushed to within inches of Max. His glare silenced the doctor. "While you're hiding behind your prescription pad, Jade, Jackson, and I are out there fighting the beast in the dark. Don't presume to know a damn thing about the reality of protecting this world or anyone in it. Come to think of it, Ian White, the kid responsible for killing his seventeen-year-old girlfriend was a patient of yours, wasn't he?" Kane hit below the belt.

"I couldn't—"

"Save it, Doc. You're what my ma would call a bad dose."

Building security stepped off the lift with big boots headed in a clear path to Kane. Apparently one of the businessmen was also a good Samaritan. "Everything all right, Dr. Maxwell?"

Kane was reminded Max had another name, Abraham Maxwell. Sounded corny, but the man using it had no sense of humor. Max hesitated. Kane backed up.

"Shall I call the authorities?" His meaty hand threatened use of his radio.

"No need," Kane said. "They're already here." Eyes still locked on Max, he lifted his badge from his pocket and flashed it at the guard.

"Sir?" The guy was undaunted.

"I'm fine, Lawrence. Detective Kane's been working a difficult case—"

"The Redeemer case? Hope you catch him soon. My sister's an A-lister too and scared as hell her overachieving will get her killed."

"What?" The guard stole Kane's attention.

"I said, I hope you—"

"Not that part! What do you mean, A-lister?" Kane brushed Max aside and closed in on the guard.

"She rolled our father's car with my brother in it when she was nineteen and stupid. Franklin was two. He wasn't hurt physically but quit speaking for a year. She became a compulsive overachiever. Making amends, I suppose."

Kane drifted from feet away to encroaching intrusively within the guard's personal space. The argument with Max flushed away in the rush of adrenaline. "Why is she scared?"

The guard edged back, confusion furrowing his brow. He didn't speak, searching for clarity from the man behind Kane's left shoulder.

"Don't stare at him. Answer the question." Most days Kane sheltered people from his intelligence to play nice, not upstage, but not today.

"Everyone's—"

"Not everyone. I asked you why *she* is scared."

"The women he takes...they're like her, overachievers maybe with a haunted youth? She figures they have demons of their own driving them. Sins. You know? She says women don't reach those heights without a catalyst."

"Kiss your sister for me." Kane smiled, smacking the guard's back a couple times, and passing Max with deliberate disregard on the way out.

"Did I help?" the guard yelled after him.

Kane swung around. "You bet, buddy. More than he ever could."

Max shook his head and stared at the coffered ceiling. Kane laughed his way to the car. He knew the women were connected. Failures made them Redeemer targets, failures hidden by youth, parents, and laws that erased records. There was no database to cross-reference abortion, or unprosecuted crimes, but the pieces were coming together.

The noose around their suspect was tightening, and Kane wasn't letting go until it choked the life out of the bastard.

TWENTY-NINE

"What the hell?" Jade raised the note from the file on Max's desk as if closing the distance between it and her eyes would dissolve the potency of its meaning. One to talk, she'd violated more than patient protocol and broke into his new offices. The ink had been smudged blurring the words but not enough to make them illegible. In black and white it read, "Convince Grey to come clean."

It wouldn't have bothered her if the note hadn't been attached to her file. The name Jade Carmichael in bold lettering ran down its side. She understood why Grey had kept certain details surrounding her mother's death and killer from her, but if Max didn't agree? She grabbed the edge of the desk staving off a wave of nausea, not certain it was fault of her concussion. Why was Grey hiding truths from her?

The two cases *were* connected, her mother's and the Redeemer. There was no other explanation for the similarities and body posing. Unless…

Icy arms of dread wrapped Jade's shoulders, driving cold pain down the length of her spine. The sound of the front door opening snapped her out of its grip.

Maggie, back from lunch. The crunch of her wrestling shopping bags under her desk alerted Jade that her intrusion wouldn't go unnoticed much longer. She had to vanish, a ghost, but her enlightenment became paralyzing. She couldn't see her way past the documents in front of her.

The file had been on Max's desk. How long had he wrestled with this? Had he just pieced it together? Was he planning to reveal all he knew to her? Is that where he was? Somewhere out there searching for her, armed to shatter her fractured constitution?

In the outer office, the phone rang. The intrusive noise, painful. Jade flinched dropping the file, praying Maggie didn't hear it hit Max's desk. She froze.

"Thanks for the tip. I'd love to chat," Maggie said. "The boss will be back soon. Must get the coffee on." Maggie paused, said her good-byes, and hung up. When she entered the hall en route to the back-room, Jade held her breath. She formulated a lame cover story, hoping it wouldn't be needed knowing in her current state she'd fail to be convincing. Maggie drifted by Max's open door oblivious to Jade's presence.

Jade slinked to the threshold in time to see Maggie disappear into a storage closet. She used the opening to skirt the corner and out the waiting room door, careful to cushion its closure. Checking the place-ment of security cameras, she dodged and weaved her way out of the building avoiding detection not sure she wanted Max or anyone to know she'd been there. Kane's animosity for Max didn't need fuel.

Outside, she opted for the narrow divide between buildings to avoid security in the parking area. Free of detection, she collapsed on a cement ledge. Her hands trembled, shedding nervous energy. The frailty of her body reminded her of the severity of her head injury. Stupid to be out, but she couldn't stop now.

They were closing the distance to the Unsub, so why'd she feel so much dread? She tried but couldn't shake it. If Max and Grey suppressed information, had they reason beyond protecting her from harsh truths?

Her mind rewound the days leading up to each of the Redeemer's killings. Always posing the same question. Her stomach churned, her mouth dried, her head pounded. She wanted to drive dark conclusions from her mind. Those efforts only made it louder.

Who was her mother's killer's successor, and why continue his legacy?

How was Grey, her trusted, revered, and beloved chief of police, involved?

The mental vocalization left a bad taste in her mouth. She spit on the dirt below her butter leather boots expecting the splatter to soil the fresh polish. It gleamed. She pulled a tissue from her pocket and wiped the spittle from her lip.

Grey responded to the discovery of Wenzel's body first. He'd hand-picked an outsider to handle it and been explicit about them steering clear, setting boundaries.

She hopped off the cement ledge, brushed off, rechecked her weapon, and left to confront the man she respected more than her biological father and ask him his connection to their serial killer. The mess in her head confirmed they were nearing the end of the case, when leads converged violently and always with consequence.

THIRTY

Amy mumbled something Jackson didn't register. He wasn't ignoring her. Alarms in his head were gaining volume, drowning out trivial intrusions. Everyone associated with the case had crossed into dangerous territory.

"I haven't seen you like this before," Amy said.

That, he heard. "Like what?" He sat, awkwardly folded, on the floor, surrounded by case-related documents dug out from a damp church cellar, with his tie off and shirt half tucked. At least his boots were on straight. "It's about as enjoyable as sifting through cow shit, but when you dive in sometimes you find a gem."

"Not the mess, Tex. The panic driving it."

He refused to glance up from the most recent sheet of interest, listings of religious groups dating back twenty years or more located within the strike zone. "I'm not panicked. I'm pissed. Coiled like a cobra raring to strike."

"You're not the type to fear for yourself." She leaned down placing a hand gently at the sight of his gunshot wound. "Who are you afraid of failing?"

Amy was the shop comedian most days, lighthearted and strong, beautiful and tough, smart and soulful with a crucial sense of timing. The fact that she was attracted to women was about as defining as her hair color of the month.

Jackson set down the papers. "Everyone. That's not news. This could go south on us, kid, and the slope's getting steep."

"You're closing in. You have leads."

Always the optimist.

"He's not waiting. I'm strutting in circles dreading incoming messages knowing—"

Homicide division's steel door bounced against its back wall with a reverberated thud that stalled at the end of Grey's hard sole shoe. "He's hit again. We have a survivor. First responders are isolating her until you arrive."

"The General?" Jackson sprang from the floor, papers showering off him. He tucked in his shirt on the way to the door, then remembered who he'd abandoned in the heap as he lit outta there. "Amy, you—"

"I've got it," she said.

"No hospital. The victim is at her neighbor's house," said Grey. "Crashed through their glass doors. They're stabilizing her before transport."

"She was driving?" Jackson asked.

"No. On foot. She's a mess, but if she's talking, I want you listening."

Jackson glanced at the paper Grey handed him. The address was fifteen minutes away at best. He'd find a way to shorten it.

Grey blocked his route. "Something else."

Jackson waited.

"She cut him. Got his arm with a straight razor."

Jackson sensed the corners of his mouth turn up. "Thatta girl. Kane? Jade?"

"On other leads, just you—"

"I'll call 'em from the truck." Jackson flew out the door. An eyewitness. Priceless. The Redeemer had to know his days were numbered. Shadow Hook was closing in on him, and that kind of pressure was sure to cost. The question was who and how many.

Leigh's assault on the Redeemer began before he crossed the threshold. Scalding brew burned his flesh blood red on impact. She'd heated it twice. Used the hot liquid to fill the maker then reheated it a second time beyond boiling. She'd maintained a sequence of scorching cups, reusing the cooling ones for a constant ready row. She threw cup after cup. First at his face, then wherever she could hit.

She'd waited in a state of readiness for three brutal hours.

Blinded, he dodged and weaved like a boxer.

And he screamed.

The sound unnerving. Unexpected.

She'd studied his work. He was a monster. Monsters shouldn't scream. He did.

Ten seconds. The window she gave herself for escape. After that, rage would take hold infusing him with an immeasurable strength she'd have no defense against. Time ticked by too fast. She was counting in her head.

Seven one thousand.

Terror fueled Leigh's resolve. The Redeemer wiped his face with a sleeve. Blood smeared beneath the dripping coffee. What had he done? Whose blood was he wearing? The screaming monster.

Six one thousand.

She hit his eyes full force with the fifth full cup of espresso. He screamed louder, adding profanities that cut into her marrow. They had teeth. What he promised to do to her was born of an evil she'd only witnessed once before, capable of killing innocence while damning you to an unbearable end.

Five one thousand.

He blinked scorched lids in a futile effort to clear his sight, sweeping his arms in search of her throat. Silent, she retreated to the far side of the door opening. As if sensing her next move, he shifted, blocking her exit. In close range, she tossed coffee at his feet. He lost balance, slipped left.

Four one thousand.

Leigh swept by flailing limbs. Night air fortifying her resolve. With one leg out the door, she released the last cup. It hit its intended target with perfect accuracy, and no effect.

Three one thousand.

This cup hadn't burned her palm. The others had. She lifted her back leg around him, planting it for the launch of the fastest race of her life. It snagged on takeoff.

Two one thousand.

Instead of impeding him further her last cup did the opposite.

Bleeding caffeine, he stared up with a vengeance born of pure hatred. He seized her ankle with a grip that said her chance of escape hinged on her foot instantaneously detaching from the rest of her body. She would've chosen that option if it'd been available. It didn't exist, and soon, neither would she.

One one thousand.

He dragged her back, clenching his hands around her throat. She didn't resist. She'd rather be sacrificed by rage than endure the lasting torment he'd envisioned for her. He lifted her off the ground by the throat. Before everything disappeared, she regretted two things. She hadn't let out an earth-shattering scream before he'd silenced her, and her timing, miserably, was dead right.

Leigh regained consciousness riding waves of nausea accompanied by a terrible awareness of her situation. Like all psychiatrists, she could identify lingering symptoms of certain drugs and indicators of attempted suicides in her patients.

What she knew scared her.

Dizzy, cold, and weak. She diagnosed she was suffering from blood loss. She could even say precisely how many liters were missing. It didn't take a genius. They were sitting in a row of jars in front of her when she opened her eyes.

Movement behind her alerted her to the Redeemer's whereabouts. She fought the vertigo for a clear grasp of her environment. Then wished she hadn't.

A kill kit, used, lay beyond her left foot. She hung suspended like a hammock, legs and arms at head level, torso arced over the cement dish in the center of the room. She wasn't wearing pants anymore. And every major artery had been tapped and prepared with valves either feeding in or draining out.

He caught her staring at the one in her left wrist.

"It's a nifty cocktail. Your heart will keep beating until there's almost nothing left to beat with. Ta-dump, ta-dump."

Her eyes shifted to the two liters of blood in the glass cylinders on the floor.

"It's yours. I have more to add to it." He signaled to three empty containers in the corner. They'd more than take her four-point-seven quota. "We have work to do before then. I'd advise against struggling, movement of any kind really."

"What happened to your arm?" Her voice came out cracked, slurring, and as broken as she was.

"My arm? Oh. Nikki. She's suicidal. Turned the razor on me when I tried to help her."

"Help her?" There was no fight left in Leigh's body. He'd taken that after he strangled her unconscious. Her mind, honed to endure through intellect, would test its mettle here.

"You'd be surprised at how many I've helped." He spoke while adjusting IV drips and checking the lines of tubes accessing her veins.

That was what she feared most, the tally of his crimes. He read her thoughts.

"Hundreds. Thousands if you count the villages in Africa, medical advances, shelters, and crime prevention programs. I'm affiliated with many in my line of work." He locked eyes, his sinister gleam made her squint. "This is a sideline."

"Were you involved in Jade's mother's murder?" She'd dissect him, and he'd be oblivious. This was her fight back.

He jerked at the words. Stabbed his finger with a needle. Cursed. Then froze for a couple seconds avoiding her. His chest heaved. "Your blood is in mine." Slowly. He drew in a calming breath. It confirmed her suspicions. She'd found a weakness.

"I'm a little young for that, don't you think?"

"Too young for the crime, but not..." She breathed shallow for a couple seconds feeling his eyes on her and the satisfaction her suffering awarded him. "...not to suffer at the hands of the criminal."

"What are you saying?" He dropped the needle and the bottle he carried. "Are you suggesting—"

"Master and disciple. You wouldn't be the first."

He rushed at her, clutching a group of lines and pulling them. Pain resonated from too many sources to register. A shrill cry escaped her lungs with a velocity that surely would have saved her life if she'd done it earlier. "Quit assuming you're the smartest one in the room. My IQ trumps yours, lady. Generational advancement."

Blood escaped several sites. He noticed and released the lines. The most painful squirted, one in her right thigh, another in her neck. It ran warm down her chest.

"You're a mess. You can't die now. Maybe later." He worked on both areas readjusting until they sat dormant once more. He sutured, with care and precision, the tear in her thigh. Her physical state debilitated. Her mind blocked it to focus.

"I'm wrong. I'm sorry. I was asking, not assuming."

He stared at her. An odd expression she couldn't place the emotion of. Regret?

"He was master of nothing." His eyes glistened under a flush of fluid, and his voice found a somber note.

"You knew him, the police chief?" She sustained a nonjudgmental tone. "Or knew of him when he killed?"

He sauntered away. Then running water. It shut off. He returned with a white, soapy cloth, wiped the sweat from her brow and the blood from her wounds.

His Armani aftershave washed over her, drowning her original theory. He wasn't born a monster.

"He's my father. Can you imagine what my mother was like?"

Horror permeated from the knowledge that the worst among us didn't occur through a random deficiency in natural evolution. They were cultivated. Manmade.

THIRTY-ONE

Jade sat in her semi-repaired Mustang, engine off, choking down haunting images knowing better than to allow anyone into the wreckage of her pain. Those who have not suffered the same are incapable of handling what they can never understand. Their words of support and sympathy come off cold and condescending regardless of intention, and she wasn't willing to worry about making the privileged feel better about their failure to relate.

Laughter resonated from a distant past as she stared at the worn photo of the two of them covered in paint. Taken the morning of the murder. They'd been redecorating while her father was supposedly away on business. Restoration had emptied the china cabinet making room for Jade to stow away. Life planned her survival before she knew she'd be fighting for it.

Her mother's character flaws? They didn't exist, leaving when she did. Erased by the hands of time. Jade's wounded mind idolized her. Longing to return to a life that would've allowed a blissfully naïve adolescence nurtured by love.

Her eyes blurred. No tears fell. Emptied long ago.

She shoved the picture back into her pocket and stared up the tree-lined drive of Dr. Leigh's lake country house.

Jade hadn't located Grey. Instead, she'd run her theory by the profiler. Hoping Leigh would put the kibosh on any unfounded suspicions. Second guessing your instincts marked the end for a homicide detective.

This was Jade's path. One of honor to close the case. Serve justice. No matter the cost. No matter who fell—she expected it'd be her. She survived for this purpose alone.

Grey's life was largely a mystery. Since his wife passed two years earlier, he'd lived a solitary existence. They were on the verge of divorce when she died. Guilt isolated. A few drinks after work, office gatherings, or Christmas parties. Outside the occasional impromptu cookout, no one knew what he did when he wasn't at the shop.

Even investigators could be blind. The Achilles' heel of the century, lives so absorbed in criminal drama, they missed each other's personal landslides.

Iris, Leigh's assistant, burst from the front door long before Jade came within knocking distance. She appeared frantic, juggling a phone and an arm full of files.

"It's not like her, Your Honor. She mentioned working at the station. Those files are with her. She'd never miss a presentation."

In a rush to dump falling papers into the back of her car, Iris overlooked Jade standing amid the foliage. Jade didn't interrupt. Preferring to listen in from the side of the drive.

"She didn't have anything scheduled outside the Redeemer case. Yes, yes, of course. I'm loading them. I'll be there in fifteen minutes."

Iris closed the door of her car with half the coat she'd dropped over the files draped outside it. She skirted the rear and slid into the driver's seat, slamming the door shut without glancing up. She sent gravel spray leaving the drive. Jade stood in the dusty aftermath watching the car disappear around the bend and sensing something eerie in the murky air.

Leigh wasn't inside, but intuition drew Jade to the house. She tried the front door. It opened. In her hurry, Iris failed to lock up. When you hunted killers, mistakes like that cost lives. Leigh had become too close to the case, a threat, and she wasn't home.

Fast and driven, Jade entered the house without a creak, squeak, or click. The house in and of itself wasn't creepy. That element Jade ushered over the threshold herself. Thoughts raced in her mind, too vicious for airplay. She pushed at them hard, still they bled through. A switch had been flipped. An alarm blaring at bomb siren volume echoed inside her. Instead of a warning, it carried a message of unavoidable doom.

Leigh was dead. If not already, soon.

In Leigh's office, Jade searched her Day-Timer, desk notes, and computer. In the most recent emails, a thank you from a university for a riveting speech delivered late two nights before. Iris had apologized for a presentation Leigh missed. Scouring through information, Jade deduced she could've been gone for two days.

Two days too long.

What did Leigh discover that made her the Redeemer's next target, and how had he found out she was a threat? It wouldn't have been difficult to discover her involvement with the case. Why the interest now?

The onslaught of questions rose with panic in her gut. She'd left Leigh in the break room at the shop surrounded by crime scene photos when they'd last worked together. The answers had to be there, maybe the killer had been too.

Had Leigh unearthed a link to the killer when she was alone at the station. She'd likely inform Grey first of any break in the case. What if he was out there making up for her sick leave and walking into a trap?

"Shit." Her mind raced down cursed avenues, and she couldn't find the brakes. A flash of Grey kicking the shop door open sent her searching through Leigh's computer file on the case. The shoe impression left at Lorenda Lainey's crime scene. She found the document and confirmed it'd been size thirteen. Grey was size thirteen according to his file, but his stocky build remained true down to his feet. Thick and wide, he wore thirteen and a half to accommodate. Only someone close to him would be aware of his special-order shoe size.

Was he being framed? Criminal deception was a safe bet. Her job was to protect him, her gut said Grey was in danger. Leigh was still dead.

She accessed the shop database and sent a request to the university for Leigh's speech, details on her arrival and departure, names and contact information for those escorting her, and that night's security camera footage.

Lorenda Lainey's file lay open on Leigh's desk. Leigh was last seen leaving the fundraiser event. It appeared she'd have a file of her own, and it'd read the same.

Their killer liked cars.

He drugged his victims for compliance and easy transport. He'd used an array of benzodiazepine tranquilizers, GHB, Flunitrazepam, known better as Rope or Rohypnol, even cherry-flavored Noctec. He killed in isolation. And kept them for weeks in the beginning. Leigh had days minus two. Smart, with a profiler's perspective, Jade prayed Leigh's intellect would keep her alive.

Iris's conversation replayed. Leigh had a hard copy of the Redeemer case files with her. Old-fashioned, she too preferred to see information on paper. He'd read them. If he found her analysis flattering, it might buy them time to find her. If not…

A mental picture obscured the desk before Jade, transforming it to a movie screen. Images of sliding into the back seat of the town car to find him sitting across from her played out in terrifying clarity. No escape. Then the needle, the injection, the hazy horror of drifting off at the mercy of a monster.

She shook her head to shatter the illusion. She knew Leigh. Worked with her. Admired her. Damn him.

A glance at the bookshelf on her left while she waited for the printer to spit out the university's response revealed rows of potential mourners. Photos of Leigh winning awards, contributing to Shadow Hook charities, bestowing scholarships, teaching, and speaking lined the shelves. She and her father outside a rustic cabin caught Jade's attention. Leaning on each other glowing with admiration, they depicted a reality Jade dreamed of. One worth protecting. Now she was truly pissed.

"I'll find you, you son-of-a-bitch, and when I do, I'll kill you." She wasn't thinking like a cop, hadn't been for a while. She couldn't walk away leaving the enemy behind. This time, the path to justice went dark. She couldn't resurface until certain he couldn't follow. For her mother, for every mother, she'd send him to Hell even if he dragged her with him.

She dialed the shop. The phone wouldn't connect. No ringtone. Empty air. It wasn't the first time her cell phone couldn't be relied on. Annoying. Time for a replacement. The next upgrade would be a civilian model.

She sent a text request to Jackson and Kane asking if either of them had recent contact with Leigh. Jackson answered first.

He'd received a message from Leigh late Thursday night. She'd found a possible link between victims. She intended to explore it and come in with her findings as soon as she had something definitive. Jackson was steps away from interviewing the Redeemer's only conscious survivor. He signed off. Better he gather evidence unhampered by the news of Leigh's almost certain abduction.

She waited a couple minutes, staring at the photo catalog of Leigh's life, delaying the bad news. Better to receive word of Leigh's fate when there was ammunition to find her captor.

Kane answered next.

> In church. Sister insists I turn off my phone. Ten minutes, and I'm out. Scary nuns.

He didn't know she hadn't been at home recuperating like he expected until now.

Leigh's computer sounded an incoming message. Jade swung the swivel high back she'd been leaning on around, jumped in, and focused her attention on the screen. A university filled with wannabe detectives had quick response times.

Leigh had arrived minutes before her speech two nights previous and left right after. Nothing obvious jumped off the contact list. And the footage from the security camera in the parking lot, at first glance, appeared uneventful. Leigh's driver brought her, got out, and escorted her to the door. He waited in the same space until she returned. The camera angle left the back left side of the vehicle in the blind spot but gave a clear image of her entering the back seat from the right on her return.

She didn't try to escape. The car didn't swerve or maneuver erratically. No apparent struggle. It didn't exit in a rush. The driver gave Leigh time to get comfortable before pulling away or…

Or the Redeemer had become a ghost. He entered the car from the blind spot, killed the driver, and pounced on Leigh the second she shut the door. A fast-acting sedative and away he drove.

A plate check all but confirmed this wasn't Leigh's regular driver. And he waited, without setting off any alarm bells, for a woman highly educated in spotting them.

A shiver slithered across the back of Jade's shoulders. She shook free of it. He was there, in front of her, on the tape, hiding in the shadows.

She texted Jackson and Kane, updating them with all she knew. She ended her message,

...and delay telling Grey. Visit the scene, get a clear picture before we break the news. Need to be sure.

THIRTY-TWO

Broken glass crushed beneath Jackson's boots as he followed the path of the Redeemer's latest conquest. The chase area was taped off before he arrived. Flags littered the distance behind him. In front of Nikki Taylor's neighbor's home, remnants of cutwork, edgy and intense, framed the once pristine French doors to the parlor in a most unwelcoming fashion. He bypassed the break point and went in the front entrance.

"Hey, Jimmy. You first on scene?" Jackson stopped the patrol cop at the door.

"Yep. Lights were all on when I got here. Owners said they were reading in bed and heard the crash. Parlor bookshelf is backlit on a timer. Layout would've kept them blind until she was at their doors. Don't know why rich folks think shrubbery is gonna keep them safe."

Jackson's lips pulled thin with regret. He skirted by Jimmy and headed in.

Nikki Taylor, shredded and sullied, lay on a stretcher, an EMT rushing to bandage a laceration on her right forearm. Jackson's boots crunched with every step. She'd broken through double panes with soft flesh. She turned to face the intrusion. He surveyed the room, not allowing her to read the shock in his eyes. Strange to find a victim still breathing, stranger still to hear one speak.

"Are you Detective Jackson? They said you were coming." Her voice was soft and solid.

"Guilty." Jackson grabbed a footstool, setting it down outside the paramedic's radius. "We want to get you to the hospital, ma'am. I have to ask—"

"Francis Carroll."

Jackson's stool failed to offer much stability in the wake of Ms. Taylor's words. He knew the name. Everyone in the department knew the name. Hard not to, given you walked past it several times a day. The inscription below it read, "Chief of Police." Of course, it couldn't have been him. He'd been shot dead during a case...

"Detective? Did you hear me? I know my attacker. Don't know where he lives or much else, but I know his name."

Her voice drowned out as the room began spinning like it'd been set atop a roulette wheel. The decades-old case had the earmarks of their current one. The only obvious link between the two was the man who broke his chops on it. Grey. And Jade.

"How old is he?" Jackson's focus snapped into narrow alignment.

"How old? Umm. Thirties."

Jackson glanced down at the glass below his feet and breathed in, cleansing breath entered his lungs.

"It's hard to say for certain. I told you his name. Why aren't you putting out an APB on him or—" She lifted off the stretcher, spoiling the paramedic's final touches to stabilize her injuries.

Jackson leaned in. "I'm familiar with the name, fairly certain it's an alias. I need details. Did he tell you his name, or did you know him before tonight?"

"Can you leave us for a few minutes?" Her tone wasn't sharp but commanded an authority the men tending to her responded to. They closed their kits and left. They'd put in an IV and were administering fluids, but she was far from out of the woods. She had a three-inch gash over her left eye and several deep wounds on her arms and legs.

"You're in shock," Jackson warned, shifting his stool closer. "Won't stave off the pain for long, and it'll smart something awful."

"I'll live, but whoever he takes his rage out on next won't. I saw his eyes. He wanted me dead, and he'd planned out exactly how."

"I don't mean this disrespectfully, but how do you know?"

"It wasn't enough for me to die. It had to be his way, by his hands."

Jackson was moved by her strength and certainty, but admiration wasn't enough. "Did he say that? Say what he'd planned?"

"No." She sat up. Battered, bruising before his eyes, and seeping from her bandages.

"Best you lay still. How long do you think he'd been in the house?" he redirected.

"A while." Nikki laid back, staring into space for a few seconds. "He could've been there before I got home. I don't know."

"What time do you arrive home normally?"

"Late, like tonight. Always late." She paused. He followed her eyes as they scanned over the patchwork of bandages.

"What is it?" He could see her wheels turning.

"The CD skipped. It was playing downstairs, and it skipped like…"

"Like someone bumped it?"

"Yeah. That would've been at the start of my bath."

"Okay. Do you have security cameras on the property?"

"One at each entrance. Seems stupid now, should've had them everywhere else." Color drained from her face. She wasn't doing well. "I was unsettled. Thought that was about my decision but now—"

Jackson was on his feet. "I've got to call the medics back. You're—"

"Listen to me! I know this man. He had a role for me to fill—"

"I am listening. I hear you loud and clear, but you can't be sure—"

"If my death was all he wanted, he would've let *me* finish the job." Emotions were taking over. Shock would be next. "Do you really think he gave me time to search the cabinets for a straight razor?"

The paramedic team entered the room waved in by Jackson. He moved the stool away and stepped back. "We have to get her in, sir. Her heart rate is unstable, and she's lost a lot of blood."

Jackson kneeled at her side and whispered, "Nikki, you said you know him, can you tell me anything that will help us find him?"

"He's tied to a few pharmaceutical companies. I'll think of the names. He's wealthy. I know he participated in an Africa safari with our company's founders last year. They may have a photo. Dark hair, green eyes, tall, six-foot-plus easy, big guy, and I never saw him drink coffee."

Jackson's mind raced ahead as he took notes. Hair could be dyed. Colored contacts could mask true eye color. "He doesn't drink coffee?"

"It's just…"

The paramedics locked the gurney into rolling position and were ready to run Jackson over.

"It was around. Fresh brewed when he came to the lab. He'd smell it, you know, sniff the air like he loved it, but he never accepted it when offered. Actually, I never saw him drink or eat anything there. Thought it was a germ fear."

"Were you intimate with this man, this Francis Carroll?" Jackson was being shoved aside.

"I made a mistake once."

The confirmation he'd waited for. "I'll come by the hospital when you've had time to rest. Until then, please don't discuss this with anyone."

"Who would I tell? I married my work, Detective. And even it doesn't care for me much."

"You cut him. You fought back, and you're alive. We care." He held her gaze. "How did you manage to outrun this guy?"

"The banister. I slid down it. Mastered that as a kid. Not so fun this time."

Jackson stopped the medic closest to him with a solid grip and leaned in on his way out. "Y'all watch her," he whispered. The young man locked eyes and nodded. He'd overheard enough and understood. This was one witness they couldn't afford to lose to suicide. Jackson paused in the threshold to face her. "I will need your help. You take care. I'll come check on you soon."

He stepped out into the cool night air. Dew was forming on the glass littering the lawn, some of it stained red, tears on broken images. He couldn't help wondering what happened to Nikki Taylor to send her into the arms of a psychopath or, and perhaps more tragically, to contemplate suicide. He'd got the rundown on her. Staring at her manicured estate, he didn't need a background check to tell him how accomplished she was. So why? What tore her apart before the glass doors?

He walked the expanse of yard between the homes. Echoes of Nikki's screams haunted his path. Midway on her property he paused by an evidence marker. A shoe impression left, undoubtedly, by the Redeemer. Jackson slid his boot alongside it.

"They're almost done in the bathroom," a CSU investigator called out.

"Thanks. I'll be right in." Jackson glanced down, then made his way to the front door, whispering under his breath. "Hope the plastic surgeon's up to the task at County. That's one warrior that deserves beauty, not battle scars."

Careful not to disturb evidence, he tucked his hands into his pockets and slid into the foyer. Static noise halted him two strides from the door.

"Anyone check the stereo system?" he bellowed. Someone deep in the back of the house answered.

"Blues. Check it out."

Jackson made a mental note and moved on.

The staircase loomed about ten feet from where he stood. If not for the attack, he could've got comfortable here. Heavy wood surrounded by natural elements and simplistic charm. No fake opulence. A photo on a sideboard called to him. Nikki was a beautiful woman even marred by glass shards and a madman, but in the picture, accepting a humanitarian award, she was stunning. Sad to think she'd been willing to destroy that.

He started up the stairs. Nikki's ghost, outrunning a killer in pursuit, traversed the landing and flew through him at the midpoint. Her thrashing heartbeat echoed on the steps.

The bathroom was the second doorway off a wide vestibule. The door was ajar. Rusty smears guided the way in. The bloody mess, exaggerated by the water told a sick tale. Jackson's eyes recorded Nikki's life before the attack, locking on its details—her broken wineglass, etched scented candles before they'd melted to ruin, fresh lilies in a vase on the windowsill, and moonlight streaming in from above.

A peaceful place to die. Was that what she'd been going for?

A tech entered the room. "He was watching."

"The house?" Jackson said. "I'd expect as much."

"No. Through the skylight." The tech grabbed a flashlight and shone it up to the glass cover above the tub. The ceilings were so high, he hadn't bothered to strain his neck yet. "Handprints on the outside. He must've been in love. He climbed the roof. It's well over thirty feet."

Their suspect was big, tall, and agile mentally and physically. Nikki was right. He'd planned everything except her last-minute desire to live.

"What are the chances for prints?" Jackson stared at the signs of intrusion. Tension locked in his gut, anger permeating from his core.

"We haven't got up there yet. You never know. You want to inspect this stuff before I bag it?" The tech pointed to Nikki's nightgown spread out over a chair in the corner, untouched by the brutality served on the bulk of the space. Jackson moved closer. French lace, cream with a pale pink ribbon woven through the bust line. Delicate. He couldn't help seeing Nikki in it.

"Take it away," he said. "Let me know if anything interesting surfaces."

"You got it."

Instead of being comforted by Nikki's survival, Jackson seethed. He'd met one of the targets. Talked to her. Seen her home, her struggle, her scars. The women this bastard was killing were amazing, extraordinary. They'd lost too many. Too many body bags, not enough bullets.

Jackson left the room and barreled down the stairs threatening Jimmy's safety on his way up.

"No offense, Jackson, but you look like one pissed off Texan."

"Oh, I am, son. And there's hell to pay." Jackson swept by and headed for the door without a glance.

"Good luck, Tex."

"Luck ain't got a damn thing to do with it."

THIRTY-THREE

Smoke drifted counter flow into a storm drain at Kane's feet, fitting given the ass-backward state of things. Rain fell as an oppressive mist, weighing down the air in humidity but never forming drops. It created a strange vortex underground that sucked at a smoldering cigarette on the sidewalk like a subterranean chain smoker. Hell had officially lit up, and Kane was finding it difficult to breathe above ground.

With Leigh missing, their careers, not just their asses, were all on the line, and it was getting harder to play by the rules. He wondered which one of them would break first. The answer was pretty clear. He snuffed the abandoned butt out with the heel of his boot and jumped into the passenger side of Jackson's truck.

"I resent the hell out of this damn fool." Jackson pulled away, cutting off the driver behind him. He gave an apologetic nod. "He has us all running around like mice in a maze."

Kane slicked back damp hair from his face and leaned into the manufactured breeze blowing from the vents.

"Jade said thirty-six hours." Jackson turned hard right and made eye contact. "Thirty-six too long."

"She's smart, Tex. Cagey smart. She'll stay alive. Hospital first?"

"Sure. Your theory on past sins and what Nikki said is too close to be a fluke. Leigh's hiding something, and that bastard knows what it is. Time to even the playing field."

The truck careened down the fog-laden streets painting a canvas of disturbed swirls behind them. In all the time he'd known Jackson, he'd never heard him complain or get nervous. He said the best training for the job came from dealing with the bulls back home. A cowboy's swagger of confidence ensured survival when you were dealing with animals that tipped the scales at twenty-three hundred pounds. "Not a piece of beef you want to make edgy," he'd say. Reading his expression, the tension of his grip on the steering wheel, and the absence of his wry sense of humor, something had spooked him.

"This won't work if we can't get the Taylor woman to talk." Kane was fishing. He didn't hold much hope in the wisdom of a suicidal victim.

"Nikki," Jackson corrected. "She'll talk to me."

Interesting. The victim wasn't a victim anymore. She had a name. "What makes you so confident?"

"I saw her eyes. She wants to catch this bad seed as much as we do." Jackson slammed against the curb at the emergency entrance. "She needs to. Maybe more than us."

"Why more?" Kane jumped out and stood in the mist with his door ajar.

Jackson killed the engine, slid out, and leaned inside, using the truck's cab as a protected tunnel. "She needs a reason to live, so I'm fixin' to give her one."

Kane slammed the door, aware of the irony between the Redeemer's victims and the cops chasing him. They were all after the same thing, justification for their existence, earned one way or the other.

Nikki Taylor was on the third floor. Her room guarded by a guy Jackson had handpicked. When they arrived, the doorman gave Kane a subtle nod, never budging from his post.

"He's taking this serious," Kane whispered as they crossed the threshold.

"Better be. No one enjoys a Texas shit kicking," Tex whispered back.

Nikki Taylor was sleeping. The doctor standing beside her bed was writing on her chart when they came in.

"Hey, how's she doing?" Jackson was first to flash his badge.

Kane didn't bother. If there were any doubt about who they were, they wouldn't have made it in.

"Her vitals have stabilized since the transfusion, and we're monitoring for infection. Apparently, she's one of the lucky ones." He shifted positions nearer to them and the door. Physically coaxing them back out.

"How long's she been asleep?" Kane sauntered to the end of Nikki's bed. Held together by stitches and gauze, she was a mess and deserved anything but interrogation, but time was not a friend.

"Since surgery. We're hoping she'll sleep through the night. She's been through enough for one day." The doctor's demeanor mimicked the doorman's, not an ounce of leeway. Kane understood why. The woman appeared to be constructed of paper mâché.

"Her mental state?" Jackson asked.

Kane recognized the sentiment underlying Jackson's tone. He was worried about this woman. The kind of worry that ran deeper than surface concern. She'd gotten to him. It happened, but never to Tex.

"I'm sad, not insane. If that's what you're asking." Nikki's groggy answer was heard by all three but was directed at only one.

"You've been through a lot." Jackson's tone revealed too much. "An attack can twist you inside."

"He has all he's getting from me. You must be Detective Kane. They were talking about you on the ride over. Are you responsible for the bodyguard? He practically followed me into surgery."

"No. You can thank Tex for that. Sorry we're meeting this way." Kane closed the distance to her bed. There was no point extending a hand. Both of hers were bandaged.

"Better this way than not at all," she said.

The girl was tough. No illusions about what the alternative would've been.

Jackson brushed by, taking the seat closest to the patient. "How ya feeling?"

"Don't worry about me, Tex. They have me on really effective meds. Can't feel much of anything."

Kane stood at Jackson's side, looming but not too close. "I have to ask you some questions that may appear insensitive or redundant. They're not meant to offend or embarrass. They are necessary. You okay with that?"

The doctor, who'd maintained his distance, shuffled closer. "If you're not up to this, the detectives can come by at a later time," he suggested.

"No, they can't. Someone else's life is hanging in the balance." Nikki locked eyes with Jackson. Kane hoped Jackson kept his mouth shut. If he opened it, he wouldn't lie. "Isn't it?"

"I can see it in your eyes."

Kane broke the spell before Jackson parted his lips. "Can you think of any reason why this man attacked you?"

He had their attention. Neither one approved of the question.

"I'll be back in twenty minutes," the doctor warned. "Make it brief, gentlemen." He made his exit as Kane repeated the unsavory inquest.

"Any reason—"

"He's a psychopath. Outside of that, nothing specific." Nikki was barely awake and razor sharp.

"As I said, it's not my intention to upset you, every detail—"

"I'm sorry. I searched my memories for details before they knocked me out." Nikki cleared her throat. "Hasn't helped."

Jackson reached for her water cup, replenished it from the jug on the nightstand, and held it near, bending the straw toward her. Nikki sipped the water as Jackson spoke.

"What does he know about you?" he asked. "How close would you say you were?"

"He'd never been to my home. I didn't think he knew where I lived. Not many do. I make a point of keeping my work and home life separate."

"You were intimate with this man, correct?" Kane thought it better he asked.

"Once. I'd isolated a compound that offered real promise to young children suffering from severe epilepsy. I'd gone to Israel to work on it. They were ahead of us in this area. It was an emotional day. I met him there. He was touring the plant."

"We'll need the name of the facility," Jackson said.

"I had a nurse write it down and everything else I could think of. It's on a notepad in the drawer."

Jackson pulled the drawer out, grabbed the notepad, and handed it over.

"Thank you for this." Kane accepted it and scanned the penned details.

"It was four years ago." Nikki searched the ceiling for words. "He was linked to the project somehow. Funding, I think. I was allowed to assist on the research side. They weren't interested in sharing much with us. The research was not widely supported."

"How much time did you spend together?" Jackson asked.

Kane wondered about the kindness in his tone.

"A couple days, on the tail end of my visa. I left for home. We spoke on the phone a few times. I quit answering. He quit calling."

"Did you ever disclose any sensitive details about your past?" Kane's patience was fraying under the need for something solid.

"Probably. We drank three bottles of champagne in less than an hour. I couldn't tell you what I said."

"Was he drunk?" Jackson said. "Did you see him swallow?"

Kane hadn't a clue why Jackson was asking if the guy swallowed, but Nikki did.

"Yes. Never saw him drink their coffee, but he shared the champagne. I saw him swallow. I'm sure I was in far worse condition. He drove us to the hotel."

"Town car?" Kane asked.

"Yes. Something new, a rental." Nikki shifted her position. Pain seared across her face, tensing her muscles. The drugs were waning. "I gave a child the wrong medicine. I was seventeen at the time and stupid. Willow died. She was five. I've never forgiven myself. I'm certain her family hasn't forgiven me either."

Where the hell had that come from? Nikki's admission sent Kane back a step. Jackson wasn't speaking so he did. "Did you seek counseling?"

"I joined a grief and guilt group through church many years ago."

"We need the name of the church, and everyone you can remember taking part." Jackson perked up.

"The church was Our Lady of Peace. Names won't help you. They weren't used to protect our identities. We were all minors."

"Jesus." Kane spoke without volition.

"That's why we haven't found a connection." Jackson faced Kane, his expression mirroring his own. "Like we suspected, nothing on the books officially."

"Who knew about the group? Was it open to anyone? Were the sessions taped? Any male members?" Kane's words flew at a pace that made it surprising he wasn't foaming at the mouth. They were closing in.

"One nun and the priest, an all-girl group. Held in the basement."

The perfect segue to a good joke. No one was laughing. Kane's stare demanded more from her.

"We always shut the doors. It wasn't the type of thing you spoke about outside, too much judgment, pain. I'll have the nurse write every-thing I can remember down and—"

An alarm wailed launching Jackson out of his chair. Kane located the source, a heart rate monitor to his left. His hand was on the machine when the doctor barged in. "All right. You two out, leave Ms. Taylor to us." The doctor crossed the room, shut off the annoying sound, and plowed by, a human barrier between them and Nikki.

"Sorry, Nikki." Jackson hesitated en route to the door. "I'll be by soon."

"I'll be fine. Your bouncer won't let any undesirables in," she said. "It's my final penance. If I help you catch him, I'll live knowing I've saved one."

At this, the doctor glanced from Kane and Jackson to Nikki and back again.

"Have the nurse call us. Leave the information at her station," Kane said. "We'll swing by and pick it up without disturbing you. You've helped enough." She mumbled something only her doctor heard as they rounded the corner en route for the exit.

"Hope Our Lady of Peace has the kettle on." Moments later Jackson hopped into the truck's cab as Kane closed his door.

"If not, we'll wake her." Kane watched the hospital lights meld in the rearview, then glanced at his friend. "She's a mess, buddy. Smart, all that, but a mess."

"Recoverable," Jackson said.

"You think? I'm not convinced." Kane didn't want to see Jackson go down the same path of heartbreak he was on, with a woman who couldn't be healed.

"Speaking of recoverable, you told Jade yet about the chief?"

"Didn't want to do it via text."

"Yeah, soon though." Jackson opened his window. The night breeze sent cool shivers across Kane's skin. "You ever wonder why I never warned you to back off?"

"Not until now." Kane had fully expected Jackson to hit back.

"Because you're thick headed, and it would've been a waste of time."

"True. It's still good advice. If I could've stopped it, I would've."

"Like hell," Jackson flashed a grin. "You don't walk away from the *one*. You love them in your mind your whole life. When you meet them, it's unavoidable fate."

Kane never responded. Jackson was right. He couldn't have stopped the train that was Jade. He was a passenger with no exit. He had no clue where it was taking him, and it didn't matter. He was on until its final destination.

THIRTY-FOUR

Jade stood in the shadow of the police station waiting for a discrete opening, the air around her charged, welcoming a storm. Grey left out the front door for Flattery's pub to fill his weekly quota of corned beef, best in the district. He'd be gone a solid hour. He pulled up his collar and quicken his pace crossing the street. Avoiding the main entrance of the shop, she entered through the lowest level of the parking garage.

A couple guys were on their way out when she crossed the parking area. Neither gave her a second glance. The service elevator was on its way down. With every descending floor she grew anxious about possible occupants.

The fewer interactions the better.

She surveyed her surroundings. Empty. When the elevator hit the first floor, she slid behind a support post and waited. Seconds passed before the alerting ding sounded at parking level C. A patrolman stepped out, strolled by a bank of unmarked units, veered left, and disappeared. Jade slipped into the elevator and pressed the top floor, hoping no one significant interrupted her ascent. The elevator stalled, doors ajar. Annoyed, she pounded at the button. The doors closed, and it rose.

Three floors above the elevator halted at the shop's second floor. Jade pushed at the buttons. Ineffective, the doors opened. A guy she remembered from the narc division climbed aboard. Deep in thought, texting, he never acknowledged her presence. He exited on the third floor turning left for the interrogation rooms. She veered right, headed to Grey's office, shoulder checking the narc member for signs of curiosity. Nothing.

Inside, she closed the door and began searching. She accessed Grey's weapon's drawer first. Found nothing surprising and moved on. If he had one secret drawer, he'd have another. She swept her hands under counters, his desk, over ledges, around the back of shelves. Then reverted to hands and knees inspecting the floor, specifically for what appeared fixed in place.

A leather footstool adjacent to Grey's desk, always there but never used, appeared suspect. Why have it if you never put your feet up? And he didn't. The top of it wasn't soiled or marred with indents from rested heels. She shifted it aside. It shielded nothing save the kickplate below his bookcase. She tested. One of the segments was loose. Pried free with an Inukshuk letter opener, she reached inside the dark space. Her fingers found a mass of brittle paper. Sliding it out, she stared down at a police manual that must've been used when Grey himself was a rookie. Too hidden to disregard, curiosity called her to thumb through its aged pages. They wouldn't move. She pulled the thick manual apart. It had been cut out like a box. She emptied the contents onto the carpet and began wading through.

The case file on the man who murdered her mother had been buried, but not deeply enough.

A quick scan of the documents said the killer's psychosis was far worse than she'd imagined. Chief of police, herald as a hero. This was what Grey hid from her. Damning evidence in the truest sense. Most disturbing was his family status. Husband. Father.

Flipping through photos of his ravaged victims made it impossible to reconcile the man and the monster. His wife "died at home surrounded by loved ones." Or so said the copy of her funeral announcement. Jade imagined the suffering the woman endured knowing she was leaving an unprotected child behind. The degree of torture he inflicted on his prey indicated a compulsion that defied containment. No way the abuse didn't saturate his home life. Jade witnessed it firsthand through the cabinet doors years earlier.

She rummaged through seeking information on the child, pushing down the mounting surge of betrayal.

Romann Carroll was away at boarding school when his father was gunned down. A picture, a surveillance photo, from the funeral showed the young man, head bent over his father's grave. Something about him was familiar, but then he was her age, her era. There was little mention of the name again. She'd do a thorough search of school and medical records from home.

The next batch of photos stalled her breath. They were of her and the cupboard she'd been found inside after her mom's murder, so young and little. The reality was jarring. Her adult eyes recognize the child who couldn't have saved her mother. The reason Carroll didn't suspect Carmichael's little girl was hiding was because she'd slid a boxed tower of china in front of the buffet door for it to appear unsuspicious before he walked in. There would've been no silent exit. An element of surprise, but then what? With the eyes of a seasoned detective, Jade knew the answer. Two victims instead of one.

The boxed china being moved aside was the shifting sound she heard before Grey retrieved her from her hiding place. He saw her mother's efforts, even at her death, to shield her daughter. Then he accepted that same protective role. She stared at the aged photo, seeing her own eyes staring back from the crack between the cabinet doors.

Carroll left the door to their home ajar. A neighbor discovered the body or ventured in far enough to see blood and call police. He didn't search for Jade or even call out to her. He kept ringing the doorbell for what seemed an eternity, anonymous and threatening. Jade hated the sound to this day.

Eventually police flooded the house. Grey removed her from hiding after hearing her soft cries. She couldn't hold them any longer. He'd been her hero. As wrong as his silence was, it was in protection of her and many others. The thought made her take stock of her surroundings. Anger surged, scorching through her veins. Carroll started a war that had been reborn in the Redeemer. She would end it.

Turning her face from the toxic photos, she noticed a framed picture, half hidden behind a Bigfoot statute, a team gag gift, Grey proudly displayed left of his desk. In it, they celebrated her graduation from the academy. She'd return the dignity this bastard had taken from him. There'd be consequence for his silence later, in her experience there always was. Now, she needed to get the hell out of his office.

Heavy footsteps approaching said she wasn't leaving as gracefully as she'd arrived. She shoved the documents back inside the mock manual, tossed it into hiding, slammed the kickplate into place, returned the stool, and slid between the door and Grey's old-fashioned coat rack seconds before he stomped in.

Judging by his gait and the way he pitched things onto his desk, he was in a mood. She debated what was worse, him finding her hiding behind his door or stooping to this level in the first place. The profanity coloring his language confirmed it'd be a bad day to be discovered violating his private space.

Staring through the crack by the doorjamb, his shadow paced the room. It'd veer close then jut off in the opposite direction. He held a file. Afraid her labored breathing would give her away, she forced a calm even flow while desperately seeking a viable explanation for being there. Nothing brilliant forthcoming.

Something stole his attention. The pacing stopped. He was beyond her field of view. Without realizing it, she leaned into the crack. Her foot nudged the door. It creaked. She froze. His shadow loomed in the background when Amy strolled by.

"Cap, the list of names. You left it on Tex' desk." Amy disappeared from view into the room, papers shuffled, and she walked back out.

For a fraction of a second, as Amy crossed the threshold, Jade was certain she made eye contact. Amy didn't flinch, pause, or alter her stride. Either she couldn't see Jade through the dark crack, or she was the smoothest detective on the force.

From out in the hall, Amy said, "You should go back, I'm sure your order's ready. A couple of us are headed over. You need to eat. You're getting grumpy."

"Way past," Grey said. "Can't keep track of my own head."

Amy laughed. "You're assuming it's still there. You know what they say about assumptions."

"Haha, smart-ass. I'm coming." Grey followed Amy out, a file in hand.

Jade exhaled, listened for their footsteps to recede, then crept around the corner and watched their backs disappear into the stairwell. Grey hated elevators. She eyed the place where she'd left the footstool. Grey had moved it. As tempting as it was, she fought the urge to pry into the manual a second time. She sent a text to Jackson and Kane: "On my way. Found a skeleton. Have to talk." When the hall cleared, she made her exit.

On the second floor, she walked into a productive screaming match in the violent crimes draft room.

"…there's not a damn thing we can do until morning. Even then, we're betting on unearthing ancient church records—" Jackson was propped on the edge of his chair near their crime scene board. Kane was pacing in front of him.

"Yeah, the nun, Sister Burr-in-my—"

"Not the nun thing again." Jackson dropped his head into his hands.

"Lives are in the balance here. All things being holy, I doubt St. Peter gives a damn how much shuteye she's had. He may have reservations recommending the Almighty marry a woman who let people drop dead over beauty sleep."

Jade crossed the room and stood at the side, out of direct aim. "What are you two squabbling over?"

Jackson came up for air. "If the link between all his victims is group therapy. Should we be looking at clergy?"

"Our guy's not a priest." Kane continued his trek, his pace slowing as he spoke.

"No. He's a sadist, not a priest," Jade agreed.

"He's making them pay for their sins," Jackson said. "You can't deny the religious overtones."

Jade stepped nearer the board. She tapped every crime scene. "The killing is too personal. There's something deeper at play here. I'd say if anything, this guy suffered because of religion. He's using it and ridiculing it simultaneously."

Kane followed her pattern, scanning the photos. "Religion is his weapon of choice. He doesn't respect it."

Jade planted herself on the edge of a desk, exhaustion setting in. Her migraine made a triumphant return. The overheads burst to blinding wattage that made her squint.

Kane came close, put a hand over hers, and whispered, "You okay?"

"Headache." Jade hadn't looked up, fearing the pain of movement.

"No, I meant after the skeleton. Grey told me hours before your discovery. Gave me the file on the first monster. I was ready to…this is the first we've—"

She met his gaze. "I get it. I'm pissed. I'll deal with him, but we're in too deep for that right now. He risked everything for us to have that knowledge."

Jackson rose, came within inches of the first crime scene pictures, then swung around like he'd been shoulder smacked by a bull. "Who sinned against this guy?"

"What?" Jade echoed Kane, both jolted out of their conversation.

"Nikki said her crime was committed when she was young. Leigh's profile included him building to an ultimate goal, a statement if you will. Whoever wronged him did so years ago. His final victim has direct connections, and there's a bull's-eye on one of us."

"We all have past sins, but none of us are responsible for the death of a child," Kane said.

Jade walked over to the information on Sara Keller. "She is. Who knows how many children died in her ward."

Kane closed the distance. "Sara Keller lost children under her care, but she wasn't a doctor a decade ago."

"What made her become one?" Jackson asked.

"And we're back where we started," Kane said. "The motivation for all the high-powered, philanthropic careers."

"No. We're close," Jade said.

"We'd be closer if the damn nun didn't make us schedule an appointment," Kane ranted on.

"Yes," Jackson said. "We can all blame the nun. Were you forced to go to Sunday school?"

"Only half Black, blond student." Kane ruffled his hair and collapsed in the nearest chair.

Jackson grinned. "Must've been fun."

"A blast."

"We'll hit the church tomorrow," Jackson said.

Kane smiled at Jackson's play of words. "And where does that leave Leigh tonight?"

Jade stared at the corpses on the board, flashes of her mother's bloody china staining her vision. "In Hell, purgatory at best."

THIRTY-FIVE

"How are things with your mother?" Max knew there was more than one root cause for his patient Jacob's behavior. He'd acted out at school earlier that day, threatening a female teacher who exhibited sympathy for his mother, and been suspended. Max fit him in at the request of his dad, a patient and officer out on extended leave due to an unfortunate accident while undercover in the narcotics division.

"Haven't seen her much, so it's been good." Jacob leaned forward, loosening a mass of blond waves to shelter his face in adolescent mystery.

"She's in treatment?"

"She's not an alcoholic, but she got a free pass to a sanitarium." Jacob's hands clenched.

"You don't want her to find help?"

"Help? If it wasn't for her, Dad wouldn't have been banking all the hours in the first place."

"In the end, your mother's responsible for the downfall of your family?"

"She started it, didn't she?" Their session was ending. Jacob located his cell phone on the shelf nearest the door. Stood, reclaimed it, then motioned to the clock. "She started it after she had me."

"It started long before then, Jacob." Max wanted to stop him, tell him his parents loved him, but those answers had to be discovered not given.

Max didn't expect to have a breakthrough with this kid. His parents forced him into treatment. His father had worked undercover in the narcotics division for four years. A car accident and addiction put him back home, the catalyst of decline for his family.

The door closed behind Jacob. It'd take time. Max was confident he could reach him. He stopped the recording, jotted down a few cursory notes, and swiveled his chair to face the window.

Night suffocated daylight with black pillows banded around her so tightly no trace of sky survived in Shadow Hook. Its grip as inescapable as the past deeds of men. Better to make peace with than war against an all-consuming darkness.

Broken families, devastated children, the world was corrupt. There were a chosen few warriors like Jade. Raging against evil, offering their lives in the hope of illumination even if they themselves had done nothing whatsoever to contribute to the shadows.

Max turned his attention to the file he'd concealed in a saddleback portfolio on his desk. Inside, he referred to Leigh's case assessment. Her voice echoed in his head as he read. The pattern of the abductions, their increased frequency, and the precision of the Unsub led her to believe the victims were a rite of passage to his true target—Jade or one of the police detectives involved. Of particular interest, his most recent activities showed an increase in risk. *It was as if*, she had written, *he'd located his primary prey and was closing in for the kill.*

Max had questions. He couldn't ignore the knot in his chest telling him Jade's days were numbered. Nor erase Detective Kane's vehement accusations from repeating in his mind. Worse still, the distinct sense that the cure for all of it was in front of them, and they'd missed it. Where the hell was Leigh? Why hadn't she answered his messages? She was nothing if not professional, meticulous, and deliberate. If she was avoiding him, there had to be a damn good…

Max lunged for his desk phone, knocking the classified file into his trash bin. He dialed the station and demanded to connect to Detective Kolter.

"It's imperative I speak with him immediately."

Twisted in the heap of papers, halfway into the garbage can, a profile headshot of Rachel Leigh stared back at him. A series of clicks alerted him to being transferred to a secondary location. Part of him wanted to hope Kane was way ahead of him.

"Detective Kane Kol—"

"Kane, it's Max. I've been texting Rachel and can't—" His voice held sufficient panic to hasten honesty.

"I know, Max. I called you earlier. You were in a late session. She's been missing since—"

"She's his mother." Max was stepping on file documents. They crunched beneath his feet.

"What? Say that again," Kane called out to Jackson, who must've been nearby.

"Rachel Leigh is the Redeemer's mother! I'm sure of it."

"She said she never had kids." Kane's voice reflected the rush of devastating clarity. "Why the hell weren't—"

"Don't waste time being angry. She swore me to secrecy decades ago. Frankly, I'd forgotten until one of my patients said something that jogged my memory. I was reading her profile. The way the case is laid out. It's textbook. Enticing her to the answer like bait. It was designed to. That's when I thought of it. He pulled all of us in knowing it would lead directly to her. It's not Jade. You were right. Leigh's the target she warned us about!"

"Christ, Max, she's been missing for two days. He's had her for two damn days." Sadness streamed through the line and bonded the men in a way Max would've deemed impossible hours earlier.

"She got pregnant in high school, Kane." Max couldn't slow the quickening in his speech. "She was just sixteen. Her father—"

"The judge," Kane clarified.

"He sent her away to have the baby to avoid family embarrassment. She returned two semesters later more beautiful than ever. They explained it away saying she'd been a foreign exchange student. She came back fluent in French with excessive knowledge of Paris."

"She gave the child up for adoption?" Kane's tone reflected his support of Max's conclusions.

"She must've. I don't even know if she actually left the country, or if that was part of the lie." Defeat forced Max to exhale.

"It doesn't explain why he'd want her dead now. Why the rage?" Kane's struggle for truth was palpable.

"Their complete abolishment of his existence might be the trigger.

Combine that and what she does for a living. Being the object of her analysis was his way of guaranteeing her attention."

"Well, he certainly has mine." The pissed off cop tone was back in Kane's voice, and for the first time, Max welcomed it.

"I've read her profile back to front. You don't have much time. The obsession will be too great for him to keep her alive long. If he's waited a lifetime for revenge, there won't be much she can say to stop him."

Max scanned the ceiling for answers. When he glanced down, he realized he'd been pacing the distance surrounding his desk with crumpled papers crushed on the bottom of his shoes. Panicked, he pulled the sheets from his soles, carefully smoothing them on his desk, aware they may be the last notes Rachel would ever make.

"Max, don't take this the wrong way. You referred Rachel to us. Said she was the best. If anyone can hold him off—"

"If you can't find her soon, I'll spend the rest of my days knowing I got her killed."

"Careful, Max. You're sounding like one of us." The compassion in Kane's voice, given at a time when he'd every right to stick the knife in and turn, made Max regret their history and its animosity. "Any indication that Leigh ever entertained the idea—"

"No. That's the thing. She'll keep her composure, but for how long after she finds out the serial killer who captured her is her son? I mean, when she knows she made him…"

"Max, I need you to think carefully back to Rachel's absence. You knew her, knew her family. Where would they have turned for help?" Kane concealed it well, but Max read the underlying dread in his voice. He was linking dangerous pieces together.

A silence passed between them. They were going to lose her.

"Was the family dedicated?" Kane asked. "Were they devout?"

"Yes." Max shifted from smoothing pages to smoothing his hair and re-sorting what could be the last sheets of Leigh's knowledge ever penned.

"Our Lady of Peace?"

Max thought for a second. "Yes. How'd you—"

"I'll call you back when I have more. I might have a way to find this bastard."

"Kane?" Max couldn't let him hang up. "I'm sorry for discouraging your involvement. You know, Jade. It's…I—"

"I know, Max. You love her."

"Not like that," Max clarified.

"You mean not like me." Kane's soul was bare, and Max could see it for the first time as Jade had all along, true, brave and wide open to be crushed. "I'll call. Soon."

The line went dead. Max held the receiver, the dial tone resonating. He stared at the chessboard sitting on his desk. In his mind's eye a man's hand captured the queen, clenched her in an unforgiving grasp, and crushed her until she exploded into dust. And he'd put her in the game with an opponent that made amateurs of them all.

THIRTY-SIX

Leigh's mind swirled down a dark vortex, flailing at walls sheathed and polished in dread. The clarity that the former police chief, the serial killer responsible for Jade's mother's murder, was the Redeemer's father left prospects for her survival in rapid decline. Damage too deep to affect. Mass blood loss sealed her fate. He'd made her so cold. She'd fight until she couldn't draw breath.

Her profile hit the mark. He *was* connected to the case involving Jade's mother's murder. She suspected a significant link. Mentor. Disciple. Quite possible. Father. Son. That was a stretch. She hadn't dug down far enough.

"I can see I've thrown you." His voice trickled in.

Her eyes wouldn't work. Perhaps the dimmed lights impeded sight, or she was shutting down inside.

"I know it's a lot to absorb." He pulled up a chair. Where did he get it? Must've brought it in while she was unconscious. She couldn't remember, even from seconds earlier.

"Truth is you haven't heard the half of it, my sordid past. Are you sure you want to know all the gory details?"

She didn't. Suddenly, the thought of hearing him reciting his deadly deeds sent the spinning in her head into hyperdrive. She couldn't stomach it, though she had nothing left to hurl.

"You still in there?"

"Yes." The faintness of her voice came as a shock. "I want to hear. I'd be grateful for the chance to understand. You said he was your father, your biological father? You were raised by him?"

The Redeemer bent down, scooped an item from the floor beyond her view, and answered without glancing up. "No. He never raised anyone. I was raised by nannies, then boarding schools, the best boarding schools. Odd how he insisted on that."

"Not...really. If he intended on grooming you for a certain life-style...developing your superior intellect and shielding you from nega-tive influence, outside his own, it'd seem logical." Where logic failed was expecting her to hold any kind of an intelligent conversation while strung up like a rag doll with every major artery tapped and prepped for siphoning. What she'd give for Jade or Kane to burst through the door.

"What are you thinking?" He'd glanced up and followed her squint to the sealed exit.

"I was thinking about Detective Carmichael." Stay close to the truth. If he perceives a lie, it's over.

"She won't save you." He spoke with disheartening conviction.

"Why won't she?" Leigh clung to the hope it was possible.

"You don't believe me?" The glint in his eyes when they met hers almost scared her from her path of inquiry.

"No, it's not that. I was thinking how both your lives were destroyed...by the same man."

"Mine first." He fiddled with papers on the floor. She listened to the soft slide of him arranging them.

"Her mother died by your father's hands. Didn't yours too? I read —" Pain made her flinch. More pain stopped her breath. "The funeral announcement you left out said your mother died at home."

He stared into her eyes with an intensity far beyond intrusive discomfort. He searched her soul. For what, she didn't know. She held his gaze, then said, "I'm sorry for what you endured. You're an intelli-gent man, highly accomplished, with obvious attributes other men would envy. You didn't deserve—"

"I was glad to be rid of her, his wife." His voice dipped an octave. "She wasn't my mother."

Leigh fought to put the pieces into place. He'd threatened her earlier, cursing his mother. Carroll and his wife were married long before his son was born. She'd done the math. The obvious eluded her.

A glance at the discoloration of her feet was explanation enough for the lack of clarity.

"Could you put me down? For a short while. I don't think can stay conscious much longer…" Her words were blended, soggy, and slow. "I understand your mother failed you terribly, or you wouldn't have ended up—"

He sprang from his chair, driven by either her slurred speech or the discoloring of her limbs. His arms slid under her, raising her up to disengage the hooks she was suspended by. It wasn't enough. He couldn't get her free. He came up beneath her, her head sunk into his broad shoulder, their faces touching.

"No good mother would ever abandon her baby to the arms of a monster." Delusion was setting in. His face appeared beautiful, smooth skin, bright oceanic eyes like hers when she was young and full of life.

"Then why did you?" He moved, fast and strong. Chains rattled, clamps snapped, and lengths of tubing swung overhead.

What had he said? Asking again meant she hadn't been paying attention. "Pardon? I couldn't hear you over the chains."

"I said…" He released a clamp. She collapsed into his arms. Heavy and empty at the same time, her limbs hung limp. His breath was warm on her ear as he spoke. "Then why did you?"

Down a long tunnel of detachment, the words found their mark. She gasped, fought for one clear glimpse of him, and locked her gaze with his as he carried her.

"Couldn't be." She was fading fast. "I was sixteen. Raped. They never caught—"

"Yes. Yes, they did. Shot him dead. Hid their mess, but not before he served a lifetime of hell on me. And you, you…" He set her on a bed that materialized as the chair had as his voice cracked and dipped. "You and your father let him adopt me."

In a death spiral of realization, his deeds became hers, her body convulsed, her senses fell numb, and the room melted black. She'd made him…so cold.

She couldn't die now. Not this way. He hovered over her wilted body. Stripped, bloodied, and depleted. He didn't want her to die. Not yet. Perhaps not at all. He'd dreamed of killing her forever, since early childhood, since his weapons training, and the complete annihilation of his innocence, his purity, his hope. He'd been told she'd abandoned him, the darkest version of the truth. Later, he'd unearthed details of the adoption in church records, never relying on the words of the sadist who blamed her for his existence.

Raped? Why hadn't he thought of that? It was true to Carroll's nature. He was a product of the damned. Retribution guaranteed his redemption, his freedom, but not anymore. He couldn't even take pleasure in killing her. She hadn't known who raped her. Impregnated her.

He kneeled beside her, checked her pulse, then flew to the outer room. He gathered the necessary transfusion equipment, set it up, checked the clock, and began the process of resuscitating his mother.

He'd acquired the finest ER room staples through a deliberately botched shipping order from a now defunct company to an overseas hospital.

Patience had been a matter of survival. Outsmart. Outlast. Outmaneuver. He'd learned it well.

His medical training came from assisting emergency staff at every catastrophic disaster he could slip into under the radar of suspicion abroad. No one cared why you were there to help after a tsunami hit just that you were capable.

He'd learned from the best. They moved fast and with a precision that put other high paid surgeons to shame. Though his training was basic, it afforded him the knowledge to control life and death.

Rachel Leigh was precariously hanging between the two when he set her IV drip and began re-administrating her blood.

Flashes of her smoothing her skirt, her fear of being raped, he'd missed it. The church medical documents lay piled on the floor by the suspension grid.

He checked her carefully, removed the feed lines, cleaning and sealing them with cotton bandages. Her skin was cold. He activated a heating blanket and laid it over her.

Information within the documents had been committed to memory. Still, he searched specific health records. There was zero indication of the pregnancy being caused by rape. No bruising, tearing, or signs of force. No suspicion of foul play whatsoever. The judge had covered all traces of the truth. He must've taken her somewhere else for initial treatment and waited until she'd healed.

Smart. Protective. Cruel. It ran in the family. His family. His blood, hers.

Why cover the tracks with such vehemence? Did he know who raped her?

Blood trickled down his arm. His laceration was seeping. Nikki. He'd left a crumb behind. One the cops would gobble up. They'd have her protected like a crown jewel. No easy way to get to her now, too risky. He'd wait. Patience. His saving grace was her history of depression and suicidal tendency that cast doubt on anything she said.

At his desk, he set down the documents and tore the protective patch off his forearm. Two areas had ripped open during his rescue efforts. While dabbing them clean, he glanced into the adjoining room. The sliding wall remained open to ensure a sightline to Rachel. No change. He opened a drawer, selected medical glue, and poured it over the split in his skin. He cinched the area until it tightened, put on a new bandage, and returned to his notebook.

Rachel would wake up. He knew precisely how far down the ladder to Hell one could descend and still crawl back out. He'd done it so many times as a boy, smaller even than her. Years of orchestrating their reunion, the sacrifices made, demanded he have answers. All of them. Francis Carroll, the demon, had been gunned down before he was allowed to do the deed himself. That left the judge, the other man who damned him to Hell. He would carry the weight of punishment for both.

A few keystrokes on his computer and a live feed opened with crystal clarity. The judge wasn't doing well. When Rachel regained consciousness, she'd see her son's version of sentencing.

THIRTY-SEVEN

Kane left the cabin's front door ajar, turned on the burner for tea passing through the kitchen, and headed to the bedroom to find a clean shirt. He returned half-dressed to find boiling water spilling from the kettle's spout.

"What are you doing?" Jackson stood in the threshold of the cabin's kitchen, leaning against the counter, staring at Kane.

"Haven't made friends with this stovetop version Jade bought. I ignore it until it boils dry, and it melts the stain off my cabinets out of spite."

"Kettles aren't spiteful."

"This one is."

"Is that herbal tea?" Worry furrowed Jackson's brow.

Kane nodded. "Hate it, it's that Irish mum thing. Love black, hate herbal."

"Then why—"

"I'm testing different kinds to find one I don't detest."

"Terrific." Jackson scanned the open shelf, struck by the vast loose-leaf variety. "How many have you—"

"Seventeen. Mango spice? That's manky." Kane wiped the sweat beads off the wood surface above the kettle, inspecting it for clouding. "An alternative to caffeine. Anything to keep me awake without fraying my nerves. Health, you know? Want to be around in the future."

Jackson sauntered over, set down two tall takeout cups of Kona coffee that had been concealed behind his back, scooped the box off the counter, and read it out. "Blueberry, vanilla bean? Y'all drinking kids' ice cream flavors thinking it's a remedy for sleep deprivation. Drink the coffee. Why does Max think Leigh is our guy's mother?"

Kane eyed the coffee. "The timing fits. Problem is, it does little to narrow down who he is. Doesn't give us a name."

"What about facial recognition? What are they doing?"

Kane stared bitterly at the tea. "I sent Francis Carroll's photo in with Leigh's to a buddy at Langley. He runs them through a computer program that blends the two for a possible child outcome aging them into adulthood."

"That's sick." Jackson flipped the protector off his coffee and gulped it. "I miss the heyday of the rotary phone."

Kane grabbed the kettle, burned his palm on the stainless-steel handle, and cursed as it dropped back to the stove. "You weren't around for rotary phones."

"Wish I was—simpler times."

Kane snatched up the coffee Jackson brought him. "It's a long shot. If there's a chance one of us laid eyes on this guy, I want to know."

"Hey, I should send them a photo of you and Jade. See what the Black dude with blond hair and hot stuff makes." Jackson smirked. "You know your kids are getting those green eyes either way."

"Ha. Ha. You're funny when you haven't slept. If we leave now, we can hit a drive through on the way to the church." Kane's caffeine imbalance put him on edge.

"Don't think the nuns will appreciate us smelling up their rectory with takeout."

"Far less offensive than me going off on them in a low-blood sugar rant."

"You do that?" Jackson flashed a pirate grin, started his truck with the button on his fob, and headed for the door staring down the stainless-steel enemy on his way past the stove. "Facial blending and aging, damn, and I was fixin' to start dating."

"We're fossils." Kane threw his jacket on, shaking his scalded hand.

"Where's Jade at?" Jackson glanced back before jumping in the driver's side.

Kane locked up the cabin. "Checking out a lead on Leigh's history. Left before I got in."

"Ships passing in the—"

Kane toasted Jackson with his coffee, then said, "Not for long. I can handle it. I'm playing the long game."

"Aren't we all? Your working theory?"

Kane jumped in. "Max thinks our Unsub brought all of us into this, targeted victims in Shadow, knowing eventually it'd lead to his mother's involvement." Kane stared out the window searching for somewhere to eat as they drove. "He must've found out who she was shortly after Carroll's death. Gave him time to plan."

"All of us, the victims, pawns played to capture the queen?"

Kane pointed to an advertisement for a nearby breakfast deli.

Jackson nodded. "They're not open until eight. You gonna bang on the door, flash your weapon?"

"That approach hasn't worked well historically for us Black dudes."

"Damn. I keep forgetting you're Black. It's the hair, throws it all off."

"I love you, Tex. You know that?"

"I do. Give 'em hell."

"Whatever it takes."

A few miles down the road, Jackson pulled in. Kane threw off his seat belt and jumped out before the truck fully stopped. "The guy's son knows us pretty well. He'll open up."

"Ah, pulling in favors."

"Small towns have benefits. Breakfast burrito?"

"Hot sauce," Jackson ordered as the door closed.

Seven minutes after he'd rapped on the front door, Kane slid back into the truck. He set two containers between them. "Been thinking, this guy blames Leigh. She gave him up for adoption, abandoned him, whatever. His victims were all taken out before they could start a family. No right to procreation. You saw the Lainey woman's body. Posed the same as Jade's mother's. Why? What does she have to do with this?"

Jackson adjusted the heater and pulled out. "It certainly brought Leigh onboard. There's also the sexual element. Chances are he slept with all the women he killed. What's that?"

Kane opened the container to his breakfast. The burrito was oozing sauce, cheese, and egg everywhere. No way to eat without wearing it. Jackson averted his stare from the road long enough to see the slop and laugh. "No worries, they'll serve homemade holy muffins to sweeten up bitter souls."

"That's me, sour as ever." Kane closed the container lid and swallowed the last of his coffee.

His stomach was protesting when they rounded the corner to Our Lady of Peace.

Inside, they were greeted and asked to wait in the vestibule while Sister Bethany was summoned. Jackson planted himself on the bench seat. Kane milled about, checking out display cases, starving.

"You in the market for a new rosary?" Jackson whispered.

Kane hesitated, his eyes drawn to the hanging chains by Jackson's comment. "Yes. We are. One exactly like that." He pointed to the top corner of a particular case. His eager tone of voice beckoned Jackson from his seat. Together they stared at a chain of pale pink prayer beads.

"Eva Summers." They spoke the Redeemer's first known victim's name in unison. They had Amy scour every religious jeweler on the books. This tiny special order church display had flown beneath the radar, not public. Sales came solely from parish members.

"How'd we miss that?" Kane shook his head, frustration refusing to loosen its grip.

"Junkies aren't usually devout." Jackson locked eyes. "We know now."

"Knowing Eva Summers' religious commitment back then could have saved lives. If that asshole shrink had opened his mouth." Kane's anger refueled. He missed the soft footsteps behind them.

"No one knew she worshipped here," Sister Bethany said. "Not even her family. It was safer for her that way. I'd prefer if you didn't curse inside."

"Sister Bethany?" Kane's expression failed to conceal his embarrassment. He hadn't expected the nun to be pretty, much less, stunning. Didn't expect to be caught swearing either.

"Call me Beth." She tucked a stray piece of strawberry-blonde hair under her habit and offered her hand. "We can speak in my office."

"Are you the church liaison for these matters, ma'am?" Jackson asked.

"Well, I suppose I'm a public relations adviser and an administrator in one. I knew Eva personally and many others in our group counseling sessions. We thought it best I meet with you."

Beth led them down a narrow hall to an end office on the left with large bright windows and a view of the courtyard. The other four offices were empty. "How did you know them?" Kane asked. "No offense, but you're too young to have—"

"Thank you. I am. I sat in on some of the sessions. I struggled with similar demons at the time. It's very disheartening, how Eva left us."

Jackson jumped in. "So she quit?"

"Died," Beth corrected, then drifted silently behind her desk and sat, hands folded before her.

Kane sat across from her slightly distracted. "We need a list of attendees."

"That's confidential, I'm afraid—"

"You should be," Kane said, the nice nun realization fading. "Most of the women on that list have been murdered. Anyone still alive won't be for long if we don't get ahead of the killer, Eva's killer. Sister, confidentially, they're being exterminated by someone who had access."

"You're not suggesting—" Her hands remained folded, their grip intensified.

"Heck no, we're not." Jackson claimed a chair near the door and leaned in. "We don't believe anyone inside the church is at fault. A contributor, someone with access, a man willing to violate your trust."

"Can you think of anyone who might fit that category?" Kane stared around the room, taking in the environment where this beautiful nun chose to hide away from the world. As it was, he didn't blame her.

"I wish I could produce a short list of names, but the truth is you'd have to search through the entire congregation and many more."

"We'll take any place to start," Kane said, staring at Jackson.

"We have a strong volunteer program. All our families are involved in some capacity. We don't make public our attendees' names, we have high-profile members who appreciate our discretion, a few in law enforcement."

The wind was picking up. A large tree branch beyond the window swayed then slapped the outer brick. "Rachel Leigh," Kane said. "Does Dr. Leigh's—"

"Yes. Her family have been members for many years, long before I arrived."

"Francis Carroll?" Jackson asked. If he hadn't, Kane would've.

"Yes. The Carroll family attended regularly until Mrs. Carroll fell ill, right before Chief Carroll was killed in the line of duty. We figured the service was held in the city to accommodate the mass of mourners."

Kane's stomach shifted from a low growl to disgruntled twisting. They'd come to the right place. "Were the two families friendly? You ever see them together?"

"Never noticed the women socializing. The men talked." Sister Beth shifted in her seat, settling her delicate hands in her lap. "They sat in different pews. Never came in together. There were rumors that the daughter and mother distrusted Chief Carroll."

"Ever hear why?" Kane asked.

Beth sat silent for a minute, then chose her words carefully. "I was very young when I came here, damaged. I've all but forgotten much of my life before. It's for the best. I remember him, though. Chief Carroll. There was a discomfort in his presence. I assumed it came with the title. Perhaps it was more. His son knew Eva."

"The chief's son?" Jackson flashed a glance at Kane that said they'd hit pay dirt.

"Yes, Romann Carroll. She admitted her feelings for him after group one night. Said she ran into him quite by chance many years after his parents' death. They had a lot in common. He picked her up a few times."

"Did you ever see him? Later in life." Kane felt the bait take, finally they had a line.

"He always waited in his car in the parking lot. The windows were tinted. I wanted to see him because Eva spoke so highly of him. I was curious, how he had matured."

"What kind of car?" Kane asked.

"A sedan. I'm not good with models. An expensive car."

"Would the church have any photographs of Chief Carroll and his family on hand?" They needed a visual to blow away the anonymity of Romann Carroll. The Redeemer had gained a name. Now they needed a face.

"Yes. I'm sure I could find one. It may take a little time." She stared at her hands, exposing long dark eyelashes.

"I could sit still for that," Jackson offered.

The nun eyed him strangely.

"Sister Rachel Leigh was abducted two days ago. She may not have much time left." Kane broke protocol.

Jackson leaned closer to Sister Beth's desk. "We're close. With your help, we may stop her from sharing Eva's fate."

"The Redeemer has her?" Beth's composure ruffled. "Right now? And you think—"

"We've said too much already," Kane cautioned. "The pictures?"

"They're in the storeroom in a box. We quit displaying them when our numbers increased, about seven years ago. He'd be young in them. We'll have to dig them out."

"I'm from Texas, Sister. We've made fortunes digging." Jackson stood and motioned for Beth to lead the way.

Kane stood and waited for her to pass him to follow behind. As she drifted between the desk and him, he asked, "The group sessions? Who were they for specifically?"

Beth paused inches from him. A waft of lavender scented the air around her. "Guilt counseling. For those whose recklessness led to the death of our most innocent."

"Everyone in the group killed a child?" Kane wore his shock.

"Yes." Beth's eyes held a glistening regret. She'd "shared the same demons as Eva."

"Why was Eva there?" Kane asked.

"Eva? She was the driver responsible for an accident. Her sister and others died on impact. There was speculation a baby was also lost. She never spoke of it in explicit detail, too difficult. Her own family couldn't find forgiveness."

Kane couldn't speak. He stood, hovering over Beth, images of broken children clouding his vision.

"I'm sorry, Detective...we didn't meet sooner. I'll pray for Rachel." Kane had been wrong about the Sister, wrong about Eva, and the church. He hoped he was wrong about the timeline on Rachel's life too.

Jackson waited for Beth to take the corner. He leaned back. "Romann Carroll. Jade's mother. This guy is slicker than a slop jar."

Kane whispered back, "Makes sense. Knowing who he is compounds the suffering." Jackson's brow creased. "He was groomed from birth. More nooses in his family tree than you can shake a stick at."

Kane agreed. "The worst kind of enemy, like a soldier. He was cultivated to kill."

Jackson shook his head, then said, "Wonder if his mother knows."

Kane checked his watch. "By now, I'm afraid she does."

THIRTY-EIGHT

Rachel wanted to die, or at least a part of her did. She knew she was out of danger the second her eyes made out the hazy image of Detective Jade Carmichael sitting on the chair adjacent to the hospital bed. Others hadn't been so lucky.

Life shed any quaint illusion that sustained her before. Reality, raw, ugly, and unforgiving, drained her defenses as surely as her son had her blood. She'd live, but with much regret. Graphic images of the women her son ravaged would haunt her until the day she joined them.

No room for mistakes. She'd used up her share. She yearned to relay every detail of her captivity, give the team a complete template to act from. And she had to know how they found her, who rescued her, and what happened to her son.

She couldn't will her body to move or her mouth to speak. No voice at a time when she needed to scream, had earned the right to. She hadn't said so many things she needed to voice. Sorry she gave her son away, sorry she hadn't searched the world for him when she became independent, sorry for every pain he'd suffered and those he'd suffered upon others. Too often it was the case, deep words that earned volume never heard beneath endless surface noise.

Detective Carmichael sensed her frustration. Her voice sounded hollow, echoing from a distant place. "Sleep," she said.

Drifting out, Rachel's focus found the ceiling. She couldn't help wondering where the drop panels were, why no track lighting? Must be a private facility. Her father would've insisted. The roof was beautiful, coffered in heavy reclaimed wood.

A doctor adjusted a device bedside. Eyelids too heavy to push open fully offered mere glimpses of a white-sleeved man's arm, raised overhead.

"Quite an ordeal you've been through." His voice was fuzzy, static.

Rachel forced her eyes downward, desperate for visual confirmation her limbs remained intact and not lost to amputation. The memory of their pasty discoloration brought a wave of terror. Covered by a blanket, she assesses the outline of legs, feet, arms, and hands.

She'd been rescued in time. Before he did irreversible damage.

"Thank Jade." The effort of the words made her dizzy.

"Thank Jade for what?" the doctor asked. He held a bottle of something, waves of white slosh inside it.

"For coming," she whispered.

The glass shattered. Her body jerked, and she was gone again. Launched into an unconscious, unforgiving oblivion. Cast into a replayed version of the hell she'd endured. Truths inside the nightmare were tattooed, seared into the halls of her mind. Conclusions she couldn't reach while awake, burned with clarity.

Her father had arranged for the adoption of her infant son while she was sent away to rehabilitate from the ordeal, as he'd called it. She never held him. She'd wanted to meet the potential parents, to be involved in the process, and know he'd gone to a loving home. Her father forbade it. Shadow Hook was too small a town. Her identity could never be revealed.

He'd failed to mention *he* knew the parents, that her son would be kept close, in the same county, at the same church. She'd seen him every Sunday for years and never known he was hers.

A satisfaction bestowed on her rapist, her attacker. To see her every week, stare at her down the pew, laughing at the reversal of justice. Her own father, condoning his attack because he didn't know who raped her, brought his child into the world and back into his vicious hands, while she sat compliant inches away and oblivious to it all.

Violation at its finest.

Her father's actions, born of a hunger to bury all evidence of the objectionable thereby erasing it, damned many. Too many.

She loved him. He thought he'd protected her future. Francis

Carroll was a respected police chief, which was all her father knew. He was wrong. She hadn't known either, until now. Her father thought he could keep an eye on the boy, watch him grow and conceal he was his grandfather. And remain the picture of propriety.

Not anymore.

In high definition, he appeared before her. Beaten and bloody, tortured in a dark place, almost unrecognizable. Minutes drifted before she realized she was awake not dreaming. Seeing a live feed on screen on the wall ahead. The hospital vanished. And in the chair beside her a monster slept. No Jade.

A monster who brought her father, the judge, to his knees.

Rachel wouldn't survive, couldn't survive anymore and yet—

"You thought it was over, didn't you?" Romann Carroll spoke with his eyes closed. "You were hallucinating, talking to Jade of all people. That's when I knew you were really gone. Glad you're back."

Rachel stared at the chair as he stood. She'd been so certain Jade had occupied it. She didn't want to take her eyes from it. As if Jade could materialize by force of will.

"He's seen better days." Romann sauntered to the screen. "Aren't you curious? Ask me how he's doing. He is your father. I thought you two were close."

Rachel didn't want to look but couldn't resist. She wished her vision hadn't been restored. Her father hung, with arms extended at an upward angle. He hovered almost on his knees, broken and unable to stand. A knife handle protruded from his right thigh, the blade embedded. The left side of his face was swollen and the eye socket flush. His other eye appeared adrift as if detached and sightless. She'd stared too long.

"His quality of life has diminished considerably. He's still breathing. Tough guy, runs in the blood."

"He didn't know." Rachel fought back the tears, the fear, the disgust. "He didn't know my attacker any more than I did. Carroll was a coward. He wore a mask. There were no physical details to narrow the field. He wasn't in the database for semen. My father believed you were given to the safest family he knew." Rachel turned her head away. "We didn't want this for you. We wanted the opposite."

"Then you should've been there!" Romann killed the feed. "That's the problem with parents today. Thinking good intentions relieve all responsibility for grievous outcomes for children. God places them in your care for a fucking reason!"

Rage permeated from him. She spoke softly. "I was a child when he raped me, when I carried you. I protected you for as long as I could. I wanted to keep you. I was too young to know how."

"What about now?" He slid a rolling stool close to the bed, leaned in inches from her face. "You want to keep me now?"

"No, not keep you. There'll always be a part of me that loves you, that wishes—"

"There's nothing left to love. He killed all of it. And I intended to serve the same on you because you let him. Now I'm not sure."

"Let your grandfather go," she whispered. "He arranged a new life for you where you could be proud of your name. He told me it wasn't fair to make you pay for what happened to me. He didn't want the stigma of being a product of rape to interfere with your right to a good life. That's why we gave you up. He loved you even then."

Romann shot up from his seat and paced across a bank of windows. He'd relocated her. Only the tops of trees were visible through the panes. Had to be on a second or third floor. Of what, she wasn't sure.

"Does he know who you are?" she asked.

"No. He hasn't seen my face."

"Then find a way to ask him without disclosing your identity," she tried.

"Why bother?"

"The damage is reversible. Don't let Carroll take anything else from you."

He didn't speak. He stormed across the room and out the door. She couldn't know if her words had saved her father or condemned him. Either way it bought her time.

The door bolt engaged, his footsteps recede, and then the distant sound of an elevator. Ten minutes passed without further noise from outside. She broke. Tears spilled down her face. She couldn't catch her breath or stop the tremors. Whatever her career had done to fortify her, it'd all been washed away. Truth, not her training, kept her alive.

Her limbs moved sluggishly, aching, resisting, still functional. She pushed back the blanket and inspected her battered body, grizzly but capable. When her feet hit the floor, the rest of her body followed, collapsing accordion style. Strength came in increments. She found her footing, a robe, and then determination.

He hadn't chained her to the bed. Peering out the window she knew why. The room was four floors above ground level. A straight drop from the window to a cement patio surrounding a pool. And empty, rolling land for miles. She'd never make it down alive.

She'd paid attention when he killed the camera feed to her father. With the remote in hand, she hit the buttons in reverse. Her father reappeared on the screen. She turned away and searched the room. The door was impenetrable, no surprise. Nothing for weapons. The cupboards held linens and scrubs. She slipped on pants, several sizes too large, rolled the waist to take up the excess length, and tightened the belt on her robe.

She removed a folded sheet, unfurled it in the air, then twisted and tugged at it testing its strength. Pain radiated through her limbs, shuddering into her core. Six sheets, minus knots and distance from the anchor. She did the math, opened the window and prayed her grip on life, sanity, and the sheet was no less than imagined.

Tying the material as tight as strength allowed, she watched the screen. Minutes passed. He hung, perhaps already dead, no movement that she could detect.

When all the sheets from the cupboard were linked, she tore the bed apart and added those. The cupboard doors were adorned with heavy iron handles. She selected two closest to the window and slid one end of her sheet rope through. Once secure, she glanced back at the screen.

Romann, the Redeemer, entered from the left side of the camera, his back in view. Her father collapsed to the floor as the apparatus suspending him released. His body flinched.

Alive.

She turned her attention to the window. She broke the screen out, her eyes followed it to the ground, shattering on impact. She threw out her rope, twisted it around her strongest arm, and scaled the empty pane. One glance down, and she was well aware it was a bad idea.

The alternative, however, was worse.

THIRTY-NINE

"Leigh's been in that animal's hands for days?" Grey's voice rang in Kane's ears and echoed down the corridor, diverting anyone on approach into an immediate retreat. "Which one of you wants to explain why the hell I'm just hearing this?"

Kane knew Grey would be pissed. The logic behind waiting for a solid lead shattered in the light of his discontent. "We didn't know until recently. Her assistant didn't file—"

"How recently?" Grey was seated at his desk, but his posture said he was primed to launch out of his chair.

"Less than a day, Cap," Jackson said.

"And you're sure she is his mother?" Grey directed the question at Jackson.

"Yes." Kane and Jackson spoke in unison.

Kane inched within spitting distance of the desk. "Everything says Romann Carroll's the Redeemer and her flesh and blood."

"Then why haven't you picked him up? That'd be a welcome surprise." It was never that simple. He rubbed salt in the wound. "What do we know?"

"His name fell off grid after he graduated. Business major, masters, and two minors. There was a trip to Saudi, on the manifest going, never made the return trip, at least not as Romann Carroll. It's likely he altered his appearance," Kane said. "He didn't resurface until his plan was in action. We have his school admissions photo. Some from the church. Hair masks half his face. Gangly, scruffy, cagey kid. No one knows what he grew into or what alias he's been using."

"We're searching for someone clean cut. That narrows it down." Grey's sarcasm was his way of letting off steam. Kane didn't respond, though Grey was right. Romann's appearance was orchestrated to mislead.

"We're cross-checking return flights from Saudi with the airlines, ship manifests, etc. Chances are he used a different means to return," Jackson said. "Judging by the foot impressions we've got the guy is a cornfed, big boy like you. We're blind until Kane's buddy sends through the facial recognition program results."

"How long?" Grey's stare, when it locked on, reminded Kane that he'd earned his position the hard way.

"He said forty-eight. He's pushing it forward," Kane said. "Should be soon."

"It'd sure as hell better be." Grey glanced out the window then back at them. "Have you notified Leigh's family, her father?"

Jackson sauntered away from the desk and spoke with his back to them. "We called. Haven't got through. We're all feelin' gut shot, Cap."

Grey glanced at the garbage can, tapped his fingers on the file in front of him, then said, "His Honor is a busy man. Keep trying. I'll know when you reach him. He'll bring this department to its knees to find her."

"He may not feel up to that." Kane grabbed the chair across from Grey, Jackson plunked down in the one next to him. "I won't say he was the cause of all this, but he kicked the first domino."

Grey appeared intrigued. His stare remained unforgiving, but he listened.

Kane explained, "Beth said the families knew each other."

"Beth?" Grey appeared confused.

"The pretty nun," Jackson clarified.

Grey shook his head. Kane continued. "Judge Leigh thought he was handing his grandson over to a pillar of the community, a man he trusted would provide the boy with the best. And, like everyone else back then, he didn't know Francis Carroll raped and killed. He certainly wouldn't have suspected he was the one who brutally raped and impregnated his sixteen-year-old daughter."

Grey's facial color faded out earning him a right to his name. "He handed the rapist his biological son?"

"Yeah. Talk about a miscarriage of justice." Now Jackson was shaking his head.

"And Carroll spent the rest of his life brutalizing the boy." Grey's stare drifted as reality settled in. "Shit."

A sickening silence seeped into the room. Its pressure crushed the air from Kane's chest. "This...is the aftermath."

"You're wrong," Grey said. "Nickolas Leigh didn't start the dominoes falling, I did all those years ago when Francis Carroll walked by me every day, and I couldn't see him. God only knows how long he'd been raping and killing before we stopped him. He's a stain on this town we can't rub clean."

The regret Grey wore was impenetrable. Kane had no desire to carry the same armor. "It stops here, no further."

"Go get him." Grey locked eyes with Kane. Pain drained his irises to monochrome blue. He handed him the file that had been sitting on his desk. "And don't worry about telling Judge Leigh. I'll notify Nickolas."

Kane nodded and followed Jackson out of the room. Neither spoke a word until they were standing in front of their case board. The evidence before them hadn't changed. The way they read it had.

Kane opened Grey's file and cleared a new space adjacent to Leigh's photo. He pinned a picture of Francis Carroll up alongside the evidence from Leigh's rape years earlier.

"You've got to be frackin' kidding me." Amy, who'd come in behind them, neared the board, reviewed its data, then handed a pile of paperwork to Kane. "The information you requested on Carroll's history. And I thought *it* was interesting."

"What about it?" Jackson said. "Not the time to be cryptic, kid."

"Offshore accounts, ownership in economic development companies here and abroad." Amy's focus stayed on the evidence. Her voice fell to a whisper. "The man had resources and apparently a whole lot of rage."

"Between us," Kane warned. "Grey knows. No one else."

"Okay," Amy said.

"And that door stays locked around the clock. Use the key code and make sure it shuts on your way out," Jackson added. "We don't wanna dig up more snakes than we can kill."

"No problem." Amy surveyed the case board. "What do you need?"

Kane flipped through the documents Amy handed him. "Any active ownership ties to the companies?"

"Three. The stock passed to his son, Romann. IHD, they develop industrial sites based on economic need, three projects overseas, one here. They joint ventured with an architectural firm."

"What's the name of the firm?" Jackson walked across the evidence stopping at Venice Beil's murder.

"Something Italian. Umm." Amy focused on Jackson.

"Venice Towers," Kane said.

"Yes. It's in there." Amy glanced between both men for an explanation.

"It's how he knew where she'd be," Kane said.

Jackson shook his head in disgust, stomped over to Kane, and snatched the file. He spread it out on the table behind them. "We find all the connections and fast. One of these buildings has to be where he's holding Leigh."

"Dr. Leigh?" Amy's sirens wailed. "He has her?"

"Yeah, kid." Jackson handed Amy the papers on the architectural company. She pinned them to the wall under Venice Beil's crime scene photo.

"There's a pharmaceutical company," she said. "They sold land here and somewhere in the Middle East." Amy returned to the table and slid papers around searching. "Here. They do research on unconventional cures for—"

"Childhood epilepsy." Kane finished the sentence. She handed him the document. He tacked it under Nikki Taylor's photo.

"Marijuana." Amy spoke without volition.

"Anything in there linked to Africa?" Jackson tapped the image of Lorenda Lainey's emaciated corpse.

Kane read a list of philanthropic donations. "Yeah. He donated enough to be privy to every move she made." He handed the list to Jackson and placed both palms on the table. The room was spinning.

"Why leave the trail?" Amy asked. "He could've further buried these connections."

"Why bother," Kane said. "He's too far ahead, nothing to fear."

"He's as dark as coffin air," Jackson added. "Hiding in plain sight."

"Not for long." Kane's phone alerted him to an incoming message.

The photo recognition program kicked out five possible identifications. He forwarded the images to the computer, keyed in his code, and opened the file so Jackson and Amy could see.

The first two images revealed were of a man too slight to be their guy, DNA leaning to Rachel Leigh's side. The next one fit the body type but didn't set off any recognition alarms. Kane glanced at Jackson then Amy. Nothing. He shrank it and pulled it to the right top corner of the screen. The fourth caught all their attention.

"I don't know?" Jackson leaned in scrutinizing the picture. "What do y'all think?"

"There's a familiarity," Kane agreed.

Amy, overzealous, intending to hit the key to move it, lost the image and inadvertently opened the last likeness full screen.

"No way." Kane put his hand on the screen. "I've seen this guy."

"Me too," Amy echoed.

"I've seen him here." Kane stared at Jackson, whose eyes gained dimension. "In our halls."

"What's his name?" Jackson's eyes trained on the image. "What's his damn name?"

The three crowded around the computer in silence. The door exploded inward. They disbanded leaving a clear line of sight to their suspect.

"Our problems just got worse, I—" The panic Grey wore intensified. "Isaiah. Why do you have Isaiah Isreal's picture up?"

Kane's expression spoke volumes, and for a fleeting second, he thought he read desperation in the eyes of their leader. "I don't."

Grey was at a loss for words.

"Meet Romann Carroll," Jackson said. "Better known as the Redeemer."

"Mother of God." Grey became a statue before the image.

"Considerably worse." Kane redirected Grey back to the sentence he'd walked in with. "Our problems?"

"Nickolas." Grey came to life. "He has Nickolas. I spoke to his secretary, and she hasn't heard from him since last week. His assistant says he didn't return from his hunting trip at the cabin. She had a friend check the area. Said it appeared he'd never arrived."

Kane knew they had to act fast. "We know who he is—"

"And, as of seconds ago, he's well aware of that fact," Grey said.

"How would he be?" Jackson didn't disguise his frustration. "I'm startin' to feel as confused as a goat on AstroTurf."

"Who do you think paid for the new software?" Grey turned in a circle scanning the room's new computers. All their eyes followed his. "His donations rebuilt this place. Now we know why."

Kane slammed the files he held down on the table making Amy recoil. "He's had access to everything, all of it, from the beginning?"

"We have to assume so." Grey held a hand to the side of his face as if fearing half his skull would dislodge. "Thank Christ out monitoring system isn't linked."

"Everything?" Jackson paced. "All the evidence, victims we were tracking, our text messages? You can forget locking that door, Logan. He's been inside the whole damn time."

The words no sooner fell from Jackson's lips, and Grey spun back to face Kane.

"Jade?" Kane said what they all were thinking.

"When was the last time you saw her?" Grey stared at Kane then Jackson and Amy. "Physically laid eyes on her?"

"She's the one who discovered Leigh was missing." Kane fought the alarms sounding in his core.

"Leigh's assistant saw her?" Grey asked.

"Had to." Jackson spoke with his head down, surfing his text messages. "She let her into the house. Jade accessed Leigh's computer, had the university send their tapes."

"Call them. Confirm it. And find out who Leigh uses for tech support and if anyone has been to her home recently."

Amy quit staring at their useless set of doors and spun to face Grey. "I spoke to them. No breaches."

Kane heard their voices but couldn't find his own. Flashes of Jade and him making love at the cabin, her beautiful face... "You don't get to die until I decide," Kane whispered.

"What?" Grey was staring, and for a second, Kane didn't know why.

"It's what Romann told Jade at the textile mill. Confident." A physical pain pierced the center of Kane's chest and spread outward.

"Hold on." Jackson fumbled with his phone almost dropping it, then turned it for Kane to read. "She was here."

Kane read Jade's last message to Jackson. His breath, again, flowed through his lungs. The grip of pain in his chest released a little. He grabbed a burner phone off another officer's desk and dialed Jade. No answer. He sent a text. She responded.

"Jesus, thank God." He leaned back on the desk, waiting on the room to stop spinning. Romann Carroll, the Redeemer, and Isaiah Isreal were one and the same and had access to everything through the station's mainframe. Assuming he had access to messages, he remained cryptic and told her to call direct when she was free.

He gave Grey the "she's okay" in an exhale. Jade reminded him that she'd talked to their suspect in the hall before heading to meet Simms. He took down some details and refocused. "Amy, search video footage of the office for this guy before Jade left for the sanitarium and everything we've got for properties the son-of-a-bitch owns within a thirty-mile radius. The timelines and strike zones narrow his window of travel time. Keep an eye out for sites west of here." Kane traced the red marks on their map of victim abduction sites and body dumps. "He's most comfortable this direction."

"He should be." Jackson handed evidence of Francis Carroll's land acquisitions to Kane. "His father owned three sites in the area."

"Wait a minute." Grey's tone stalled the conversation. "Wasn't Jade working Leigh's connection?"

"Yes," Jackson said. "She's been actively working the link and fleshing it out."

"And he would've read it," Kane said.

"You guys better huddle and fast, the clock is ticking on Nickolas and Leigh. If you thought we made headlines before, imagine what'll happen if we lose a judge and doctor at the same time. My days are numbered as it is." Grey sunk to the edge of a desk and absorbed the case board.

"Bad choice of words," Jackson said.

"He slept with Lainey." Grey's eyes locked on her photo.

"What? Why the hell didn't we—" Jackson was about to lose it on his boss.

"We didn't know who he was," Kane cautioned. "Until a few minutes ago, it didn't matter because Isaiah donated money to us and her charity. Uncomfortable. Not criminal."

Grey folded his hands. His head dropped shielding his expression.

"What?" Kane's anxiety refueled.

"When he was in the hall with Jade, he acted like…"

"Like what, damn it?" Kane hovered over Grey, a rarity for most as he stood six-three, but he was still seated.

Grey dropped his hands and looked up. "Like he was making a play for her or—"

"He knew her." Kane spoke while acid burned the back of his throat.

Amy, who'd been doing a site search while they debated, sprung from her seat. "I have two industrial sites, one's empty land, one's a business center under construction, and two private residences."

"Find them. Bring him back in a body bag," Grey stomped out of the room rubbing his temple in the same spot as earlier. His voice gained octaves as he walked out. "Kane, keep your head clear! He's played with us enough. Don't give him more ammunition."

"The chief's going to give himself an aneurysm." Jackson walked over to Amy, who'd sat back down to continue searching. "Find this on our monitors." He flashed her his phone, directing her to find the hallway incident and any other times the Redeemer walked the halls in the last few weeks. "And assume he's seeing this while we are."

"The industrial site is our best bet. We'll go in quiet. Alert backup. They can meet us if there's any sign of him." Kane realized they'd been leaning hard on Amy. "You okay with this?"

Amy smiled up. "Okay? I'm pumped. Go get 'em, Sugar Kane. Oh, and try not to get dead."

"Sweet." Jackson snatched the jotted down addresses from her hand as if he enjoyed the fact they were being forced to do it old school.

Grey walked back in and threw new cell phones at Jackson, then him and Amy. "Stole these from narc. New numbers are programmed in, and there's one for Jade." He handed the extra to Kane and walked back out. If they didn't catch the Redeemer in time to save Leigh and her father, Grey's career would likely be the case's final casualty.

"This is close." Kane stared at the industrial area on Amy's screen. The area was familiar. Heavily wooded, there'd be plenty of ways for the Redeemer to escape if he knew they were coming.

"Not close enough for Leigh and her father." Jackson locked eyes. Kane read in him the melancholy he'd carried into every body discovery. They had a destination, and odds were they'd arrive too late.

"It's been days, I know, but they're special to him. We have to pray he's taking his time." When the words left his mouth, Kane regretted voicing them.

"Time in his hands?" Jackson spoke on his way out the door. "Damn if we find them alive, but that's not the same as saving them. Time for that may be long gone."

FORTY

"Leigh's a fighter, Max." Jade's words skated on the narrowest pathway over the dark void of despair. "She knows what he's capable of."

"But Rachel. When she learns he's her child…" Max's proper posture disintegrated. He slumped into his armchair.

"He's taken precious lives, but not his mother's." Jade's tour of Max's office landed her in front of a photo of them at a department fundraiser. He'd been her confidant for so long. She scanned it for faces she recognized while she spoke. "It's easy for him to kill women he's conquered. It'll be difficult with Rachel."

She turned as Max dropped his head back. "She'll die like everyone else he's come in contact with."

"She loves life. What she does, she does with passion. That passion may keep her alive. Her will is strong. Bringing your fantasy to life can turn into a nightmare…even for a killer." Jade's attention was drawn back to the photo. "She can't die. She dies, he wins. He can't win."

"He's already won." His voice was thin. "This is so not a game."

"Max, how do we find justice in the face of darkness?" Jade watched for his reaction. He stayed pressed into the chair, tipped back, head resting, eyes closed. "We get comfortable in it and seek her out."

"What have I done? I left you vulnerable, a lamb tied to a bloody stake." Max stretched his hands behind his head, not relaxed and easy, but as a precaution should his skull start crumbling.

"Can't blame yourself without taking us all down." She glanced one more time at the photo then made it to the seating area in three strides.

Max tilted his head up, stared at the handset on his desk, shaking off the cobwebs.

The office was closed. Sunday. No one in the building. The halls were quiet. The mood of the place, its purpose, silenced visitors. Today, Jade found it particularly dreary. If it were a battleship, the enemy's guns were locked on.

"You've got to quit spending so much time here." She plunked down on the lounger opposite his desk. "It's damn depressing, unhealthy."

He'd sent his informal, panic-driven conclusions on the case to her home computer. She assumed he'd be guilt ridden, Leigh being his friend and colleague. The odds of her survival were about a million to one. Jade was invested in that one percent.

"I handed Leigh to him." Max released his hands from behind his head. He held a photo in his right hand. She couldn't see what of.

"He had his sights on her long before you were in the picture. I'm past the anger, the injustice of it." Jade slid off the lounger and stomped back to the fundraiser photo for one last look. When she spoke again, her voice gained an eerie stillness. "Anger can make you clumsy, useless. Emotions can be dangerous. This bastard isn't making me useless. He was groomed to take life. I survived to stop him. Everyone fears him…he has no idea how much he should fear me."

"You think emotions make you useless," he said. "There's more damage than you'll ever know. I don't know why I couldn't see this."

"He was out in front of us, hard to catch. Missing pieces, can't see the whole picture without them." Jade followed his stare to the phone. "Kane *will* call. We are close. Jackson and he are narrowing sites."

"I don't know what's worse, its ring or its silence. Neither is good news."

Jade walked to his desk, then rounded it, coming up beside him. The draft she created rustled papers perched on its edge. He jerked upright slamming the picture down. His hand covered all but an indiscernible fragment.

"This case even has Tex jumpy. You're not alone. It'll all be over soon." She was the therapist this time, and he the one in need of counsel.

"How many will we lose before the end?" Max rubbed his eyes with his left hand. "I couldn't tell Kane everything, all my suspicions."

"What suspicions?" Jade stayed beside him hoping her closeness offered comfort.

"If I'm right, I'd only be jeopardizing him further." He turned to the window, rubbing his eyes. The sun found a crack, piercing a pathway to him.

"He'll figure it all out, everything, soon enough. He has to focus and take the Redeemer, Romann, Isaiah Isreal, down. Don't worry. I'll be there."

Jade patted him on the shoulder and said, "Got to go. I'm meeting him and Jackson at the warehouse."

Max hesitated, removing his hand from its shielding position over his eyes. His stare locked on Jade's reflection, ethereal in the intensity of the sunbeam. His gaze met hers. His eyes glistened, freshly flush with sorrow. She smiled and mouthed the words, "don't blame yourself." Before he could respond, his phone rang. He snatched up the receiver, snapping out of his trance.

"Kane?"

Time to make her exit before things became too uncomfortable. Kane was calling en route to catch a killer, and she would be by his side when he did.

"Have you found Rachel? I'm going out of my mind," Max's tone said, the irony of his words was wasted on him. Jade could hear Kane's laughter through the phone.

"If nothing else, you guys are finally working together," she whispered. "It's about time. You'll be good for each other."

"There's nothing remotely funny about this situation," Max barked.

Kane laughed louder. Max's face reddened. His welling tears were gone.

Jade smiled and slipped out the door listening to Max's ethical tirade. Anger was a cop's survival tool. Instigating it. Feeding off it. Understanding it. Different from rage, it soothed and motivated when you learned how to use it. Romann Carroll let his anger turn inward, fester, and poison. Jade's was building constructively. It'd crest at the peak moment to decimate the bastard.

The photo in Max's office flashed into view in her mind. A man laughed in the backdrop. Romann Carroll had lost his anonymity. Lost his hiding place. She knew where to find him, and with any luck, Rachel Leigh, alive.

FORTY-ONE

Leigh's leg wounds were hemorrhaging, taxed by the climb and vertical suspension. The roped linens, set adrift by icy winds, billowed in crimson-capped waves. The sheets she clung to brushed the brick wall below her feet. With every inch, she encountered more evidence against survival—bloodstains gaining girth.

She refused to continue looking down, dreading a miscalculation of cloth and courage. Glancing up, the distance between her and the ledge she'd traversed grew in such small increments it was discouraging.

This crap actually appeared feasible in movies. Reality revealed the glaring impracticalities better not experienced firsthand.

She'd twisted her arm in the material for extra control, but the constriction slowed her descent. Staring at the wall alleviated the dizziness but did nothing to stop the moments of inertia. At this pace, her captor was certain to return in time to cut her lifeline or have a cocktail at the drop zone.

Fuck it. Rather die fleeing than let him finish the job. Even the voice in her head lost dignity.

She untangled her arm, underestimated the resistance it provided, and watched her life and the wall flash in front of her face. The sheets flew through her hands. Weak, her grip was useless to fight the fall.

Bleach and blood burned her palms. She flailed, bashing elbows, wrists, and legs into the raw brick. More pain. The stupidity of her decision landed with the impact of the ground. She hit with a force that exploded through flesh, muscle, and sinew, shattering to the core of her marrow.

Torn sheets, ravaged, fell aimlessly covering her broken body. Pall blankets, shutting out the light, and with it, hope of escape.

Romann hadn't run a race since track and field in high school. Then, there wasn't an opponent on campus he couldn't defeat. Assessing the condition of Nickolas Leigh, the damage, beyond his capabilities to repair, said the enemy had advanced way out ahead. His plan for justice became the one race he'd lose.

He screamed until it echoed back at him. The warehouse was unfinished inside. Hollow. Its walls coated in cement and the reverberation of his rage. The other sites were equipped with resuscitation gear, but he hadn't intended on letting the judge live.

Until now.

The desire to take this man's life had manifested into a twisting panic at the thought of his death. He'd wanted to kill Francis Carroll, but Grey had robbed him of that. The judge became his stand-in. Romann reigned eighteen years of torture down on him, merciless and vile. And he'd remembered many of Francis's favorite tricks. He saved the best for last because initially he needed him alive. At the sight of him now, it appeared they weren't necessary.

The man was dying.

With the turn of a handle, the chains released, and Nickolas' body fell with them in an indiscriminate heap onto the concrete. A twitch. No sound. Unconscious. He scooped the man up, avoiding the knife he'd left protruding from his exposed thigh. Harder to muscle than expected, he staggered to a pile of packing blankets and collapsed. Nickolas's breathing was ragged. He grabbed a padded blanket and pulled it over his body, around the knife handle. Removed a syringe from his pocket, prepared it, and administered the contents into Nickolas's limp arm.

He stabilized Nickolas's head with a makeshift neck brace. The oxygen tank and mask he'd carried from his trunk waited at the room's entrance. He retrieved them, set the oxygen flow, and positioned the mask.

Nickolas fought unconsciously against the cover over his mouth. Signs of a cerebral contusion. He'd hit the old guy over the head with the humanitarian award by his desk when he'd abducted him. If the flailing worsened, he'd have to sedate him, the likelihood of him surviving would drop considerably. He restrained his arms and legs, this time mindful of preventing further damage, then administered to his injuries.

Precise and fluid, his movements matched those of any skilled ER doctor. Contents of his advanced first aid kit emptied as he set broken bones, cleaned and dressed open wounds, and placed ice packs over Nickolas's damaged eyes. He was sure to lose sight, partially if not completely, in his right. His left would heal if he lived long enough.

Nickolas inhaled the pure oxygen more deeply. His hands clenched and released. If he was coming to, pain would knock him back out. Not much time for answers.

"My name's Isaiah, Mr. Leigh. I'm here to help you. Can you hear me?"

Nickolas's expression said he was fighting for vision. The drugs and oxygen were working.

"Don't fight to see. We have your eyes covered for protection. Be still, you've suffered severe injuries, and we can't risk further damage. You're safe. Remain calm. I have important questions I need answered to stop the man who did this to you. Ice chips, for your throat."

Nickolas opened his parched lips and welcomed the ice then whispered, "Rachel?"

"They'll bring your daughter home, but we need to know. What do you know about the family who adopted her son?"

"Nickolas."

Romann retreated. "We know who you are."

"No. My grandson, Nickolas," he slurred, fighting the pain to speak. "What does this...have to do with him? Is he safe? He isn't hurt?"

Romann heard his real name. For the first time in his life, he knew who he was, who he could've been. Reality hit with the force of an enemy's blade and cut deep into a cold place that once was the heart of him. He was Nickolas Leigh. Namesake to the dying man he'd brutalized for the sins of a man who'd done worse.

He couldn't speak.

"Is he safe?" His grandfather's voice was thready, weak, and desperate at the thought of harm befalling the one who'd beat and tortured him to the brink of death.

"He's..." The Redeemer bowed his head. Defeat crushed his six-foot-three frame. Dead for years, Francis Carroll demeaned him still. "He's out of harm's way for now. I'm not sure we can guarantee he'll remain safe."

"He's innocent. He doesn't even know who we are. Protect him, please." Nickolas Sr. faded out.

The injury to his thigh caused critical blood loss. He'd die if the laceration wasn't repaired quickly. Nickolas put his hand firmly on the blade, whispered, "Forgive me, grandfather," and pulled.

He calculated down to the most finite detail, anticipated the moves of law enforcement long before the game began, yet here he stood covered in the blood of his grandfather, the only man who loved him. And he'd killed him.

Aside from a miracle, Nickolas Sr. would be dead in a matter of hours. Hospitalization wasn't an option. The cops were closing in. He'd lost his protective veil of anonymity.

He'd performed miracles. They had no idea how many. He was the Redeemer. And he vowed to see a few more before they stopped him.

He snatched rubber tubing from the soiled floor, swung it around his upper arm, tapped hard on a clear vein, and whispered, "Hang on, Nickolas. The strength of the blood in our veins has a will that survives even in absence of humanity. For us, it's never over, even when it needs to be."

FORTY-TWO

Warm rain on cool grass turned the green grounds enveloping the Carroll estate lush. Shadows Hook was established in the mid seventeen hundreds, and this was one of its oldest preserved homes. Aged sugar maples billowing in a flourish of wet leaves lined the property. Smooth stone structures with arches and clean lines fenced in the lair. Its beauty, breathtaking and distracting to most, was wasted on Jade. Though she wondered who originally occupied the residence—an early president? What would they think of the current owner and the fate of their legacy?

She bypassed the front entrance, clinging to the manor's moist walls around its endless left side. Struck by its breadth and stature, she stared up the layered bricks until they blended into sky. The fortress loomed, intimidation befitting its owner. Its facade as well orchestrated as his.

At the edge of the west side she paused, glanced around the corner, ducked back. What the hell was that? A ghost-trail at the far east side of the property. She peeked again, this time holding her gaze long enough for clarity to set her feet ablaze.

She ran, abandoning protocol, until the sheet rope morphed from speculation to certainty. It ended sixteen feet or so from ground level. She flew up the patio stairs two at a time, never questioning if a captive could survive the crude escape route.

Rachel Leigh laid, a broken bundle, at its end.

On her knees, Jade searched Rachel's wrist for a pulse. She couldn't find one. Rachel's flesh was cold. Jade's throat tightened.

"No."

Her fingers sought the side of Rachel's neck. Oddly positioned, it didn't appear broken. The same could not be said for the rest of her. The left ankle had sustained a compound fracture, the right shattered, left arm broken and twisted the wrong direction. If Rachel was alive, better she stayed unconscious.

A pulse, intermittent and faint, beat under Jade's fingertips.

"Fight, Rachel. Don't you fucking let go."

Jade pulled her phone from her back pocket, dialed Amy, and hit call. Nothing happened.

"Shit. Not again. Not now!"

Service showed two bars, fading in and out. She typed in, "RL escaped, at back of old Carroll estate, dying," and hit send, cursing the transmission indicator until it delivered.

Scanning the place, it appeared devoid of life. The Redeemer was, in typical fashion, long gone. It would've taken time for Rachel to coordinate her escape. Still, if he doubled back, they were sitting ducks.

She set the phone on the frigid cement, gathered the torn sheets, and protected Rachel's battered body as best she could. Every effort exposed more damage.

Careful not to shift Rachel's neck or head, she cushioned the surrounding area. Covering her exposed limbs, she noticed wounds and sutures. Her mind ran gory, graphic scenarios. Each intimately disturbing. Whatever Rachel endured, it hadn't killed her will to live. At least, not until after she scaled the wall.

Her phone alerted help had been dispatched.

Having done all she could, Jade leaned in and whispered, "You don't stop fighting to live. I had to, so do you. They'll be here soon. We know who he is. And I won't let him hurt anyone again."

Rachel wasn't moving. A photo reel of victims reinforced their department's tally of failures. Jade wasn't prepared to add Rachel to the list.

Distant sirens offered hope. They weren't enough. Jade moved within an inch of Rachel's ear. "Your father needs you. This isn't your end. Fight."

Rachel moaned, soft anguish.

Jade adjusted the sheets once more, stood, seeing the flash of lights on the horizon, then disappeared back down the stairs. She caught a glimpse of the heap of sheets before the house blocked her view and the irony hit.

The killer's mother was dying this time not hers, and strangely, the pain in her chest felt the same. Death was death. Mercy was mercy. And she would prevent one to grant the other.

"I've passed this place a hundred times." Kane eyed the warehouse as he and Jackson neared a side entrance.

"Me too. I'm startin' to think mandatory sweeps of vacant buildings is in order. We need to know who's in our backyard." Jackson hugged the wall right of the door making room on the left for Kane to take lead. He lifted a Glock 19 from his side holster.

"Mexican metal?" Partners were familiar with each other's weapons. This was new.

"Seventeen rounds," Jackson said. "Getting shot is a great incentive to expand ones firearms collection."

"Only one guy."

"A round for every life he snuffed out or tainted."

"Try explaining that to Max." Kane reached for the door handle, turned the knob, and heard the latch release. "We're in."

"Carroll's evaded us like a ghost, and now he leaves the place unlocked? Either we're in the wrong warehouse, or he's waitin' on us." Jackson nodded the go-ahead.

"Three floors, six thousand square feet, he'll have more than one escape route." Kane opened the door and slid into darkness with Jackson at his back. He wasn't thinking of the Redeemer, what he'd done, or what was at stake. He was wondering where the hell Jade was. He had to push hard at it. Refocus.

Jackson whispered from behind, "What's with the windows?"

Kane noticed a roll of black construction paper in the light cast from the doorway. "Blacked out. You were right. He's waiting."

They froze, listened for movement, then pulled out their flashlights to sweep the ground level. Obstacles deliberately scattered the floor. A crude warning system they avoided with cautious steps. The cargo elevator stood with its doors ajar, a welcoming ambush. The standard elevators were out of service. Kane searched for stairs. Jackson found them first.

"Watch for land mines," Kane warned, not sure what awaited them.

Jackson nodded, guided the entry door's pin back, and eased it open like rattlers were waiting on the other side. He leaned his head in. "Black as coal," he whispered. He pried the door ajar with his boot, fit his gun hand in, then cast his flashlight beam into every dark quadrant. "Hold up." Tucking the light into his belt, he reached down, scooped dust from the floor, and tossed it in. He stood with the door open enough for Kane to watch the dust illuminate a laser triggered alarm system cascading over the staircase like a vertical spider web. "Up for an uncomfortable climb?" Jackson asked.

Kane waved Jackson back, made his way to the building's exit, and slid out. Once they were both outside, and the door shut behind Jackson, he exhaled. "Round back."

"So you agree you're no Tom Cruise?" Jackson smirked.

"He's cool, but I'm bigger, fewer wrinkles according to Jade." Kane didn't pause for Jackson to respond.

They moved behind the building evading elevated security cameras. Once around, Kane pointed up. An escape ladder, out of reach. Jackson stared at it and the long stretch to where they stood. "Okay, Spider-Man, how are we supposed to—"

"The sign." Kane motioned to an adjacent building's advertisement. It made a slippery but possible access route to the second floor. It appeared new. With any luck, Romann Carroll hadn't recognized it as an alternative way onto his property.

"You're certifiable. You really expect that to hold us?" Jackson shook his head, then tucked his Glock away and folded his hands together for a makeshift step. "I'm startin' to feel like spit on a skillet here. You first."

"Thanks, Tex."

"Don't mention it."

Nine precarious footholds, two nearly fatal slips, and one annoying as hell squeaky walkway, and they'd traversed onto the escape ladder, climbed up one flight, and entered on the third floor. Kane paused inside the window until Jackson's large frame cleared, then whispered, "He's here. I can smell him."

"Hope you're the only one with that talent." Jackson scanned right, then nudged Kane. A faint light came in waves from the far back.

"Back hall."

"Yep."

Kane moved in silent, heart pumping adrenaline into his bloodstream. A glimpse beyond an opening revealed a dark passage. Two hallways flanked a back room deep in the building, casting dying daylight. Accessible by either side of the warehouse floor, they inched into the hall nearest them. Intermittent streams of light illuminated their path. Halfway down the echo of a voice froze them in place.

"Not here old man. Don't you die."

Jackson made eye contact fueled with the exhilaration Kane lived for. That moment when you knew you'd driven a predator to the end of his rope. Kane couldn't wait to see this one hang. A believer that no human deserved that fate, it was difficult to see this man as human. What he left in his wake proved otherwise.

As they inched their way down the corridor, the faces of the Redeemer's victims flashed into memory. Kane let them bleed out onto the dark walls, imagining their will empowering his own.

"That's it, a nice even rhythm. I told you, we're survivors," Carroll said.

Who was he talking to? Old man? The answer hit as Jackson whispered, "Judge Leigh."

"Shit." Kane wanted to rush in and take Carroll down in time to save Leigh. Rescues didn't happen that way. Ever. Something unexpected always impeded a clean retrieval. And Carroll had far too much to lose to go quietly. He'd use the judge as leverage.

"Go back," he said. "Circle around, left flank. I'll wait until you're in place. We can't give him room to run."

Jackson nodded, backed out of the hall, and disappeared. Any attempt Carroll made to shift positions they'd hear. Unfortunately, sound traveled more than one direction. Kane waited, giving Tex sufficient time to reach the far side. Only seconds had passed when a crash rang out.

"Shit." Kane breathed. No hiding now.

Kane launched out of the hall, hoping Carroll wasn't armed. No such luck. Bullets sent shards showering over his right shoulder as they sunk into the doorjamb overhead. Pieces of layered paint exploded in a flurry of color. A warning? Carroll was a damn good shot. Kane's gun tracked Carroll. Advanced weapon's training shifted his aim to the kill shot, but he couldn't fire. Carroll used Judge Leigh as a barrier, hiding behind where he laid brutalized on a heap of blankets. Bullets whizzed by, a swarm of bees coming for him. He aimed into the window behind Carroll. Glass fractured but remained in place. Storm glass.

Tex was right. The bastard was prepared.

And he was firing two weapons. Ambidextrous. Kane fired back. Drawing him away from Jackson. The barrage turned full force on him.

Carroll's shots struck a half-wall, sending chunks of plaster and wood into Kane's midsection, right side. It knocked him off balance like a tree cracked in half by a lumberjack. A muzzle flash burst in Jackson's direction. Its report rang in Kane's ears as he hit the floor. He scrambled and came up firing to pin Carroll from going after Tex. Too late. Carroll vanished. Kane rushed to Leigh. Midstride, he smacked the annoyance of debris from his side. His hand came up bloody.

Recognition brought pain. He'd been hit.

Clutching his abdomen with his gun hand, he swiped Leigh's neck with his left. A pulse.

With the echo of bullets ringing in his ears, he heard the sound of a fresh magazine being snapped in place as he entered the hall Jackson should've come up. A shadowy figure approached. He prepared to fire knowing at close range, trapped inside the corridor with nowhere to hide, they'd both end up dead.

"You got him?" Tex. Out of breath.

"No. He went your way." Kane's side burned. He pushed at the pain.

"Bullets. No Carroll." Jackson's eyes traced to Kane's injury. "You're hit. How bad?"

"A scratch. Go, go. I'll circle back."

Jackson glanced at his watch and flew back down the hall. Kane headed into the room where Leigh Senior lay dying, then down the opposite hall. Pain shadowed his every step. He met Jackson in the open warehouse floor.

"What the hell?"

"He's good, not invisible." Jackson moved in a circle around where Kane stood bleeding and baffled.

"Leigh. The last time I had him was behind Leigh." Kane rushed back to where it all started, the pain intensifying.

"I'll be damned." Jackson kneeled behind Leigh. "Snake in the pipes." A door in the floor opened to a metal ladder.

"He doesn't get away that easily." Kane released his side and climbed. Legs faltered. He slipped down a couple rungs, regained control, and grimaced through the burn stretching its tendrils into his guts.

"Kane." Jackson matched his place on the ladder, advanced, taking the lead.

No way to be sure if Carroll would wait to kill them on the second floor or rush to ground floor to escape. He had the means to get out of town, even country. "Coward. He's running." On even ground, Kane clasped his side. His much-needed oxygen intake became scarce beneath his shallow panting. "Hit your light. Stairs. Ground floor."

Jackson found the staircase in one sweep, threw the door open, and cut through the lasers clearing several steps a stride. Alarms wailed overhead. Kane followed Jackson down in a driven stumble, waiting for his legs to buckle beneath him. When Jackson opened the first-floor door the corridor spun with a momentum Kane couldn't stop. His vision cleared in time to see Jackson hit the ground in a barrage of bullets.

Jackson cried out. He'd used the metal door as a shield but caught one in the shoulder that knocked him to his knees. Kane snatched him back inside the safety of the cement stairwell. Face clenched in pain, Jackson's gun arm hung slack. Whatever attached it before wasn't doing the job now. He switched his gun to his functioning arm, shook his head, and wrestled to stand.

"Stay down," Kane cautioned. "Better odds."

Propped against the wall, Jackson said, "Backup?"

"Too late." Kane stepped over him to face Carroll. Pain blinding, clamped his teeth shut.

"Sinners in a cyclone, partner." Jackson placed a bloody hand on Kane's boot. "Odds aren't great."

"I know, my brother." Kane grimaced, glanced down at his trusted friend, then lifted his foot free and bit down hard. The shock on Tex's face said he expected him to form a plan, think it through. He hoped his enemy did too.

One chance to nail Carroll first, that's all he prayed for, that and a quick response team. He'd have seconds after the door opened. If Carroll got past him, Tex was as good as dead. He couldn't defend himself with a rubber arm. And "couldn't hit the broad side of a barn door," as he put it, left-handed.

The trouble with catching a killer was confronting what they did best. Kill.

Kane threw the door open and stepped into the line of fire. This is what he did best. For every victim, serve.

The world ceased spinning. Time lost force. Pistol smoke hung in the air. And Carroll's bullets found a sluggish inertia. For a breath.

The pain in his side hit with crippling impact. With his pistol drawn and trained, he centered Carroll in its crosshairs. His body betrayed.

He couldn't breathe. As if his gut paralyzed his lungs for fear of movement. Couldn't control the shakes rippling out from his core. Something was terribly wrong. Not a scratch. He'd known that. Far worse. The Glock, heavy in his hand, had been replaced with a concrete replica. He had to fire. He'd be sure to miss if he didn't raise it.

Out of nowhere, Jade's hand locked over his and the weapon. In a split second, her body braced against his. Her strength shifted the muzzle into alignment. "Together," she mouthed the word. As one, they pulled the trigger.

Kane watched blood splatter explode from Carroll's neck. Then a cattle prod of fire brought him face to face with the warehouse floor. Metal, dust, and gunpowder saturated Kane's nostrils on the way down. Jade faded to black, but before he lost sight, he saw her smile in Carroll's direction. That "got you, you son-of-a-bitch" smile. If it was the last thing he ever saw, it wasn't bad.

FORTY-THREE

"Carroll's old estate?" Grey was yelling at Amy. He forced calm into his voice as they worked their way through a maze of cops in the shop's reception area. "Site C. You're sure?"

Amy flashed him the text as they exited. "It came from Jade's cell."

"New or old?" Grey jogged to his parking spot, Amy following behind. His car wasn't there. He cursed Kane for messing with the assigned spaces, scanned the lot, found the car an aisle over, and jumped in. He paused long enough for Amy to belt up, flooring it out of the parking garage.

"New or old?" he demanded with eyes glued on the road as he accelerated.

"What?"

"The cell, new or old?" He was yelling again.

"Old one." Amy's response sounded oddly like an annoyed teenager.

He glanced at her. Young. Almost a decade younger than Jade, and he thought of *her* as…not now. "Old number's dirty. She's given Carroll her location and news of Leigh's escape." He hit the lights and weaved through traffic.

"You think he'd go back to finish Dr. Leigh off? Run the risk to get to Jade? What is it?" Amy's face was registering alarm on more than one level. "What aren't you saying?"

Grey didn't want to reveal too much. Better the kid didn't get pulled in. She had a tough enough climb ahead of her without the scandal that was certain to take out more than *his* career. "Ambulance?"

"En route." She paused. "Jade never answered me." The shallow tremor underlying Amy's tone belied her tough exterior.

"She's in pursuit. Jackson checked in when he and Kane hit the warehouse. They're in the heat of it. We'll hear soon."

His assurance masked a lie.

And the twisting in his gut never led to anything good. It didn't bode well for his team of detectives. Scattered all over, seeking a maniac in the dark.

A maniac with connections. He hated the things he knew. Putting a voice to them now wouldn't help his people in the field.

Amy rode silently beside him until the Carroll's land came into view. She repeatedly checked her phone. He didn't bother. No news wasn't good news. He suspected his inbox would stay tragically empty.

He left a skid of black rubber on the curve of the estate's front drive and sprang from his seat. Amy cut him off before he rounded the back corner of the house.

"Me first, boss."

Grey would've protested, but they breached the view to a mass of human destruction. Seven stairs led to an upper stone patio lavishly appointed and horribly spoiled by the broken body at its center.

No words. Grey folded to his knees beside the woman and brushed the blood-soaked hair from her face to check for signs of life.

Sirens climaxed entering the main drive, then stalled. Medics would be on site in seconds. An eternity too long.

Rachel Leigh's pulse was barely obtainable. She reminded him of smashed china. You might glue it back together, given you had all the pieces, but it'd never be pretty again. He thought of Nickolas seeing his daughter this way and was almost glad odds were slim he ever would. Gauging by the number of days he'd been missing, he was already dead.

Grey glanced up. The team behind him poured out of their truck and went in hard to secure the site. Amy loomed over Rachel, afraid to come nearer. "Here," he ordered. "Take her hand. Talk to her." Time to break the kid in. "Stay with her all the way to the hospital. Outside her door through surgery. Never leave that post until I send someone to relieve you. Got it? The order has to come from me directly!"

Amy kneeled beside their barely living victim wearing her pain. She nodded her pledge, heard the "all clear" over her radio, then waved in medics. She held Rachel's hand and never let go while they worked.

Grey exited in the same flurry as he'd arrived. With ambulance lights coloring his rearview, he got on the line with dispatch. Kane and Jackson's backup were arriving on scene. And what was coming through his speaker didn't sound good.

Shots fired. Shots fired.

Grey glanced at the thick manila envelope on his back seat, flipped his sirens on, and weighed heavy on the pedal. He was tracking the dominoes back in time, and they lead to one fatal mistake that opened the door to more death and destruction than Shadow Hook had ever seen. This was the fallout from letting a criminal escape justice.

Ram it! Now, now, now. Entering main warehouse. Officer down...officer down.

Static filled Grey's ears. He couldn't hear the valuable information being broadcast any longer. His officers found the Redeemer. He'd placed the burden of catching a killer squarely on their shoulders, and they'd done it, but at what cost?

Call dispatch, we need a second ambulance.

Voices filtered through. Grey pulled his wheel hard left and headed to the hospital, praying he'd find his men alive when they got there. The contents of the manila envelope flew out across the back seat.

A picture of Jade's mother, standing in a police examination room, young, battered, and terrified, landed on the center console.

Grey slid it onto his passenger seat, his eyes burning, he whispered, "Domino number one."

FORTY-FOUR

Jackson recoiled dodging a bullet thundering into the stairwell's outer concrete wall above his head as Kane disappeared into the barrage. Tex was pinned two feet from the door with no line of sight. It'd happened too fast. Kane, forever the weigher of options, vanished. No hesitation.

A scream echoed, Kane's voice, warped by agony.

Seizing a left-handed grip on his weapon, Jackson pushed up hard into the cold wall dragging his dead arm in a blood smear to full height at the threshold. He stuck his head out expecting to have it blown off. Instead, he saw the Redeemer take a bullet to the neck. The impact picked him off the ground and crumpled him like yesterday's newspaper.

He would've cheered if Kane hadn't collapsed into the same dust. He didn't witness what leveled him, only his body dropping to the warehouse floor unmanned.

Clutching his injured arm, fighting for balance, Jackson made it to Kane's side. The enemy mass lay still yards away. Sliding on his knees, he turned Kane over. He'd landed on his arm. Face still intact. Unconscious, breathing, weak.

Searching in frenzy, he found Kane's flashlight tucked into his belt. He pulled it free, switched it on, and surveyed the damage.

He sent the beam where Carroll's body went down. Motionless. Dead or dying. The Redeemer's carcass was no longer a threat. His weapon launched out of his hand and out of reach with the impact to the ground, a difficult crawl away. If he tried, he was a dog Tex would put down even left-handed.

Blood seeped from Kane's side. Crimson ink in the flashlight's beam. The left shoulder of his jacket was ravaged, bleeding through, not gushing.

He lifted Kane's head onto his lap. "Don't even think about it. You're a hero, cowboy. Can't miss the parade." Kane never made a sound. "Goddamn."

He grabbed the radio from his side. Amped the volume and bellowed into it. "Detective Swan here, where the hell's our backup? Officer down. Suspect secured. Send medic ASAP. What's your ETA?"

"*Entering the building on—*"

"Now, now, now!"

The door burst open and with it a stream of light and armed men.

"Here." Jackson waved them in. They secured the Redeemer and a path for the medical team to retrieve Kane. "He's shot midsection, not more than seven minutes. Laceration to left shoulder. Think one grazed him."

"We got him," a voice said from behind. "What about you?"

Jackson unfolded to full height. "I'm fine." A medic rushed in, reaching for his wounded shoulder. He yelled past him to those around Carroll. "Is he dead?"

"You're not fine, Detective. And certainly not if you ever want to handle a weapon again." The medic waved in a second gurney for him. An EMT kneeling beside Carroll commandeered it.

"I've got a pulse," he yelled. "Hurry. He's critical."

Jackson watched them load Kane, then walked with one bloody hand on the gurney that carried his partner to the ambulance. He glanced back at the scene. Carroll's body was lifted and transported with a medic's hand stuck inside his neck.

"We'll fight hard to deliver them alive," the medic said.

"You deliver my partner alive!" Jackson shifted aside for them to load Kane in. Unsteady, he claimed the seat at the head to ride with him. "That bastard has a one-way ticket to Hell, and I'd hate for him to miss the train."

The ambulance doors closed, and the sirens swirled with the tires.

The younger of the two working on Kane turned to administer an anesthetic into Jackson's shoulder.

Jackson flinched out of reach. "Keep your eyes on him. They can see me after."

"But, sir, you're risking—"

"After." His tone was enough. The kid never bothered him again.

His phone, buried in his chest pocket, buzzed. Automatic reflex, he reached for it to no avail. His shoulder screamed in pain. The feeling wasn't gone. A strange tingling sensation snaked down his right arm and into his fingers. The arm wasn't paralyzed, but it sure as hell didn't work right.

He fumbled extracting his cell phone with his left hand and answered. The EMT mumbled something admonishing.

Grey shot questions down the line as fast as he could answer. "Kane's down, unconscious...don't know yet... no. Creep's still breathing. Took one from Kane in the neck...yes. See you there."

Kane moaned, coming to. "Cowboy up," Jackson said.

"Jade?" Kane whispered through broken breath.

"Let's worry about you. She wasn't caught in a shooting gallery."

Fighting, Kane's eyelids fluttered. He writhed in agony. "Did we get him?"

"Yeah, buddy. You got him."

Out again. Jackson searched the medic's eyes for reassurance.

"Your partner's a fighter," the kid said. "Like you. Stubborn."

By the time the hospital came into view, Jackson's anger and urgency couldn't be concealed. He followed Kane into the operating room until a nurse forced him out. He eyed a chair outside the door. It appeared to slink further away on his approach. A nurse behind him shouted a room number. He swiveled to confront her. His momentum sent the hall spinning around him. When it stopped, he was on a gurney.

"Hey, I need—"

"You need medical attention, and you're getting it," the nurse barked.

His eyes closed against his will, and the fire that fortified him burned out. His head hit the pillow as hands shoved him in place. They didn't give him time to find Grey, talk to Jade, or ask someone for Kane's prognosis.

Damn unfinished messy business.

All he could think of fading out was that Kane was the doctor's priority. He hadn't seen the ambulance carrying Carroll. With any luck it'd slowed down because there was no longer a need to save his life. With any luck, the Redeemer was dead.

FORTY-FIVE

A nurse entered the hospital's operating wing corridor. Max's head came up. She shook hers preparing for an apology. "He isn't out of surgery," she said. "I'm sorry."

"The other detective? Jackson Swan. How's he?" Max wore the worry of a man invested.

"He's being moved to recovery. That's what I came to tell you. I'll come get you when Detective Swan wakes."

"Yes. It's urgent I speak with him. Any word on the extent of damage?"

Tex was shot in the arm. Nurses said he'd been difficult. He wasn't mortally wounded, but he was a cop shot in his gun arm.

"They won't have anything conclusive until he is healing." The nurse stared at Max. "Are you feeling okay? You look pale."

"Don't like hospitals," Max replied, staring at the floor to avoid more than a couple seconds of direct eye contact. When he glanced up, she pursed her lips to speak but said nothing. On her way out, she paused and turned back. "His surgeon's the best I've seen. Your friend won't hold much of anything for months, but with Dr. Mills, there's hope of full recovery. It'll take time."

"None of them will be fit for the job anyway," Max whispered. The nurse left, and Max collapsed against the back wall wearing defeat physically.

He wasn't responsible for the fallout. If Jade had been told everything sooner, Kane might not be down the hall having a surgical makeover on his liver, kidney, and/or spleen. The doctors weren't sure what the bullet nicked. Their assessment was obscure at best. Life could've been different.

Max held pieces, and Grey set them on the game board.

Pieces, that's who they were now, broken pieces.

Grey marched in, an aged manila folder dangling from his hand.

Max stiffened to full height to face him. He'd come alone. His hands were weak, clumsily they lost grip and dropped the contents of the file over the floor.

Grey dropped to his knees clambering to retrieve the documents. Max locked onto one particular evidence photo that slid his direction. He spun it with the toe of his shoe until it faced him right side up.

"Is that who I think it is?" Max asked.

Grey reached to dislodge the picture from under Max's foot. Max stood firm, reached down, and snatched it up.

"Yes."

Not many photos of this time period had survived. Jade's father had eradicated all traces of her mother's life. She'd salvaged few pictures from her youth that Max knew of. None like the one Max held. In this one, she wasn't smiling. In this one, Jade's mother had clearly been beaten and raped.

The hall, once empty and endless, compressed to a claustrophobic cell. Max never knew her mother was the victim of rape. It made sense. Not a topic of discussion for an eleven-year-old daughter, so Jade wouldn't have been told. It cast new light on that strange expression her father wore when he thought she wasn't looking. Max had seen it more than once and wondered what lurked behind his distant eyes.

Max swept through the papers and located the initial complaint report and locked on the date of the attack.

Grey backed away, then stood at full height.

"You knew." Max stared up at him from his position crouched on the floor. Grey's face lost all pigment.

"Jade?" Max accused. "You didn't think in all her years of therapy she should've been—"

"Told?" Grey said. "Told what? More devastating truth? More haunting history she could do nothing to change?"

"This explains the discord between her and her father. The reason he couldn't reach out. You don't think that would've healed her?" Max's voice gained octaves with every word.

"No! I don't! I think it would've made things worse. There's nothing healing here." Grey waved the half empty file at Max. "You don't understand the half of it."

"I don't think anyone has been given the luxury of understanding. You denied them that, and they're all in operating rooms or dead!" Max wasn't holding back.

Grey quit waving the file, stepped closer to Max, and when he spoke again, his voice left no trace of defense. "They'll be all right. The doctors haven't said anything else, have they?"

"Jackson may have lost his career to the bullet in his arm. That's his reward for waking up a hero. Kane isn't out of surgery. They say his challenge will be infection and intense pain. And he deserves that? Jade—"

"Dr. Maxwell?" The nurse was back. Her expression reflected the intensity of the room. "Your detective is coming to. If you'd follow me."

"This is Captain Grey of Shadows Hook's Violent Crimes task force." Max stepped aside, gathered the remaining photos from the floor and slammed them into Grey's stomach.

"Sorry, sir." The nurse nodded Grey's direction. "This way."

"How is he?" Grey asked.

"The surgery went well."

More obscurity.

"Does he know?" Max asked.

The nurse paused before rounding the corner. "No. Would you prefer—"

"I'll tell him," Grey said.

Max cast Grey a glare, too late to be forthcoming. The damage inflicted, the fallout begun. Max wanted to vent, accuse, but knew it wouldn't change a damn thing.

His thoughts turned to Jade as he walked to see her injured partners. How her vibrant green eyes had gained new depth when he saw her last. She'd been at peace with her decision to start a new life with the man in the operating room fighting for his. He took solace knowing she had been removed from active duty because of her concussion, and it wasn't her on the operating room table. He glanced at Grey gritting his teeth. They'd both failed to protect her, and the fallout had only begun.

FORTY-SIX

A sea of wreckage surrounded Grey. Its waves eroded the solid ground beneath him, shuddering in the hollows of his breath, fracturing the façade of his integrity.

Every operating room he glanced into on the way to recovery was worse than the last. The fallout. Each, a segment of a pinwheel layout, was visible through the windows in the adjoining hall. A coiled path intended for staff.

In one room, nurses bandaged Rachel Leigh following what must've been a massive blood transfusion in the war to save her life. Used bags piled high in a metal tray, dripping. The scene was macabre. The smell made him grimace.

Her father occupied a bed two rooms away. Doctors worked frantically, an eye surgeon at his head, another repairing a leg wound, and one holding cardio paddles. Amazing, Nickolas had fight left in him.

They passed Kane's room last. Only his head was visible beyond the wall of attendees that worked at his side. Unconscious, his face appeared oddly serene. Not in the clear yet.

With every step Grey took, the floor sloped a little more, if only in his mind.

The nurse leading him moved aside to reveal a back waiting area where Jackson was waking. Another redressed Jackson's wound from the shooting at his barn.

Grey couldn't stop the tightening in his chest. He had a theory that was full of holes, like his detectives.

"In operating rooms or dead," Max said and wasn't wrong.

Max stomped by, circled the foot of the bed to stand at the opposite side. His distancing a deliberate statement about Grey's guilt in mishandling the case history. Max's eyes hid none of his fear, even less of his accusations.

Grey waited for the nurse to finish, then claimed the chair she abandoned.

"Kane?" The word fell from Jackson's lips before his eyes opened.

"Still in surgery, buddy. No news yet." Grey gave him a few seconds to process.

"Carroll?" Jackson strained to shift positions. The toll visible.

"Stay still. They're transferring you to a room in a couple minutes. That'll be uncomfortable enough."

Max grabbed an extra pillow from a linen rack behind him and propped it under Jackson's injured arm.

"Wow. A shrink and my boss." Jackson focused in on Grey. "Not the welcoming committee I hoped for."

"What happened?" Grey needed facts, fast. The media storm was swirling floors below them.

"We pegged him for a runner and walked into an ambush. If I hadn't been shot, Kane wouldn't have risked going in without help. From where I bled, it didn't appear he had a choice." Jackson's voice gained strength. "And where the hell *was* our backup? We gave 'em plenty of time."

Grey leaned back in the chair. "Carroll put a delay router virus in the system. Tech will be sweeping it for weeks. Said it's a mess in there. The whole thing's being dismantled. We didn't see it. Our messages got through. We didn't notice the time lag."

Max released an exasperated sigh. "There's a lot about this completely out of the realm of your control. You shouldn't—"

"No offense, Doc, I don't need you or anyone telling me what I should or shouldn't feel guilty for. Kane isn't out of surgery." Jackson suffered visible agony pulling himself higher up on his pillows.

"You're right." Grey shot Max a glare. "The fallout is *my* responsibility. You did your job. You caught Carroll. We owe you."

Jackson locked eyes for a second, then turned to stare at Max.

"What are you doing here? Really. I'm not one of your patients. Or am I?"

Max searched for the right words. Grey jumped in before he found them. "No. You're not now and won't be."

Max raised an eyebrow. "I'm concerned about what all of you are going through, and I'm here if you need me."

Jackson turned his attention back. "You said fallout. So, this isn't over? Help me out here. I'm a little hazy, but I'm pretty sure I saw Carroll take a bullet and drop like a hammer. What am I missing?"

Max closed the distance to the bed. Jackson shifted uncomfortably. Grey wanted to toss Max from the room. He wasn't the enemy. The enemy was the past, and there was no apprehending it.

A seasoned hound, Jackson sensed trouble afoot. "Where's Jade in all this? I want to talk to her. Can you send her in?"

Max sent Grey a cautionary glance. Jackson caught it as the nurse returned.

"Your room is ready, Detective Swan. We should get you moved to a more private location." The nurse swept by, unlocking the bed wheels and lifting side rails.

"Excuse me. I'm sorry, hon." Jackson gestured for the nurse to step aside. He glared back and forth between Grey and Max. "I don't know what's up with y'all, but I expect answers and quick. Jade had better be my first visitor the second I'm set up in the new digs. Which one of you is delivering the okay on Kane?"

"Max will," Grey offered. "The second he knows he's in the clear. I'm headed back to the shop. I'll be back tonight. Max is staying."

Jackson stared at Max. Max nodded his reassurance and headed out behind Grey to get out of the nurse's way. She stopped them before they made the door. "You better take the staff stairs at the back. Our lobby's swarming with media. They say there's never been a case this awful."

"Not publicly," Max mumbled.

Grey wanted to punch him. He was in enough trouble. His crumbling credibility wouldn't survive an assault on the house shrink.

"I want to talk to Jade," Jackson called after them.

"You need to rest. Please." Grey heard the nurse plead with Jackson. He hoped she could keep him occupied or tranquilized until he had answers.

"I don't know how you're keeping a lid on this." Max headed for the main elevators. "They deserve the truth."

"Keep quiet. Call me the minute Kane's status changes." Grey paused before turning down the hall leading to the back staircase. "And don't tell them a thing. I will after I...they're in enough pain."

Max's worst fears were realized. He should've told Detective Swan what he suspected. He almost had, but Grey shut him down.

Grey worked the case, handled the media, and pulled the pieces together. Max wondered if the picture he arrived at was nearly as tragic as his own. He glanced at his hands. They shook. Ten minutes in a room alone with Kane or Jackson, and they'd read him like a book.

He informed the nurses' desk where he could be found, then pressed the elevator for the second-floor cafeteria. He needed distance.

When he walked in, the place was overrun with journalists spinning angles, amped up on bad espresso.

He overheard one speaking to her paper over the phone. "If the detective dies, I'll lead with that. If the killer does, we'll go with the 'Police End Reign of Redemption' version. If they both live, hell, I don't know. Save me six above the fold."

Max walked by head down, staring at his shoes. The headlines in his mind were worse. God forbid one of them connect him to the case.

He found a table in a far back corner, a space before the expanse of windows, swung his work satchel off his shoulder onto its top, and melted into a chair. Depression crushed his tall form into a spineless mass.

Work was a healthy path to survive guilt and anger, a lethal combination, or was it?

Journal in hand, he pulled his ballpoint from his breast pocket, inflated his posture, and mapped facts. Sunbeams, muted by the film on the outer windowpanes, drew an arrow over his paper from where he'd written *Redeemer* straight to *Jade*.

Grey had secrets. He wasn't alone.

He didn't tell Grey about Jade's visit to his office. Grey knew more than he'd revealed. He always did, though *he* did a brilliant job of concealing his suspicions. Max's burned through his flesh in bold scarlet across his face. Bluffing was never his strong suit. And what he knew wouldn't be buried.

Buried, he thought, a horrible word.

He lived by facts. Realizing he'd plummeted into a realm absent of clarity unnerved him. He wrote down the names of those involved, linked them to recent events, added in the details he'd learned from each, and connected them in sequence. The sunlight shifted until only its tip remained illuminating the last two letters in Jade's name. The dark overtook the labyrinth that emerged and scared him.

"You working the case?"

Max jerked upright, slamming his journal shut, appearing more than a little guilty to the female journalist he'd overheard spinning headlines. He'd attracted attention, deep in thought, scribbling with intensity.

"No." He rose, aware of the scattered papers he'd amassed. He gathered his things, refusing to make eye contact, and brushed by her. He eyed the barista at the coffee bar. Should've ordered a latte first.

"Thought we could—" the journalist hollered over heads.

"I'm a doctor. Have a patient waiting." Max embellished and let the reporter's voice fade as he fled the cafeteria and made for the elevator.

He stared down the descending numbers as the elevator came to meet him, forcing his lungs to slow their air intake. Breathe. The elevator opened. He hurried onboard and fervently pressed the close door button, leaving would-be passengers waiting. Without intention, he pressed the button for the floor Carroll occupied. One lower than Jackson and Kane's. He ascended in silence until the chamber shuddered to a halt. He stepped out and drifted down the hall, eyes scanning information boards. No nameplate on Carroll's room, and none needed. Security darkened his door. Max cursed protocol under his breath until he recognized the cop as a former patient's partner.

Smiling, he asked, "Any word on prognosis, Terrance?"

"Don't know, Doc. Was a revolving door for a while. It's quieted down." The doorman stood staunch.

"How's Mike been? Think we've got him on the mend," Max said.

"He's good. Thanks."

"Getting an update for Grey. He's waiting on Kane and Jackson." Max gave him a can-you-believe-this-mess headshake.

"Sure, we'd all be happier if the perp kicked it." Terrance waved Max in.

"We sure would." Max slid inside, waiting on the threshold for the door to seal behind him.

The man on the bed didn't warrant his "Redeemer" pseudonym. Vulnerable to the accuracy of a breathing machine, trapped in a deep coma, with half his neck mangled, and suffering partial, if not complete, paralysis, he wasn't scary anymore.

Or was he?

Max stepped forward. Close enough to lift the information from the end of the bed and scan it for details, a comfortable distance from the body.

"Neck quadra. paralysis. Trauma sustained at base of neck, six and seventh vertebrae, monitoring swelling—" The air compressor sounded. Max eyed the man on the bed, then the machine.

He returned the clipboard to its place, meandered to the far side of the room, stared out its window at news crew vehicles amassing below, then walked to the head of the bed. Hovering over Carroll, he eyed the life-sustaining machine. Its cord lay inches away, its electronic panel at perfect height for an armrest.

Wouldn't take much. One lazy, haphazard mistake, and they'd be rid of him and his murderous bloodline would die with him. Or would it? Max leaned in, close enough to hear the artificial breath leave Carroll's lungs. Then, the Redeemer's eyes snapped open.

Max slammed into the machine. Air stalled in his chest. He barely registered the nurse's voice as she rushed in and shoved him aside to tend to the patient.

"You've got to be careful around the equipment," she admonished. "It's highly sensitive. The least little—"

She turned, following Max's stare to Carroll's open eyes, then said, "It happens sometimes. Trust me, he's not awake. Chances are he never will be. Guard said you're the police shrink?"

Max couldn't look away. He stayed locked in a stare with Carroll's dead eyes until the wall stopped him from drifting further. "Genetic testing ordered?"

"Yep, isn't back. Really, don't let the eyes unnerve you."

"It's not the eyes. It's what's behind them." Max spoke under his breath. She couldn't understand what he meant, soon everyone would.

Her voice faded as Max inched out the door. Visiting hours were over at the hospital, but his patient wasn't there. He needed to find her. Certain of it now, she deserved the truth.

FORTY-SEVEN

Kane woke disoriented which worsened with his awareness of the hospital bed and memory of the serial killer's bullets that put him there. He let moments pass staring at the sunlight of daybreak edging through the window, grateful the last face he'd seen was Jade's after they'd plugged Carroll and watched him fall.

Kane found breathing on his own reassuring. He lifted his covers, inspected the bandages around his midsection. He expected those. A slight pain outside his left shoulder said he'd been nicked. No memory of that. Or much of anything between firing on Carroll and waking.

The IV in his hand itched, his stomach churned against him, and his headache was a three-alarm. Other than that, alive.

He doubted Carroll could say the same.

He searched for the remote to summon a nurse. A slight man in scrubs entered before he pushed the button.

"You're awake. I'm Dr. Mills. Patched you up last night. I'm off in an hour. Thought I'd check on you before heading out. How are you feeling?"

"Like the worst flu on earth knocked me on my ass. Otherwise, not bad. Meds must be working. How bad is the damage?"

"We were pretty concerned before we got in there. Essentially, you got lucky. The bullet grazed your spleen. We removed it, the bullet, not your spleen. Could've been far worse."

"When can I get out of here?" Kane stretched, lifting up on his pillows. Pain shot through to his back with a force that caused instant nausea. It must've shown on his face.

"The nausea will dissipate soon." Dr. Mills stepped closer and wrote something on the chart at the foot of the bed. "It'll be a few days before you can move around comfortably. You need time to heal here, then bed rest at home for—"

"Thanks, Doc. I'm in the middle of the largest case Shadow has ever—"

"I know. We all know. If you want to outlast him, you'd better—"

"Outlast him?" Kane struggled with the control to shift the bed upright, clenching back the urge to vomit. "Carroll's alive?"

"Depends on your definition. Machines are regulating his breath and—"

Kane's temperature rose. He had a sudden urge to throw off the blankets, spring from the bed, march down the hall, and empty a new clip into Carroll's life-sustaining equipment.

The doctor seized his wrist, tapping his pulse. "Calm down, Detective. He's not going anywhere, if there's a hell on Earth, he's in it. Better him here than in paradise."

As much as Kane longed to see Carroll dead, the doctor's words rang true. If an afterlife existed, and there was even a slim chance the Redeemer would find redemption there, he was better suffering here with the rest of humanity.

Mills released Kane's wrist. "Gotta finish rounds before I head out. If you want a future in your career, stay put."

"No long-term damage?" Kane asked.

"Nothing that'll keep you off the job permanently. No. I recommend you avoid bullets. An inch can make the difference between life and death. Luck, I've found, runs out sooner or later." Mills headed to the door.

"I tell my partner that all the time." Kane couldn't help thinking how he'd given Jade the last laugh. Criticizing her for being reckless then ended up on the operating table. He couldn't help recognizing an echo of his father. He'd no interest in her trading places. Soon she'd be off the job and out of harm's way. "Have you seen my phone?"

Mills paused in the threshold. "Your boss claimed it when they brought you in. The desk phone works if you need to use it until you get yours back."

"And my partner?"

"Detective Swan's injury is complicated." The doctor clenched his lips. "We don't know if the paralysis will be permanent. We haven't discussed worse-case scenarios with him. We'll give it some time."

Kane felt sick again. Not from the nausea. "Thanks for saving my life, Doc."

"My job." Mills's smile faded. "I'm glad you got him off the streets. I'd be lying if I said it was easy to know we're keeping him alive."

"Then he's finally sharing the fate of his victims. Having his life in the hands of someone who sees it as worthless."

The door closed. The case flooded back, and all its unanswered questions begged for his attention. He buzzed the nurse. She came in a minute later.

"I need patient information, something for nausea, and a phone book. And I need to know how fast I can get out of here."

"Well, you look like crap." Nikki sat at Jackson's bedside waiting for him to stir. When his eyes opened, a calm came with the sight of her. Some good had triumphed.

"You look like an angel." He smiled at her then down at the hand she was holding. Gripping back sent a dull ache through his injured shoulder despite the meds.

"Liar. More like a rag doll or a half-wrapped mummy." Her smile wasn't damaged. It was all he saw. That and her beautiful blue eyes.

"It's kinda sexy." The Redeemer no longer a threat, he wasn't wasting any time.

"Wow. You're terrible." Nikki shook her head, her smile intensified.

"You don't know the half of it." He rubbed his eyes with his free hand and left the other in hers. "How long have you been here?"

"Just arrived."

A nurse walked in with a breakfast tray and overheard the tail end of their conversation. "She's lying. She's been sitting there since the crack of dawn."

"Hush, Estell. I thought we were friends." Nikki shifted to make room for the tray. "Besides, look what he did to stay in here with me." Jackson clenched her hand. Painful or not, now that he had it, he wasn't about to let go.

The nurse moved the tray, positioning it within reach of Jackson's good arm, and smiled down. "Try to eat. You'll feel better. How's your pain?"

"Fine as cream gravy." Jackson was laughing at Nikki.

"If it worsens, hit the button."

"That's dangerous. Talk about instant gratification." Jackson smiled at the nurse as she left, then back at Nikki.

"That's a whole other conversation." Nikki released his hand, leaned over to the tray, and angled the water glass for Jackson to drink from its straw.

"One we should have." Jackson swallowed down half the glass. "One of many."

Nikki reclaimed his hand. No denying their emotions, rare beyond measure, a safety. The start of something good. The attraction, though intense, was secondary.

Their trust caused him to insist she stay when Max flew in, staunch and dismal to deliver "bad news." Jackson heard him out, his heart sinking with each of Max's admissions about Grey, his past connection to Carroll, the cover-up, and finally its cost. When Max was done, he quit pacing and collapsed, head in hands, into a chair by the door. Neither spoke for a brief eternity.

Jackson broke the silence. "Does Kane know?"

"No. He knows about the cover-up, well most of it, but—" Max's large form diminished under the burden of knowledge.

"Any chance you're wrong?" Jackson knew the answer. It burned in the fresh resin coating his eyes. The truth hurt, its pain crippling.

"Grey didn't think so. He's working on confirmation. When Jade didn't show up at the hospital after you both were shot, we knew. He wanted to be certain before revealing anything to Kane. He owed him, and you, that much. When there was no answer at the cabin, he hit her place, everywhere he could think of on the way out."

"And he's gone out there alone?" Jackson wanted to punch something. Max seemed a viable option, but a glance in his direction said he couldn't inflict more damage.

"Amy's helping him nail things down. I assume he took back up."

"Right." Frustration had Jackson clench down on Nikki's hand. Instead of pulling free, she matched his grip. "Did he find anything yet?"

"Said he'd call me the second he did. He's waiting on his contact at the DA's." Max stood and paced the room again. "I want to be wrong. No one has laid eyes on her since she discovered Leigh. That's two full days and one night."

"Give me your phone." Jackson snatched it from Max with his left hand. "I need the whole truth before I let either of you near Kane."

FORTY-EIGHT

"You want to lecture me about consequences?" Grey yelled into his office phone at the district attorney. "Bodies are littering the place. Those consequences will hit hard and heavy at your doorstep if this isn't wrapped in pretty paper."

The two men discovered an interest in law together as kids. Generations later they stood firm on very different paths. Both precarious.

Grey needed a back door for information. His buddy would help as long as he didn't get his hands dirty. Cops had an innate disdain for criminals, closely matched only by their revulsion to lawyers. Amazing how many of them got in the way of the law.

"You're supposed to be in *our* corner. I'm asking you to lean on her a little. I need that list of properties, Matt."

He arched his circling of the room near the door and slammed it with a swift smack without breaking stride.

"Work for the good guys?" He avoided the awards and commendations on the walls of his office, ignoring the warnings pouring from his cordless, knowing if the truth hit the papers, they'd all fall. "Working for them doesn't make you one of them."

He hung up, speaking to the empty room, "I ought to know."

Attacking the pile of papers littering his desk served as a distraction until the printer in the corner switched on. He loomed over it willing it to quit warming up and print.

Annoyed at the thundering rapping between his ears, he rummaged through his desk drawer for extra-strength something. Only to realize it was the pounding of his heart that wouldn't be silenced.

Paper slid free from the machine. He snatched it up, still warm in his grasp. A list, fourteen names flanked by addresses, blackened the paper. He read down. Four large corporations associated with the case, three charitable foundations, two newly constructed architectural buildings, the textile mill Jade was hit at, a pharmaceutical company, the Carroll family estate where Rachel Leigh was found, a land holding in Upstate New York, and a residential address that froze him in place.

An old, familiar residential address.

The room around him lost clarity. Crisp edges, blurred. So too did the page he held. The heartbeat, loud in his ears before, muffled to a distant drone. A deep pain opened in his chest. A dull, raw ache to mark the beginning of a regret destined to make its home there and never leave.

He'd sent teams to the properties. They'd go in alone to all except the last. That one he'd cover with them. The places Jade should've been found didn't hold her, which meant the Redeemer did. Even sustained by medical equipment, he had what they all held so dear under his grasp.

Jade.

His hands were shaking when Amy opened the door. Her perplexed expression deepened with concern. Accustomed to barging in at any inappropriate moment, she hovered on the threshold. The dead weight in the air pinning her there.

He waved her in. "Shut it behind you." Moisture trickled from his left eye. He turned away. He'd seen unimaginable horror over the course of his career. Disheartening waste that tarnished forever one's perspective on the world, but he'd never broke.

Grey Grant didn't cry. His ex-wife said, "you can't get blood from a stone or tears from Grey."

He wiped the stain with his sleeve, pulled his gun from its drawer, then lifted his holster from his coat rack and strapped it on. Amy closed the door behind her, moved in, and adjusted the strap across his back.

"Thinking you'll need to use it, Cap?"

He met her worried eyes. "You never know."

"Carroll's out. In a coma, I thought." She followed him to the doorway.

"It's not for Carroll."

"This case, it's far from over, isn't it?"

She was young, impressionable, but brilliant. "Yes. Far from."

"Where we headed?"

Grey let her pass under his arm. He held the door ajar and paused, staring at his office, wanting to remember how it once was. Fearing after today, it'd never be the same.

He wasn't one of the good guys anymore.

"The last address on the list." His voice lost its command, solemn in anticipation of what lay ahead. He handed the sheet to Amy. She studied it on the way to his car.

Grey's assistant stepped out of her office, leaning on her doorframe. "Captain, head office called twice. They want to know how long Detective Kolton will be on leave. Sorry, sir. Should I tell them—"

"Tell them he'll be back whenever he's damn well ready and not a second before. And if they have a problem with that, tell them I'll call them back when I'm done mopping up bodies." Grey's voice rang with zero tolerance, but he placed a hand gently on his assistant's arm as he passed. Reassuring her his venom wasn't for her.

She nodded and disappeared.

Cold air outside tempered the heat rushing through his veins. The day was somber, overcast, and cool. The sun knew better than to shine today. Grey hesitated. His car was sitting in its rightful place. No one there to steal his front row parking space. He unlocked it and sank into the seat feeling he couldn't get much lower.

Amy slid into the passenger side, shut the door, and began programming the GPS.

He put his hand over hers, lifting it from the computer keyboard. "I don't need directions." He released her hand and gripped the wheel. "I could find it in my sleep."

"These are Carroll's property holdings?" Amy's expression remained concerned.

"Yeah." Grey flew from the parking garage out into traffic, never diverting his eyes from the road. "They didn't all start that way."

"How'd you—"

"I knew the previous owner." No point in giving her more information. She'd find out soon enough. He hoped she was ready. He wasn't sure how she'd handle the truth. The one thing he knew was after today, she'd be like the rest of them. Damaged.

Amy shifted her position. Sat back straight, eyes dead ahead.

Stiffening up, he thought. Smart kid. She knew something ugly was coming and chose to brace for it revealing strength of character. Good.

She'd need every ounce.

He brought her for more than one reason. Loyalty provided insulation when walls crumbled. And he could hear the brick and mortar collapsing as he drove.

———

The leather seat at Amy's back was as cold as Captain Grey's curt answers. If the dread rising inside her was the equivalent of a cop's gut instinct, she understood how it couldn't be ignored. Afraid to ask more questions for fear Grey would slam the car to the curb and deliver a leveling truth, she offered quiet compliance.

Her phone rang, breaking the deafening silence in the vehicle. Jackson, with more bad news.

"I'm sorry, this isn't a good time. I'm with—"

"I know you're with Grey." Jackson's words were fueled with urgency. "Don't let him know it's me. Listen and give short answers."

"I can't make it tonight. Apologize to your family for me." Amy did her level best to avert suspicion but wasn't sure why she needed to.

"Are you in the car?" Jackson asked.

"Yep, me too," Amy said.

"Running down locations?"

"It's one night, I know."

"One location? Okay. Did he request backup?"

"Yep, meet your family there?" Amy gave Grey an apologetic grin when he glanced over. He didn't appear concerned about the call.

"Text the address to this number when you hang up. Can you do that?"

"Sure. I'll send you the link for the restaurant. Wish there was more I could do."

"Delay him if you can." Jackson's voice reassured her she should trust her gut. Something horrible was on the horizon.

"Don't know if I can. I'll do my best." Amy hung up, typed in the address, and forwarded it to the number Jackson called in on. Truth was they were further away from it then Jackson was leaving from the hospital. He could, in theory, get there first, but he was barely out of surgery and not mobile. Nothing made sense.

"Something wrong?" Grey asked. She'd been preoccupied too long.

"Cops and dating don't mix. Sorry."

"Well, she's got you meeting her family." Grey cracked a half smile then turned his attention back on the road.

Amy stared out the window afraid her thoughts could be read in her eyes.

"Why didn't you ever remarry?" Redirect, she'd learned that one early on.

"I married the job. Tried a mistress for eighteen years but that ended badly." He never made eye contact. "You can never please both. Sooner or later, they both either leave or give up on you."

She hoped that wasn't true. It felt true, and she realized, lesbian, straight, black, white, or other, rookie or captain, atheist or devout, they were only people, and none could escape the trappings of pain.

FORTY-NINE

Kane glimpsed Max rushing into Jackson's hospital room and followed him. The nausea medication was working, and the nurse made concessions for short walks. Rounding the corner, he caught the tail end of a conversation that stopped him.

"...my worst fears realized. I wasn't sure until—" Max was patrolling the doorway. Kane ducked back. "At first, I thought I was losing it, but now..." Max sounded unnerved in a way that sent shivers up Kane's taxed spine.

"You're certain?" Jackson sounded abnormally incensed, even fired up. "This started with her then. Doc Rachel was right?"

Kane struggled to pick up broken phrases between overhead announcements, nurse and patient chatter, and the hallway's squeaking gallery of wheelchairs, rolling beds, and IV stands.

"Not just that, I checked the log. There's nothing on it since the day Jade came to tell me she was quitting and found—"

"Quitting?" Jackson's voice thundered out the doorway. "Why in Sam hell didn't you speak up?"

So much for doctor-patient privilege, Kane thought. All it took to break it was a pissed off Texan.

"I don't want to believe it. Neither of us has reached Jade since that appointment, and now he's not talking, ever!" Max sounded remorseful, enraged, and on the verge of a breakdown. The case had cracked the shrink. Not good. Kane missed details beneath a blanket of confusion.

Medicine aftertaste dried his mouth. A tray with a water jug was left in the hall within reaching distance. He glanced longingly as a nurse scooped it away.

"How do you intend to deliver the news to Kane?" Max asked.

Kane leaned in, rubbing his throat.

"No one is telling Kane a thing until we have something solid!" Jackson winced in pain. Kane sympathized. His side burned through the painkillers. Whatever they had to tell him he'd rather it came from Tex. His distrust of Abraham Maxwell, doctor or no, hadn't completely vanished.

"When did this happen? How could it?" Jackson wasn't asking, he was deciphering. "If your calculations are correct…and it's been two days…"

Max hesitated. "Yes."

"You know what you're telling me?" Jackson's voice cracked. Whatever Max told Jackson had him twisted up, a rare feat.

"Calm down." A woman's voice. "Is there another way to verify this?"

"Outside seeing it with my own eyes? No. Nothing I can trust." Jackson again.

"I can go," Max offered.

"No offense, Doc, but you're not qualified." Jackson shifted and grimaced. Pain from a wound the doctors hadn't admitted could cost him his career. Kane clenched his teeth at the thought of Tex grounded. He was in no condition to be hunting down anything. "Amy and Grey should reach the scene, if it is a scene, soon. Amy will let me know. She's the only one of you not treating me like a mushroom."

Kane recognized the ding signaling an incoming message on Max's cell. He'd always been annoyed at Berlioz announcing Max's importance in symphonic display.

Jackson read an address out. "Five-forty Vine Avenue. Is that relevant?"

Max paused, weighing the question or checking documents, Kane couldn't see. Max was deep inside the room. Kane had no means of checking the address either. No cell. They all relied on technology too much. He searched, instead, his memory banks. Had he ever heard the address before?

Had Grey said it? Did it relate to any of the crimes?

Voices from the past flooded his mind, the addresses of all the crime scenes, old cases that shared identifiers. The hall got noisy. Competing for his attention. A patient teetered into a nurse carrying a tray, sent her off balance. The tray crashed to the ground.

Five-forty?

The hall stretched linearly into a line reaching to infinity at either end, the people and objects therein blurring into streams of muted color, with Jade in clear recollection at its center. She was laughing at their favorite Chinese restaurant celebrating the purchase of her house. The waitress said which house numbers were good luck and which to avoid.

"Fifty-four, don't do," the waitress warned in broken English.

"I know that one." Jade's expression lost its glow. "Means certain death."

"Not certain, you translate badly," the waitress argued. "Chance of—"

"Certain death," Jade repeated. "I know, lived it. They say I was lucky to survive."

The hallway bled through erasing the image. Kane's skin formed an icy barrier trapping everything beneath, including his heart, in a cold grip. Perspiration trickled from his hairline, tracing his cheekbone. His breathing labored under clenching chest muscles, and his eyes lost the clarity of definition, discerning only distorted shapes in monotone color. Hospital unrest rang back into his ears underpinning words he dreaded.

"Jade was Carroll's target." Jackson's voice quaked. "All of this to get to her?"

"Not just her, but yes." Max sounded certain and afraid.

Carroll was being kept alive by machines. He couldn't hurt her now.

"His elaborate plan was constructed with her at its center, and whatever his end goal was…he guaranteed it'd play out with or without him." Kane heard Max collapse into a chair, the burden too heavy.

The wall Kane rested on became unreliable, greasy. Against his will, his body slid down it. Clutching a hallway chair for stability, his hands shook along its wooden edge.

"The address. Max, can you check it against Jade's file?" Jackson asked.

"I can…I guess if—"

"Just do it!" Tex was yelling, something he never did. "Nikki, my water please."

Kane inched up the wall again.

"You need to stay calm." Nikki cautioned. Kane guessed she'd become a permanent fixture in Jackson's life. He'd taken an interest in no one until her. Kane knew how that felt. What it did to a man.

He glimpsed inside, breath shuddering up from his lungs. Max scrolled through his emails, typed a line or two, and waited.

"Well? Any connection?" Jackson's tone shielded nothing.

Max's voice cracked. "Her parents' old address."

"The house her mother was murdered in?" Jackson barked. "And we're in here? She's been out there on her own—"

Kane abandoned the doorway and stumbled into the next room. A male patient lay sleeping. A duffel bag, left on the adjacent bed, sat open, clothes and personal items inside. Kane scooped it up, threw the strap over his shoulder, and weaved through hall traffic to a visitor's washroom.

His night nurse, Vanora, had just come on shift. He glimpsed her heading his direction, bent his head down, and kept moving. He knew he wouldn't last long before the morphine wore off and his injuries crippled him.

For Jade, he was willing to die trying.

"Detective?" Vanora spotted him, caught up, and had a hold of his arm. "What are you doing? Your room's the other direction."

Kane stared at her through a haze. "He's got my partner. If I don't go, she's dead."

"If you go, you might be." Vanora was young, soft.

"I'd rather that. Let go." Kane's eyes remained locked on hers.

"When was your last dose?" Vanora was reaching into her pocket for keys.

"An hour ago." Kane prayed his desperation was contagious.

"In here." Vanora shuffled him off to a side room equipped for minor surgery. "Your enemy is infection and direct trauma. Lift your shirt." Tears stained her sable skin.

Kane raised up the cloth exposing his dressing. Vanora checked it, redressed it with extra bandages, then pulled out a needle. "Give me your arm. This will help with the pain. I give you four hours."

"I was guessing three." His stare held intense gratitude. "Why are you doing this?"

"If you don't come back before, then you'll end up on a floor somewhere." She glanced up from her crouched position tending to his wound. "Come back before then."

"Why?"

"Help you? Every woman here wishes him dead. Our whole town needs this nightmare over, not just you."

Kane nodded, straightened his clothes, and headed to the exit.

FIFTY

Kane watched Jade's childhood home come into view through the cab's smeared glass. He envisioned her, little, innocent, hiding in closets.

The cabbie wasn't familiar with the area. He passed the street and backtracked. Approaching from the west, the house was visible before the strobe of flashing lights encroaching from the east.

Grey sent patrol ahead of him and Amy. They'd all arrived within seconds of each other. Too many red lights. Kane counted three cars. Grey's pulled in as the cabbie closed the distance.

Lights were on inside the house, windows glowing soft gold. Cops littered the sidewalk edge of the front lawn. Kane's eyes fixed on one descending the front steps running east toward Grey.

That's when he noticed the crime scene tape being set out.

Jesus, no.

There were lots of reasons for it. It didn't mean anything definitive. The red lights circling the car roofs caught the corner of his eye. He squinted, shutting them out.

He must've been staring. The cop with Grey recognized him. The expression he wore was…

Kane smacked the cabbie on the shoulder, stopping him in front of the stairs leading to the front door, beyond the stretch of lawn where Grey and the cops were approaching.

Grey shouted. His words muffled inside the cab. Kane needed inside that house. He couldn't outrun Grey. Being a yard closer gave him a head start.

He threw the car door open before the cabbie came to a complete stop. Sheer adrenaline fueled him. Five steps up he wondered how the loose trousers he wore had turned to lead. He scaled the staircase, beyond the sea of arms reaching to impede his climb. A footfall from the landing, strong hands caught up and gripped him, ending his blind rush.

Stopping time so he could read the horror in the faces of those men closest. Hear the anguish in Grey's plea. Smell the night air mix with the scent of despair and blood.

And die inside.

"Stop him!" Grey's voice cut through the confusion. His officers rushed to tackle Kane on the stairs. "Careful. He's been shot, abdomen, supposed to be in the damn hospital!"

The men eased from rugby scrum mentality to no-touch football. Grey flew past them knowing when he reached Kane, there'd be no way to prepare him. A lifetime of being a cop, and he had nothing in his arsenal to offer. He'd seen horror. Survived its effects. Suffered the scars. This was different. This was worse.

Patrol entered the home on his orders seconds before he and Amy arrived. Time was the enemy. If there was a chance, he'd try. And where the fuck was the ambulance? Neco, first on scene, reported back with all the restraint of an officer holding the line despite personal devastation. Revulsion. No time for regret, that'd come later.

Grey confiscated Amy's phone off the seat. The responsibility of communicating what followed was his burden alone. As he flew up the lawn, she waited, as instructed, beside the car.

One of his newer acquisitions, a player-sized ex-military RN, seized Kane by the shoulders. Kane struggled free and crossed the threshold.

Silence.

The men outside froze, afraid to follow.

They dreaded what lay beyond the door.

The dining room sat left of the foyer. The glow Kane witnessed coming from the windows was cast by tower candles lining the room. The men he evaded never pursued him inside. Only the huge man followed at his back. Three steps were required for a clear view, one inside the threshold, the next across the hall, the last between open French doors.

Three steps and his world imploded.

A stone altar occupied the room left of center, three feet high, six in length. No more than thirty inches wide. And on it laid Jade. In the room with him and yet not there, he feared he was alone in ways the word failed to capture.

Sleeping beauty. Silken hair gracefully encircled her face. She wore layers of sheer white. Her lips accented in a false shade of red. It wasn't her. Was it the body that once housed the most amazing soul he'd ever known? One he couldn't save, couldn't protect. One he'd miss every second of every day that breath stayed in his lungs. Or was she still in there, waiting to be rescued?

The world transformed into a static place of lack and emptiness. Anguish failed to describe the tear that ravaged the core of him. It physically ripped open, turning his soul to glass, broken at the center, shattering out in a burst of defeat so the slightest emotional touch would leave him in useless shards.

Then, the flush of rage. Jade never wore lipstick. His Jade never did. It wasn't his Jade. She'd smear it off with her sleeve when she woke up. She had to wake up.

His infiltration robbed him of energy. Legs, once leaden, solidified and became near immobile. He struggled the last steps to reach her.

Her hands rested one atop the other. Arms sleeved in draping fabric at her sides. He knew her body. Every curve, every edge, the hard and the soft. All altered. Lacking.

When he touched her hands, she was cold.

But too cold?

"No! Damn it, you wait for me!" The voice of a broken soul deeper than his human overtone burst from him unrecognizable.

Tears burned bitter streams down his face. She'd been discovered seconds before. He leaned in, ear pressed near her lips and nose. "Not a sound!" he yelled behind him. Everyone froze. "She's breathing! Medic, medic!"

Her heart rate was so slow, her breathing so shallow they'd assumed she was gone.

"Move!" a burly voice commanded from behind him. "Bring me his siphon! What's your blood type?"

"I'm O negative," Grey called out rolling up his sleeve, racing into the room.

Time that had been stagnant now rushed forth with the speed of racing hooves.

"Get over here! She's got seconds."

Kane's hand clung to hers while the burly cop tore clothes, slammed needles into veins, and manually pumped Grey's blood into Jade's fading body. Arms weren't an option, nothing viable in her neck, he took out a knife and before Kane could protest, he sliced a gash in her upper thigh.

Pain hit Kane and sent him down on one knee. His wound pierced him here and in memory. In monochrome color, he remembered Carroll waving in and out of his gun's scope, Jade stepping in to stabilize his aim, and the shot that sent Carroll down. Flashes of the scene as he was loaded into the ambulance outside the warehouse resurfaced. No Jade. She hadn't been there. He'd wondered why. Jackson's voice echoed through time. Jackson dismissed concern for Jade because he hadn't seen her. It had all been in his blood-deprived mind. She had never really been there.

She'd been here, dying for two days.

He turned away from the bloodbath soaking him. Carroll's siphoning equipment was makeshift at best. He didn't know if the blood was Grey's, Jade's, or his, and it didn't matter. It was one and the same now. For the first time, his eyes searched the walls. They'd been painted red. Rust beneath the candles' flames. His skin bristled. The temperature inside was artificially reduced like a freezer. And the candles were heavily scented, masking?

Masking blood.

The man fighting for Jade's life was crushing the bag Grey's blood flowed into back into a hole in Jade's thigh.

A woman cried out. Not Jade. Amy, defying orders, clung to the doorframe.

"Jade, wake up." His plea was a desperate whisper. Hands were on him again. This time he couldn't fight them. He collapsed into them. Falling back gave him a line of sight to the coffered ceiling. Blood red.

Grey stared into Kane's void eyes before EMTs took over. Filmed and scattered by panic and drugs. Painkillers couldn't help Kane's agony now. He'd pushed it too far.

"What's the ETA on the second ambulance?" he yelled.

The newly arrived EMT was doing what he could, which wasn't much, to prevent shock from killing his detective.

He held a clear view between Kane and the doorway. A line of sight no more than three feet off the floor. He couldn't raise his eyes above that.

Couldn't watch her being ravaged, this time to save her.

A patrolman stood in the threshold near Amy. Patched through to the hospital, he relayed information. "They're saying a low dose of morphine. Wait! Conflicting reports. Could've been back-to-back doses administered."

Grey barked but never called the man closer. "I don't give a damn what's in his system. What do we do now?"

"His pulse is dropping," the EMT said.

"Well stop it! Kane? Kane, it's Grey. Look at me," Grey called to his detective to no avail, still tied to a lifeline for Jade. He grabbed the RN siphoning his blood by the shirt with his free hand. "What'd you do in battle?"

"Shoot him with Narcan to counteract the—"

"Meet the ambulance, get a gurney, and run the stairs," Grey barked at the patrol. "Tell 'em to have Narcan ready." He watched Kane fade out. "Christ, can we have one thing go our fucking way?"

The second EMT, who hadn't fully rounded the door, disappeared back out it. The draft he caused brought the white silk Jade wore to life in butterfly waves. White attracts the eye. Grey's were on her before he could avert them. Dear God.

Tears burned his face, a silent river never before unleashed. The agony was physical. His chest bared down so hard it forced him to catch air in broken gulps. She was his daughter in every way that mattered, more than blood, he chose her. The serenity in her face, harsh tribute to the girl everyone failed to protect from monsters. Her father, friends, lovers, her shrink, and him, all walked with her on the path that led to a blood-filled room, painted in hers.

He was alone, Kane unconscious in the EMT's care, Jade near death beside him.

"Where are the fucking medics?" They heard him at street level, and he didn't care. Tears blurred his vision when the medics came, and he didn't care. Amy slid in beside him wearing streams of her own, and he didn't care. They wheeled Kane away and tapped blood bags fighting to save Jade. He collapsed wondering if he'd ever care again.

FIFTY-ONE

"Can't be normal, Carroll's eyes springing open. Disturbing." Amy loomed over the man responsible for the desecration of the people she'd come to love and the police department she considered home. No matter how deeply she peered in the windows, she wouldn't find a soul. This house was empty. Her eyes wandered over the mass of electrical boxes, wires, and tubing that kept him alive for the past weeks coming to rest on the medical machinery's company logo.

"Doesn't happen in all cases, but sometimes." The nurse was on her way out of his hospital room having run a gamut of checks.

"What are his chances of waking?" Amy asked the nurse leaning in to close Carroll's eyelids. "No. It's fine. Leave them."

The nurse shrugged her shoulders. "Not good, but it happens." She slid a clipboard into a wall slot, wrote her name and shift on a white-board, and moved on to tend to other patients.

Amy waited seconds until she was alone, then pulled it out and read.

A clatter of noise made her peek her head into the hall. A brain injury fundraiser bulletin board moved by two interns had lost a leg and toppled over. Nurses came running. Some helping stabilize the giant corkboard, others scooping seas of leaflets from the floor.

Amy ducked back into the Redeemer's room and returned the log.

Sunlight streaming in the window drew her. She peered out at the hospital grounds below, a walkway lined by aged shrubbery and trees. He didn't deserve a window or sunlight, even if he couldn't appreciate them.

Where was justice? His victims had been ravaged in ways that were, quite literally, unimaginable. The investigation was still piecing together how he'd kept victims conscious while he robbed them of blood, the drug cocktails mixed with precision drainage.

Amy thought of the sheer terror and torment the women would've experienced dying that way. What Jade experienced. She couldn't push the image of the old woman who lived next door from her mind. Amy stopped her from approaching the house where Grey and Kane were fighting to save Jade. She'd fallen into her arms sobbing. "No," she'd pleaded. "Not again. No more." It made Amy realize the woman's pleas were those of every good citizen of Shadow Hook. Of every victim he'd murdered.

She was warned not to do that, associate with victims. Hard to avoid when they were friends, neighbors. Maybe not Wenzel. That didn't mean his head being blown off was okay with her. Kane and Jackson were big brothers on the force. Brothers who were up one floor in hospital beds down the hall from victims in critical care.

And Jade, her big sister on the force. What she'd lost.

She stepped back, midpoint between the patient and the window. From there, her reflection in the glass was pronounced. The uniform.

At twenty-seven, the uniform meant everything. Her life, a life in turmoil because of the man on the bed.

The image of Kane, wrecked and dying, wouldn't leave her any more than that of Grey, broken by waves of anguish that pronounced his commitment and loyalty to his team, making it worse to witness, impossible to repair. Jade's room was across from Kane's, steps away from each other but neither conscious nor able to console the other now or maybe ever.

She wandered to the side table, grabbed a cloth from its top, and lowered the alarm volume on the digital panel of the ECMO life-sustaining machinery. Simple. Removing its backup battery was more complicated, but doable. She dunked it in a sink full of water, dried it with the cloth, then replaced it.

It helped that she'd dated a specialist in the field when the technology was introduced. Her girlfriend had been intrigued by the machine's capabilities. She'd spoken of nothing else. Amy's former lover was responsible for introducing the technology to area hospitals and fine-tuning procedures to prevent operational errors. She taught Amy everything as practice. Amy thought the role-playing was sexy but useless, until now.

There were avenues that led to machine error. She walked down the one most certain, watched the cycling ventilation cease, and left.

Halfway down the hall, a laundry service hamper waited outside a room being cleaned. Amy wiped perspiration from her forehead with the cloth she'd taken from the Redeemer's room, tossed it in, and descended the stairs back to check on Kane, Jade, and Jackson.

Her family.

She knew being in homicide there'd be decisions she'd live to regret. She just couldn't see how this would be one of them. And she'd promised the old woman, never again.

None of the names he'd been called by the papers fit, Romann Carroll, Nickolas Leigh II, or the Redeemer.

Victim. That fit. They wouldn't call him that.

His was a dream world or purgatory. Reliving the highlights up to the moment the bullet ripped through his neck. He'd endured many forms of torture in his life, never a bullet. It would've given Francis Carroll away. So would scars. He'd avoided both. He thought it odd how the bullet's impact registered but not the pain. Perhaps he couldn't feel pain anymore.

Death was knocking or had arrived. The EMTs discussed his dismal condition on the ride to the hospital. They didn't want to save him, not if he was the one they'd read about, but they fought to anyway. He wanted to speak. He couldn't open his eyes or utter a sound.

He slept. He'd never been so tired. He didn't want to wake. Life held too many demands. Sleep was nice. Except for the bad dreams. There were lots of those.

Threatening intentions added degrees to the hospital's thermostat and tainted the air with the sour scent of vengeance. A familiar bouquet. He sensed someone near. Once or twice, he caught flashes of them lurking. Glimpsed them from a long, dark hallway, murky figures at the far end.

Who else was staring into the dark? Leigh wouldn't survive long without him. His mother needed him.

He counted shadows, calling them by name. Some were too distant to reach. They couldn't hear him. The second-rate cop Wenzel, Eva Summers, Lorenda Lainey, Venice Beil, stood sentinels. His earliest conquests wore masks of black nearer the end where Francis Carroll waited. His mother, grandfather, and Jade stayed close. Their faces were clear, could've heard their voices.

Only Jade spoke.

"Are you ready to be redeemed?" she said.

This was another nightmare. He wasn't afraid of nightmares. He wasn't afraid of death. Carroll was another matter. A category all his own. He didn't want to go that way. He'd placed so many between him and his biological father, but were they enough?

"You have the power to redeem me?" He doubted it.

"I do now." She appeared oddly peaceful. She'd earned the right to avenge. They couldn't have saved her in time.

"My life is not worth taking." His voice echoed down the tunnel though his lips were taped around a breathing tube. His shadow people nodded their agreement.

"Every life has worth." A beam cast from off stage cut the blackness. Jade stepped into the blinding light, glowing at its center. Inclined to believe her, a part of him aspired to argue. Thoughts flew through his hands. He grabbed at them catching nonsensical bits and pieces, unable to grasp complete clarity. What he couldn't comprehend was why she mattered, but she did.

"I'm dying?" he asked.

"Yes." Light refracted off Jade's back in ghost wings making her appear angelic.

"By your hand?" Darkness outlying moments ago bled nearer, closing in, bringing Francis with it.

"No, at the hand of someone once merciful. This is what you do, invoke cruelty."

"Is that what I've done to you?" He'd manipulated Jade, used her, fashioned her actions to serve his purposes, but had he made her cruel?

"You believe you've been successful in violating me."

"I never violated. I—"

"Did you think I'd become you? That I should chose now to retaliate?" Her face, feet away, bore no anger. "Did your mother retaliate? Did your grandfather?"

"He didn't know who I am." At the mention of Nickolas Leigh, he detected the onset of pain in his chest. He *had* a merciful father, a grandfather, all along. His lungs surged against a depletion of oxygen.

"You knew who he was at the end. You tried to save him."

Pressure wrapped his upper torso squeezing like a python. "Is he dead? He's in the dark."

"Not yet. He's down the hall in intensive care. You'll see." Her tone belied the ominous nature of her words. "Why? Are you afraid of ghosts?"

"I'm not afraid of you. Are you a ghost? Is Rachel?" He'd been shot and taken to the hospital. That he understood. He feared if the ineptitude shown in the past stayed true, she would've died before being discovered.

"I want to discuss *my* mother now—we'll talk about yours later." Jade remained stoic a few feet away. "Were you present when Francis killed her?"

In the other place, his chest heaved, his body thrashed. "There isn't time."

"Answer quickly." Her expression revealed none of the panic marring his.

"No. I wasn't there. He wouldn't let me come then, afraid my sympathy still existed." He had no voice. His words were thoughts, nothing more.

"Did Francis Carroll expose you to all his crimes?"

"Yes."

"Are you certain?"

"They were his templates for grooming me." A burning sensation trickled up his legs and arms, seized them, and exploded back down his limbs seeking his heart.

"For making you truly into his likeness, his son?"

"I'm nothing like Francis—"

"Your father."

Through the agony he searched her face for signs of cruelty. "*He* raped women." "And you don't?"

"I have never, and would never, take a woman by force. I have no need." He protested with the sting of rage burning at his core, or was that physical pain?

"You don't agree with rape?"

The intensity of the suffering was trumped only by his anger. She knew better. She had to know him by now. "You know I'm vehemently against it."

"Because it was how you were created." Her green eyes smoldered in waves like a dangerously deep sea.

"Yes!" he hissed, collapsing into the vortex where his heart should've existed. The darkness trickled behind Jade, enveloping all but her.

She drifted close and whispered, "Me too."

An arrow hit him dead center, burning through and exiting his back. What did she say? Clarity was excruciating.

"You almost killed me, brother. I'm the one who understood. The only one like you." She reached for him, placed her hands on his chest, and stared into his eyes.

He saw it then. His eyes staring back at him. He memorized Jade's eyes when he tortured her but failed to see it. Francis Carroll's eyes inside hers. "No. No. It couldn't—"

Laughter silenced him. His father's laughter. *Her* father's laughter.

"This is what happens when you take a life," she said. "Mistakes are made. Mistakes that can't be undone."

His pain was blinding, the truth no lesser agony. "Kill me now. You hunted me. Finish it!" He wanted to let go. Death would free him, the final salvation from a tortured life that shouldn't have been lived.

"If I wanted you dead, you would be." His imaginary Jade released his chest. Oxygen flooded his lungs. "You should wake up."

"Don't you see? Daemon cognoscit(It's Latin) semen redemptio—a demon seed knows no redemption. You said you came to redeem me?" he begged.

"Redemption is found by the living. It takes time. Time I'm giving you. Time to suffer the truth. Wake up, brother."

FIFTY-TWO

Beau Carmichael slept in a wingback chair beside Jade's hospital bed in the private care facility she'd occupied for months. A perfectly comfortable sofa bed with extra pillows and blankets sat, untouched, a few feet away. His clothes were rumpled, and a half-read newspaper lay askew as if it'd fallen from his grip when he succumbed to exhaustion. An unopened cooler sat on the counter where, undoubtedly, his wife had left it for him. Grey had no sympathy.

He stared down at the man he believed did the most damage to Jade, despite the Redeemer's attack that left her in a coma. Beau abandoned her when she was so young, vulnerable, and needed him most. And that day was the day Grey assumed the role of her protector and provider.

"You're in my chair." He kicked Beau's foot stepping past to stand by Jade's bedside, forever the buffer between the two. "If you make this a habit, I'll ask them for another rocker."

"Huh? Um, I didn't know you would be here this morning." Beau sat up, wiping sleep from his eyes.

"I check on her every day on my way in." Grey's attention focused on Jade. Her color, regulated breathing, and overall state. "Why are you here?"

"I'm her father—"

"You are less her father than I am. A fact I've known for a very long time, and one you can no longer deny." Grey didn't give the man the dignity of facing him. Instead, he adjusted Jade's covers.

"Are you arguing parental credibility standing over my daughter now?" Beau was on his feet.

Grey turned to face him, owning the couple of inches of height he had on him. "No. I don't have to prove my position in her life. I have one."

"Where do you get off thinking—"

"I suggest you leave. Apparently, you have a knack for it." Grey stepped in close. "I'd like to be alone with her. You've done enough. Don't you think?"

"I didn't almost get her killed." Beau overstepped.

Grey had turned his back. He swiveled back around. "What did you say?"

"It wasn't me that—"

"Oh yes, yes it was. If you had been a man back then when her mother and she needed you, you would've stayed to protect them instead of running. You wouldn't have left them open targets." With every sentence, the words gained volume, and his voice hardened. "Jade wouldn't have witnessed the brutal homicide of her mother. And I..." Grey leaned in towering over Beau. "I wouldn't have pried that poor child out of a fucking cupboard only to end up here! Watching her trapped again! Get the fuck out!"

"You can't make me—" Beau was stumbling backward around the chair. Resisting leaving but recognizing what would come next.

"The hell I can't!" Grey pressed the security button on the handset for Jade's bed adjustments. A male nurse rounded the corner before his hand released having heard the loud exchange from down the hall. "I'm Captain Grey. I want this man removed from the premises, and any visits go through my approval unless it's one of her partners I've given clearance to. Understand?"

"Yes, sir," the nurse said, moving in to escort Beau out.

"I know you blame me for everything, but someday she will wake up and me being back in her life will be her decision." Beau shook the nurse's hand off his arm and headed for the door.

"And I'll be here, right beside her, still. Telling her to stay the hell away from you and your halfhearted bullshit!" Grey lowered his voice as the two men exited. He claimed his chair, kicked it in closer to Jade's bed, and sat down taking her limp hand in his firm grip. "Where I've always been until you don't need me anymore."

It hurt to see her like this, but inside he believed Beau was right about one thing. She would wake. The decisions would be hers, and they'd all repent. Him included.

FIFTY-THREE

"Who will you save?" Kane stood center of the lecture hall, the podium his barrier of protection from the agents in training. "You're tracking a serial killer. So, who do you intend to save?"

He scanned the room registering eager faces yearning to triumphantly declare their answers. Over the last three months he'd spent teaching, he'd heard every possible response. Grey all but forced him to run the class, rejoin the living, forward momentum.

Little did Grey know, he wasn't living. He breathed, existed, nothing forward about that. And waited.

"The victim." The overachiever in the third row blurted out.

"Everyone…in consideration of potential victims." The overachiever's archrival in the second row challenged.

"Justice." He didn't see where that one came from. Almost comical, he thought.

Faces of the audience blended together in a panorama of naïve passion. He stared down at his notes, blurry-eyed, seeing none of the words he'd written.

"Stand if you think the answer is the victim." Half the class launched from their seats.

"Stay standing." He eyed the man in the second row. "Stand if you think the focus should be on saving all victims, potential and otherwise." A third of those still seated joined the towering ranks.

"On your feet if you aim to save anyone." All the remaining students left their seats. Kane surveyed them slowly, sentries of faith awaiting his sword.

"That's not possible, and they're all damn naïve to think so." The comment came from a usually quiet young woman at the back, hidden but still seated.

"You're all wrong," he said. "Except, maybe her. You hunt a killer to catch him and stop him from killing again. If you're focused on saving anyone, you'll likely end up dead."

He flipped a switch activating the overhead and listened to the gasps from above and around him. Nothing pretty about death or the aftermath of failure on the screen.

He examined his notes for a second leaving them to bask in shame. "Sit down."

When he turned his face upward again, the crowd appeared somber. He'd got their attention. They were afraid now. As he met their eyes, he left no doubt about the severity of his statement.

"Is that how you caught the Redeemer?" a woman five rows up with dark hair dared asked.

"Yes." His tone warned off venturing further. "And it's why my partner isn't here."

The room fell silent, no shuffling of books or repositioning of feet. He locked eyes with the brazen woman making a mental note of her, then his eyes swept down. For a fraction of a second, he thought he saw Romann Carroll hiding in the crowd.

Reality told him he was hallucinating again. It happened less frequently than it had in the days immediately following Jade's rescue. The first few weeks he argued with her regularly, and she argued right back. He engaged in full-fledged conversations regardless of who else was in the hospital room or how insane they found it. After a month or so, he threw sentences in the air, cursed her at night, cried to her in the morning. Now, a half-year later, he glimpsed her less and less behind the static form on the bed he visited. He searched the audience again. No demons, none he recognized.

"This is what we had to go on." He pointed to the projection of Eva Summers as they'd found her. "The information in your packages should lead you to a killer. Study it. Live it. And have your conclusions in by the twenty-seventh."

Max said fewer hallucinations meant progress, indicative of making peace with reality, but then Max had his own issues.

Reality was cold, cruel in Kane's line of work. Without Jade by his side, there was nothing on the other side of the equation. There never would be.

He couldn't recall teaching the remaining half hour of class, but the students always returned with fervor. Grey was appeased by his participation. He asked no more of him.

Not yet.

Kane appreciated that no one, not Grey, Max, or Tex, bothered to reason, justify, or qualify Jade's condition away. They let it be what it was, heart-shattering failure wrapped and packaged in despair. She was alive, but not.

Jade appeared in dreams to him as she had in life, beautiful. Even on the cold slab where Romann Carroll left her, she was serene.

Kane remembered collapsing there. He was removed by stretcher and readmitted to the hospital he had escaped from. There were complications, more surgery, loss of consciousness, and confusion. In the end, Grey reassured him Jade hadn't been violated like the others. Carroll had switched out her painkillers for a sedative, brought a car, and picked her up, then kept her alive until the game's end.

The medic's report estimated she'd been bled for several hours. Her heart had come to a deathly crawl while the bullet from Kane's gun ended the Redeemer's reign.

No one admitted seeing her that day. Kane never mentioned her assistance during the previous shoot out when he regained consciousness.

She was his mistress even then.

Leigh's assistant missed Jade at her house, and later messages could've been sent from Carroll. His full access to their communication network gave him the advantage. This was one of the things that plagued Kane the most, never knowing what Jade's last words really were. No one looked at Leigh sideways when she swore in the hospital that Jade had sat at her bedside, held her hand, coxed her to fight for her life, but then she didn't carry a gun to do her job, and she'd been near death. She survived against the odds. And so had her father, the judge. He was grateful, saw all of them as heroes, though through impaired vision, and saved their reputations and careers.

Jade left Kane in her childhood home in the room where her

mother was murdered. Carroll restored the house back to its original state. The only difference was the wall color. Years ago, a pale blue hue. When Jade returned, the walls were red. It took Carroll countless hours of painstaking work to repaint them over and over and over to get the proper pigment.

You see, blood turns brown when it dries.

Kane quit driving by the red house two months earlier before the city tore it down. Quit sitting outside watching it from his car, reliving it. Now it lived in his nightmares, and they rarely happened while he was awake.

Grey kept the link between Jade and Romann Carroll out of the media, although they confirmed she was his biological sister on the paternal side. The father who raised her until eleven came to sit vigil by her bedside on occasion, but not relentlessly like Kane. Grey assumed that role and shouldered the grief that accompanied it. Kane made the arrangements for long-term coma care with the help of all those who loved her. He insisted on only the best.

All he wanted was for her to wake up. He prayed for, hoped for, begged for it.

The thought shrank and disintegrated from his mind when Beth entered the room. Student stragglers eyed her, especially the men.

She was a redhead, but more strawberry blonde. He didn't hate strawberries or blondes, he was one, after all. He didn't see her like they did. He only saw Jade that way.

"Organic tofu wraps," she announced lifting a takeout bag. "Park bench or office?"

"People will talk." He folded his brown leather organizer, slipped it into his satchel, and swung the strap over his neck. The theater emptied.

"Ah, let 'em. Jade knows the truth. I told her yesterday, you're not my type." Beth smiled. She glowed when she smiled. She wasn't wearing her habit anymore. Dark denim and powder blue wool suited her better.

"And what did she think?" He walked beside her.

"She agrees. Said you're too broody for me and, tragically, madly in love with her. She also said God's too perfect. Instructed me to keep looking."

Beth came to the hospital the day Jade transferred. Grey supported her visiting Kane during his recovery because Jade couldn't. A routine

Kane first tolerated then grew to depend on. When she gave up her habit, she'd been witness to him yelling at Jade while she lumbered in her coma, cursing God until he couldn't speak and lashing out at everyone who cared. Oddly, it was her raw humor about his failed faith that got him talking. She joined in, instead of gawking awestruck, she gave Jade a right tongue-lashing. It worked.

"What does He think of you calling off the wedding?" Kane couldn't smile. She did that for the both of them.

"It was His idea." She grinned and held the door for him. "Why don't you ask Him? Just so we're clear, my contemplation of leaving has everything to do with healing my demons and nothing to do with helping you slay yours."

He believed her. Her faith was rock solid. When she first explained she wouldn't be a nun for much longer, she'd said her time had served its purpose with joy in her eyes. No regret. The emotion that freed her, claimed him entirely.

He walked out, squeezing past her in the tight threshold, then paused in the warm summer breeze letting the air drift through him. "Will you ever allow me to get the door?"

"Nope." She walked with him down the stairs and into the campus park. "So, bench then. Something odd happened today during my visit."

"Really? Jade playing matchmaker with a nurse?" He kept walking, eyes ahead.

"No need, have my hooks in one already." She laughed. "I don't know. You going over after class?"

"Can't. I'm meeting Tex at the firing range." He eyed her. "Odd how?"

"That should be interesting. How is Jackson?"

"Ornery, especially if you slap him in the shoulder. Can't hit a barn door if he's standing in front of it. Other than that, he's good. You said odd."

"I'm sorry I missed their wedding." Beth disbursed the wraps and napkins between them on the bench. "Call me crazy, but she's different."

"Nikki has your vase on display in their front hall." He waited for her to take a first bite then tasted his. His appetite had returned, but he'd had trouble gaining weight. A vegetarian by proxy, he couldn't eat red meat anymore, and he was running five miles a day chasing demons. "How?"

She pulled a tall cup from the bag and handed it to him. "Tea. It was as if her face held more expression. Like…"

Kane stopped chewing.

"She's in there. Closer to the surface." Beth chewed watching a goose swim by tending to goslings. "You heading up tonight…after the gun range? I know Jackson is expecting you to wait for his recovery before assuming your old duties."

"He doesn't have to worry." Kane set down his half-eaten wrap and stared across the water with the hot cup in one hand, the other gripping the bench's edge. "Tex has no aim. I fire at ghosts." He paused for a second. "Yep. Doing night shift."

Beth's hand patted his. She shook her head. Her hair glistening in the sun became flames of vibrant copper. "She'll come back to you."

"I'm waiting." He turned back to the water, following its reflective surface to the far edge. "You never said what drew you to the church meetings where he chose his victims."

Beth's interest shifted downward. She hesitated and then said, "No, I didn't and wouldn't. Everyone else I told is dead."

FIFTY-FOUR

"How long until Kane stops hallucinating?" Grey forced Max to meet him at the station, reasserting his honor of the badge and right to continue wearing it while denying Max home advantage. They relied on each other, but it was an uncomfortable alliance.

"Maybe never." Max stood halfway between the door and the chairs, unable or unwilling to relax. "I can't give you a timeline. Kane's wounded, perhaps irrevocably, and not eager to discuss a thing with either of us."

"Have you spoken to Jackson?" Grey's hand leafed the corner of a pile of documents he'd turned over before Max entered. "They're spending time at the firing range. Regular Friday night dinners at his house."

"You're following him? I think that's less than wise." Max held his gaze as if refusing to acknowledge the walls adorned in awards and photos.

"He's *my* wounded detective. Hell yes, I'm following his activities. Sooner or later the question of reinstating him will be addressed. Everyone from politicians down, want to give him the key to the city, permanent sabbatical isn't an option. And, in case you haven't noticed, we're a little short on detectives. Quit hovering. Sit down."

A buzzing tone indicated a call waiting. Annoyed, Grey silenced

Max before he could get a word out, picked up the receiver, and spoke to his assistant. "Who is it?"

Max relented and sat, eyeing the papers under Grey's hand.

Grey spoke into the phone, eyes locked on Max. "Tell him I'm working on it, and I'll call him back." He dropped the receiver back into its cradle.

"You know he'll never trust you again." Max spoke without lifting his gaze from the desk.

"Yeah? I wonder which of us he trusts less." Grey pulled his hands from the desktop and folded them over his stomach as he leaned back into his chair. "When he snaps out of this, and he will, he'll realize how deep Jade dove into the case. No one could've stopped her, but he'll always feel like you should've."

"I should have?" Max leaned onto the desk.

"Yes, you. We were working the worst string of homicides to come through here. What's your excuse?" Grey controlled his volume. He didn't want their conversation seeping beyond his office walls. "Look, the one to blame is living on a feeding tube, but that doesn't mean we're outta the woods." Grey leaned in, his tone smoother. "I can't have him back here unstable. No more hail Marys."

"You mean, you can't have him talking to ghosts," Max said.

"You heard him in the hospital."

"It isn't that uncommon. It's a way of making peace—"

"Making peace? He was cursing Jade, day and night. Flat out fighting every stupid choice she made." Grey's voice echoed back on him. He huffed, indignant.

"Still, there's precedence for it, and he hasn't reacted like that in months."

"That we know of." Grey rubbed his hands together and stretched his fingers, arthritis and age creeping in. "And Jackson?"

"Jackson is Jackson. Tough stuff. Not willing to talk, but he's on solid ground and, I believe, wrangling Kane in beside him."

"Belief isn't enough. I need assurance Kane won't lose it before I hand over a loaded weapon."

"You sure he wants his job back? It ruined his life, cost him Jade and their future." Max left the chair, shifting his weight in front of the desk. "Has he asked to come back?"

"That isn't the point." Grey stood, meeting Max eye level across the desk. "*This* is his life. It's what's left, and I'm not sitting around waiting for him to lose that too. He has purpose here. He needs it."

"Like you did?" Max stepped back.

"This isn't about me. Don't make it." The room was getting hot. Perspiration matted Grey's shirt to his back. He shifted his shoulders to break free of the clinging fabric. "I'm picking up the pieces to protect him. Someone almost finished Carroll off at the hospital. There's nothing conclusive yet, but I don't know what'll surface, and I'm worried about what's lurking in the shadows. Kane, Jade, Jackson, the department, they've paid enough."

Max waited midpoint to the door. "Who did you assign to the attempted homicide?"

"Amy Logan. Not a whole lot to choose from. She's solid, and God knows head office doesn't see catching Carroll's would-be killer as a priority." Grey walked around the desk and passed Max, his hand on the cold doorknob.

Max met his stare. "Does Kane know everything?"

Grey inched closer. "He knows, and that knowledge is likely responsible for him being incapable of accepting Jade's condition."

"Let's face it, none of us are capable." Max smoothed the creases from his brow. "How are you sleeping? Me, I see her every time I close my eyes. Can't tell me you don't when you're alone in the night. She's always there. I suppose she always will be for all of us. I don't know if I'd call that justice."

Grey stared out at the approaching night beyond the window, mesmerized by the swirling gray clouds approaching from the north. "Carroll's done killing. You, me, Kane, Jackson, and Amy, we're left to live on, fumbling in the dark. You may not see that as justice, but it's the way it is. I want her back as much as anyone. She just can't find her way to us."

Max stepped by him and whispered, never looking back, "Don't count her out. There's fight beyond measure in that bloodline."

FIFTY-FIVE

"Complications?" Kane echoed the voice from his cell phone. "What the hell is that supposed to mean? You said she was stable!" His voice crackled back at him, annoyingly bad connection, but he couldn't risk hanging up. "I'm ten minutes out. She better be fine when I arrive. Do whatever you have to!"

He hadn't had time to clean the gunpowder off his hands before Jackson and he were thrown into high gear by the emergency call from Still Waters, the medical center caring for Jade.

"They said her breathing was labored? What else?" Jackson demanded clarification.

Tex was worried but doing a far better job holding it together. In the six months since the Redeemer case ended, Kane knew he'd become a reactive slave to emotions. Another reason he wasn't job ready, heck he was barely legal driving.

"He said they were monitoring brain function, something about oxygen depletion. Christ, I don't know. I couldn't hear half of what he was saying between the bad connection and gunfire."

"I don't trust those yahoos." Jackson stared ahead, rubbing the meaty right hand of his injured arm across a denim-clad thigh. "Watch the curb."

"Yeah. Me either." Kane thought for a moment. "Then who do I trust outside you?"

Jackson said little on the remainder of the ride. When they pulled into the care center parking lot, he spoke up. "Jump out. I'll park and come in. Go find out what the hell is happening."

Kane abandoned the truck near the entrance, flung the building's front doors open, and ran to the back left of the L-shaped facility where Jade's room was. He parted a few nurses outside her doorway with an aggressive shove, and then nearly lost his footing inside the threshold.

Her primary doctor was wiping saliva from under her mouth. The aftermath of removing a breathing tube from her throat from what he could see through the maze of staff. A horrible wet gurgling sound, and then...Jade was coughing.

"Keep coughing for me as hard as you can," the doctor said. He was speaking to her. The doctor realized Kane was in the room. "You have company."

Kane made his way through white-clothed bodies to an open spot at the bedside, treading as if the floor was made of thin glass. "Jade?"

His line of sight cleared, and there she was.

The tube removed and mucus cleared, she stared up at him. "Not my finest," she whispered in broken notes. "Hour."

Jade. Not a compromised version who didn't know who he was. His Jade.

"We'll give you a minute." The doctor cleared the room. Pushing a chair in behind Kane as he left. "Sorry about the entourage. Not every day we witness a miracle."

Kane collapsed into the chair, not feeling his legs. "Never thought I'd see one." He enclosed her hand in his. "Hey, partner."

"How...long?" she asked, taking in the room for the first time.

"Roughly six months. You only missed the bad weather. Spring is almost here. The town will throw a parade for sure now." He couldn't quit staring. "Damn, it's good to see your eyes open."

"I'm so sorry. You got hurt. And I, I got dead."

"No, no. Today is a good day." He hugged her gently fighting the urge to crush her in his arms. He hadn't come up for air when he heard Jackson come in.

"Well slap me stupid. You kidding me?" His smile exploded behind his eyes.

"Hi, Tex." Released, Jade smiled broadly, chuckled, and spoke, her voice cracked and full of effort. "Good to see you too."

"I've seen you practically every day, kid, but usually looking like a statue. Move something, would ya!"

Jade reached up to welcome a hug, and Kane's phone rang. He glanced at the number between smiles with Tex and Jade. Grey was calling. The man had nothing if not great timing.

"It's unbelievable," Grey said before Kane could utter a word.

"I know, right? Did the doctor call you?" Kane was squeezing Jade's hand in his free hand while she talked to Tex.

"Yeah. Did he call you too?" Grey asked.

"No. I'm here with her. You gotta come see this for yourself." Kane couldn't contain his elation. His cheeks hurt from using long dormant muscles, but his grin held.

"With who?" Grey's tone was one of confusion not joy.

Kane paused, his mind replaying the conversation. "I'm with Jade, Cap. She's awake. What—"

"Jesus." The line went dead quiet. Tex and Jade stopped talking and were waiting for an explanation for the sudden change in Kane's expression. "So is her brother."

"He can't be." Kane shot to his feet. The joy of the moment lost. "How in the hell?"

"What is it?" Jade demanded, though raspy in her delivery.

"Hold on." Kane muffled the phone into his chest. "Grey. He says Nickolas Leigh is out of his coma. He's immobile but..." He spoke back into the cell phone. "Where is the justice in that? I hope he's paralyzed from the neck down."

"No," Jade said calmly. "Awake is exactly what he deserves. He has to live...with what he did. He's at our mercy now."

"What?" Kane was speaking to Grey again. "I'll tell her." He hung up and sank back into the chair wide-eyed.

The green of her eyes deepened. "What?"

"I should've shot him when I had the chance," Jackson offered. "Sorry, kid."

Kane shook his head in disbelief and then said, "Your mercy, Jade. You're the valid next of kin. Grey's on his way here, he said, Nickolas's care, because you're awake, will be decided by you."

Jade's eyes followed the outline of her fragile form beneath the blankets, drifting to the scars on her exposed arms, then to the men flanking her bed. When she spoke, something cold lingered in her voice. "That's justice, a whole new beginning for us all, and...one he won't like."

A LOOK AT BOOK TWO:
DARK DIVIDE

The clock is ticking down on twelve lives in a restricted forest warded for its treacherous terrain. With the latest victim being a friend Jade vows to bring home, she accepts help from a man detached from society and hidden for decades deep beyond the borders of The Divide. Alone in her pursuit, with new FBI partners anticipating her failure, Jade finds her greatest ally in the hunt to save lives may be more qualified at taking them than the criminal she seeks. And once inside, the only way out for her, and the carefully selected sacrifices of the accomplished captor, is a high stakes trade no detective should be forced to make.

COMING SOON.

ABOUT THE AUTHOR

As a thriller author, owner of a successful developmental editing company for authors, a ghostwriter, and journalist, J.L. Hughes is grateful to be immersed in her respected field working with other accomplished writers. On the inside cover of dozens of novels, she contributes as editor or ghostwriter to both fiction and nonfiction in every genre from true crime to fantasy, sci-fi to horror—all for the love of story.

J.L. and her family enjoy city life against the adventurous backdrop of the Rocky Mountains.